The Feet Say Run

A Novel By

Dan Blum

G/H

Gabriel's Horn Publishing

Other Writing by Dan Blum

LISA33
https://rottingpost.com

Contact: editors@gabrielshornpress.com

Published in Minneapolis, Minnesota by Gabriel's Horn Publishing

Publisher's Note: This novel is a work of fiction. Names, characters, places, and incidents are either products of the author's imagination or used fictitiously. All characters are fictional, and any similarity to people living or dead is purely coincidental.

Cover design: Elsa Blum

First printing September 2016
Printed in the United States of America

For sales, please visit www.gabrielshornpress.com

ISBN 10: 1-938990-21-8
ISBN 13:   978-1-938990-21-2

For Katherine, William and Charlotte

- Illyria -

If there is an actual name to this island, it is unknown to us. We have chosen to call it *Illyria*. We're not exactly sure where the name comes from. Some book perhaps. But it no longer matters. It has become our own—mythic and melodic-sounding. As though, if we keep calling this place Illyria, keep pretending it has some magical allure, people will want to come. Someone will come rescue us.

I am not complaining, particularly. Well, maybe I am. But I probably shouldn't be. So far fate has proven a fair enough agent. The beaches are sandy, the water clear and turquoise, the reefs plentiful. The island is wreathed in a soothing white foam. On shore there is the shade of palms and palmettos and eucalyptus. At least we think it is eucalyptus. We call it eucalyptus. Maybe it is just some kind of fancy magnolia though. Who the hell knows?

There are fruits in relative abundance—though what they are, we aren't sure. Some are purple. Others are yellow. Some vaguely sweet, others sharp and abrasive on the roof of the mouth. There is a variety of coconut that grows in conjoined pairs to look like the buttocks of an African woman. We call this ass fruit. When I offered some to Conrad, he said to me, "I'm not into that shit." As though I were suggesting something perverse. As though fear of this fetish object outweighed the need for sustenance.

"What shit are you not into?" I asked.

"Ass fruit," he said. "Ass."

"It's not real ass, Conrad," I said.

"Well, it's not a real fruit either," he said.

"What do you think it is then?" I asked.

"A joke," he said. "A sick joke. Like the rest of this place."

God is playing a joke on us. That is a common theme here. It was funny the first time someone said it. Now it is just annoying, like a child saying, "knock-knock" to you over and over, more and more emphatically, as you refuse, just as emphatically, to ask, "Who's there?"

The other common theme here is that none of it is real. We all died when the boat went down. And this is all just a dream. Conrad suggests this a couple of times a day, each time choosing a different angle, a different inflection, in a vain attempt to keep the joke fresh. If you suggest, gently, that this joke no longer strikes you as uproarious, Conrad will immediately jump into a long denial that he is joking. *"I'm not fucking kidding,"* he will tell you. *"I really mean it. I think this is all a dream."*

Perhaps Conrad is right. Because honestly, I did not believe, until my current predicament, that deserted islands still existed. I thought these islands were all owned by former tennis pros and former tyrants, or inhabited by caricatures of primitive tribes who sell carved bamboo flutes to flabby tourists in checkered shorts.

If it is a dream, if this is my Land of Oz and I am soon to wake up, then it is curious how, from time to time, little bits of Kansas wash up upon our shores. Whenever we wander further down the beach, away from our settlement, we find Styrofoam packing peanuts, Styrofoam bowls, #3 plastic take-out containers with their familiar, triangular *recycle* symbols (apparently the previous owners of these containers ignored this particular environmental imperative).

The restaurant take-out containers are the most distressing. More mockery from The Almighty. More of his levity. Ha ha. We bring them back to our camp and wonder what twenty-first century foods they once held. Pad Thai or Kung Pao Chicken or Shrimp Korma. From some restaurant from the other world. Thank you, God, for delivering us this practical joke. Ha ha. You're fucking hi-*lar*-ious.

In truth though, these containers have become invaluable to us. We eat out of them, wash them out at the little pool in Piss Brook, store our meager salvaged supplies in them. If there is truly one thing we should thank God for, it is those non-recycling sinners.

In our first days here, we found a means of killing a dove-like bird that is here in abundance. We creep up on it quietly, then all at once we start hurling rocks at it from all directions. It is the same low-tech technique the Iraqis used for shooting down American planes in our first Gulf War. Just throw up flak in every direction and hope something falls out of the sky. Actually that is something else that I am no longer sure is real. Gulf War I. In my current, delusive state, I am no longer clear whether it really happened, or was some very popular video game, and Gulf War II was just the long-awaited next release, with its improved graphics and better villains and four-and-a-half star rating. Perhaps, since we have been here, Gulf War III has broken out. Or been released.

But back to the doves. With the doves, this method worked once in every ten or twenty tries. Moreover, some of us were hit by rocks. Conrad compared us to a circular firing squad. And for the effort, we each got no more than a single bite of precious meat.

Frigate birds watch us from high overhead—out of range of our stone-age weapons. There are also pelicans and sandpipers along the coves. But the only other bird we have succeeded in slaughtering—a heron of some sort—tasted much like a discarded sneaker might taste. There are also lizards and little pencil-sized snakes, but thus far we have passed on these particular *specialites de la region*.

So much for Illyria's fauna. Now a word or two on the topography. The interior has proven rocky, thick with vines, and difficult to penetrate. There is a single volcanic peak in the middle, which we call Mount Piss. We call it this because the streams that run down from it are of a yellowish, sepia color—piss water. This includes our drinking source, the much despised and much revered Piss Brook. It is probably just some dissolved mineral. Iron would turn it orange. Maybe zinc? Who knows. The taste is strong and unpleasant, but it is moderately cool, given our subtropical latitude. It is keeping us alive. Probably, if we could contact the civilized world, we could bottle it and sell it for its curative powers and make great mountains of money.

Our first shelter was rigged out of bamboo and palm fronds. It was set on the beach, and we soon learned there was no way to keep out the sand crabs. They came out in large numbers every evening. It would have been one thing if they scampered in from outside. But it was stranger than that. They just rose up through the floor of sand. They tunneled in, materialized among us, little uninvited sprites, climbed up out of the ground like the living dead and crawled across us as we slept.

"We're not high enough above the water," Cole said. "What if a storm comes up?"

"He's just afraid of the sand crabs," Conrad said to me, snickering.

"The first really high tide will wash us out," Cole said, ignoring the snickers.

"He's right," Monique said. Although her vote meant little. She is Cole's lover, and seemingly agrees with everything he says and does. If he becomes the *de facto* king of our little group of seven, which now seems likely, she will be our queen.

Our next shelter was built just above the beach, using a cliff face for one of the walls. It was roomier, and easier to close off from the creatures. It was quieter too, farther from the surf. But that was worse, in a way. Because now you heard all of the human sounds more precisely. Cole snoring. Gloria talking in her sleep. My own imperfectly muffled farts.

One night, a rain came and our new shelter was tested. At first we just felt a kind of mist, soft and cool, that had found its way through the thatch. But then it got heavier. Droplets.

There were groans. Curses. Aborted snores. Rustling.

And then it was no longer just droplets raining on us. It was the cliff itself. Mud from the cliff started slopping on us. Little shit bombs. Dripping through our roof. It was raining crap. "Fuck!" Conrad shouted. And it was an accusation, directed at Cole, who had chosen this location.

Another splat. Another curse. And then we were all up, groaning and cursing our miserable fate—surely the world's very last castaways, on what is surely the world's last desert island, somewhere mysteriously out of reach of our GPS-bound, cell-towered, trawler-traversed global village.

Maybe Conrad was right. God, that sadistic little prick, was playing some kind of joke on us. God was the house cat and we were his mouse and he was taunting his mouse over and over, carrying it and dropping it and picking it up again, half-swallowing it and regurgitating it and kicking it like a soccer ball, before finally disposing of it.

So it's shitty metaphor. What can I say?

We got up in the middle of the night, abandoned the shelter, huddled together on the beach. We were sunburnt and bitten, chilled and miserable. Hungry, filthy, greasy-haired, exhausted. Tears mixed with the downpour; our pathetic, mortal cries with the thunder of heavens.

After a while the rain stopped. We sighed, calmed, leaned against one another. Relief. Then it started again. There were no more tears by then. Just silent misery. Half-sleep. Each of us with his or her own private thoughts. My thoughts were of Dawn. (I am capitalizing Dawn not as a statement about the mystical meaning of sunrise. In fact I am not referring to the sunrise at all. I am referring to one of our company, Dawn, the youngest in our party—a nineteen-year-old girl who had won my sympathy. But I am getting ahead of myself.)

When Dawn finally came (sorry, this time I *am* referring to the sunrise), we straggled up and pretended—as one does on a red-eye flight when the lights pop on—that we'd actually had a night's sleep.

Only there was no stewardess, no orange juice and coffee, no magical, mile-high toilet to whisk away the miserable night's rumblings in a screaming blue swirl.

Just another day here on Illyria.

This is my question about aboriginal peoples. Did they always feel as short of sleep, as exhausted and worn out, as we always feel? Or did they find a way to sleep through all of those night sounds and crawling things, hunger pangs and gas-emitting neighbors?

Our third shelter was set on a long, flat rock, above the waves and a half-mile down the beach. It is interesting how quickly one develops a sense of home. Just moving that half-mile seemed unsettling. An unwelcome abandoning of the familiar. We filled empty ass fruit shells with sand and carried them up to our rock to soften the floor for sleeping. And by adding more overlapping layers of thatch than we had before, by covering it with a paste made from clay and eucalyptus sap, we managed to keep dry inside. We called our new residence Versailles.

By then, the inevitable had happened. Cole was our leader. We hadn't exactly chosen him, and he had never asserted his authority directly. It just happened.

Was he wiser than the rest of us? More generous? Had he provided for us in some impressive way? No. He possessed what Human Resources questionnaires refer to as *leadership qualities*. And most of us, let's face it, are natural followers.

It started with his suggestions. We should do this. We should do that. We should set the shelter closer to the brook. The women should gather the fruit. "You!" he would say, narrowing his eyes at Andreas, "Work on finding firewood." It was as though he had been waiting all his life to play this role, to have the chance to tell someone to gather up the firewood. And of course it was natural to direct his first order to Andreas, who had been in his employ on the yacht before it went down. And then from there it was easy to direct "suggestions" to the rest of us.

We are a pack of primates. And Cole is our alpha male. Tall, burly, handsome in a bushy-browed sort of way. Real estate developer in his previous life. Resourceful man of the jungle in our present life. Dipshit in both lives.

With his background in real estate, so he insinuated, it was only natural that he should oversee the construction of the shelters. And though the connection seemed tenuous, nobody challenged him. Conrad, who in our previous life was Cole's cousin, despises him. For myself, I dislike him as well, but more or less indifferently. I see that he is only of average intelligence, perhaps slightly more self-centered than what might be considered average. He is lacking in irony, introspection, humor, really anything that might make one actually like him. But I am too old to worry about these things. I have seen too much of humanity —and at its very worst. Let someone else figure it out.   Just tell me what you need me to do and leave me alone and don't ask me any questions.

Our next construction project was a dove coop. Gloria, our kindly widow (yes, dear reader, it goes without saying that our group is made up of "types," a microcosm, as it were, of humanity at large, and that one of these types, inevitably, must be our kindly old lady), had the ingenious idea of raising doves rather than just throwing rocks at them.

"Good plan," Cole said, nodding wisely, and somehow managing, in his nod, to demonstrate the importance of his judgment.   His ratification.

It was a big step for us. Our move from a hunter-gatherer society to an agrarian economy. But it was something else also. A recognition that we might be here for a while. That we had to plan for a future. And for me it was a recognition of this:

I am done running. I am here now. There is nowhere left to go.

With great effort, we caught three of these birds alive—surrounding them and dropping a heap of branches on them.   We put them in our coop.

"What if they're all the same sex?" I asked.

"I don't think they're all the same sex," Cole said.

"Why not?"

"That one looks like a girl."

"Why do you say it looks like a girl?" I asked, wondering if Cole had noticed a wiggle to its tail, a shape to its figure.

"It's more colorful," Cole said.

"The male birds are more colorful than the females," I said. I am no John James Audubon, no Roger Tory Peterson, but I believe I am right in this.

"Either way," Cole said.

We turned the birds over, looked around their tails, but could find no conclusive evidence of maleness or femaleness. Then one morning Conrad called us over. Two of the doves were dead. The third, the apparent victor, seemed to have been bloodied.

"Maybe they were all males," I said.

"Or maybe with doves it's the girls that do the fighting," Cole said.

I was skeptical of this, caught Conrad's eye.

"Just because the males are colorful, doesn't mean they're girly,"

Conrad said.

"So much for doves being symbols of peace," I said.

"Unless of course they aren't really doves," Dawn offered up.

We all looked at her. It was rare for Dawn to speak up among the group.

"True," I said. Because it's not as though Dr. Doolittle is here with us and can just ask them if they're doves. Or Crocodile Dundee. Or whomever. What we know, or think we know, about the rain forest, we have learned from the packaging on our health supplements and our beauty aids and our enviro-friendly paper towels. The TV shows that bring wild nature into our living room. *Here, high in the cloud forest, the spectacled monkey is tending to her young. The little ones will need to learn much if they are to survive the harsh winter.* Actually, scratch that. No harsh winters in the cloud forest. But you understand my point.

Though bloodied, the dead doves still had meat on them. We brushed off the ants and flies, washed the corpses off in the stream, put them on the barbeque spit.

In the next days, we caught more doves. This time we observed the brush they pecked at in the wild and brought them piles of it. And we separated the doves into pairs that appeared to be of opposite sex. And lo! Dove eggs started to appear. Like magic. Like Easter eggs. Like… actual…eggs!

In time, one of this second set of doves died too. This time though, apparently, it was from natural causes. (Strange phrase: natural causes. Because what could be more rooted in nature than being pecked to death?) But we nonetheless had eggs. And while we ate some, we left some of them alone. And one day we witnessed the miracle we had dreamed of, but never quite believed we would see—a little beak pecked through one of our eggs, pecked its way out into the world. Within a couple of weeks we had a little collection of chicks. We had done it! Our poultry farm had been born!

Again we returned to our construction. Our next project was a little shelter along a rocky outcrop, to protect us from the sun when we were fishing and crabbing. And then Cole and Monique decided they wanted to sleep in privacy. So we built a second shelter alongside Versailles that we called Fontainebleau.

"Why," Conrad grumbled, "should we be putting all this time into another shelter just so that dirtbag and that douchebag can go at it in private?"

I wondered what you get when you mate a dirtbag and a douchebag. There must be a good punch line. Please write me if you think of one. 1 Delirium Terrace. Illyria. Earth. 02483-7676. to insure proper handling, be sure to include a self-addressed, stamped envelope. And a life raft.

"Well," I said, "the next shelter we build after that could be for you."

"Yeah," Conrad said, "but it's not like there's anyone I'm likely to be screwing."

"Well don't you want to be able to pleasure yourself in private?" I asked.

Conrad looked uncomfortable at this, but said nothing.

"And won't it be nice to be rid of them?" I asked.

Personally, I was relieved when Cole and Monique moved out. It had grown tiresome, those nights they waited until they thought everyone was asleep and then started moving and rustling, whispering and slurping. And then those guttural sounds, like a pair of native frogs. Only nobody was ever really sleeping during their nocturnal choruses. We were all just pretending we were asleep. All too uncomfortable to say anything about it. To interrupt them.

"I think it actually turns them on," Conrad used to snarl. "They know we know they're going at it. And they know we know they know."

"It's difficult," I say.

"I'm saying something next time."

And he did. A couple of nights later we started to hear it again. Unmistakable. Rustle. Breath. More rustling. Sighing. Frog calls.

"Hey Monique," Conrad called. "Can I get some of that?"

Suddenly the sounds stopped. Silence. The whole shelter went silent. Pretended to sleep. Like even Monique and Cole were asleep and the only one awake was Conrad and nobody had heard anything at all—the grunting or Conrad or anything. Monique and Cole frozen *in flagrante delicto*. A final rustle. Monique discreetly slipping off her little pole of Cole. Then more silence. Everyone pretending sleep. Until we actually *were* asleep. One by one. Like in that children's story.

> *Goodnight Cole.*
> *And goodnight Pole.*
> *And goodnight, o empty soul.*
> *Goodnight stars.*
> *And goodnight air.*
> *Goodnight misery everywhere.*

Two days later Cole began organizing work on Fontainebleau. He must have waited an extra day so it wouldn't be as obvious why he was doing it—that it was related directly to Conrad's comment. Since we were all pretending we had never heard it.

Bit by bit, Cole has seemed to be developing the island. I imagine that, if a rescue ship ever comes, while the rest of us are celebrating, weeping for joy, he is going to take them for a tour, show them all the improvements, try to sell his development for a profit.

For Conrad, the last straw was one morning when Cole put up a great big bamboo cross over our little encampment.

"It's embarrassing," Conrad complained, pulling me aside.

"Embarrassing before whom?" I asked.

Conrad thought about this. "What would a pilot flying over us think, looking down and seeing that?"

"I don't know," I said.

"They'd think we're…we're fucking missionaries."

"I haven't noticed any planes," I said.

"Well, it's still embarrassing."

"I have given up on embarrassment," I said. "At my age it is pointless. I am who I am. Let the pilots think we're missionaries then."

"We're castaways!" Conrad said, as though asserting membership in some privileged class.

"Doesn't it strike you as odd," I asked, "that we are a thousand miles away from civilization, and you have brought with you to this place that one absurdity of living in a society. Self-consciousness? Embarrassment?"

Conrad didn't hear me, though. He looked off in disgust. "What gives him the right? He just does whatever he wants. Without asking anyone. After all that shit about making decisions as a group. I knew it was all bullshit."

"Just think of it as a couple of big sticks," I said. "It doesn't have to be a crucifix. It doesn't have to mean anything."

"It crosses the line," Conrad said. "You know what it is? It's state-sponsored religion. How does he know we all believe? How does he know some of us aren't atheists? Or Jews? Or Hindus?"

Conrad, in his past life, was a labor lawyer or something. An advocate of some poorly-paid group, or class, or underclass. "You don't look like a Hindu," I told him.

"That's stereotyping," Conrad said.

I considered this, puzzled, but didn't pursue it. "Maybe you should talk to him about it," I said.

"Right in the middle of the camp!" Conrad exclaimed, still

smarting. "That's the problem. It's like…government fucking property. He should have put it up somewhere else. In front of *his* shelter."

From what I can tell, the Sovereign Nation of Illyria is about evenly divided between Republicans and Democrats, three of each with one independent—your humble chronicler. We have no social safety net, no taxes, a total lack of laws that would make a libertarian proud. On the other hand, our foreign policy is aimed at peaceful coexistence with our neighbors. And we consider ourselves to be pro-environment. For example, there is no peeing in Piss Brook. Strictly enforced. And we have started husbanding our excrement for the precious resource that it is, and putting it to use it in our farming experiments. You see how this place is the very inverse of our past life? Civilization in negative? Here our very stools—the quintessential waste product—are a measurable portion of our net worth.

It is remarkable how seamlessly our political disputes have moved from our former life into this one. Cole and Conrad still argue about tax policy, for example. And what to do with illegal immigrants. Although, should we die here, as I assume we will, it is unlikely any of this will ever matter again. You see the absurdity, the futility of these arguments we engage in? We have no problem of illegal immigration on Illyria. Nobody has shown up offering to do our laundry or to bag our groceries.

I find myself wondering: if a mutiny were to occur, with whom would my loyalty reside? True, I don't like Cole. I don't respect him. Only I don't think Conrad would be a very good leader. Of course, Conrad and Cole are not the only two possibilities to lead us. There is Andreas—shy, handsome boy of twenty who had been the deckhand and cabin-boy on the yacht. He is bright and level-headed, from what I see, and the only one of us who does not appear to be suffering, who seems to see this as just an extension of his summer, a further break from college. What comforts does one need, after all, at age twenty?

Or perhaps we should try a matriarchal structure, like the Samoans had. Choose Gloria, chattering old lady, as our chieftain. Gloria is perhaps seventy, a widow, grandmother to a dozen grandchildren. She smiles when she speaks of them. The oldest is a lawyer with the Justice Department. The next oldest has a very high grade point average at Temple University. She had been knitting a sweater for her youngest grandchild when the boat went down, and somehow the wool made it onto the lifeboat. She washed it out and dried it and has continued with her project.

One night I am next to her by the fire as she holds the sweater up, imagines her grandchild inside it, considers the proportions.

"Very handsome," I say.

"Yes," she says. "Too bad he will never have it."

"If you believe that," I say, "then why continue with the sweater?"

"Well, I have to do something," she says.

"Of course."

"You have children? Grandchildren?" she asks.

"I have a son."

She looks understandingly into my eyes, as though she knows what I feel. Only how could she know? "He must be suffering at losing you," she says.

"I haven't seen him in thirty-five years," I say.

"Oh," she says with a start, and politely changes the subject. "I think it must be harder on the young ones. I mean, we've had our time. Right?"

I have to admit I resent slightly Gloria's intimations that we have something in common in our accumulated years. That we must share the same values. I must be as good, as upstanding, as resigned to death as she is. Gloria worked as a cafeteria lady in a local elementary school, was our cook on the yacht, and is our cook again on the island. She has a stocky stature, and I always imagine her in her white cafeteria uniform, arms folded under her shapeless, megalithic breasts, looking out over the children. The hairnet and sagging stockings, the cakes of flour-white make-up.

She has a slap-your-hands-together, let's-get-down-to-business kind of spirit about her, is chipper in a way that I find unnervingly mindless, as though she is dealing with the seven-year-olds at her school, and— aside from some greater understanding of responsibility—is much at their level. I see her helping out on some field trip, there in the back of the bus, happily, even joyously, singing *Ninety-nine bottles of beer on the wall* with the children. I can safely say that nobody here on the island has warmed to her in a way that I imagine the singing children might have.

Has Gloria considered me as a possible object of romantic interest? Clearly, I am not capable of this, not merely because we have nothing particularly in common, but because my heart already belongs to another.

I have yet to say much of myself, so let me offer a few words here. I am a man in his eighties. My name is Hans. The hairs on my head have been reduced to a few scattered strands, sparse as the hairs on a coconut or the hairs on a testicle. I am a refugee, a wanderer, a retired refrigerator salesman, human organ dealer, warrior on the wrong side of history. I am in love with a nineteen-year-old girl. I am speaking, of course, of the aforementioned Dawn.

Dawn, Dawn, Dawn.

Dawn is Cole's step-daughter. Of course, if the others knew my feelings for her they would be shocked. Or if they weren't shocked, they would at least feel obliged to pretend to be shocked.

And yet it is true. I am in love with a nineteen-year-old child. And what of it? Why should such feelings be wrong in an eighty-five-year-old and not in a twenty-year-old? At what age does it become wrong to love? Wrong to yearn for youthful beauty? Or do you doubt that I am capable? Let me say that I have been assured by professionals, by those who should know, that I have the genitalia of a much younger man. My erection is as firm as a senator's handshake. So should I not endeavor to contribute my genes to our little colony before I expire? Should our gene pool include only those offspring of our alpha male, as though we were a troupe of gibbons? Do we really want five Cole juniors for the next generation, five male models, admiring themselves in the reflection in the cove, wondering who is the fairest of them all? Or worse still, all vying to be the leader, dividing up the island, buying and selling their beachfront real estate?

I did not choose this predicament. I am sleeping just a few feet away from a beautiful nineteen-year-old girl. Am I not still a man?

It was not supposed to end like this, with us huddled together on a beach somewhere, wondering who is going to die first. How did I find myself on this excursion, after those years ensconced, alone, in my villa by the sea? I was living the life of a recluse, an old salt, an old masturbator, when one morning, on a day just like any other....

Scratch that. I am not ready to tell about that. We will get there. In due time. But now I see I must go back further. I must say something more of myself.

- Germany -

So what is my particular crime? The reason God might choose me for this fate? Or, to put it another way, my own place in our little microcosm of humanity?

Let me begin with my entrance into the world. It is true that life may be said to begin at conception, but I know little of that magical moment, that miraculous one-in-a-million accident in the super-collider of my mother's uterus (long, dark tunnel in which so many packets of energy swim by unnoticed, until that one quantum event that creates the universe out of nothing). Nor can I speak of the months that followed in which I appeared, variously, like a little pea, a fish, an eyeless salamander, and so on.

I do know this: I was born in the town of Edelburg outside Leipzig in 1923. My father owned a small factory that made brass finishings—belt buckles, door knobs, faucet heads, platters for serving tea. He employed fifty local workmen and I grew up in relative comfort. Edelburg was a pretty, old town that fanned out along the peaceful Saale River and scrambled up a steep hill to the ruin of an old castle. If you think of charming town squares and little fountains, medieval three-story houses with steep roofs and crisscrossing beams built into the walls, if you think of crooked streets and flower boxes on the railings of the bridges that cross the river, that was where we lived.

Our house was off from the middle of town, not so old as to be narrow and warped and not so new as to be devoid of charm—with a high ceiling, a wide central staircase, a dining room of fine dinnerware.

I remember playing hide-and-seek along the walls of the castle, imagining I would find some treasure there, playing make-believe with my friends where some of us were defenders and some of us were invaders. And I remember fishing along the banks of the Saale with my father. We would drive up along the stream to where the valley got steeper, the scenery more rugged, hike another two miles upstream from the pull-off, and drop in our lines. And I remember my mother, giant as any Teutonic mythical figure in her high heels and sweeping skirt, taking me to the *Kindershule* for my first day of school and letting go of me—I remember the feeling of running off with the other children and knowing she was still watching me, *would* be watching me the whole time until I entered the building itself and disappeared from sight.

My father worked hard and made sure I knew it. "Everything I do is for you," he would tell me. And if he had just come back from the drinking hall, and was tipsy, he would say it with tears in his eyes. At those times he would hold me, like he was yearning for something from me that I had no capacity to offer or even to grasp. He tried. I will give him that. He loved me. But he was not someone who it was easy to love back. When people greeted him on the street, *Guten Tag, Herr Jaeger*, I sensed both their deference, because he was someone of means, and also a feeling that the respect he was afforded was due to his position alone—that in truth people found him to be curious, awkward. He seemed ashamed of himself around more educated men, ashamed around more manly, athletic men, comfortable perhaps around business acquaintances, but also disparaging of them. "They love only their money," he would say.

Yet he was himself fascinated by money, envious of those who had more. He hid it in jokes, in some devious smile when he talked about someone else's stash. But he also had dreams for my education, for my rising above this tawdry grubbing for gold.

In some ways he always seemed to be searching for his place. A serious man, with big dreams for my education. But he also had a sly smile, especially when speaking of the hypocrisy of others—the licentious priest, the corrupt judge, the bribable policeman. These were subjects of both high comedy—a kind of joyous release—and also instruction, for my benefit, about the human condition.

He was lonely in his marriage. This I sensed in the quiet that settled over our dinners, and in the things he would say to me in those weepy, lovelorn, drunken moments. "My only child! My life! Some day you will understand." I don't know if my mother ever loved him. It is unfair to say she married him solely for his money. Who knows what she felt. I will say that by the time I was aware of them, she was nagging and controlling, and he was henpecked.

My mother was devoted when I was very young. She loved babies. Little ones. She reduced herself to a happy babble of baby-talk around them. As I grew older I saw other sides to her. A coldness and pride. Giving the waiter a hard time at the restaurant. Referring to the housekeeper who had mislaid something as *Ein Idiot*. Arguing with the sales lady in the department store about a barely visible thread in the wrong place on a coat she had purchased. If my father was only partially comfortable with the respect he was afforded, my mother accepted it as her due.

And then there were times it went beyond mere pride and she showed an almost willfully contradictory quality. I remember walking along a garden once and saying something like, "roses are the sweetest-smelling flowers."

"There are many *wonderful*-smelling flowers," she replied. And then she made me stop by every new blossom that was not a rose, to inhale its fragrance. "This one is magnificent. See? I don't know what you're talking about. And this! It has a wonderful smell! What are you saying?"

"I didn't mean 'sweetest' in the literal sense. I only meant..."

"But still! And the lilacs when they're blooming...you can smell a block away!"

Let me skip ahead to 1935. I was thirteen. My mother took me and Hilda, my former governess, to a popular local restaurant for lunch—the Dorfschenke on Bruckenstraße. Everyone knew this place, with its big, porcelain boar's head sign hanging over the cobble sidewalk. Hilda had been my governess until I entered *kindershule*, had stayed friends with my mother, and was always excited (or at least pretended so for my sake) to see me, to see how much I had grown, to dote over me.

She was younger than my mother and the only one of my parents' friends who I liked. Their other friends, in married units of two, used to interview me at my parents' dinner parties about my favorite school subjects. I would say recess or lunch, elicit the requisite smiles and laughter, and disappear upstairs. Hilda was different though—all light and spirit. She told stories of what I was like as a baby, asked who was the class clown, told stories about the pranks they played on their teachers in her day. I remember once, when I was eight, she had asked me to guess her age, and when I guessed sixteen she laughed delightedly and gave me a big hug and I felt her breasts (pretty and pointy and brassiere-bound) against my cheek. She was a comely red-head, full of sparkle, and I was in love. (Yes, at age of eight, I was in love with a twenty-year-old. So why should I not, at the age of eighty-five, be in love with a nineteen-year-old?)

Now, at lunch, and looking at our menus, Hilda started asking me about girls, teasing me. My eight-year-old's love had matured, ripened into thirteen-year-old's lust, and the hug, the breasts against my cheek, had taken on a more erotic quality in retrospect.

"I bet they're all crazy for you," Hilda said.

"Shush," my mother said. "You'll give him a swollen head."

"Aww, he's going to be a heartbreaker," Hilda said. "Is there any special girl?"

There was indeed a girl in my class who struck me as almost infinitely beautiful, my mind immediately leapt to her, but this just caused me to blush.

The waiter arrived. My mother fancied herself a great gourmet, and always had to ask questions before she ordered. No matter how simple the food. (She is the only person I have ever encountered who could ask, with a straight face, "How is the glass of milk prepared?") The menu had a French-Alsatian influence, and in this case so did the waiter. He had a thick accent, a slightly superior, overly elegant manner. So the elements were all there for one of my mother's scenes.

"What's in the Limburger sandwich?" my mother asked.

The waiter tilted forward slightly. "Madame....it iz...a *sandvich*."

My mother looked puzzled, vaguely annoyed. "I know that. I can see that. That's why it's called a sandwich. What *kind* of sandwich is it?"

The waiter continued in the same manner. "It iz.....with bread. Toast. You see? A sandvich."

Now my mother turned red, her voice raised slightly, "I *know* it's a *sandwich*! Of course it's a sandwich! That's why it's called a sandwich! Of course it has bread. What sandwich doesn't have bread? My question is, what *kind* of sandwich? What's *in* the sandwich?"

Hilda shot me a little smile, we were conspirators together now, watching this drama.

"It has zee Limburger-r-r," the waiter said, rolling the last 'r' majestically, for greatest anger-inducing effect.

"Yes. Thank you," my mother said. "It says that. I can read. I mean, besides bread. Besides Limburger. Is there mustard? Is there sauerkraut? Butter? Marmalade? I mean, *really*!"

"*Pardon, madame*," the waiter offered, with a perfectly executed half-bow. "It has zee mayonnaise. And zee tomato. Vould it pleez you?"

But, as was her fashion, once she was inflamed, my mother wouldn't let it go that easily. "Thank heaven!" she declared, rolling her eyes. "We now know what is in the sandwich." Then she turned again to the waiter. "*All* sandwiches have *bread*. That's what makes them *sandwiches.* I was asking what was *in* the sandwich. *Besides* the *Limburger.* Why didn't you just say so? That's what I was *asking.*"

The waiter tried again. "No, madame. Just zee Limburger. And zee tomato."

"I see."

"Zat is zee sandvich. Vould you like?"

"No, I would *not* like," my mother said. "I don't *like* Limburger."

"Ah."

"Do you have any other cheese?"

By now Hilda was positively laughing. Only she managed to do it in a way that included my mother, which made it seem like a comedy that we might as well all be enjoying. "I think you should get something else," she said. And then, to the waiter, "Just bring Frau Jaeger the Schnitzel. And a beer."

And soon enough she had my mother laughing as well. It was 1935, as I have said, and as the astute reader has undoubtedly already noted with a nod of recognition, even perhaps, premonition. Hitler's buffoon face was everywhere like a movie poster for some feature whose arrival we were still awaiting. Swastikas hung from flags at the town hall. And somewhere in the dark distance, prison camps had already swallowed up the country's Communists and journalists and resistors. And yet how happily life went on! Like there were two Germanys, one a grotesque re-imagining of the other.

I had sensed some tension between Hilda and my mother over politics.

"I just don't know where it's all heading," Hilda had said, years before.

"It's not heading anywhere," my mother had said. "It's just like America in the south. With their Negroes. Give them their own schools. Their own restaurants. Their own whatever. Let them keep to their own. What's wrong with that?"

"I worked for a Jewish family for a while. I didn't see anything wrong with them. I didn't see how they were…parasites."

"Oh, that talk of parasites…that's just Hitler. He loves to get people fired up. He's just trying to prove himself."

"Well, far be it from me to speak ill of the chancellor…."

"Don't tell me you are going with the communists, Hilda. You know what's happening to them."

"I'm not going with anyone."

"Your problem," my mother said now, "is you are thinking too much about politics and not enough about finding a man."

"My problem," here Hilda's smile returned, "is I don't want to settle for just one. I like them too much. And I'm not even including Hans here."

The debates had ended though—not because Hilda and my mother had reach agreement, but because all open talk of politics had ceased.

After lunch we walked along Bernstraße. My mother saw a plateware store with a Limoges set that interested her, and hurried in, leaving me alone on the sidewalk with Hilda.

"So yes? There is no girl you are interested in?" Hilda asked.

"Well…there is…one actually."

As I said, there was a girl I thought the very essence of feminine beauty. The female ideal. This in spite of the fact the she was still completely flat-chested, that her knees stuck out like knots from her spindly legs. But her soft, dark eyes, her thick dark hair—it was too beautiful to bear. Her name was Sylvia Bayer. Her father had died before she was born—supposedly of some left-over wound from the Saone.

There was a story about her—that her father had been a Jew. Which would mean, according to the recently passed Nuremberg laws, she was to be considered a Jew. Nobody knew for sure. She lived the life of a Protestant girl, with a Protestant mother. But we had all heard the rumor. Still, she didn't act differently. Had her friends. And nobody treated her differently—each maybe waiting for someone else to say something, deciding, by the inaction of the others, that somehow her lineage had been validated. Or maybe it was like she existed in that Germany that had not changed at all.

If you have guessed that this girl is in some way related to what has become of me, so many years later, you have indeed guessed correctly. But at the time her ambiguous status only added a kind of additional mystery to her. My mother had said disparaging, nasty things about Jews and I had more or less accepted them on their face. A few of my teachers had gone even further. And we had all gathered at assemblies and listened to Hitler's radio addresses. But surely Sylvia must be different, I thought. Surely everyone doesn't mean to include her. Otherwise, why would she still have her German friends? And how could she be so *normal*?

She had been in my class since the beginning of the year, but it was as though I just noticed her one day, out of the blue, even though she had been there all along. So it was not love at first sight. More like love at first awareness. There she was one day, just like any other, at the desk two over from mine, and it was like I was looking at her for the first time. This mythical creature. Right there in my classroom. Surely if there were something to the rumors, if there were something that wrong with her, someone would have said something? Done something?

"Is she pretty?" Hilda asked me while my mother was still in the store.

"I think so," I said.

"Well tell her. Tell her you think she's pretty."

The thought had not even occurred to me, and now seemed terrifying. "Do you think so?"

"Sure. Just say it casually. And then ask her out to the movies. Here, you can practice with me. Tell me I'm pretty."

"I can't say that."

"Why? Do you not think I am?"

"Of course I do. It's just...."

"You're just like your father," Hilda said with a smile. "All nervous around girls." I had never thought of my father in that way, or of Hilda speaking enough with my father to even find this much out. "We're nothing to be frightened of you know. Okay, so now tell me I'm pretty." She fluttered her eyelashes absurdly, comically.

"You're...."

"Yes?"

I swallowed. "You're pretty."

"Not like that!" she said. "Like you're just making conversation. Like it's easy."

This time I looked at her, gathered my voice. "You're pretty."

"There. You said it. Was that so difficult?"

"That's different," I said.

"It is not. Don't let it be. So what's the lucky girl's name?"

"Sylvia."

"What a pretty name. And to think how you are depriving her with your silly shyness. I want you to ask her out. And then I want you to report back to me."

And so the terms of my quest had been set.

- Illyria -

It was supposed to be a party. Handful of idle rich, boarding a gleaming yacht while the masses gathered at the marina and looked on, dockworkers and locals and lowly, land-bound vacationers, all left in a cloud of smoke as we pulled away, iridescent, oily film spreading out over the water—our parting gift. Two weeks of sun and sea and self-satisfaction, cutting the ocean like a claw, returning tanned and toned and condescending and indifferent.

When the yacht caught fire, there was just enough time to pack up some of our belongings, along with the survival kit, and load them all into the skiff. We had a lighter for fire, plastic bottles for water, a flare gun that has since failed us. We had a few personal effects—lipsticks, nose-hair scissors (mine), Preparation H (Monique's, apparently, and with new, extended tip for easy application), Allegra, toothpaste, floss, combs, what have you. Of course, most of the personal items are long since used up. We have pen and paper, upon which this journal is being recorded. And we have a few random bits of reading material that happened to have been stuffed in the right day-bag: an old copy of *Vogue*, the novel *Great Expectations* that Andreas was reading for a class, some magazine about cigar-smoking called *Aficionado*. How much is there to say about cigar-smoking? Holy crap. And a flyer for some resort where you can "swim with dolphins." What an adventure!

We have the damaged skiff itself, but it rests lifeless on the beach, useless but for a place to sit. The clothes that were salvaged are a haphazard mix of evening wear and bathing suits, underwear and t-shirts and Dawn's once-charming sailor suit. It all hangs about the branches outside our shelter, is soaked in the rain and dries in the sun. It is amusing how we have preserved our modesty here. We slip our tattered clothes on and off discreetly behind bushes and rocks. Except

Conrad, who has taken to nudism (if a primitive can truly be said to be nudist).

The men have beards. Our bodies are covered with sores and bites and stings. And we're all thin and scrawny as coyotes in winter. Still, daily existence, survival, seems to have been established. We have learned which roots are worth eating, which cause stomach cramps, which taste like poison but can still be swallowed without apparent harm. We have learned to build spearheads out of rock flakes and use a vine to tie them to sticks, and we have learned to use our spears to catch fish. And we have a steady, if meager, supply of dove eggs.

One day Andreas accidentally left Cole's Swiss Army knife in a pool of salt-water and destroyed it. Cole swore at him, upbraided him in front of us, told him he'd never work on his boat again. Which was unlikely, in any case, since Cole's boat is somewhere at the bottom of the ocean.

Andreas was surprisingly calm in the face of Cole's fury. He just looked down somberly at the ground. And in time, Cole settled down, "forgave" Andreas. "We all need to be more careful," he said, looking out over the rest of us. And then he added, absurdly, "I'm going to give you a pay raise."

Andreas looked away, unsure how one expressed thanks for a make-believe gesture of magnanimity.

Conrad shot me a look at me.

I shrugged. "It's capitalism," I said.

"It's bullshit," Conrad said.

"Yes. That too," I said.

"Well, I'm gonna talk to Andreas," Conrad said, "and tell him he doesn't have to take that."

"What did he take?" I asked. "He took a pay raise."

"A pay raise he'll never see," Conrad said. "But that's what they do. They keep you going on promises. *Serving the man.* I'm going to talk to him."

Later I saw them talking together. I saw Conrad kicking the sand irritably, and Andreas nodding, listening, looking off. And for a while after that there seemed to be a bonding between Andreas and Conrad. Conrad had identified a member of the working class, and was turning him into a young revolutionary. This became clearer one day when Cole was looking for someone to shovel our excrement into furrows of freshly planted something-or-other (we had not settled on a name, some sort of starchy vegetable).

"Whose turn is it?" Cole asked, looking from one of us to the next. Andreas had been the first to be assigned this particularly odious chore (made more odious by the absence of a shovel). Then Conrad and I had taken our turns. It had never been stated explicitly, but there was a tacit understanding that the women were to be exempted. Who could ask Dawn, our young innocent, to mine our open latrine for its magical properties. And surely Cole was not going to besmirch Monique, his own lover, with scooping the lode of an octogenarian's ass.

We looked at one another, said nothing. "Who went last?" Cole asked.

"Hans did," Monique offered helpfully.

"So that means we're back to Andreas," Cole said.

Now Conrad looked at Andreas. We all felt the sense of injustice. For a moment nobody spoke. We were each waiting for someone else to say something. Dawn left the group, wandered down to the beach, as she always did when she anticipated a confrontation. Andreas looked off. He had a handsome face, bronzed and chiseled and wreathed in golden curls. Most of us had seldom heard him speak. "Is it?" he asked.

"Seems that way," Cole said.

"What about you?" Andreas asked.

"Me?"

"You," Andreas said.

Conrad nodded agreement, pleased, *pleased* that Andreas had spoken up. The revolution was spreading. It was no longer just the intellectual elites—himself. It was now the proletariat as well.

"I don't take a turn," Cole said, aware that this was an important moment, that everyone was watching suddenly.

Andreas looked at Conrad for support. "Why not?" he asked.

"I have all kinds of work nobody else has," Cole said. "Mental work. And it's plenty difficult."

"That's bullshit," Conrad said. "What fucking mental work?"

"Designing stuff. Planning."

"Well what about my mental work?" Conrad asked.

"What mental work do you have?" Cole asked.

Conrad looked at me for support. "He masturbates," I said. "It requires concentration."

"Hans!" Conrad felt betrayed.

"What?" I said. "I was sticking up for you."

Gloria blushed and recovered and raised a hand to volunteer. "Well, gosh! I'm not helpless yet!"

But if Gloria took a turn that meant Monique would have to take one as well. And so Monique rallied to Gloria's defense. "That wouldn't be right! We can't...it's not...." And she looked up at Cole.

For a moment Cole looked off, said nothing. He cleared his throat. He started three different sentences, and swallowed each in turn. At last, and muttering something about whether there was anywhere left that was free, he stormed off to the shit-farm.

The loss of the knife was unfortunate. Now we have only sharpened oyster shells for blades. But it would become more important later as a symbol, the dawn of our glorious anti-Cole revolution.

Perhaps our single most precious possession is our Bic cigarette lighter. Only it has started to run low on fuel. So now our fire must be kept lit all night because we know there are only a few dozen lights left. We have tested rubbing sticks, smashing rocks that look like they might release sparks, but of course we have no idea what we're doing. And so someone must stay up and babysit the fire, and during the day also someone must always be on fire-duty, and someone else must make sure there is a good supply of wood, and the fire has to be kept strong enough that it will survive a sudden downpour. In fact, it is so critical to us, the thought of losing our fire so terrifying to us, that a second hearth, protected under a canopy, has been built and is always ready for lighting should a sudden rain storm threaten our main blaze. And yet even with these precautions, it seems every couple of weeks we need to take out our magical fire maker and say a prayer and expend a droplet of its precious oil.

Sometimes, when Conrad is on fire duty, I sit up late with him, keeping him company. We look out at the stars, the moon, see if we can remember all the state capitals, the presidents. We tell stories to amuse one another. Conrad's first time, he tells me, was with a distant cousin. They did it in a car. I ask for details. What kind of car? Back seat or front? Top or bottom? Just once? The next day, he tells me, their families played tennis together, and they acted like nothing had happened.

"Did you ever do it with her again?"

"Never. I wrote her a letter. Worded carefully in case her parents read it. She wrote back, ignoring what I'd written and telling me all about her new boyfriend."

"Did you ever talk to her about it?"

"Never. I saw her three years later. Her family was rich. We were the poor side of the family. I could tell she was ashamed of what she'd done. Not the fact that it was incest. The fact that I didn't have money."

I slapped what felt like a bug crawling on my neck, felt a crunch.

"Too bad," I said, wondering if it was true, or if Conrad just always felt he was judged for his lack of money, or if, in turn, this little story was the beginning, the source, of Conrad's worldview. I looked at his half-wild face, filthy and fire-lit and orange. "What does she do now?"

"She's a sales rep for a home-made pasta company. How can it be home-made if it is distributed by a fucking sales rep?"

"Good point."

"Did your mother have a sales rep for her baked fucking potatoes?"

"My mother didn't bake potatoes."

"Capitalism requires bullshit."

"Maybe life requires it," I say.

"But capitalism rewards it."

"Well, maybe life rewards it. Do you know crows hide food from each other? They even wait until the other crows aren't looking and then they hide it. And then afterward they act all innocent."

"I'm not sure I follow your point," Conrad says.

"My point is crows are bullshitters too. Maybe all species are."

Conrad thinks about that for a while. "Not dogs," he says.

There is a long pause. The crackle of the fire. The breathing of the waves. Life functions of the planet.

"Okay, maybe not dogs."

"I hope you don't die first," he says. "This place would be lonely if you went first."

It's nice of him to say this. I feel fonder of Conrad than I have felt in a long time. "I'll try not to," I say.

"Can I tell you something?" he asks.

"Sure," I say.

"You know what I can't stop thinking about?"

"What?" I ask.

"Well, it's more a who than a what," he said.

I feel a slight discomfort coming over me. "Okay, who?"

"I know it's crazy."

"Maybe you should...."

"She's a child. I know it. And yet..."

"Dawn?" I ask.

"I know," he says. "She's less than half my age. But...oh my God. There's just something about her...."

Dawn, you must resist him. He's wrong for you. You must resist all of them.

He goes on. "Have you seen her when she's washing in the cove?"

"Your feelings for her are wrong," I say with some conviction. Shall I pretend that I was astonished at my own hypocrisy? Of course I was not.

"I know," Conrad says. "I know. It's just..."

"Maybe you just want her because she's Cole's step-daughter. Maybe this is really about Cole."

"Maybe you're too old to feel it anymore," Conrad says. "But...I don't know...."

I add a stick to the fire. I think of saying goodnight, leaving him out here alone. His punishment. But I don't feel tired anymore. "I want her too," I say finally, sadly.

He looks at me.

"I'm in love with her," I say.

"You're...?"

"Yes."

We are quiet for a long while.

"Christ," he finally says.

"Nothing I can do about it."

"You didn't have to tell me, though."

"I wouldn't have. If you hadn't told me first."

"But now...I'll feel like I'm betraying you. If...."

"If you succeed with her?" I ask. "Don't worry on that account. You have no hope."

"And you know that for a fact somehow?"

Do I know it for a fact? Or do I just wish I could be as certain as I sound? "Yes," I say.

"She's told you?"

"No."

"Then how do you know?"

"I understand her."

We sit quietly. Something in the fire pops.

"Well you certainly have less hope than I do," he says.

"It is in our nature to cling to hope," I say.

"You think the world is really still out there?" Conrad asks.

"What do you mean?"

"I mean, maybe there was a nuclear war or something. Who knows. Or some epidemic. And the rest of the world has been wiped out. And we're all that's left."

"Maybe," I say.

"So tell me about *your* first time," Conrad says.

- Germany -

Did you catch that? How I finished that last part with Conrad asking about my first time, and how cleverly it brings us back to Edelburg and Sylvia? I am starting to get the hang of this. And isn't Dawn really Sylvia herself, Sylvia's surreal after-image, her ghost?

So let me return to my childhood. Only maybe *that* is the part that is dream, and the island part is real. Have you considered that? An old man's reflection on Eden, on some mythical past, as told after his banishment?

Hilda had been to our house often, visiting with my mother, and each time took me aside and asked me about Sylvia. Whether I had spoken to Sylvia yet. And her impatience fed my own. One weekend there was to be a dance at the school and I became determined to ask Sylvia out at the dance. I had told a friend about my interest in Sylvia, and of my plan to ask her out, and my friend had told his friends, and so by the time of the dance everybody knew—knew even that this was the night I was going to do it.

Perhaps my father sensed my distraction, and the reason behind it, as well. Because on the night of the dance he asked me to dine out with him—just the two of us. Can it be said that you truly know a person only after you have seen him or her order in a restaurant? By coincidence, he also took me to Dorfshenke, and we were served by the same waiter, which made for something of a controlled experiment as to which of my parents was the more difficult, more embarrassing to be with, and in what way.

My father was just getting to the point of our conversation—my studies, my future—while in my own mind I was entirely focused on my upcoming encounter with my beloved, which of course was a thousand times more important than something as insignificant as my future.   It made for a   lopsided question and answer session—longwinded, penetrating questions, briefest, vaguest of answers. And in the midst of this, the waiter came over and attention was drawn to the menus.

I ordered a Schnitzel. My father however could not make up his mind, seemed unsettled by the choices. "How spicy is the Schweinwurst?" he asked.

"It...has zee little, how do you say, zee little...pinch. It's not... extremely spicy."

Was I always just looking for fault in my father? Did his aversion to spice not seem overly dainty, effete, even...cowardly? Was there no room for some masculine pain in one's diet?

"I see," my father said, still unsure. "Hmm....so is that like...*very* spicy?"

"No," the waiter replied, his posture conveying at once distance, respect, condescension. "I would not say zat. It iz a bit...medium, sir."

My father, still did not feel he had a precise calibration of spiciness necessary for his decision. "I don't really like too peppery. Would it be...peppery?"

Now the waiter looked at me just long enough so that I knew he recognized me, knew he remembered my other parent. And somehow both of my parents were my fault. I was the common ingredient, after all, the source of the issue. "It iz not...very peppery, no. But if you don't like zee spice perhaps you would enjoy somezing else."

"Oh I see," my father said. "And the Szegediner Gulasch? How is that?"

"Zat is a bit spicy as well. I would say medium."

"Ah." My father considered. "Is it *very* spicy?"

"No. Not very. But again...."

There were newly placed flags with swastikas at the party headquarters just outside the restaurant. The SS were already sending 'radicals" off to unknown fates at concentration camps and Germany had recently retaken the Rhineland. In a few short years the Dorfshenke would be a steaming ruin and those of us still alive would be searching for stale pieces of bread in the pockets of dead soldiers. But right now my father was not ready to reach a firm conclusion about his order. He was still trying to hone in on the *exact* level of spice.

"Is it more...*sharp*?" he asked the waiter.

"Well, if you don't like spice at all, again...it might be sharp."

"I see." (Pondering, coming up with an idea). "Can you make it milder?"

"Sadly, Szegediner Gulasch is a stew, a goul*ash*." I had no doubt the waiter was thinking the equivalent, in his native French, of the contemporary English, *"It's a freaking stew, dipshit!"* What he said was, *"Pardon*, sir, it iz already prepared."

"I see," my father said, looking back at the menu.

I was starting to squirm. Imagining the waiters talking about us in the kitchen. *Herr Jaeger! Blödmann!*

"Should I...give you a moment? Come back?" the waiter inquired.

My father considered this new question. But now he seemed positively paralyzed by the complexity of the dilemmas before him. Did he need more time? Hmm. That was difficult to say. Perhaps yes. On the other hand...perhaps not. And so now, he could not even decide whether he needed another moment, and so lost track of whatever decision he might be arriving at as to his order. Moreover, there was the new predicament, the new problem of which question to consider first— whether he needed more time, or whether he would like the Goulash. And so he just sat there, inert, as many long seconds ticked by, requiring the poor waiter to stand there, desperately trying to maintain his pose of Alsatian superciliousness, while his other tables were beginning to turn this way and that, looking for him.

At last, and through some process I cannot begin to imagine, an idea rose forth. "Would it be possible to *try* the Szegediner Gulasch?" my father asked.

"Vati, please...." I said at last, face in my hands.

"Perhaps, vee can do zis," the waiter said and hurried off.

My father turned to me as though I were deaf and had not heard this exchange. "They're going to bring over a taste."

"I know," I said, still looking down into my hands. "I heard."

What was it about my father? Why did he not fit in? He surely sensed that his requests were *off* in a certain way. Made light of them. Made excuses for himself. And yet he couldn't help himself. He needed. He was everything and it's opposite. He condemned all vices —greed and envy and hypocrisy, he mocked them and laughed at them, and yet, deep inside, he was in a constant battle with them, with himself, red-faced with envy and shame, confidence and clumsiness, pushiness and hesitation. He was a child inside a man. And uncomfortable with that too.

After the waiter had returned with his miniature bowl of goulash, and my father had finally tasted and ordered his meal, he turned back to the subject at hand. How were my grades holding up. What did I think about university? I could learn our great literature. Goethe. Schiller. Or study music. My father was a great Beethoven fan. Or what about science? Medicine? But then, when I merely shrugged, a contrary idea

seemed to take over. An idea that, I soon realized, was the reason for
our dinner. Well then, he said. If I had no other plan, it was time for
me to understand that I would be taking over the business one day.
"There are going to be a lot of opportunities," he said. "You know what
there is a big demand for?"

"What?" I asked.

"Brass band instruments. They can barely keep them in the stores.
And if we begin an actual military campaign...you can imagine...." He
was excited. It was a new era. A time not of actual combat of course,
no, but certainly of pomp, of military music. And here he was. Right in
the middle of it. He had spent two years retooling his factory of brass
fittings to make trumpets, trombones, tubas. And re-branding his
company. "What do you think?" he asked. "You want to join your
father at Jaegermusik? That is our name now. You could start this
summer."

He leaned over and put his hand on my knee and gave it a friendly
shake that was as frightening as if a bear were attacking me. I thought
of Sylvia. Of the dance that I was in danger of being late for. Was there
really a choice? "All right," I said. So this was to be my future. Hans
Jaeger. I would make musical instruments. For the war effort. I would
help provide the musical accompaniment to the atrocities. Are the worst
of human tragedies not on some level also the greatest of human
comedies?

I was still feeling unsettled when I arrived at the dance; still
perhaps in the glow of shame of the scene at the restaurant, as though I
surely must be awkward like my father by both birth and association.
And now the girls all looked different from usual. More glamorous. I
couldn't have said exactly how they were different. They just seemed
particularly lovely. As I got older I could better recognize the art behind
the effect, the sweeping skirts that came to just below the knee, the high
heels and make-up and decorative hair-pins. But then they just seemed
untouchably beautiful. Unapproachable. The way their still-narrow
hips swayed in time to some popular melody whining from the little
four piece band on stage.

And there she was among them. My pubescent Sylvia. Shining,
black hair around that pale, moon-face. Starry night of a girl. My heart
started to beat at the sight of her, only more with terror than with joy. I
remembered Hilda's advice. Just be confident. But that seemed scary
too. Because it was so impossible. Sylvia turned her head in my
direction and I looked away quickly. Had she seen me staring at her?
Had she noticed the hundred other times I had stared at her? Had my
friends told her friends, and had her friends in turn told her, that I was in

her thrall, and that tonight was the night, that I was going to ask her to go out with me?

I watched the dancing, drank the grape juice that was offered by the organizers (*ersatz* wine to fortify me to declare my *ersatz* love).

The next song came up. Her partner wandered off. She was alone for a moment. This was it. My friends watched as I left the safe harbor of their company and headed off into the swaying ocean of dancers. I caught her eye. Only this time I didn't look away. I continued forward. "Would…you…like to dance?"

She nodded yes. I took her hand. Soon I felt her other hand, softly, against my shoulder. There was no technique. It was all just an imitation of the dancing we had seen older teens do. We made conversation about our classes, teachers. I felt a bit calmer. Yes. I could do this. How remarkable it felt even. To actually be touching her! To have her touch me! Soon the melody wound down. We broke off. But she was still there before me. Waiting. Waiting as though she knew what was coming. "Would you…go steady with me?" I asked. (Forgive me. I don't recall the exact phrase that was in currency then, in our little provincial world, or how it would be said in English. But it was something to that effect.)

"I don't think so," she said.

Just like that. It hit me like an electric shock.

I waited for her to say more. To qualify it in some way. To explain it. But there was nothing else. Nothing to ease the moment. No face-saving, "But I would like to be friends." No explanation, "I think you're really nice but…."

I was too stunned to say anything more myself. Only…how to just walk away? What to do? In retrospect, and now that I can laugh at it, it reminds me of something from that American cartoon of Lucy and Charlie Brown. "No. No, I will not go steady with you. Goodbye." But in the moment we were stuck in a kind of death-grip of discomfort. I just stood there. And she just stood there facing me.

"Is there anything else?" she finally asked.

"No," I said.

And then I bowed forward slightly. *"Heil Hitler,"* I said.

Those words, so startling now, just came out like that sometimes— especially among those of us who had grown up with them, who had been taught them at school, when we were still too young to even know what they meant. It was simply the way to greet someone. It was just hello, good evening, have a good day, and differed from those other greetings only in that it was more formal, and therefore, at this moment, rather horrendously clumsy.

She made no reply, just looked at me.

And then, somehow, I was back with my friends, had navigated through the dancers, tacked my way through what had become a sea of shame, thinking not only of my rejection but of the last, blindingly idiotic words I had uttered. *Heil Hitler.* What was I thinking? What kind of idiot! And…and to a girl who everyone says is Jewish! Suddenly, I wanted to disappear, to melt into nothing, to crawl out of the room unnoticed and never return.

My friends surrounded me. "What did she say? What did she say?" they all wanted to know.

"She said no."

"She what?"

"She said no."

"That's it?"

"Yes."

There was both laughter and sympathy. "She's conceited. Thinks she's too good for everyone."

"Yeah."

"She didn't give a reason? Nothing?"

"No."

"Wow." A snicker. "That's bad."

Within a few minutes of course everyone at the dance knew. Her friends. Friends of her friends. *She said no to him. Did you hear? Sylvia told him no.*

It seemed more than just the end of my hopes for Sylvia. It was the end of my hope for love itself. For escape. I saw myself at Jaegermusik, suffocating under my father's gaze and hand. Trapped.

Later, and just as everything was coming apart in ways we still had not imagined, Sylvia and I were able to laugh at this false start. But in the days immediately after my stupendous rejection, my imbecilic, *Heil Hitler*, I wanted to climb under my bed like a four-year-old, squeeze myself all the way up against the wall, and never emerge.

And now let me ask a question. Do you sense the impending doom? The inevitable? Do you wonder at us all going on blithely, blindly, unable to see the coming war years, the disaster that was right before our eyes? At least remember this. Inevitability is something we imagine in retrospect. History was somehow all destined. Predetermined. Only what about randomness? That cackling fool that bounds in, changes the plot line entirely. That causes anarchists' bombs to misfire, that causes a momentous meeting to end prematurely when one of the world's leaders has a sudden case of the runs? That causes lightning to strike a yacht and the rod to fail and a gas-line to catch fire?

I spent the summer at Jaegermusik, which occupied space across the street from the original Jaeger factory. The rooms were dark and dry and thick with a hundred kinds of grime and dust. My father seemed so anxious, so self-conscious around his employees, you might have assumed *they* had the power to fire *him* and not the other way around. And there was no escaping those moments my father came over and made a show of me before his employees. "So what do you think?" he would say to them, his hand on my shoulder.

"Nice boy," they would reply.

"Good worker."

At the same time, they kept a distance from me. They still knew that anything they said might get back to the boss. And so I had nobody to talk to, to confide in. I answered the telephone, assembled the instruments, tested them. I had learned to play the clarinet with some facility. The other instruments, the horns, I could only blow little farts with, a single note on each. But I learned the trade. I learned how to bend the sheets of brass into tubes and polish them with an astringent sponge, how to clean the lathes and how to pull a tiny filament across a closed valve to make sure there was no room for air to leak out.

As for Sylvia, I had seen her in school every day since the dance, but hadn't spoken to her. Hilda had made a sad face at my rejection, had cheered me, and I was soon over it. In fact, the following school-year I couldn't help noticing how many pretty girls there really were, when you looked about. Any one of whom I might choose as my next imaginary beloved, I might dwell upon and develop some story around and stare at from afar. I was no longer focused on Sylvia, but in some way I was still lovesick—for romance itself, or for what, in my fourteen-year-old's mind, I imagined it to be.

On the other hand, I found myself oddly friendless that year. I am not exactly sure how it happened. Whether I felt contemptuous of everyone around me, or they felt indifferent to me, I don't really know how it began. I had started to find my childhood friends grating, immature, and yet had failed to make any new friends. And suddenly I was alone.

I joined a school arts club and enjoyed painting nature scenes, and I remember once being called *a girl* for it. Oddly, it was not by another boy, but by a girl. How strange, it struck me. First that a girl would consider it an insult to call someone a girl! And then that it was so obviously, so provably false. I was demonstrably *not* a girl. And my accuser, most certainly, *was* a girl. What did it even mean, to be accused of this thing? How was I to respond? By saying, "You're wrong! I'm not a girl!" Instead I just looked at her. Speechless. But it surely added to my confusion.

My mother too seemed frustrated with me. She wanted me to join the newly formed *Jungvolk*. What you might think of as the cub scouts, prelude to joining the *Hitler-jugend*—the Hitler Youth. She wanted a young Nazi she could be proud of. I would like to say that I resisted joining on moral grounds, that everyone else was eager to grow into the military uniforms they would one day wear and that I was a pacifist and a humanist and a resistor. The truth is this: I had been a bed-wetter until the age of thirteen, and though it hadn't happened in a year, the thought of camping out with other boys, of having an accident and being discovered, still terrified me. This is the reason your honorable and courageous narrator did not join the Nazi youth movement!

My father's politics were more ambiguous than my mother's. When he saw a great, National Socialist celebration, full of confetti and swastikas and masses of marching soldiers, what he noticed were the musical instruments of the band, the proud identifying features (if any could be found) of a Jaegermusik creation. And his hand beat, at once triumphant and mocking, with the pompous tones of the music. Underneath though, he seemed more nervous than ever. I have no doubt that, seeing the way the weak were persecuted, sent away, disturbed him. Perhaps, secretly, even sickened him. Was he not one of them? Inadequate in some way? And wasn't all of this rage and hatred a bit... alarming? Wrong even? And so he hesitated, shifted from day to day. And in the end, and weighing all of the mixture of his thoughts and feelings, he arrived at a political philosophy of a shrugged, "Who knows?"

Meanwhile, my parents were arguing more. My father had long been a subject of my mother's complaints. He didn't know how to dress. He had no idea where anything went in the house, was always leaving something unsightly in her showplace. And he didn't pay the slightest attention to what was happening with his son. This was a more frequent refrain. I was wasting myself. Doing nothing. A disappointment. And it was this particular refrain that was most likely to set my father off, both because I was not quite so contemptible as my mother portrayed, and because whatever contemptible qualities I did possess were surely not his fault.

My father stammered out his defenses, absorbed what blows he could not dodge, tried to play peacemaker, until suddenly something came over him. You saw him go dark, silent. And you knew it was coming. He had been pushed too far. He fumed, sputtered, raged. At these times my mother often simply stormed out of the house, or slammed the door to her bedroom. The house fell into silence for a day.

Or two or three days. And then it all just reset somehow. System reboot. Nothing resolved. Everything back to how it had been before the argument.

They never argued about politics. But when my father came into my room in the aftermath of one of their explosions, something vaguely political hung in the air. My father sighed, looked off. "I just don't know what it's all coming to. She's just…unreasonable. The whole country…everyone always shrieking." He never quite said it, but somewhere along the way, he had arrived at something like a conviction, had turned against the regime, even as he hardened against my mother.

If I had any friend at all in that time it was Hilda. A coolness had descended between her and my mother. But she still came to see me. She took me out for ice cream once, and saw I didn't look well and started asking, with such genuine care and concern, what was the matter, that I suddenly started to cry. Maybe it was that she had once been my governess that brought me back to myself during my childhood. Or else it just made me miss that time. That state of innocence. There I was, a teenage boy, and suddenly in tears. "I don't know," I cried. "I'm not happy. I'm just not happy."

She came around the table and hugged me. "My poor Hans. I wish your mother were more…understanding. Of everything." And then, "You should know what your father goes through. How much he loves you."

They were strange words. But it felt good all the same.

In late spring, one of the teachers at school organized a bicycle trip into the Austrian Alps. The escape, the freedom, the thought of being outdoors all appealed to me, and I persuaded my parents to let me go. Fitness, community, were patriotic pursuits after all. I must say something of this trip, not only because it is still one of my happiest memories, and not just because it unexpectedly placed me back in proximity to my not-quite-forgotten love, Sylvia, but because it will fulfill that most essential and basic of all writing requirements, recording how I spent my summer vacation.

We were all to meet at the train station with our bicycles, ride the trains through Germany and then Austria, and arrive a day later in Salzburg. We would sleep in hostels. Bicycle high up into the mountains. Hike and sing. Experience the great outdoors. And so on. I did not realize until we were all at the station that Sylvia was also signed up to be on the trip.

There were ten of us in all, and a leader, Herr Klampf, who was a young, well-liked history teacher at our school. He put us all in an excited, cheerful mood from the start. The train to Salzburg left late in the day and stopped for five hours just outside Nurnberg due to a switching problem. So there were many hours for us to gather in the corner of the club car, rucksacks spread out all around us, and get to know one another. Surprisingly, I found myself not only sitting next to Sylvia, but talking to her easily. About bicycling, the Alps, school, the teachers, at last even other kids in our grade, and who we liked and didn't. Somehow, thrust together in this entirely different milieu, we were no longer bound by that distance that had been imposed on us, or that we had felt obliged to maintain during the school year. Of course, I remembered my great, ignominious moment at the dance, and she must have too. But whatever she thought of it, she showed no desire to embarrass me with it, or let it interfere with the flow of conversation.

Her aura of unapproachable beauty was gone now that I was of the more worldly age of fifteen. And yet, beside her in this setting that was so full of anticipation, I felt I could admire her prettiness more realistically, see her for who she was, and still feel privileged to be the one who got to sit next to her. (Of course, the process of a seeing a woman realistically, understanding what is inside of her, is never complete, even after twenty years of marriage, and surely had barely begun in those hours in the club car, whatever I may have believed). She had a soft face, plain in the sense of being smooth and calm and undramatic, but with a soothingly milky skin and eyes that were full of light. She had a slight country accent—I couldn't say whether there was any Yiddish or Jewishness in it—and a simple way of putting things.

The group passed the time playing parlor games, organized with a kind of childlike enthusiasm by Herr Klampf. The first game was something called, *Das Überbringer*, the messenger, which involved one person acting out some peculiar call or gesture and two others trying to imitate it, with the rest of us voting on who did the best imitation. There were many rooster crows, flared nostrils, impassioned tiger roars. There was something about the time and place, about Herr Klampf and the late hour and the adventure we were all embarking on that freed us of our usual social inhibition, allowed us to be friends with one another, regardless of what clique we belonged to in school.

The next game we played was called *Ball aus Wolle*—ball of wool. For this game Herr Klampf produced a ball of wool and placed it on a table. Teams of two were on each side of the table, and the object was to blow the ball of wool across the other side of the table, where the other team was trying to blow it back at you. Sylvia had trouble with this game, as she found herself smiling and laughing too much to produce any breath. And this in turn only produced more laughing.

I told Sylvia she smiled too much, and that she had to try to not smile for a whole sixty seconds while the rest of us watched and timed her. Everyone liked this idea, and we looked at her while Klampf looked down at his watch and told her when to start. But she was too happy to succeed at this challenge. The best she managed was to smile with her lips closed. And her inability to straighten her lips was itself cause for more smiling, more laughter. And how pleasant to feel that this time I was the cause of it.

The train had started again after our long delay. We passed through Munich, continued on through the black forest. But by then it was after midnight, and gradually we all turned quiet and exhausted. In this dreamy state, the night-filled countryside whirring by, glimpsed through the reflections in the window, I found a pretext to touch Sylvia. We were among the only ones still awake and she was leaning against the window, and I told her I wanted to borrow her back to write a letter against. Lean, bony back. She turned and smiled at me and looked back out the window. What was she really thinking though? Did she *like* me? And what did I myself feel? Was I again in love with her? I definitely liked being next to her. When the letter was done and there was nothing more to do but sleep, my next move toward a special closeness between us— something that would set us apart from the others—was apparent. I leaned myself against her. That same smooth back, that shoulder, now with a sweater draped over it. The train rumbled. I felt her warmth, her fresh scent, closed my eyes, caught bits of sleep.

When the sun came up we had crossed the Austrian frontier. Farms, valleys, mountains were all around us, and I spent the hours contentedly, just staring out at the passing scenery. Sheep herds clustered tightly on the hillsides, huts perched high up on slopes, snow-peaked mountains hung in the distance. Villages came up suddenly, passed by in a blurry moment, were gone. Back out into the open.

Nothing more happened right away with Sylvia. I got to know some of the rest of the group. Most outgoing and prominent was a girl named Alika. She was quite attractive as well, with a confident face, golden hair that often had a wildflower in it, and strong, bicyclist's legs. Alika acted like she was a lot more grown-up, more sophisticated and worldly than the rest of us, and the truth was she was all of these. She was more socially adept, indifferent to our more childish games, interested in Socrates, Goethe and Herman Hesse. She had the fascinating habit of drawing people together into a little social group where she was the center and brightest light, and then suddenly slipping away from it to go off by herself, leaving the group empty, devoid of its core, wanting to follow after her. What did she do by herself? Why did she do that? Someone finally asked her, and she told us, though the words scarcely made sense to us. She was practicing something she had read in her Hesse. Now it would probably be called meditating. "It helps me figure things out," she would say, rather mysteriously. She didn't make a point of her meditating. But somehow, it felt like she still made of point of it by not making a point of it.

Still, all in all, Alika was pleasant to be around, helpful when there was work to be done, open to everyone.

My best friend on the male side was a boy named Ernesto, from a working class district along the river. He had a bit of urban roughness in him. He was interested in American Jazz, used lots of slang, had red hair and a grimy beard. He was a regular guy, never needed to show off, and everyone liked him.

As we approached our destination late in the morning, the mountains wrapped themselves around us more tightly. A mountain stream wove along beside us. Startlingly beautiful. Only around the next bend they were even grander, pastures rising halfway, speckled with flowers, and then cliffs, glaciers, magnificent peaks. None of us had known exactly what to expect. We'd seen paintings, but they'd all seemed more magical than real. And the black-and-white photographs didn't convey very much. We all watched excitedly. Ernesto, who had scarcely been out of Edelburg, was especially enthralled. Alika seemed captivated as well, but there was something in it that struck me as less spontaneous.

Afterward, perhaps the next day, I told Alika—for what reason I can't imagine—that I could tell she wasn't quite as excited as Ernesto and me, that she was sort of pretending. Perhaps it was my way of hiding the fact that I had myself been a bit false in my demonstrations of excitement. I could see on Alika's face that she was taken aback, a bit offended. But she handled it calmly, even gracefully. "You think?" It was the first but not the last time I would say something pointless and unpleasant to her (and would have its mysterious echoes so many years later, in another world).

We arrived in Salzburg late in the morning and had a picnic at a public park by a fountain. It was Sunday, and Herr Klampf said a few prayers and read a brief Biblical passage from Matthew. I watched Sylvia during this. She said, "Amen," at the end with the rest of us, eyes averted. If anyone had thought of in any way challenging her

Christianity, or making her feel different or inferior, there was something gentle and welcoming in Herr Klampf's manner that made this impossible.

In the next days we settled into the truly remarkable scenery. We rode our bicycles along little, zigzagging roads high in the Alps. We rambled high above the chalets, through wildflower meadows, heard distant cowbells even when it seemed like there was no sign of humanity anywhere. We cooled off in streams of glacial run-off, the glaciers themselves looming above us in odd, animistic shapes, tongue or snout or bear-claw. We climbed switchbacks up mountainsides, passed by thundering waterfalls, played, in spite of our exhaustion, in alpine snowfields. We dove into water that was so cold it felt like liquid ice, and forded streams, pants off to keep them dry, packs bundled over our heads. We rode our bicycles up seemingly endless passes, coasted down for miles on the other side. Once we climbed all morning on our bicycles to some very high pass with a view of an endless sea of mountains. We paused, celebrated, took out our canteens and drank big gulps of metallic-tasting water. We could see, down the other side of the pass, the hostelry, just a couple miles of downhill away. We started off, only to encounter headwinds so ferocious that pedaling downhill was hard work. We had to stand on our pedals, push, fight against the current.

We experimented with all sorts of low-budget food. Rice mush. Oatmeal mush. Cabbage mush. Bratwurst. Blutwurst. Bockwurst. Every meal had its assigned cooks and dishwashers, and though there was a certain amount of drudgery, there was also a pleasant camaraderie. And we washed each other's hair with buckets of stingingly frigid stream water. It was impossible not to gasp and wail when that ice water hit your scalp and ran down your chest and back.

This was it. A kind of ideal of health and spirit and community of our young empire. Yes, there was another side to this new empire, a side our little group, led by Klampf, chose to ignore. But how, looking from one young face to the next, was it possible not to feel a certain excitement at the future? At what was just over the next pass?

In time I got to know the other members of our group better. There was Friedrich, tall and lanky and extremely soft-spoken. At first he was so quiet I barely noticed him. But when you began to pay attention you realized he had the deadpan delivery of a professional cabaret performer. He liked to repeat something someone else said, just changing the emphasis from one word or phrase to another, and so reveal the absurdity of it. Though he gradually became more a part of the group, I can't say anyone ever really got to know him personally.

And there was Reynart, a gangly, fussy sort with an naturalist's interest in the flora and fauna. On the second day of the trip, he received what he thought was a mosquito bite above his eye, and his whole eyelid swelled up. He told us he was allergic to mosquitoes, and thereafter donned a mosquito net over his head when he was outside. Nobody was sure where he'd gotten it, if he had brought it with him, but somehow, draped over his thick-rimmed eyeglasses, tucked into a dark gray jacket he always wore to keep his arms protected, it really made him look like a giant mosquito—or at least one of those mutant creatures, half-man half-mosquito. He was thereafter dubbed *Mosquito Man*.

While on the subject of mosquitoes, there were times the mosquitoes were so thick you could kill eight of them with a single swat of your leg. There were times you ran down to the stream to fetch water and could see the mosquitoes hovering over it like a waiting haze, and you raced back inside as fast as you could, splashing out half of the bucket of water as you went. In time, people started to look enviously at the mosquito net. It became a topic of conversation among the more serious hikers who passed through with their overloaded rucksacks. How well does it work? Where did you find it? How well do you see through it? Can I try it on?

At the start of the trip Herr Klampf had given us a brief talk about the rules. Absolutely no alcohol. Absolutely no hanky-panky between the boys and the girls. No going off and hiking without permission. But what was the purpose of such rules but to create a set of goals to be achieved in breaking them?

On our first evening out in the woods, Ernesto came up to me when nobody else was around and told me he had a little whiskey. Did I want a drink? I had only had alcohol a few times. But I told him sure. So we took a walk down toward an open area by a little lake. Then he opened the flask. It tasted like poison. We passed it back of forth. I forced myself to swallow. It was getting darker. He took out a cigarette and we shared it, and then decided to go for a walk along the lake. And then up a trail. The air was cool and the trail floated under us pleasantly. Perfect evening. The thickets chirping on either side of us. The path wandering pleasantly around one bend and then the next. I am not sure how far we were away from our hostel, but no more than ten minutes of walking, when we was something ahead of us that suddenly made us both stop.

A shadow. Or not a shadow. A shape. Moving. We both froze in place. What was it? And then something even more startling: A pair of eyes. Alive. Something that, without even placing it, naming it, made my heart begin to pound. Looking at us out of the darkness. Low. Lean. Those piercing eyes. And then the sound. A call. Howl. Otherworldly. Terrifying. Had it just appeared there? Or had it been watching us for a long time? Watching us approach, and then howling as we reached a certain distance? Was it alone?

"Ernesto," I said. Not moving. Not taking my eyes off of it.

"Hans."

"What is it?"

"A wolf."

For another instant my gaze met the wolf's. And in that instant there was nothing else there but those eyes.

And then we were running. Running back from where we'd come. Not thinking to look back. Not thinking anything. Just running. Propelled by some instinct that was too powerful to even think of resisting. That moved our legs for us. The feet say run. And then you *are* running. Running like there is no such thing as fatigue, like you could run like that forever. Back down the trail. Back and back. Away from that vision.

At last we slowed. We looked around. Nothing around us. Silence. Only…where were we now? Was this the way we'd come? Where was the lake? The hostel? Maybe it was just the darkness. Only…it wasn't about to get any lighter. Where were we? Somehow we had to find our way back. And soon. Had we missed a turn?

We started tracking up and down the path. Looking for something familiar. Feeling some new, impending dread. I remember Ernesto saying how he was scared. Starting to sob. And my own sickening feeling. Fear. Alcohol. The after-image of that animal. All turning in me.

Both of us trying to stay calm. Quieting each other. Listening. And at last hearing distant voices. At least we weren't too far. Only where were the voices coming from? What saved us was the darkness itself. Once it was dark enough we could make out a light showing through it, and we found a path that headed toward the light, and there it was: Our hostel.

Our first night in the mountains and I'd already broken two of the three rules Herr Klampf had set for us. (Years later I read that the last wolf sighting in Austria was in 1933. It was now 1935. So perhaps ours, albeit unrecorded, was the very last. And its howl was for its entire species. Who knows. Or maybe it was a ghost.)

The next time I drank with Ernesto, it also had some rather ill consequences. We were staying high up on a steep hillside, and there was a particularly lovely spot along the hill where a little wooden bridge crossed a stream. Now, at that spot, I saw Alika and Herr Klampf together. I was looking at them from a distance. And of course I had that tipsy feeling. But…what were they doing? Were they touching each other? I couldn't tell. Certainly they wanted to be alone together. Off by themselves. And course, she was definitely the type to go for a teacher, a group-leader, if only to show how far ahead of the rest of us she was.

I was bothered. I don't know exactly how I justified how bothered I was. But something wasn't right about it. Then, when I looked again, they were gone. Only they weren't coming back in my direction. Where had they gone?

It seemed like forever before I finally saw Alika again back at our camp. And now the mellow inebriation had waxed into a sour fatigue.

"So," I said to Alika, voice dripping with suggestion, "I saw you and Klampf walking together."

She just nodded.

"I guess there's something going on," I said, pushing it further.

"Excuse me?"

"I said I guess there's something going on. Something between you two."

She looked at me. "Is that what you think?" she asked irritably. Then she walked off. I knew, as soon as she was gone, that I was an incomparable fool, that I would spend the rest of the summer trying to prove to Alika that I wasn't, through and through, the fool she had obviously concluded that I was. What was it about her that made me into a different person though? I had felt some peculiar need to bring her down, to elevate myself to her level, but the opposite always seemed to happen.

A week or so later Klampf asked me if I'd like to go for a walk with him, and I said sure, and we went off and he asked me how I was enjoying everything and told me some about himself, he wrote poetry and so on, and wanted to spend a little time with each of us individually to get to know us. I saw how completely absurd my presumption had been.

"So what do you think of all this?" he asked. "Are you enjoying it?"

"I am," I said.

"Good. I just want everyone to have a good time."

I nodded.

"That's all we can really do," he said, looking off a bit regretfully.

He wouldn't say more. But sometimes you can recognize a

person's politics so easily. In just a few innocent-seeming words. In just a phrase, an inflection, a gesture. And this is even more the case in a society where you are not allowed to speak freely. You convey meaning with just the tiniest of hints.

More than half of the trip had passed now, and nothing had happened with Sylvia. Maybe I just had found no good pretext to touch her again. Or maybe I was savoring, in some way, that feeling of attraction and promise. Or was I faintly ashamed of my desire for her, of her ambiguous status? Yes, there was some tacit agreement not to challenge Sylvia's racial purity. But did that mean the others would accept my becoming involved with her? And what would happen when word got around at school? Yet there was still some special connection there. We liked being around one another. And how many times had I almost touched her. Almost put a hand on her shoulder. Yet something had always held me back. Looking back, I think it had nothing to do with who she was, except for this: She was a girl. Foreign. How could I touch that?

Once, late in the trip, Sylvia and I went together to fill a bucket of water at a well. We took a path that led to a little clearing, and once there we were all alone. We found ourselves talking about the others, enjoying our distance from them, even in some way acknowledging that we were enjoying this moment of privacy together. As Sylvia was drawing water I quite spontaneously put a hand on her arm. She started ever-so-slightly, and continued what she was doing. Nothing more came of it. We separated. Shy as deer.

That same day, I was to commit one more *faux pas* with Alika when I interrupted her when she was off by herself, appearing to be doing nothing. This time she finally snapped at me. "Can't you see I'm occupied?"

"Sorry," I said.

"Just pay attention," she said. "I was somewhere important."

What did that mean though? She was somewhere important. Where could she be? Did she really "go somewhere" in those trance-like interludes?

With the trip nearing an end, I had yet to violate that last admonition. No hanky-panky. I had not so much as kissed Sylvia's hair.

On our last full day we rode into Innsbruck and actually went out to a restaurant. I ordered some kind of chicken dish over spaetzle, and after weeks of woods and hostels, of surviving on undersized portions of mush, it was a the most perfect, exquisite, exalted dish of food I had ever tasted.

And then we were on the train ride back to Germany, quietly watching the scenery. I found Sylvia off alone, looking—perhaps it was my imagination—a bit wistful. She was leaning up against the train window, staring out, far away in her thoughts.

I sat next to her. "Something the matter?"

"I don't want it to be over," she said.

"Me either," I said.

Already I was thinking again of my father's factory, classes, my mother's pestering. I leaned against her very gently, ran my hand over her hair. She didn't move away, so I continued, moved my hand over her arm, over her hand. She took it in hers, squeezed it. I looked to see if anyone was looking. And then I rested my head in her hair. "We can go back there someday."

She said nothing, squeezed my hand again.

"Do you remember the dance?" I asked.

She turned to look at me. Suddenly she flashed that closed-lipped smile. "Of course."

"That was pretty embarrassing."

"I'm sorry," she said.

"I guess I was kind of an idiot."

"You weren't," she said.

"I felt like one."

"I just didn't know you."

"I know. I know." I felt myself blush. "So...have you... reconsidered?"

"Maybe."

"Well, can I take you out sometime?"

"You think that's a good idea?"

"Yes."

"You really are an idiot then."

But my arms had wrapped around her. And she was not exactly resisting.

"I'm sure my mother wouldn't let me," she said.

"Why not?"

"She doesn't want anything that...you know.   Could bring attention."

"Is it true?" I asked—what I had wondered for so long.

"Is what true?"

"That your father was Jewish? That you're..."

"No. It's not."

"Then what are you worried about?"

She didn't answer. I pressed my lips into her hair in something like a kiss—marveling at myself, even as I did it.

The late evening light of summer was fading. It was an overnight train and we all had sleeper-car berths. When there was nobody left in the car with us, I took Sylvia into my tiny room and we kissed. We teased each other in ways that are too childish and foolish and intimate to faithfully reproduce. We played endlessly, discovering one another, while the dark of the countryside whirred by, while the moon hung outside the window, raced alongside us like it was peering in, wishing us well. And so in the last hours of the trip I violated that last proscription.

"Would it matter to you?" she asked, in the middle of our embraces.

"Would what matter?"

"If my father had been Jewish."

"No," I said. Which I suddenly felt more certain of as I said it.

"So you don't think they're all parasites?"

"I just know what I feel about you."

We did nothing more than kiss and caress and fall asleep together. That was it. The train chugged through the night. Sylvia slept in my arms. I didn't want to move, didn't want to fall asleep and so end my dream, awaken out of it.

Did I have some prescience about our returning? Did I have even the faintest hint of what was to come? It was just the opposite. Because wasn't it inevitable that in time people like Klampf, good, decent people, would prevail? I pictured how I would become not just a student of Klampf's, but, in time, a friend. I imagined telling Hilda the news of my success with Sylvia, and her pleasure in it. Most of all, I imagined myself with that sweet, pretty girl. All of the pleasures we would share. Only at last I did fall asleep, and when we awoke we were back in Germany. And the earth under us, once more, had shifted.

- Kelualua -

I have spoken of my erection, of which I am justly proud. Leaning tower that refuses to topple. Ancient obelisk that still stands amid some ruined temple, proudly defying history, the elements, time itself.

It must be said that I am equally proud as regards my rectum. My crapping appliance, as I think of it. At eighty-five years old, it still functions according to specification, provided it is properly lubricated with apricot and bran flake and morning coffee. Please do not believe I am boasting. I have no miraculous talents. I am no great humanitarian. And though I consider myself to be intelligent, there are surely others who are more so. This then, this physiological stamina, is what makes me remarkable. This timeless, dark gallery. After all of these years of wear, it still manufactures its singular product, its predetermined shape, as surely and precisely as a pasta press. Perhaps some spelunking proctologist may one day discover in it, illumined for the very first time by his helmet lamp, hidden works of art, cave paintings, the next Lascaux.

My wife went into a coma on my seventieth birthday. I spent the next three years in a waking trance that mirrored her sleeping one. What was there to live for? I will tell you. I will tell you what pleasures remained for my aging soul: The crapper. Old man's throne. There, in my polished granite bathroom, on my great seat above its reflecting pool, reflecting regal rear, there alone I could be anything. Deep sea fisherman, strapped to his fighting seat, battling a mighty marlin. Traveler through the space-time continuum. Young Lothario wooing his maiden. Ben Affleck. (Something peculiar just occurred to me, which will confirm for you what a lowly writer I am, if there is still any doubt. You now have a more detailed description of my rear, my nether-countenance, than of my actual face—the one I present to the world! And yet the eyes, supposedly, are a window into the soul. And what is the blind, Cyclopean rectum a window into? Still, what would be the point of holding back, when my fate, my death on this deserted island, is nearly assured? Why not open all of me up to the sunshine? Truth unto its innermost parts, no? Why else am I writing this, after all?)

But I was telling you of the days of my wife's coma. They were surely among my loneliest. For the first time in sixty years, I had no companion, almost no human contact. I'd driven off the housekeeper and ceased changing my sheets. My underwear I changed on an "as needed" basis, according to my own judgments. The only human sounds I heard were those of Ugueth, my groundskeeper, talking to himself, slashing the brush with his machete, humming that old hymn, *Rock o' My Soul,* just a bit too loudly. Where he actually learned this old spiritual I have come to wonder—perhaps on the History Channel.

Ugueth and I had found a curious equipoise. I paid him. I never told him what to do. He told me what needed to be done, and I always said fine. And he would head off to his task, mumbling something about always knowing his place, just doing what he is told.

"Nice weather," I would say to Ugueth. "Hope it holds."

"De wedder nice indeed, cap'n," Ugueth would say. He called me captain, for no apparent reason. Further, though we were in the middle of the Pacific, on the remote island of Kelualua, and though I had met him on a trip to Kenya, he spoke fluent Caribbean. Where had he learned it?

"You want I cut de mango, mon?" he would ask.

"Yes, please," I would say.

He not only slashed the mango off the tree with his machete, but also, with a few deft cuts, peeled and sliced it with that same all-purpose tool. He could have done the Ginsu Knife infomercial, but for the contemptuous way he dropped the plate of mango slices when he was done.

"Thank you," I would say.

"Just doin' as I be told, cap'n."

Sometimes I would try, very gently, to challenge him. "Ugueth, I haven't ordered you to do anything. I didn't tell you to cut the mango."

But he would have none of it. "Das' right," he'd said. "Das' what dey tell us. We want it like dis. We happy, cap'n. No worry. It good good. No worry a'tall."

I waded into the sea, listened to the hush of the waves. I played my onanistic games of chess against my laptop computer. And, alas, I sat on my faithful throne, roiling the royal reflection. The Thinker. The thinker and his ignoble twin, The Crapper.

My awakening from this existence began in small ways. I watched American television. And not just any American television. I took pleasure (if that is the word) in the low and tawdry. Game shows where women bounce and shriek and embrace their host at the sight of some material object they have just been given. Situation comedies where people insulted each other back and forth, on and on, while the laugh-track cackled, louder or softer, calibrating the insults. Reality shows where dewy-eyed lovers caked in TV make-up made mawkish speeches and handed out roses.

It may not seem so remarkable. But it was the beginning of a new life. A life of indulgence. Of shamelessness. I read American magazines at the check-out of the grocery store. *Us. Self. People.* One day, on a whim, I put a copy of *The Star* on the check-out counter with my other purchases. Was I not superior to this, I asked myself. Did I not feel ashamed, appalled at myself? I did. But in another way I was determined to go through with it, as another septuagenarian might be determined to run the Boston Marathon. I would liberate myself from the shame. From all shame! I would conquer it. Should I not, at this age, and in this state, just do as I chose, without regard to bettering myself, to society's judgments, to anything but my own caprice?

I ceased my daily walks in favor of being driven by taxi. I asked Ugueth to add more rum to his rum punches. I voted for my favorite American Idol.

And then—my final indulgence. Because who was there to be ashamed before? Who, even, had the right to condemn me for it? Who understood, had thought more, about such moral complexities, than myself?

I asked the question rhetorically, over and over.

For weeks I stared at the deliberately vague advertisements in the back of the weekly paper. Laura's Luscious Ladies. Exotica Escorts. An ink drawing of a leg coming out of a slit skirt. Below it the words, *Mistress Angela And Her Angels*.

And how remarkable, the artistry—a few simple lines traced by a human hand, yet capable in its way of conjuring a whole world, a storyline, of arousing a soul from its slumber and changing the form and shape of the viewer! Who was this anonymous master who had etched this? Who had invented this alluring scene out of nothing?

Mistress Angela And Her Angels.

I returned, over and over, to the drawing. Skirt. Slit. Leg. Insinuating itself. Stepping forward. Through the stage-curtain. Promising some dreamed-of life back-stage.

I deliberated. I who had been faithful lover, faithful husband, who had lusted in my heart so many times through the first seventy years of my life. At last I made my phone call. Human heart beating. Alive again.

Was this not, in some way, God's plan for me, now that my beloved wife was held to her hospital bed, curled up and weightless like a dying bird? Now that my son had done with me?

"Yes, perfect. I am free tonight at nine." And tomorrow. And for all the days after.

Sound of taxi in my driveway. Tires grinding across the shells and coral. The doorbell. Bloody blur of red chiffon through the textured glass side-pane.

"Hello. Come in."

Little, Vietnamese woman. Tight red gown bunched in layers. Matching red lipstick.

I smiled at my home delivery. "Nice to meet you."

"Herro." Quick little curtsy. "My name Weeeeta. Nice to mee *youuuuu.*"

I don't remember any conversation after that, though there must have been some. What I remember was her hiking up her dress and straddling across my lap, one hand reaching back to grab my crotch, bronco-rider holding saddle horn.

"You fee lilla sited?"

"Excuse me?"

"You fee lilla sited? You so big an hod."

"Again? I'm sorry?"

Feeling something. Excited. Yes. That was what she had been saying. *Excited.*

You feel a little excited?

Yes. As a matter of fact, I *am* feeling a little excited. Thank you for asking. I *am* rather big and hard. I am glad you pointed that out.

The penis is an idiot for flattery, is it not? How eagerly it rises to meet its flatterer, climbs like the proverbial beanstalk, up through a cloud of jockey underwear, up and up, through an opening in the clouds, through the Y of unzipped fly, ever upward, at last to meet that angel of heaven who spoke those sweet words of praise.

Rita paused, lowered the straps of her gown and showed off her breasts. "We talkie talk price okayyyeee?"

Mercenary in the battle of the sexes. Waiting until just that moment. Until I was hardened and softened and helplessly betrayed my compromised negotiating position.

"N...now?"

"Ya-Ya. Talkie now good."

Thus followed her price list. And as she explained I imagined a little price tag dangling discreetly from each orifice. I made my selection.

Shiny, black hair spreading out over my crotch—jumping and shaking like some exotic Pekingese chewing at a bone. How very strange. Meaningless. Like applying a machine. And yet not. More than that. A woman. Alive. There was no denying that.

Dainty wipe of chin. Arms slipping back into the straps of her gown. Hurried, closed-lipped trot to the bathroom.

Was this the encounter I had imagined while staring at that advertisement? It surely was not. As soon as she was gone I felt disappointed. I visited my wife, confessed to her senseless form, penitent before the reliquary of a saint. And yet over time the experience, the recollection of it, began to change in my mind. I saw the straps of her gown fall from Rita's shoulders, saw her proffered breasts, her lips descending toward the center of me. I heard her siren's flattery. Felt my organ's reply. *Yes. Yes, I am tall and handsome. I see you noticed.*

True, it was an empty pleasure. So what of it, I thought to myself. Crapping, after all, was an empty pleasure too, was it not? But nobody ever said, "Crapping is such an empty experience. How terribly wrong to take satisfaction in something so empty."

Soon I was again scanning the back pages of the weekly. Phone numbers, scrawled in suggestive, feminine fonts. And now just the phone numbers themselves were enough to make my heart beat faster.

I received another visitor. And then another and another. I thought less often of my wife. I accepted the limits of the experience and took pleasure in it. At times, in the throes of post-coital depression, my old self came back to me, and I felt ashamed, felt as though I had to put an end to it. But I always came back to that same thought. Why shame? Before whom? It made no sense. Moreover, as I grew more accepting of these encounters, the variety of my visitors fascinated me. All so different—the many variations of the female form, the many ways in which it is bedecked and painted and adorned. A botanical garden, a jungle of flowers, each surrounding that pinkish, sexual centerpiece. Not so much human forms as Christmas trees—all breasts and baubles, shining and dangling, with that one magical toy hidden below, that one special present—glowing, secret, behind a dainty ribbon of G-string— that will make everything better, that will transport you to somewhere where everything is wonderful.

It is true that, like so many gloriously wrapped packages of childhood, as often as not, a slight disappointment lay hidden under the shiny magnificence of the wrapping. Sometimes, they were toys best anticipated in the process of the unwrapping, in the first flash of what lay hidden inside.

And yet in another way at least it was all human. It was all *something* rather than *nothing*. The scents and accents and poses. The fake names. Tiffany and Samantha and Gina, Misty and Tanya and Brigitte. There was the illusion itself, the call-girl persona, and then those occasional glimpses of the human hidden underneath. Tart bouquet of a tart's breath. Nervous laugh. Centipede scar of Caesarian section. Or the little, under-the-breath cellphone arguments they sometimes had—with some unnamed boyfriend or family member or manager out in another world.

Didn't all of those imperfections, the hints of an actual human, hold their own fascination? Didn't they turn each rendezvous into its own masque, its theater piece? You offer your suspension of disbelief, and yet are aware at the same time that it is all a show. Presented entirely for your pleasure. That none of it is real.

Even the sexual imperfections were fascinating in their way. Insistent nose, knocking on abdomen like a woodpecker. Or, from my reclined position, the broad view of a blank back. Indifferent. Inert. Turned away. Nipples big and brown and wrinkled as prunes. Love-handles of a retired belly-dancer.

Do you see, Sylvia? Do you see how it is all one legato line, all of my lifelong quest, that stretches back ever further, across the world, back to that night in the sleeper car?

- Germany -

And so…the night in the sleeper car.

How right I was to want to stay awake through it. To savor it. To savor the feeling of her against me. Because how suddenly the dream was over, and we were awake, and we were back in Edelburg.

And strange, how startling, walking from the station and seeing those signs that had suddenly appeared in shop windows. *Juden nicht willkommen.* I was walking beside Sylvia and looked at her and she smiled back bravely, but I could see it troubled her. We said nothing of it. Just kept walking. I couldn't help feeling it was as though they had been placed specifically for me, for my return. A warning. We passed a news stand and saw the boldface headlines of the newspapers declaring a strike against Jewish businesses. And a copy of *Der Stürmer* that showed a hideous caricature of a hunched-backed Jew on the cover. I tried to put my arm around Sylvia but she slipped away. Had it really changed all that much so suddenly? Or had I just not noticed it so much before? Or maybe my memory is playing tricks. Confusing chronologies.

"What's wrong?" I asked.

"Not here."

"Why not?"

"Because."

That first day I thought it was just a kind of shock about returning. About the signs. But then in school she kept her distance as well.

I finally got a moment alone with her by the running track behind the school. "What's going on? What's the matter?"

"Nothing."

"Why won't you talk to me?"

"This is a mistake."

"Why is it a mistake?"

"Because...."

"So...what about the bicycle trip?"

"What about it?"

"Didn't you like it?"

"Yes."

I tried to put a hand on her, but she turned away.

"So what's wrong?"

" Just forget about me, Hans."

"You don't like me?" I asked.

"Of course I like you."

"I don't care if you're Jewish."

"I'm not."

"Is there somebody else?"

"No! Of course not."

"Then what is it?"

"Stop, Hans. You're just making this more difficult."

"Will you at least talk to me? Just meet me somewhere where we can talk?"

She thought about that.

"Someplace private," I said.

"Where?"

"The ramparts. Around the back."

I could see at last she was considering it. "When?"

"Tomorrow. Right after school."

"Don't you have to work?"

"It's my day off."

At last she agreed. And so the next day I climbed up the path the to the ruin, walked around the wall, found a spot that seemed both secluded and gave a view out over the countryside. In a few moments I saw Sylvia coming around from the opposite direction. She seemed anxious at first, but then when she saw we were alone, there was her smile. "Hi."

"Hi."

She settled up against me. "This is nice. I haven't been up here in ages."

"Maybe we can move in. You can be the princess."

Soon we were kissing. "I thought we were going to talk," she said after a while. "I thought there was something you wanted to talk about."

"Do we have to?"

She smiled. "You lured me up here with false promises?"

"No, I wanted to talk," I said. "it's just, now that we're here, I'm liking this."

"I see."

Ein Küss auf der Prinzessin.

We looked out at the patchwork of fields and old farmhouses, little hamlets in the distance, huddled each around its steeple. Endless Christendom. All of it bathed in a golden light of late afternoon.

"So what were you going to say?" Sylvia asked. "Before you decided you didn't want to?"

"I was going to say...I like you."

"That's it?"

"Yes."

"We came all the way up here for that?"

"Yes."

"You tricked me," she said. But she was smiling. "I thought you had something important to say."

"I did. I like you. Isn't that important?"

Now she caught my eyes. "Well, I like you too."

"Really?"

"Yes."

And so she relented. We started to meet there whenever I had off from work. At school I knew I wasn't supposed to show her attention. But after school we found our spot. If it rained there was a dry patch in the ruin under a crumbling flight of stairs.

"How's my princess?" I would say when I saw her.

"She's behind in her homework," she would reply, or something like that. "And it's your fault."

And then we would be in each other's arms, and that hardness of mine would press against her in delirious torment.

"Am I really your princess?" she asked once.

"Sure."

"Would you rescue me?"

"Absolutely. I would fight off all the dragons and ogres."

At other times I told her we should run away together.

"You're crazy," she'd said.

"I'm not. I mean it."

"Where would we go? What would we do?"

"It doesn't matter."

"See? You *are* crazy."

"We'd have each other."

How my mother found out about us was not exactly clear. Maybe the rumors started with the others on the bicycle trip. Maybe we weren't as careful as we thought we were. Maybe I was followed up the path to the ramparts. My mother never spoke of it directly. It just became apparent, gradually, that she knew. She'd tell me to be careful. Or to be home by a certain time.

She would say something about the Jews and try to catch my eye. She would point out nice, Aryan girls on the street. "Now that's the kind of girl you should be going with."

"You don't know her, *Mutti*. She's loud. And annoying."

"What are you talking about? She speaks in a whisper! I know her mother."

And then I would be offered a list of people she has known who were much louder, and far more annoying.

We were the first house in Edelburg to receive an electric refrigerator—a big, fat box on four spindly legs, with a head-shaped cooling mechanism above it, so the whole thing looked like a prototype for a robot. My mother explained how the food lasted longer, and how she disliked the ice man anyway. He was always coming late. Dismissing him would be a great relief.

Two delivery men came in and assembled the device, my mother studiously overseeing, making conversation with them while interspersing reminders of possible hazards—scratching the floor, dinging the wall, tracking in dirt.

My father greeted the new appliance skeptically. "I still like my Schnapps with an ice cube in it though," he said.

"Nonsense," my mother exclaimed. "It ruins the flavor. How can you not notice that? The flavor's gone. It's perfect when it's chilled in the refrigerator. It's cool but it's not cold. It's not diluted with ice. I think it's excellent."

The refrigerator was her decision after all, her purchase, and nothing could be wrong with it. What was more, how inferior was the refinement of her husband, that he could not perceive the obvious perfection of this new appliance.

"Until it breaks," my father said, with a chuckle.

"Breaks? Why should it break?"

"Why shouldn't it break? Everything breaks. For what it cost...."

"Ice!" my mother exclaimed contemptuously, as though its shortcomings were laughably self-evident.

"And what if there's a blackout?" my father asked.

"And what if the ice-man gets sick?"

(Had I only had powers of prophecy, I might have seen my very future in that grand appliance, I might have seen how one day, long after my mother and my home and my very childhood had exploded into the faint, invisible dust of irretrievable memory, my life would one day bring me back to that humming machine.)

Once, only once, when I knew both of my parents were out, I had Sylvia over to my house. She stayed a block behind me as we walked, and slipped in a side door I opened for her inconspicuously. Once inside, I showed her all of the rooms and paused at the refrigerator. She had never seen one and I remember opening it and letting her reach in and feel the cool air, and then describing my parents' argument over it. One benefit of growing up with my parents—I became adept at making fun of them for Sylvia, and it always got a laugh. I did their voices and turns of phrase, *and what if there's a blackout? And what if the iceman gets sick?* and soon we were both laughing gleefully. (In truth, I remember my recounting, embellishing this particular argument a good deal more vividly than I remember the original dispute).

From the magical coldness contraption, Sylvia and I turned to my father's gramophone and listened to a few of his jazz recordings. American Jazz was officially banned as degenerate music, but this particular regulation was widely ignored. After all, who could say exactly what was jazz and what wasn't? If anything, the ban only added to our sense of doing something mischievous and secret and exciting. We were sneaking around my father and the Nazis both. And then, after listening to a couple of these records, we played a movement from Beethoven's third symphony. Sylvia had never heard anything like it, and even through the thick static of the gramophone, was entranced by it.

"It's wonderful."

"Someday, we should go to a symphony together," I said. "And hear what it really sounds like."

"I'd love that," she said.

"Well then we will."

And then there was nothing more to show her. Only what a luxury, to have all of that house to choose from, to decide in which room, on which bed, we would caress and kiss and lose ourselves in our struggle with desire.

If only it had ended there. If only time had stopped. Sadly, the days chose to continue forward. One day there was a school assembly. The principal, a round little man with a big rear we used to call *die Aubergine*, the eggplant, on account of his shape, gave a speech about subversives and enemies and the wrongs that had been perpetrated against Germany. I sat in back, indifferent to the flow of words, pleased to be freed for the day from the rigors of algebra, to be free to sit in the cool and dark and let my thoughts wander. After his speech we were shown a short film. We stood up and saluted as a black-and-white image of Hitler appeared, sat quietly as he gave a rambling, shrieking speech that covered much the same material as our principal had—albeit with far greater passion. The seemingly limitless crowd before him cheered thunderously. When it was over *die Aubergine* came back onstage and came to the apparent reason for this impromptu get-together. "One of your teachers, Herr Klampf, has been arrested. I hope you will all learn from this." And then the assembly ended—with a big, enthusiastic, keep-up-that-school-spirit, "*Heil Hitler!*"

For a moment, I just sat there, stunned. I looked across the assembly at Sylvia, tried to catch her eye, but she wouldn't look at me. And she abruptly stopped making plans to meet.

Klampf was replaced by an older man who drove in all the way from Leipzig, and who taught us the new history, all about the super-race to which we belonged, the perfidy of Versailles, and above all, the Jewish World Conspiracy. I vaguely remember wondering about it. Actually considering it. Only if such a conspiracy existed, wouldn't that mean that Sylvia would be a part of it? And she just didn't make a very persuasive conspirator. (What's more, this particular teacher was not only short and bow-legged, but had a pronounced body odor, and soon had his own nickname, *Edelpilzkäse*—the Bleu Cheese. And so whatever lessons he offered in the super-race were rather undermined by his own example. (That I was actually tested on this "history," that I dutifully wrote essays about the Jewish Conspiracy, and received a 100 from Herr Bleu Cheese, is a testament to the average high school student's prodigious powers of regurgitation.))

A week or two after the assembly, after Klampf's arrest, I found a chance to talk to Sylvia in the hall. "What's wrong?"

"I can't see you anymore."

"Why not?"

"I just can't. It's a bad idea."

"I don't care if it's a bad idea."

"What if I told you I was lying all this time. About…being Jewish."

"I don't care about that."

"But it matters."

"Then I'll just have to rescue you."

"You're sweet. But you're also crazy. It's not a fairy tale though. It's not about dragons."

"Are you?" I asked.

"Would you really rescue me?"

"Yes," I said. "You know I…"

"Don't say it," she said, as though she knew the rest of the sentence. "Just go. People could see us. That would be bad for you."

And so ended what might be called our second romance. Our second epoch. This one was real at least, as opposed to being entirely in my own mind. Yet there was still—right up until its last moments—something almost make-believe in it. And if it sounds that way, it is because that is how I remember it.

I was back home more, keeping to myself and feeling confused and dejected. My mother tried—with mixed success—to be more indulgent toward me. "Don't look so glum. It's for the best," she would say, though she never said what "it" was, that was for the best, or how she knew so much. She made me dinners she knew I liked, bought me my first timepiece. I knew she was both rewarding me for my break with Sylvia and trying to distract me from my loss. Although in my unhappy state her company seemed more tiring than ever. And at last her patience wore off and I heard her complaining to my father about his ambitionless son.

At home things were changing as well. One day I found a scarf that belonged to Hilda amid a pile of coverings and blankets on a sofa in the living room, and I used the excuse of needing to return it to her as a chance to visit her at her apartment. I remembered her place from when she used to a take me there as a four-year-old—a third story apartment along Ravelplatz, a narrow winding lane in the old town that opened to a cobbled square. A rain shower had just passed through, and the stones were back out in the sun, warn and shining. The plantings around the little fountain were still dripping.

I announced myself, skipped up the steep, narrow stairs. She greeted me in a floor-length dressing gown. "Hello, Hans! What brings you to this part of town?"

She looked down at the scarf, gave me a wary look. "I just saw this at home. I thought maybe you needed it back."

"Thank you." She looked into my eyes for something. I couldn't tell what. "Do you want to come in? I'll make some tea."

Then I was sitting across from her. I hadn't realized how small her apartment was until that day, or how the floors sloped toward the middle of the building. But it also had its charm. The walls were covered with modern-looking paintings. A big Chinese vase marked the front entrance. An old fortepiano sat against a wall—wooden frieze of fauns and lutes decorating the casing. With her reddish curls and billowing gown, Hilda looked a bit like she belonged in that scene.

She came back, served us tea. "So tell me what is new," she said. "Did you find a new girl yet?"

"The same one, actually," I said.

She looked at me, and I told her about the bicycle trip and about Sylvia. Then I told her about the rumors about Sylvia. She didn't seem surprised.

"It must be very difficult for her," she said.

Again, there was nothing specifically political in what she said. But it was enough to make clear where she stood.

I told her about Klampf getting arrested, and about how ever since then, Sylvia had refused to talk to me.

"I see," she said.

"What do you think they'll do to him?"

"I don't know."

"Why was he arrested?"

"I don't know. Although...."

"Yes?"

"I have an idea." And then, "You need to be careful yourself, Hans."

"Why do you say that?"

She looked at me. Then she closed her eyes. "Is it possible?"

"What?"

"Nothing."

"What?"

It took a long while to get her to continue.

"You know I don't talk to your mother very much anymore," she said at last.

"Yes."

"We don't agree on much."

"I know."

"Most kids your age...share their mothers' views."

"I know."

"They're taught things in school. And their parents are afraid to disagree with what the teachers say. If they do disagree. And most don't. But the ones who do, who do have doubts...they're afraid of their own children, some of them."

"It's not like that here. At least...it wasn't."

"It will be now."

I went over to the fortepiano and played the opening of a little Mozart sonata I remembered from my piano lesson days. How much I preferred the sound to the music produced by our Jaegermusik trumpets and French Horns. I stopped in mid-phrase and Hilda went on.

"Your mother talked to me recently. She knew about what had happened on this bicycle trip somehow. I don't know. People talk. She wanted to know what I knew. How far it had gone. It's almost funny. Like I am still the governess in her mind, and I am still supposed to know her son better than she does."

"I think you *do* know me better than she does."

She smiled at that.

"What did she say?" I asked.

"You can't talk about this. To anyone."

"I won't."

"Promise me."

"I promise."

"She didn't say anything. But...I have this feeling that maybe she is the one who reported Klampf."

I felt a strange chill. "What?" And then, "Why?"

"Because. Because she blamed him for allowing something to happen between you and Sylvia. And because she wouldn't want to report on Sylvia herself."

"You mean because she had no proof?"

"No, no. Who needs proof just to make an accusation? She wouldn't want to say anything about Sylvia because if Sylvia were declared to be Jewish, and thrown out of school, it would reflect on you. Her son would be disgraced. And so would the mother. And so maybe —this is pure speculation—she made an accusation about Klampf instead. First because she needs someone to blame. And second... because perhaps it would disrupt things between you and Sylvia. Which...apparently...it has. I have no proof of any of this. None at all. Do you understand? I'm just thinking about it. And it's bothering me."

"Do you really think my mother would send someone off to a camp?"

"People don't think about consequences. She's angry. She wants her retribution. Her proof that she is right. That she has been wronged by him. And here is how she can get it."

"He was a nice man. At first I wasn't sure. But he was. What did he do, even?"

"I have no idea. Who knows. What does one need to do? He was probably in an opposition party."

It took me a few moments to absorb this. To see how it changed so much. I played a few more notes on the piano while I thought. "So what do I do?"

"Stay away from the girl. For her sake."

"I want to tell my mother...."

"Not a word to your mother!" Hilda exclaimed.

"Why not?"

"You want me joining your teacher?"

Hilda came and sat beside me on the piano bench. "I'm so proud of you," she said. "I knew you would be somebody special."

"I haven't done anything."

She put her arms over my shoulders from behind, held me almost like there was something romantic in it. Like I could have turned and kissed her. She rested her head against my neck. "It's all such a mess."

"What is?"

"Everything. Me. Especially me."

- Kelualua -

Succor of a succubus.

She arrives. Clomps in on platform heels. "You so sessy!" Robs me of my semen. And is gone.

Such was the scope of my existence. Until the day all of it changed.

Would you like to hear it?

One calm, sunny morning I was sitting out on my patio, playing a game of chess against my laptop. The trade winds were just starting to pick up, and this caused me to look out over the sea and take in the view. And on this morning I saw something sticking up out of the water, weaving from Cole's side of the beach, weaving toward me. For a moment it was the head of a snake. Then a floating stick. But moving somehow, propelled. Then it was close enough to see more clearly and it was a snorkel, wandering almost randomly, like a big pen, signing a message along the water's surface. I watched it move for a few minutes. Then it started speeding more quickly, propelled by flippers that now splashed up behind the snorkel, heading straight toward my beach. A creature crawled up out of the surf, flopped up the sand. It high-stepped on giant, grasshopper legs, webbed feet, looked right at me with its insect eyes and its strange proboscis. At last it removed its mask. A soggy rope of hair tumbled down. The face of a girl. Lovely, teenage girl.

She was catching her breath, peeling off her flippers, holding a hand up. "I'm so sorry," she said.

"Why are you sorry?"

"For bothering you."

"No bother," I said.

"Oh please," she said, still gasping for air.

"What?"

"I didn't mean to…I just need to catch my breath."

She bent over, inhaled, held up a hand to fight back my welcoming words.

"Are you alright?" I asked. "Can I get you something?"

She recovered a bit. "I'm fine. Thank you." A last heavy breath. "I'm sorry to trouble you."

"No trouble," I assured her one more time. "What happened? Are you okay?"

"I'm fine…I…I was just out at the reef, snorkeling, and this giant eel swam right under me. I'm sure it was nothing. Really. It's just…it came up from behind me, so I didn't…" she paused, panted, "I didn't even see it until it was passing under my mask. I felt it along me. I'm sure it was harmless. I just…panicked."

"Perfectly understandable. Let me get you some water or something."

"No. Really. It's not necessary," she said.

"Please."

I got up and headed into the villa then, pleased to be of help, pleased just for the human interaction, and knowing that she would need to wait for me, knowing that once I returned with her water she would be too polite to leave without some conversation.

I returned, held out my hand, "I'm Hans."

I still felt self-conscious about my name sometimes, as I did about my German accent. I do not record my accent here, as I don't really hear it myself, but I knew it was there. I knew that, with my age and my origins revealed, of course people would wonder.

"I'm Dawn," she said. "We live next door. I didn't realize how far over I'd drifted."

"No more apologies," I said.

"Sorry. I mean…."

But I cut her off with a wag of my finger.

She looked down at the table next to us, the chess board, the computer. "You're in the middle of a chess game," she said.

"Yes. Do you play?"

"A little. I'm not very good. And I'm…I'm interrupting your game," she said.

"I'm playing my computer," I said. "My computer is very polite about waiting."

She looked puzzled. "So why do you have a board out?"

"I don't like staring at the screen. So when the computer makes a move, I make the move for it on my board. And I can keep up the pretense of a real game that way, with a human opponent. Even if it is a ghost."

"You must be very good," she said.

"Fair," I replied modestly. In fact I am an expert at chess. This is not merely a boast. It is my official ranking. One level below master. Two levels below grandmaster. I used to set the computer at master-level, thinking that I wouldn't improve unless I played against a better opponent. Only when I turned eighty I thought, why am I still worried about improving? What is this ridiculous compulsion? And when am I ever going to play a human opponent again anyway? I am eighty-five! There is no reason to better myself anymore! And so I started setting the computer to a lower level so I could beat it. Why not taste a bit of victory before my demise? Yet how little satisfaction I have gleaned from these victories, knowing that my companion is not trying, is merely toying with me. And how lonely, really. Never to be able to compliment my opponent if it makes a nice move. Never to be able to question it if it makes a blunder. Never to sit back after the game and discuss the gambits and pitfalls, the elegant pins and hapless pawn structures.

Sometimes I actually imagined a human form across the board from me. My own father who had taught me the game, who'd had a brass set handmade at his smelting plant at Jaegermusik. My son, who I had taught in turn. *Well done. I didn't see that. Would you like some more tea?* Only my father was long dead and my son long ago disowned me. And what was in their stead? A companion that had no soul, no form, that was just thought itself, just chess moves. The last bit of my past that I can hold onto. The moves themselves. Appearing on the screen suddenly as though from another world. As though from my own, long-lost son. My anxious, uncertain father, who left me alone in the world. The empty seat across from me where they take turns as my opponents.

And now this girl, Dawn, was looking at the board, head tilted, eyes moving along all of the lines of threat and counter-threat in the position. The water on her skin had dried to a few little traces. Her hair was already starting to shine in the sun. And I had my chance to take her in. Pretty in a way that was so very rare—that has neither embarrassment at itself nor vanity. That had no interest in drawing attention to itself. That just is. But who could help but notice something that young and that lovely?

"Would you like to play a game?" I asked.

"Well…."

I encouraged. And at last she agreed. I gave her white, and was pleased with her sensible opening. It is not fun when I defeat an opponent too easily. There is no challenge, and it is awkward besides, pretending to be more engaged than you are, not wishing to hurt feelings, to show off, to win too easily, gracefully dodging the offer of a rematch, knowing it will only cause your opponent further humiliation.

Fortunately, it was clear she at least knew something of the game. The fundamentals. And she was more at ease now, enlivened by the challenge, by the dance of pieces on the board. She leaned forward, studied silently. When she moved a piece, it was always done in a tentative way, a question in her expression, a diffident hand reaching out to take my pawn and replace it with her own. "Probably a mistake," she would say. Yet, though sometimes it seemed like it might be a mistake, I found myself struggling to find a clear way to capitalize on it. By the middle of the game I had still failed to obtain any defining advantage. Was it luck on her part that she had not yet stumbled? Had she really seen that taking my bishop sacrifice would have led, inevitably, to a checkmate threat? Or had she not even seen that my bishop could be taken?

By now I was no longer thinking of giving moves back, keeping the game interesting, gently pointing out her mistakes to her. Now I was just engrossed; wrapped in the story unfolding on the board. Thrilled with this living intelligence across from me—one leg curled under the other now, towel that I had brought out for her draped over her shoulders.

The waves lapped. The sun baked. The lizards paused, throats throbbing. Ugueth passed by pushing a wheelbarrow. "Good morning," I called.

"So 'tis," he said. He set the wheelbarrow down and approached. "Shall we open dee umbrella for de cap'n?"

I introduced Dawn. "That would be nice," I said. "Thank you."

"I jus' followin' de orders," he said merrily. "What else I do?" And he hummed some African-sounding ballad as the umbrella fanned upward above us.

We continued our game. An hour passed. By now the board had reached its late state, had emptied out like a tired party. The kings came out from their hiding places, out into the fray. "I think this is a draw," I said finally.

"I'm sure you'd win it eventually," she said. "With my isolated pawn."

But this was just more politeness. Trying to make me feel better. "It's a draw," I said, with more conviction this time. "I don't have a way to victory."

"Okay," she said, apparently as pleased as I was at this outcome. "Draw."

We talked over the game, complimented one another on particular moves – that most pleasurable part after those years of the cruel silence of my computer.   She rose, shook my hand, agreed to come back the following day for another game.

And so...Dawn.

- Germany -

There are so many practices we humans take for granted. For instance this business with flags. This piece of cloth that we are supposed to venerate, and salute and pledge our allegiance to. But how did we all agree on a rectangular piece of cloth? Why does not each country have a fluffy pillow that must be worshiped, or a particular stuffed animal? And we would have rules on the correct way to display and remove and dispose of our national stuffed animal, and which hand to salute it with, and how it must be addressed, and what should happen to individuals who do not properly respect it. You see how strange it is, this idol-worship for these cloth rectangles?

And yet we all do it. Every nation must have a rectangle of cloth with which to represent itself—no matter how much they hate one another and differ from one another in every conceivable way. They may have opposing religions, opposing economic systems, they may rape one another's women, bomb and kill one another, but they all agree, yes, it must be a rectangular piece of cloth by which we are known, and this piece of cloth shall be us, and we shall worship it. (Perhaps this is what we are missing here in Illyria; we need a flag, perhaps a likeness of Cole, or Cole and an ass fruit, or possibly humping an ass fruit, shitty flag for our shitty little island).

You see what a great comedy it really is? All of those swastikas everywhere. All of those soldiers marching this way and that, saluting this shape. And where are they going? There is nowhere they actually need to go. Just up and back. Around the square and down the boulevard and across the platz, random as a bot in a Pacman game, and everyone lining their balconies to watch the parade, raising their right arms in salute, because it is important that it is the right arm, and it is important that is straight, and it is important that the posture is straight, because this is the proper way to worship the piece of rectangular cloth, just as marching around randomly is the proper way to honor that piece of cloth, only why not raise a leg, or flex your fingers in a particular way, or roll your head in circles, but no, it must be the arm canted forward and upward, firm and erect, and all of it in glorious unison, a million Cialis-perfect erections.

And amid all of that aimless marching, all of the bunting draped everywhere with its geometric swastikas, that idiot voice bellowing his madness over all of the radio, that comic figure with his Vaudeville mustache. Wild cheers. Arrests. Bonfires of books. Brownshirts with their buffoonish band music.

One day all of it actually passed through our town—the whole Nazi circus, passing through Edelburg. The whole town was draped in swastikas. The soldiers in perfect lines like advancing furrows of corn. Everybody out and cheering. And at last that man we had seen pictures of a thousand times. That God. *The Führer.* There in his motorcade. Everyone saluting. My mother (who had placed a framed photo of her hero in our foyer) there with me in the stands across the street from the house, chin high, arm extended, *Heil Hitler!* My father across from us, out on the balcony of our house with Hilda, Hilda still ostensibly visiting me, her old charge, and yet the two—Hilda and my father— suddenly alone in the house together.

And how strange it seemed suddenly, as though in that moment of the motorcade's passing, everything was in reverse. I was back at my own house, and seeing the wrong mother, there with my father. And then, as the wave of salutes rose as the motorcade approached, Hilda and my father ducking down, climbing under the table of the balcony, their spontaneous act of defiance, refusing to salute, hiding so nobody would notice, and then discovering one another under the table.

Because that was how it happened, the two of them finding themselves together in the shadow of the table-top, alone amid the throngs and the excitement, alone and suddenly aware of this bond between them, this common refusal, this intrigue, finding one another under the table and looking at each other as though to ask, "What are you doing here?" How long they had been just employer and employee, how many years he had behaved perfectly toward her, and now here they were, reaching out for each other, swept up in the delirium, the cheers, the obscene, shocking, thrilling violation of Hitler and my mother both.

That was how it happened. The pieces all rearranged. As in a dance step. Everyone unlocking from one partner and finding the next.

Actually, there was more to it than that. Because why was my mother so late to recognize her husband's affair? The answer is simple. Because at the very same time, and by some comic fate, my mother was preoccupied with concealing her own illicit romance. And so each of them creeping and slipping out and making excuses, and neither recognizing the odd behavior of the other, until at last something happened that made it impossible for my mother to carry on her charade any longer.

The muffled words from the other room. "I don't understand."

"What don't you understand?"

"But…it's not possible."

"Of course it's possible."

"But.."

"Do you think you're the only man capable of getting a woman pregnant?"

And then pause. A change of tone. "Who is it?"

No reply. Nobody. Just a spirit. Passing through. As though it was an immaculate conception, the spawn of my mother and our leader, as though yes, she was bearing *his* child, was blessed with this great, patriotic duty.

And so in my fifteenth year my mother was pregnant. And then, in a twisted sort of symmetry, Hilda was pregnant as well. And my real mother was not pregnant by my father, and my mother-surrogate and symbol was.

Mutti's lover, it turned out, was an industrialist who ran a munitions factory a mile outside town. The plant had started to run all night, and in the winter, when the leaves were off the trees, you could see its lights in the distance. I remember this vividly because, once I knew who my mother had taken as a lover, the lights seemed to represent not just the industry of war but also the industry of love, the heat of their passion.

For a while my parents still shared the house. But they ceased speaking to one another. My father blushed red with embarrassment around me, wanted to find a way to explain, to wax philosophical, to take me under his wing and help me understand. But he never quite found the words. He stumbled. Stopped and started. Took me to the barber and could not decide, without some extended discussion and deliberation, whether my hair should be come down to my ears or stop above them—as though getting this right was the solution to everything. My mother meanwhile started to dote on me, wanted me in an alliance against my father. She was still occasionally fixated on the refrigerator. "You see how much better the cheese tastes from the refrigerator? Your father doesn't know what he's talking about. All he knows is sheet metal." The argument, evidently, had been going on continuously in her mind, even though she only chose to tune in to it now and again.

My own reaction was to lash out at both of them, to ridicule them for having acted with such moral authority for so long. I was angry, confused, but also, I must admit, vaguely pleased. I knew I had them. They had no answer.

My father started spending nights at Hilda's little, lopsided apartment. One afternoon, when he was busy at work with a supplier, I went to Hilda's myself and listened to her version of events.

"You know, I always admired him," she said. "Such a nice man. And then it just happened. After all that time. I hope you don't blame me."

"Blame you for what?"

"For…for splitting up your parents' marriage."

"Should I blame you? Or thank you?"

That got a wry smile. "I think you judge him too harshly," she said. "He means well. And all men are silly lambs anyway. Right?" That was how she saw the male sex. A tribe in need of affection, forbearance, mothering. It was what made them bearable.

I had dinner with the two of them one night. My father did his best to hide his awkwardness at this new situation. But it was still excruciatingly uncomfortable. He asked about school. He asked about how my mother was. We talked about the factory. When he ran out of specific questions he resorted to asking me, "So what else?" And then, after my shrug, "So what else is doing?" And then, "Come, tell you father what else is new."

Hilda broke in eventually. "Boys his age don't share anything important with their fathers. You know that."

My father chuckled at that. Then he commented that the food had gotten cold. He chuckled again, as though to retract it, as though it was a joke. Hilda rolled her eyes at me, smiled. "I bet you could probably teach your father how to reheat something, couldn't you?"

After dinner my father asked me if I would go for a walk with him, and we strolled along the river. "A lot of changes for a kid to absorb," he said. "I'm sure it is unsettling."

"It's fine," I said.

"Life doesn't always go the way we expect," he said.

I sighed, could think of no response, wished the entire conversation a speedy demise. He went on. "I don't approve of what your mother has done. Or of my own…things happen."

I nodded, tossed a stick into the river and watched it float under a bridge. What I felt or didn't feel I still am not entirely sure, other than a great desire to not discuss it.

When I visited next it seemed things had changed between them. She was six months pregnant and had a weary sort of look. She no longer smiled at my father's idiosyncrasies. Whatever had seemed cute or charming seemed to have grown a bit frustrating. Now she had a way of cutting him short, of telling him what to do and say. My father was now running around trying to please her. In a way, in just a few short months, he had fallen into the same pattern with her as with my mother. Trying to please. Never quite succeeding. Although Hilda had him doing things he would not have done for my mother without a bitter fight.

A year later, when their child, Georg, was five months old, my father volunteered for the army and was sent off to the Rhineland. He was almost frantic in his agitation as he explained it to me. There was no resisting it after all. And this way, he could at least be sure he was an officer. And there were good things about the Reich too. Things to be proud of. It wasn't all bad. Most of all (and here he put his hands on my shoulders, looked me in the eyes) he was doing it so I wouldn't have to. I could get an exemption, because somebody needed to run the factory, which after all would be necessary for the war effort. He was sparing me.

I knew I was supposed to be in awe of this gesture. I was supposed to embrace him and tell him I loved him. Only something in me resisted. That need of his. That need for us to be one. The same. For his son to appreciate him. I looked away. *Danke, Vati.* Those were the bland, empty words that I found. "I'll watch the factory."

That was it. And then the day came, and he was in his uniform. Goodbye, my sweet boy. Holding me against him. Face red with tears.

"Goodbye, *Vati*." And then, at last, and almost under my breath, almost as an afterthought, "I love you." It was not something I had ever said to him before. Years later, I would have reason to be pleased that I had produced those words. How deeply he must have been moved to finally hear them.

I still passed by Sylvia daily in the hallways at school. Caught her eye spilling out of school at the end of the day, even once found her walking nearly beside me, the two of us acting as if we were strangers. How excruciating that was. Our enforced separation had only filled me all the more with thoughts of her. Dreams. Only on rare occasions, when I was sure nobody could be paying attention, either because we were in a busy crowd or alternatively, because there was nobody around, did I dare look into her eyes, smile, try to convey that I had not forgotten her.   And then she would smile back.   Though what it meant now was harder to discern.   Some recognition, some reference back to when we had been happy together?   Remembering that train ride back from Austria?   The times we met by the ruin and looked out over the countryside?   The day we slipped into my parents' house together?

And what was her life now?   Was it possible that she was still happy?   Still refusing to let her situation take that away?   Was she trying, still, to maintain her pretense, and now that pretense of race depended upon a pretense of calm and happiness?   I never attempted to speak to her in that time.   There was no way to know what was going on inside her.

And so I didn't even notice right away when she was no longer at school.   It was a few days, perhaps, before I became aware that it had been a little while since I had seen her.   That it wasn't simply that our paths had not crossed.   I wondered if she had gotten sick.   Then I wondered if something had happened to her.   But evidently I had not been following the news.   When I mentioned it to Hilda she told me that Jews had been forbidden from attending public school.

So this was it then.   Her pretense had failed.   She had been revealed. Banished. And now her complete absence brought her back to me most intensely.   So long as I saw her from day to day, knew approximately where she was and that she was near, it was not as essential to focus on her.   Now that she was gone from the present, the past all came back with a powerful vividness.   And with it came both the fear that she would disappear completely—and my childish promise to her.

We had never even said from what exactly I would rescue her.   Had I really meant it?   We had just been playing, dreaming.   But now it took on a more serious quality.   She had denied her Jewishness after all.   I was sure her mother must have told her never to admit it to anyone.   Never to act it.   That if you acted it, if you acted afraid, they would know.

I frequently made a point of walking past her house on Bernstraße, even if it was a few blocks out of the way, in the hopes of seeing her.   One Saturday morning, weeks after I had last seen her at school, I stopped across from her house.   There was a little church and a cemetery across the street and I sat down at a bench in front of the churchyard and pretended to read.   I could make out movements in the house through the changes in the darkness of the windows.   Dark forms growing, coming nearer, then further away again.   I was determined to sit there until somebody came outside. They couldn't spend the day in there after all. Could they?

At last she emerged, hair tucked into a cloth coat, beside her mother. I remembered those days I had stared at her when we were both still children. How I would look away if I saw her look toward me. How much more of a young woman she was now. It was the first time I had seen her mother. And now it struck me how strange it must be for this woman. An "Aryan" with a child who, by law, was Jewish. Giving birth to her and raising her and loving her and knowing that somehow, according the government, she, the mother, was good and proper, and her beloved daughter was branded. *Untermenschen.* Vermin. And possibly…no, probably…even in danger.

Because where was it all leading after all? And then it occurred to me how much I had in common with this woman I had never spoken to. How we were the two people in the world who cared about Sylvia. And how I could not go on any longer without talking to the daughter. Without doing *something.* Only, when would Sylvia ever be apart from her mother now? They walked off without noticing me, and I decided to continue waiting. When I saw them returning, some time later, each carrying a bag of groceries, I got up and walked toward them. At least it was not yet a crime to talk to a Jew.

I smiled, feigned a casual spontaneity. "Sylvia! What a surprise. How are you?"

She started, looked anxious. "Hello, Hans."

"Hello!"

"Mother, this is Hans. My friend from school."

"How do you do?" Her mother shook my hand, looked for something, surely, in my eyes, in the meaning of my friendliness.

I turned to Sylvia. "How have you been?"

"We're good," she said. "Fine."

"Here, let me carry that," I said. And without waiting for her to offer it, I took her grocery bag from her. Then we were walking back to her place together, the three of us. I only had a moment. "Oh look, the strawberries look perfect, don't they?" I leaned the bag toward her, and when she leaned in to look I whispered to her. "I'm going to come to see you tonight. Listen for me whistling."

I told my mother that Hilda had invited me to stay over, and I did go over to Hilda's for dinner and stayed into the evening. I watched Hilda dote upon her baby, my half-brother Georg, who was already roly-poly and smiley and cooing, Hilda kissing him and cooing back to him. But it is not a fascinating sight for a teenage boy—watching a mother with her baby. And my mind was entirely elsewhere. Late in the evening I went out again, crossed town and came to Bernstraße, which was empty and dark. I went back to the same bench by the

cemetery and waited until it seemed not just her house but the entire
street was asleep.

A horse whinnied in the distance. A train rumbled far off in the
night. Then more silence. I walked under a lamp to check the time.
Little waves of anxiety, excitement, anticipation, came and went.
Almost one in the morning. Good time. I started whistling quietly by
her front door. Paused. Started again. *Wenn die Sonne hinter den
Dächern versinkt*—When the Sun Sets Over the Rooftops. That sweet
lilt of strings and saxophones and voice that had always given me a little
pang.

I thought I heard the faintest sound from inside, and went quiet.
More sounds. And then the doorknob turning. It was happening! I
could almost feel the very darkness, the quiet, the suspense. The door
opening slowly, nearly silently, as though by itself. I took a long, steady
breath and slipped inside. I stood in what seemed like total darkness. I
felt a hand take mine. Then two fingers touched my lips. *Silence.* Then
her arms around me. Holding me. For a long time I just held her, felt
that warmth and femininity against me. And then she took my hand and
we tiptoed upstairs, to her bedroom. By the feel of her I knew she was
in her nightgown, and I was startled by that sense of her bareness
underneath it. I slipped off my shoes and climbed, as silently as
possible, into her bed with her. Meeting of lips. All without seeing
anything at all. Without having spoken a word. At last she whispered
to me.

"Hi."

It was meant to be amusing in its casualness, its simplicity. I could
sense her smiling.

"Hi," I whispered back.

"How have you been?" she asked.

"I'm okay. And you?"

"We're getting by."

"Did you forget all about me?"

"Of course not. Never. Did you forget about *me*?"

"Not likely."

"I'd wondered sometimes if you'd met someone else," she
whispered.

"I meet lots of people," I said.

"That's bad," she said.

"Don't worry," I said. "I don't meet any Sylvias."

"I don't meet anyone at all. Ever. So you don't have to worry."

"Good. I hope it stays that way."

"You can thank the Nazis."

"I will."

Then, in the struggle between the desire to communicate, to share our feelings, and the urge to come together, to satisfy that other ache, our physical wants gained the advantage. My hand felt her nakedness under her nightgown. She reached between my legs. Undid my clothes.

"Do you like that?"

"Yes."

"You know it's a crime, having a Jewish girl," she said.

"I thought you said you weren't Jewish," I said, teasing.

"I lied. Do you forgive me?" She stopped stroking me for a moment, waited for my answer.

"Yes."

"Promise me you forgive me."

"I promise."

Then she continued, fondled me more urgently. How different is the hand of a girl. I reached that climax of pleasure and shame that I had known in our visits to the ruin.

"Sorry," I said.

"Why are you sorry?"

"Your hand's a mess."

"You're silly. Don't be sorry."

She got up as silently as possible, cleaned herself off, lay back down.

"Actually, technically I wasn't lying," she whispered.

"What do you mean?"

"According to the Reichstag I'm Jewish because my father was Jewish and my mother is a quarter Jewish. I'm five eighths Jewish, actually. Just the wrong weighting. And according to the Synagogue I can't be Jewish because my mother isn't Jewish. So there is no group that will have me. Not even the Jews."

"I will have you."

"I see. So you think I'm that easy?"

But I could sense her smiling.

I told her about my two new half-brothers, the one by my mother and the manager of the munitions plant, the other by my father and Hilda. I told her about my father volunteering. About my taking over at the factory. She was amazed at all of it, but the last was what seemed to strike her the most.

"How can you run a factory when you're in school?" she asked.

"We have a manager," I said. And then, "It's supposed to keep me from being conscripted. We're making parts for firearms now. Along with our trumpets. Which we call bugles now. It was all my father's idea. To keep me out."

"That's incredible that he did that," she said.

I hadn't thought of it as incredible before. "I suppose it is," I said. "Is he okay?"

"I get letters. He says he is fine. Managing supplies or something. If there is really war though…I can't imagine what he will do. My mother would make a better officer than he would."

She smiled at that. "I'm glad you came."

We whispered about where we could go. Switzerland. Poland. France. How we could slip across the border together. Or I could take a horse and cart across, and she could hide under bales of hay. I thought how I needed to talk to Hilda. Come up with a plan.

"I don't care what happens to me anymore," Sylvia said. "What's the worst that can happen? What more can they do?"

"Stop," I said. "It matters. Because we're going to be together."

"My mother is trying to find a way for me to get out."

"Has she come up with anything?"

"Not yet."

"I want to go with you," I said.

"What about the factory?"

"I don't care about the factory. I hate it.

- Kelualua -

"It be bad day today, cap'n," Ugueth says. "Bad bad."

"What do you mean?" I ask.

"De storm a-comin."

Or *coh-meen*, as Ugueth pronounces it.

"How do you know that?" I ask. It is a calm, partly cloudy day, the waves lapping gently against the jagged corals off the beach.

"Some of we know de way of tings. De nature, mon."

I keep Ugueth as much for his companionship, his mystical powers, his hymn-singing, as for his actual groundskeeping. The remarkable thing about Ugueth is that he is a media creation. He could not exist without so many old TV shows and commercials, movies and geography books. Where else would he have learned this? In Nairobi where he drove a taxi before I hired him? In Kelualua?

"But what tells you it is going to storm?" I ask. "What specifics?"

"No specifities, cap'n," he says. "We just know dee way."

Later in the day though, it is still calm and sunny. I ask Ugueth where the storm went.

"It move de nort of here. Very close call. We lucky dis time."

The following day was the day Dawn was to return for another game. After that first game I had played with her, that match we had fought to a magnificent draw, I had gone to sleep full of excitement, dreaming dreams from the chessboard. I kept replaying the game in my mind, seeing Dawn herself, that tentative hand of hers, reaching out to make a move.

This time she arrived by foot, up the front entrance. Ugueth, high up in a palm by then, stopped hacking at his coconut to watch her walk up the drive. He came down and served fruit salads under the broad leaves of my agave.

Three hours later Dawn and I each had a victory.

And so began our competition, the two of us perfectly matched and playing to many draws—always at my table above the sea. We kept to the same seats, symmetrical to the longitude lines, which I finally commented on. "You know what's curious?"

"What?" she asked.

"You always take that seat. You're the East. Dawn in the East. And I'm the Sunset in the West."

She wasn't sure how to answer that, or what I was suggesting, and managed only to offer to trade seats with me.

As for the play, that too followed a pattern. Like a piece of music, a chess position is never a single moment in time. It is only truly meaningful in the context of the whole—where it started from, where it is heading. And when you look back on it, you remember it as you remember a melody—always flowing, moving forward. And with so little to distract us, the chess games seem to drift on endlessly.

She was too polite to point it out when I made a mistake. But sometimes she would look at my move and say, "Hmm," in a certain way. And gradually, I learned that this "Hmm" actually meant, "That looks like a mistake to me." I would look desperately around the board, see my fatal error, ask meekly for my move back. "My knight is left vulnerable," I would say. And she would always act surprised. "Oh my goodness! I never would have seen that!" She was surely the most polite chess player ever to have lived. Yet it was not mere decency that motivated her. Rather, she was like myself. She hated the thought of an exciting game, a fascinating position, disappearing just like that because of a foolish blunder. To a chess player, each game is its own story. And how disappointing when the storyteller makes a wrong turn, takes the tale somewhere absurd, somewhere from which there is no going back.

"You can't keep giving me moves back," I said one day.

"I'm not giving you moves back."

"You are though. Every time you say *hmm*. You can't keep doing that."

"What am I doing?"

"I forbid you to say *hmm*."

But this exchange just caused her to change tactics. Now when she saw I'd made a mistake she would get up and take a break after my move. She would get herself a refreshment. This was an opportunity for me to reconsider my position and take my move back with the least amount of shame, since she had not invested any time in thinking about the position. And at first it worked. She would return to the board relieved to see the position had been slightly, but critically, altered. Eventually though, I caught on. I learned to respond to her rising for refreshment by searching the board madly for my mistake.

Of course, among real competitors there is no taking moves back. The rule is called *touch-move*, which means, once you have touched a piece, you must move it. (Or, to put it another way, there is no unnecessary touching of any kind. Chess is a purely ethereal game.) But neither of us held to this particular requirement.

Most days she swam around the stone wall that separated our villas as she had on the day of our first meeting. She climbed up the beach, I wrapped a towel around her shoulders. Ugueth served limeade made from fruit he had picked from the lime tree at the edge of the property.

"For de cap'n and de new lady fren,'" he would say, with what seemed more than a trace of innuendo.

"Thank you," I would say.

And we would begin.

There were times the sun baked relentlessly. There was not even enough breeze to jostle the bougainvillea. On those days what seemed most alive was the board itself—alive and fantastic. A dream. Full of adventure and scheming and heroic sacrifice, a little kingdom, teeming with activity—every now and again a giant hand reaching in, hand of God, reaching down and moving something, adding a twist, altering everything.

In time, games accumulated, one and the next, into a recurrent dream, each starting the same, each turning some unforeseen corner, winding up somewhere unexpected. In the middle of it I would look up and think, who is this child across from me? Who or what has sent her, who is choosing her moves for her? My son? My father? Returned in this feminine form? Once or twice I even felt a tear form in my eye. *My son, is it you*, I would think. *My Serge who will no longer speak to me. Is it you inside that girl? Say something.*

"So tell me. Where did you learn to play?" I asked her.

"My housemaster."

"Housemaster?"

"At Darby. It's a boarding school. He taught me the openings. We played in the evenings. After I finished my homework."

Was there something hesitant in the way she said it? I couldn't help feeling a twinge. The presence of this other older man. This other opponent. Had he reached for her, reached across their secret field of intrigue? Touched her? Had she responded, taken his caressing hand and given it a kiss and held it against her fluttering heart? Had he been in love with her? Of course he had! He had to have been.

And yet why was I even wondering this? Why was I so certain that any man, any man of intellect and taste, must surely be in love with her? Why would I assume this unless I was in love with her myself? My lovely Dawn. My dawning Love. How I thought of her at night, even then. Her bronze skin and golden hair and all-consuming eyes. Her bare shoulders that I allowed myself to feel as I settled my towel over them. And yes. Her breasts and legs. Her most private parts that I was left to merely imagine. This naiad who had landed upon my shoreline, who had joined me in my lonely kingdom by the sea.

It is true that when we dwell on something over and over our imaginations will begin to take over, elaborate endlessly. And now, I imagined this housemaster, back-lit, dark and false and infinitely inferior. I created out of nothing a rival. I saw him caressing her. I even saw him in her chess moves. Had she made that very move before, I would wonder, with that other, most foul opponent? Had he played the very same variation of Queen's Gambit with her that I was now playing? Was I not, through her, actually playing him, this crude and ill-bred and lecherous housemaster? This black knight?

Surely such fantasies, such absurd thoughts, would fade, I thought to myself. Would get washed away by cleansing reality as I got to know better this strange girl. And yet, as the weeks passed, as we spent more and more time together, I noticed something even more peculiar. I struggled to get to know her any better than when we first met. Strange to say, it is hard to get to know someone who places politeness above all else. How can you comprehend someone who will never say anything that is critical of anyone? How can you know what truly dwells inside the heart of someone who is always looking to say what she thinks you most want to hear? Who, when asked what she would like for lunch, invariably responds, "Anything is fine. Whatever is your preference." What are the true, inner thoughts of such a person?

Dawn confessed to me, after much prying, that she did well in her school, whose full name, it turned out, was Darby-In-The-Fields, located in some horsey reach of New England.

"What's the worst grade you ever got?" I asked.

"I don't know."

"You don't know?"

"It doesn't matter."

"I'm just curious. You won't be bragging. Because I'm asking you a simple, factual question."

"I don't want to say."

"Did you ever get a B?"

Silence. Slight smile.

"An A minus?"

"I'm not saying."

"You never got less than an A."

"I'm sure there were lots of students who did better than me."

She needed to leave at three in the afternoon three days a week because she had a babysitting job. Of course I doubted that she needed the money. She just seemed, as far as I could tell, to want to be busy.

"Don't you get bored," I asked, "spending your afternoons with an old man?"

"I'm fine."

"But…" I dared venture a bit further. "But what about friends your own age?"

"I don't have any here. Not on the island."

"That's too bad," I said.

"I'm just visiting my step-father here for the summer."

Only why would she visit a step-father without her mother? I wanted to ask about her mother. But something caused me to hold back. Maybe it was the fact that she was in boarding school. Or that her mother remained unmentioned. Regardless, I now had this new sense of her —of her passing her days in this beautiful place with nothing to do and nobody to share them with. How I wished I could do more to rid her of her loneliness, to transport myself magically back in years, to someone whose company might be more than merely tolerable, might delight her.

I brought her books sometimes and she read them and always claimed to like them. She baked cookies for me once, carried them across the hidden "land route" that entered through a keyhole gap in the wall between our properties. We even tried other board games sometimes. The Japanese game of Go. Another purely mathematical game called Hex. But we soon fell back under the spell of the chess board. The thousand and one stories it told.

What was I to Dawn? That was impossible to say. But there was no doubt that I was entirely in her thrall. Though I continued to receive my late evening phantasms, my heart now belonged to this towel-wrapped maiden, this Scheherazade who spun her tales with the play of her chess pieces.

- Illyria -

It was a while before we settled on the name of our island. There were so many choices when one thought of it. Floral ones. Like Freesia. The free state of Freesia. And ones based on diseases. Giardia. For a long while, this one seemed the most fitting. But not so appealing. Then, as our hunger grew, there was Anorexia. Dementia. And my own favorite, Claustrophobia. There was also Amnesia. Land of Forgetting. And ironically, happy ones. Ambrosia. Euphoria. But we have always come back to Illyria. That place that should not exist. That possibly does not exist. That just possibly is a dream.

Our settlement, on the other hand, has always been Delirium. The lost settlement of Delirium. To be covered, someday, in volcanic ash. All of us mummified. Uncovered a thousand years later. Placed under glass in some natural history museum.

Now, Conrad and I sit by the fire, eating ass fruit, licking the hard outer shell, which has a strong, nutty flavor. We are ass fruit lickers.

We have been exploring new topics of conversation.

"How many animals can you name that start with the letter *S*?"

"Snake."

"Sheep."

"Sea gull."

"Shark."

"Snail."

"Seahorse."

"Starfish."

And so on. We will discuss celebrities. TV jingles. Sports team nicknames. I have never watched sports. And yet somehow I have learned that it is Cincinnati *Bengals* and the Kansas City *Chiefs*—as though a recording has been playing in my sleep. Or as though humans living in America simply carry this knowledge in the same way birds know they should fly south for the winter and beavers are born understanding dam-building, hydrology and the art and science of logging.

We discuss favorite songs, episodes of the mesolithic, *Three's Company*, car commercials. We compete for who can name the most breakfast cereals. And we look, for the fiftieth time, through the pages of our one copy of *Vogue*. There is cover story called *Bikini Ready*. Under it is the subtitle *How Sixteen Vogue Staffers Are Prepping for the Coming Months of Deshabillie*. The assistant editor, someone named Leith Speer Barton (personally, I think she should drop her middle name), offers: "I start the week with a batch of juices from Liquiteria, and they're just around the corner, so it's super convenient! Green Juice with Apple, Lemon, and Ginger is my favorite! Might try an Organic Avenue LOVEfast as well. Pre–bikini season seems like the perfect time for one!"   Jessica Kantor, West Coast Editorial Assistant offers, "Recently tried Sergio Carbajal's Powersurge class at Fitness Factory."

"Who the fuck is Sergio Carbajal?" Conrad asks.

"I don't know," I say. "I keep rereading that sentence though. I'm starting to feel like the name has some hidden meaning."

"How are you readying yourself for bikini season?" Conrad asks me.

"By eating ass fruit," I say. "What about you?"

"By starving. How's it coming?"

I look him over. "You look slim."

"Thank you."

We read on. Alana Black, fashion Assistant, "plans to order a set of Core Fusion DVDs from Exhale Spa online, and also have a Blueprint Cleanse."

"What the hell is a Blueprint Cleanse?" Conrad asks.

"No fucking clue," I say.

"Do people really read this shit?" he asks.

"Somebody must."

"I mean, people who aren't stranded on desert islands losing their minds?"

"I have no idea. Since we're stranded on a desert island."

You are thinking, perhaps, that I have chosen the most ironic examples from this magazine. But everything is ironic, no? What of the full page ad of a perfectly shaped model in her perfectly ironed panties and biting into a perfect, glistening orange—zesty spray splashing out joyously? It is a skin cream ad, apparently. Something called Novena. Or the ad for the Blue Lagoon collection, featuring a model with turquoise make-up, looking like she is in mid-orgasm, background of birds of paradise flying across enchanted lagoon? Or the Party Scene section: "Is that Ted Danson (looking dapper in Zegna—his favorite Eco brand) and Chevy Chase (the evening's emcee) greeting like old friends from the same frat of funny?"

"What do you think Ted Danson is doing right now? Right this second?" Conrad asks.

"Wearing his favorite Eco brand?"

"Maybe Zegna isn't his favorite Eco brand anymore. Maybe he has a new favorite Eco brand."

Oh, here is something I forgot to mention:

Gloria is dead.

Sorry. I should have mentioned it sooner. Do you remember her? Well, she fell ill and started vomiting. Her skin yellowed. We had no idea what it was. Was it contagious? Was it some form of cancer? Was it bad magic? Bad airs? Tree demons?

As she deteriorated we built a new shelter, just for her. We told her she would be more comfortable there. But really it was so we wouldn't have to be around the retching. And so we wouldn't catch whatever she had. Dawn tended to her, applied wet cloths to her forehead, talked to her. In truth, there was nothing anyone could do. This is something I have come to realize here: Of course primitives must believe in shamans and totems and rituals. Because it gives them something to do. What else is there? If only we could shake sticks over her, chant, do *something* to help—not her but us, the survivors—help us feel less guilty about our indifference over her death.

I will say this about Gloria. She fought bravely until the end. Whatever the fuck that means. I really honestly don't know. But it's something you say. And Cole said it in eulogizing her and everyone nodded in agreement. She kept knitting until her very last day. She ceased to wash, to change her clothes, to eat. But she kept knitting. Repetitive motion, devoid of meaning any longer, just going on, ticking the seconds with her needles. I would not be surprised to discover she had already been dead for some time before her hands finally stopped, that the last row of the sweater had been completed after her death.

Near the end we debated quarantining her. Dawn ignored this debate, did what needed to be done, and went to Gloria. She held her hand, was just *there*, a fellow human, so Gloria would not have to die alone. What a pathetic comment about the rest of us though! How ready we were to take advantage of the fact that Gloria never complained. She understood her place, we told ourselves. Ever the hired help. The cook. She knew when it was time to go, we told ourselves. But it is never time to go. And toward the end you could see the fear in her eyes.

Only who was she to us? She was old. Like me. Her beauty so long gone it could not even be imagined. Nobody needed her. That was the truth. Her stories of her grandchildren were tedious. On her last day—but while she was still alive—Cole and Conrad discussed cremation versus burial. She briefly revived during this conversation and they looked over at her sheepishly and smiled and asked her how she was feeling. She looked away, fell back into her stupor, and their conversation, in softer undertones, resumed. They agreed on cremation. But then, after she'd expired, nobody could really bring themselves to put her body on an open fire. So she was buried down the beach under a wooden cross.

We each tried to memorialize her, said a few words, shared a memory. Cole recalled her cooking. Conrad said she had been a simple woman with a good heart. This was it? This was all we could think of? A wave of embarrassment swept through us. And there was something unspoken between us as well. We were all looking at one another, wondering who would be next. And if it were me, what they would say about me? What stories would they share with one another? "He farted at lot."

Do you judge us, Reader? Are we heartless? Let me ask you then. How many tears do you have for this woman? Oh, sure, you can say I never really developed her as a character. How can you be expected to care? But let me tell you this: She was a good woman. She believed in God and never made a point of it. She loved her grandchildren and did things for people and tried and never said a bad word about anyone. No? Still nothing? She could have been anyone's grandmother. Your own! Yes, your grandmother, dying alone in a faraway place, with no child or grandchild there to comfort her! Nothing? You are heartless!

Days later I am sitting back with Conrad again.

"Too bad about Gloria."

"Yeah. It is."

We have been working on repairing the skiff. And now we discuss whether to sail off on it and hope it takes us somewhere—if not back to civilization then off to the stars, to our end.

It is early evening and the others are still about. Dawn is talking quietly with Andreas. Lately he has started building what he hopes will be traps he can drop by the reef. And she has been helping. She pulls her hair back, smiles up at him.

"Fucking Ted Danson," Conrad says.

"I didn't even know Chevy Chase was still alive."

"Did you think he was funny?" I ask.

"Who?"

"Chevy Chase."

"For a while. More amusing than funny."

"I liked Caddyshack."

We are both watching Dawn and Andreas. Watching as they leave their trap behind and head down the beach. Watching as their two forms seem to merge into one.

Of course, I think. Of course she should choose Andreas. He is young and strong, handsome and polite. Only why is it that I am trapped inside this old man's body? That I must either live the charade of pretending to have an old man's thoughts, or disgrace myself by declaring my impossible love? And should I not be happy for her, after all? Happy that this kind and lonely and mysterious creature at last has a companion?

"I think I'm getting ready," Conrad says after a moment.

"Ready for what?" I ask.

"Ready to launch the skiff."

"We have no fuel. No sail. All we can do is drift."

"I know."

- Germany -

1938.

The year a tiny bit of history came to our town.

My father had been sent to the East. My mother was tending to her new baby. Her lover, who we all just referred to by his last name, Fleulen, had moved in with us. I'm sure I didn't like him for the fact that he was my mother's lover, but it is also true that I didn't like him because I didn't like him. What my mother saw in him, as far as I could tell, was that he was emphatically the opposite of my father in every way. Firm and concrete, proud and unapologetic, pipe-smoking, card-playing, opinionated, pro-Nazi, and, to listen to him, one of Germany's greatest military strategists of the last half-century.

I had been spending more and more time at Hilda's little place on Ravelplatz. She too had her baby of course, but Georg was easy and agreeable and I felt more comfortable there. She doted on Georg, but still had enough attention and affection left over for her former charge. Sometimes she told Georg, "I bet you can't wait to see your daddy again." And we wondered together what my father was doing and how he was faring.

The memory of the night I'd spent with Sylvia was still vivid, and I confided in Hilda about Sylvia, about her situation. We talked about various plans for helping her out of the country. The barriers to legal emigration had become nearly insurmountable. That left hiding her as I crossed through a checkpoint, or slipping across an unprotected strip of border. The more we considered the first option the more implausible it seemed. I could ride a horse-drawn wagon, and we could hide her in the back, under bales of hay, or boxes of clothing, or what have you. But somehow the sheer melodrama made it seem unlikely. What did we know about how thoroughly vehicles were searched? And how would I fare answering the questions of the border guards? Would I start shaking? Sweating? So the plan, in the end, was a simple one. Take a train together to a town nearest the Swiss border. From there slip off the main roads and down country lanes and finally slip into the woods. Walk five or ten miles and find some unprotected stretch of border.

We envisioned leaving in a couple of weeks. It was early November. November fifth, to be exact. November 5, 1938. I was with Hilda when we heard the news over the radio. A German diplomat had been shot in France. *By a Jew.* We'd never heard of this diplomat. Who had? But suddenly it was all over the news. This abominable act! Committed not just by *a* Jew. But, rather, by *the Jews.* This high crime! For a few days the diplomat clung to life. But the fury of the official broadcasts was astonishing. The demands for revenge. And then, on the day I had marked for my next visit with Sylvia, this obscure diplomat, now elevated to the level of a great personage, died of his wounds—martyred himself for the cause of all of us violated Germans.

Hilda and I just looked at one another.

"I think you need to do this *now*," Hilda said. And then, "If you're going to do it."

I nodded.

"I'll buy some things for you," she said. "You'll need foods that keep. That don't take up space. And blankets. Only if your pack is too big...it might be suspicious. If anyone asks where you are going, say you are running away from home together, looking for farm work."

The wireless was broadcasting stories of rioting breaking out all over Germany. Anti-Jewish rage. Synagogues torched. Storefronts smashed. From inside Hilda's apartment though, we heard nothing. It was like any other night. Would it really spread to our quiet little town?

I left for Sylvia's before midnight. The crooked alleys in Hilda's neighborhood were all calm. Maybe none of it was true. There were people out here and there, maybe more than usual —groups of threes and fours, mostly drawn out by the news, wondering what they would see. But it was a chilly night, and that seemed to keep people moving.

As I walked toward the river I could hear more voices. And then there was something. A lamp store. Brodsky's Lamps and Lampshades. Smashed to ruins. Shards of glass everywhere. Just as the radio had described it. Why had it happened here though? What was this strange, magical connection between the radio and this pile of debris? Is that what it means to be a social species, that we will simply do what we believe others are doing? We hear words on the radio, people are destroying Jewish businesses, and like pre-programmed automatons, we interpret this message as an instruction?

I moved on, walked along old streets, under medieval arches, and out to the less ancient, less huddled part of town. Across all of it was a sort of crystalline quiet. A milkman's wagon passed —the horse clopping and snorting. Along the next block I scared up a yard of chickens, startled myself with the sudden clucking and scattering. Peaceful Edelburg. My storybook town.

I was most of the way to Sylvia's when I approached something again. A commotion. I drew closer. A crowd of figures, milling around a square, Vanderplatz. Watching something. Watching what? There were voices. Shouts. I approached. Peeked through a pair of shoulders. A man was being pushed by several men. They were shouting at him. Trying to get him to push back. He was older, had a frightened face, kept trying to back away, but there was always someone behind him, giving him another shove. His hair was disheveled. Beside them, on the ground, was a hat that had evidently been knocked off his head. What did they want from him?

A woman, who seemed to be his wife, was restrained by two other men. One had her arms. The other had a hand in her hair. She was crying, protesting. She wore a heavy coat that bunched in the neck as they pried her arms back. When she spoke, the hand in her hair drove her down lower, until at last she was on her knees, and drool was dripping from her mouth. Now the man protested the woman's treatment, begged on her behalf, and this resulted in a fist hitting his stomach. He bent over, breathless, as other blows started to land on him.

What an unreal quality it had though. This one little act. This one droplet of cruelty amid the sea that seemed to be sweeping the country. You could even sense a kind of self-consciousness among the perpetrators. Acting out this bit of violence, getting themselves comfortable with it, acclimated to it, this act that they had heard was happening everywhere, trying this new thing out, yet having trouble identifying this old couple, these actual people, with the criminal *Juden* of the broadcasts.

And then, after the first blow, how much easier it seemed, the next punches coming so much more naturally, the hatred starting to feed on itself, the inner pleasure at inflicting pain. Yes! This was going to be a beautiful thing, this new violence! It was just a question of adjusting to it. That the victims were old and helpless, that there was nothing that they had actually done to deserve it that anyone could name—wasn't that really part of the joy? Wasn't that liberating in some way? Because if you could beat these people, punch their elderly faces and kick their sides, with all these others watching, doing nothing to stop it, didn't that give you a kind of power, not merely over your victims, but over everybody, everything? Could you not take it even farther, see how far it could go?

There were maybe only six or seven young men actually involved in tormenting this couple, and maybe a sixty or seventy watching silently. Many no doubt shocked, horrified, wishing it would stop. But silent as an audience watching a performance in a theatre. Silent as a group of schoolchildren watching a bully pick on someone smaller and weaker. Each thinking maybe now someone should stop this. It has gone on long enough. Someone should intercede. But who? How? Others just incorporating it. Accepting it. Who knew.

And then there was that awkward moment. That end without an end—the victims just lying there bloodied. The beating done. Only there was no curtain to lower upon the scene. And that lack of a proper ending seemed to reveal, even to the perpetrators, the pointlessness of what they had done. Did they just walk away? Bow to their audience? What? At last it occurred to one of them to spit on the couple. And then the others recognized the virtue of this, and added their spit. And their beads of spit landed like hateful, little exclamations points on their victims. And thus having found a suitable denouement, they turned away, headed off, whooping, breaking into some Nazi song—as though it were the final number in a musical.

Kristallnacht had come to Edelburg.

For a while the crowd stayed where it was, looked on at those two heaps of suffering, as though still expecting something more to happen. Wondering if it is over. Wondering if they should offer assistance, call the police, deposit their own spit. In the end though, they did none of these. Instead they just watched for a while more and wandered off, left to sort out their own thoughts.

I was one of the last to leave. I watched them stagger up. Alive. Moaning. I briefly caught the man's eye. At least someone get him his hat, I thought. But I didn't. I left. Just as the others had.

Just a few more blocks to Sylvia's, and now I felt even more urgently the need to reach her. I was aware of forms passing this way and that. More than would normally have been out at that hour. I heard muffled voices. But it was difficult to see very much. The night was moonless. Who were they? It was hard to make out.

I waited across the street for a while, until it seemed there was nobody around. Then I slipped around the back of Sylvia's house and tossed a pebble at the window. A moment later I was inside. I was in her arms. That same shocking nakedness through her nightgown.

Pressed against her. We tiptoed up to her room, just as we had on my last visit. I undressed. Slipped into her bed. At first I was still seeing that scene at Vanderplatz that I had witnessed. That vignette. And then our lips were joined. And in another instant it was gone. As though a great wave came over consciousness itself, obliterating everything. Because how could this beautiful sensation and that horrid memory coexist? Or maybe I just willed it away. I just wanted the pureness of the moment. No past and no future. No words. Just the sensation, the great ocean-wave of desire, flooding everything. So that when the bed creaked it was as though reality itself had given us a little nudge. *No, you cannot forget me. I am right outside. I am waiting for you.*

Sylvia froze. We heard a rustle from another room. She carefully pulled away.

"We have to be quiet."

"I know."

"You're crazy to come here."

"I said I would rescue you."

"I know. Is that what you came for?"

"Yes," I said. And then, caressing her again, "Eventually."

"You mean after I let you have your way with me?"

"Yes."

"Could be a long wait then," she said. But I knew she was teasing, could sense a smile in her voice, even in the darkness.

"That's okay," I said.

"I'm just kidding."

"Good."

"You can have me. If you can do it without making the bed squeak."

"You were the one who made it squeak."

"I was not. It was all you."

Then I was over her, pressing, inside her, slow and careful, our breathing steady, measured as though we made some primitive engine. *So this is it*, I thought.

When it was over, exhaling its last, we spoke. Whispered.

"Hans."

"Yes?"

"Nothing. Just making sure you are still there."

"I'm here."

"Did you like that?"

"No. It was horrible."

"Shhhh. You'll make me laugh."

"Of course I liked it."

"Have you heard the wireless?" she asked.

"Yes," I said.

"What do you think?"

Then there was no blocking it out any longer. "I saw something. On my way over here."

Now I wondered who that couple was that I had seen. There were not so many Jews in all of Edelburg after all. Sylvia might have known them.

"What did you see?"

"I don't know if you want to hear it."

"What's going on? Tell me."

"We need to do this thing. Now."

"We just did that thing. You want to do it again?" How she could continue to joke at her own misfortune and danger amazed me.

"No, not *that* thing," I said. I sensed her smiling. "How can you still be joking?"

"Because you're here. With me. And it makes me happy."

"Me too."

"I feel safe with you."

"I wish I felt that," I said.

"I just want to feel happy. That's all I want to feel right now."

"Me too. But…I mean it. We can't wait anymore."

I told her the plan, relayed to her all of the advice Hilda had given me. *Just act calm and casual. Smile. Like we have nothing to worry about. We're just out looking for farm work.* But my heart was already racing. What if…what if…what if. What if people challenged us? What if we were questioned? What if we were caught at the border?

"What do you mean?" she asked. "You want me to leave right now?"

"I mean tomorrow morning. It's not safe for you to go out tonight."

We lay quietly. Maybe if I had acted right then. At that moment. Or a week before. Yes, just a week before. Or even if I had done things differently that night….

I don't know whether there had been voices outside for a while and I just became aware of them once we were completely still, or whether they had just started. But we both became attentive to them at the same instant. We stopped our breathing. Listened. Did not dare admit to one another our thoughts. Yes. Definitely voices. Movements. Very close. Freezing both of us. *Don't move.* Because moving, somehow, would only show the other that the sounds were real. That they meant something. And at first we were both telling ourselves that they meant nothing. That they didn't exist. They were a dream. Like when you wake up frightened, feel there is something menacing, and are afraid to move.

And so we both just stayed frozen. *Don't act like it exists. And then it won't exist.* Only a few seconds later it was happening. Undeniably, horrifyingly happening. A knock on the door. Another nudge from reality. More than a nudge though. More like a piercing scream.

November 10th, 1938. *Kristallnacht*, as it would later be called. Night of the broken glass. Night my life would change irrevocably. What stands out now, so many years later, is Sylvia telling me she just wanted to be happy. The girl who wouldn't stop joking. Smiling.

I just feel happy.
Ich bin froh....
And then in the next moment....

There is no Romeo and Juliet in this story. Not even the movie version, starring Leonardo Di Caprio. It is not even, *When Harry Met Sally*, with Meg Ryan, or *Love Story*, starring Ryan O'Neal and Ali MacGraw. If you want a romantic hero, fleeing with his lover through the night, I would suggest, *Ivanhoe*, by Sir Walter Scott.

The next frantic moments are of the sort that are played over and over, pondered, reconsidered over the course of a lifetime, never completely understood. The two of us frozen in bed together. The sounds of Sylvia's mother getting up, hurrying down to the door. Then Sylvia bolting up like out of a nightmare. Whispering to me. "What do we do?" Clutching me. "What do we do?"

My own mind racing frantically. "Hide."

"We can't hide. There's nowhere to hide."

"I don't know."

"What do they want?"

"I don't know."

Sylvia, "You need to get out of here!"

Banging on the front door now. Shouting. *Öffnen Sie die Tur! Open the door!*

Trying desperately to process a hundred thoughts, calculations. And suddenly up. Racing to get clothes on. What if they catch us escaping? What if they catch me with her? What if she just goes to talk to them? If they just want to talk? Frighten her? If it is just her? Maybe it'll be okay. But...if they see both of us together? What then? What if what if what if?

Her mother stumbling upstairs. Voice through the door. Trembling. Desperate. "Sylvia!"

Crying. Sylvia crying. Thinking take her with you. Out the window. Take her with you. Do it *now!* Her mother, frantic, "What do I do? " Maybe hearing us. Thinking what on earth… Only what did it matter now?

Sylvia, "What do they want?"

Through the door still. "They won't say. They…they just keep saying open the door."

Take her with you! Out the back window. Racing to the window. Looking down. Then back to Sylvia. Dressed now. Sitting on her bed. Ready. Waiting. Frozen. They'll just talk to her. Threaten her. I'll come back tomorrow. Unless. No unless. She hasn't done anything. Look at her. Who could hurt her? She hasn't *done* anything! Unless. Unless they find me with her. Okay. So that's it. I need to go. The door downstairs swinging open. The voices. Shoes. Take your shoes. Your coat. Back to the window. Nobody out there. Darkness. Throwing them out. The footsteps on the stairs. Not even a goodbye. Not even a last glance. A last catching of eyes. Sylvia! Just climbing out the window, dangling, letting go, landing, scrambling for my things, running. Running. Running because the body says run and the body is in control now. Like that night. *The wolf.* Only now…the legs just moving. Running. Slipping, tripping, up again, running.

Because how could I know, could I have known? How could I have known that, on that night, they were also arresting? Thirty-thousand. Sending them off to camps? How could I have known? But maybe…maybe I did know. Something. Not that. But something. Your hero. You see now?

This is why we need stories. Why we need heroes. Because we are the opposite. We are pathetic creatures. Our instinct is flight. Or mine is. Or was. Maybe just mine. Wondering, as I ran, what was happening to Sylvia who I had left there. What at that exact moment was happening? And what was she thinking? Was she thinking she would be okay? This was what was safest? To just hide her fear, act, as she always had, the part of someone who has nothing to be afraid of? Should I have taken her? Or maybe this was our best chance after all. We did the right thing. They will harass her and leave her and we will run away together the next day. Better than the odds if they caught us together. Trying to flee together. If they looked in her bedroom and nobody was there, and they looked out the window, and….

And and and….

Only sometimes you make the right decision, don't you, the one with the best odds, and it doesn't work out. Right? Wasn't that what happened? Only…was that really why I left her like that? Leapt out the window? Because of some calculation of odds? Wasn't it more that, after so many half-thoughts and instantaneous considerations, I did it because I was impelled to do it? *The feet say run.* How can you fight that? Only how terrible not to even look at her. Not to say goodbye. Nothing. Did that haunt her afterward? Did it leave her to wonder? To doubt? To doubt that I would have come for her? What I felt for her? How important that came to seem. Because to have had that to remember, that last glance, that last intimation, something. *I am happy.* Those words of hers. *Ich bin froh.* And why did I not think to stop at some point, turn around, see what was happening? See if there was anything I could do? Why was I still running?

By the time I got back to Hilda's, heart pounding madly and out-of-breath and realizing that I had not worn my coat or shoes the entire way, that I was still carrying them, that I was freezing cold, what I felt was more than just foreboding, more than just fear for her sake, wonder at what had happened in the second and minutes after I'd left, but…those words. All of them.

All that fucking crap about rescuing. Oh my God. What was wrong with me?

Do you see? Do you see now? *I did not even look back at her!*

Hilda opened the door for me. Frightened at my state.

"What…?"

Only I couldn't speak. That last image. Sylvia sitting up. Composing herself for her persecutors. And then the instant after I had gone. Only what had happened? Maybe it was all okay. Maybe they would slap her. Break things in her room. Frighten her. What had she done? Nothing. *Nothing!* Her father had fought in the war!

Aware now of Hilda's hands were on my shoulders.

"Calm down."

Trying to talk to me.

"What happened?"

"I can't. I can't I can't I can't."

"Was she there?"

"Yes."

"Did something happen to her?"

"Yes."

"What?"

"I don't know. I can't say. I don't know."

"What happened?"

"I have to go back."

There was a pause. "You need to calm down. Get your thoughts together."

She made me drink a cup of tea.   The sky was brightening.
November 11.

"What happened? Tell me."

"I have to go back."

"Wait. Wait until a respectable hour. When people will be out."
Then the baby was awake. Hilda feeding him. "I'll walk with you."

Hilda pushing Georg in his pram. Me beside them.   The sky
brightening. People out. Another day. Like any other. Only not.
Telling Hilda the outlines of what had happened. Reaching Bernstraße.
And then at the corner by the house. "We'll wait for you here."

And going up to the door and knocking. Her mother's voice.
Anxious. Wrong. "Who is it?"

"It's Hans. I'm…Sylvia's friend. I carried her groceries…once.
We met." Silence. "Is Sylvia there?"

The door opening. Her mother just staring at me.

"Is Sylvia there?" And then, "I'm her friend. I need to know."

"She's not here."

"What happened to her?"

And then her mother in tears.

"What happened to her?"

I don't remember her inviting me in. I just was inside. Sylvia's
mother gathering herself enough to talk. Yet still measuring her breaths.
"Was…that you….last night?"

"When?"

"I heard a voice. In her room."

At first I thought of lying. Only then I realized that at that instant
she just wanted someone who knew Sylvia, who cared about Sylvia.
Nothing else mattered. "Yes," I said.

And then she was holding on to me. Sobbing.

"They took her."

And then it hit me all over again. If only I had just taken her out
the window with me! She would be with me now. There was nobody
behind the house! Nobody would have seen us. Only. Only how could
I have known that? Didn't we do what made the most sense? Or what
she thought…because she always believed…she could just will her way
through it, maybe not smile, but show them who she was, that
innocence, that…ease, like she belonged, like she had nothing to be
afraid of. Hadn't I done what she had wanted me to do? Had thought
best? It had always worked for her. Why wouldn't it work again?

Only why hadn't I at least looked at her? At least said goodbye?

"Where?" I asked. "Did they say where?"

No answer. Shake of the head.

Years later I would wonder why Sylvia? Why was she among the thirty-thousand? The very first thirty thousand? Was her self-possession what in the end had damned her? That defiant happiness? She didn't violate any laws. She just refused to submit. To act ashamed. To hate herself for who she was. That was it. That was what was threatening. Unacceptable. That was disobedience enough. Her sheer calm was disobedience enough. Her very loveliness. That was her crime. If Jews, after all, were so filthy, so hideous, how could she be? She must be destroyed.

That was what I thought about years later. What I thought about then, in those days, was this: Her joking and laughter. Her words. *I feel safe with you.* The madness. The running. Her mother clutching my shoulder, wailing into my shoulder. And this: if only if only if only if only if only if only.

- France -

The war is a distant memory. I am in the town of Annecy—famed for its beautiful setting along Lake Annecy in the French Alps. Its fresh-water canals and islands, its arches and bridges. I am fifty-seven and single and have returned to Europe for the first time, as neither conqueror nor refugee, but as that third and most reviled variety of foreigner—tourist.

I had discovered museums in my forties, and discovered that I hated them in my fifties. I just wanted to be outside. To be on the move; to watch others of my species, strangers, also on the move. Annecy was the perfect place. No museums. No cultural experience to be had anywhere. Just mountains. Watery reflections of mountains. Gardens. Canals. Something to paint in every direction, and a magnificent absence of paintings.

My father might have been disappointed in my indifference to the visual arts. Yes, he was eager for me to join him at his factory. But he had also dreamed I would be a man of learning. I would rise above the tawdry world of business, the factory he had left for me, and study art and poetry as he never had. He looked up in awe and bewilderment at the celebrated painters and poets, full of his own insecurity, unsure exactly what made them great, but still wanting a sort of nearness to them. Had there never been a war I might have done something entirely different. Although I have no idea what it might have been. I had no particular calling. Or if I did, it was too mixed up with what my father wanted for me to know if it was mine or if it was his. Probably I would have stayed in Edelburg, at the factory, and spent my life dreaming of some other life. But who really knows.

So there I was in Annecy, France, at an outdoor café one morning. And there she was, this attractive woman at a table two over from mine.

She was dipping a brioche into a *chocolat chaud*, and reading. What I noticed, what made it hard not to look at her, was that she was so difficult to place. Her skin was unwrinkled, and yet it was finely striated in a way that seemed to suggest a kind of aging. Her hair—was it blonde, or gray, or something in between? Was she German? Italian? Young? Old? Her book, I saw, was in English, with illustrations, and she was writing in it. Like me, she was alone, enjoying a cool, sunny morning. In no hurry.

We exchanged smiles. That was all. I paid for my breakfast and was on my way. And the next decades would have taken an entirely different course had I not run into her again, two mornings later, in a different café, on a different canal. And yet this same scene. She with her book and brioche. I with my newspaper and my *Guide Michelin*. And this time, as we made eye-contact, there was a recognition of our having seen one another before, and that seemed to make it more awkward *not* to acknowledge one another than to at least say hello.

"You speak English?" I asked.

"*Un petit peu*," she said, smiling. And then, "I'm from London."

"Ah, you're British?"

"Indeed."

"We seem to be following the same route," I said.

"So we do."

"Staying here long?"

"I haven't decided." She set down her cup. Seemed happy for the conversation. "I'd planned to just spend the night and head higher into the mountains. But it's so lovely here."

"And there are many more cafes to try," I said.

"Precisely."

In another moment I was invited to join her for breakfast. Her book, I now saw, was a guide to alpine wildflowers.

"You're a naturalist?" I asked.

"I don't know what I am. I'm one of those naturalists of a century ago who went up into the mountains and drew sketches of flowers. Only I was born a century too late."

"I see."

She was tall and lean, faintly freckled, boney, dressed for a hike in the hills. Her posture though belonged more at an afternoon tea.

"And what brings you to this part of the world?" she asked.

"I'm recuperating," I said. Which in fact was only partly true. I was still recuperating from my kidney transplant. But I was essentially better. Only I was in no hurry to declare myself so.

"And where are you from?" she asked.

"Many places," I said. "Shall I go in reverse order? From here backward?"

I offered an abbreviated chronology, and we wound up ordering more coffees and talking for a long while. At last I asked, "So where do you go to look for your wildflowers?"

She looked me over. "Are you fit for some walking?"

"I'm quite sure that I am."

We drove higher, parked at a little mountain village, walked along a high meadow. She pointed to gentians and bellflowers and buttercups. She described everything in detail, periodically interrupting herself. "This must be terribly boring to you."

"Not at all," I said. "I'm very much enjoying learning. As long as I'm not going to be tested on it." As the day wore on, I learned to recognize the pink bouquets of rock jasmine, the sunbursts of alpine aster, the tiny, downcast mantles of snowbell—a sea of Lilliputian penitents, streaming across the valley.

Some of the flowers were so tiny you had kneel close to see the intricate patterns and colors.

"I must have walked by flowers like these every day as a boy and never noticed them," I said.

"You had other things to notice," she said, with a suggestive smile.

"So I did." Only at this moment, were not the slyly beckoning petals of *Veronica urtificilia* as alluring in their way as any milkmaid of poetry or song?

What a different world this was, high above the other one, the one we normally inhabited. When you changed your focus, it was remarkable how these little bursts of yellow and crimson and blue added to the beauty of the mountains themselves.

We walked along a brook and then zigzagged up a hillside high above it. Mountains came up behind the crest of the next hill, seemed to rise with us as we rose. Jagged, snow-capped peaks. We lunched along a rocky ledge, drank metallic tasting water from our canteens.

Her name was Annabel.

She was a tireless traveler, an early riser, a believer in comfortable shoes, in healthy air, in the salutary effects of fresh fruit and yogurt and reading dusty, old novels. She had worked, in a previous life, as a public relations photographer, had lived what might be considered an avante-garde existence, had gotten pregnant by someone from the recording industry, had married him.

We were on our third or fourth walk when I asked what had happened.

"He died in a traffic accident. We were having difficulties. And he went out drunk. And he crashed up his car. And that was that."

"Sorry."

"We were headed for divorce. His family wouldn't talk to me at the funeral. They blamed me, evidently."

"I can't see how it was your fault."

"I'd just told him to go eff himself." She sighed. "Those were the last words I said to him, as it turned out. Only in the unabbreviated version."

After that she took her little girl to stay at her mother's for a while. To get some babysitting help while she recovered. And she never went back to her old life.

This then was Annabel's reincarnation. Lover of travel and solitude. Calm and intrepid and unquestioning of herself or others. I had found my companion. My fellow wanderer.

"And your daughter? What does she do now?" I asked.

"She's at Cambridge. She's studying literature. Involved with some boy who wants to be a poet."

"Do you like him?"

"I do like him. He seems nice. Only…a poet?"

"Excellent field," I said. "Terrific career prospects."

"Exactly."

We had crossed into Switzerland, were lunching in a perched valley, looking down from high above a world of tiny hamlets and steepled churches and shepherds' huts. In the distance were clusters of little, milky-white dots trailing off like the tail of a comet—herds of sheep. In the foreground, and just where the land fell off in a rocky ledge, an unseen spirit had laid out wreaths of rhododendron that shimmered in the breeze.

"How far away do you think that steeple is?" I asked, pointing to a spot in the distance.

"In space?" she asked. "Or in time?"

"I was thinking in space," I said. But I knew what she meant. That nothing looked quite real. That the scene could have been painted, just as it was, two hundred years before. That perhaps we truly were looking back in time.

This is what I remember. The two of us wrapped in our sweaters, sharing our baguette, having that whole world entirely to ourselves. That feeling that you could head off in any direction of your choosing, see what is around this bend or that; only limited—sadly—in not being able to explore in every direction at once.

When had I last felt that? Some memory was trapped inside me, reaching for the surface—as though those sprigs of color in the wildflowers were lost jewels, awaiting rediscovery, and the paths that were sprinkled with them took me not only outward, forward toward some new vista, but deeper into some legendary past. And then, suddenly there it was before me, and I was pedaling through the Austrian Alps, and I was fifteen. And there were Sylvia and Alika and Ernesto! So many lifetimes ago. And how astonishingly young and innocent and free of burden we were! And now the day was doubly intoxicating, held in it a breath of that previous life, as though the breeze itself, the scent it carried, came all the way from that other world, that lost world that lived on across some distant mountain-pass of memory.

"I had no idea rhododendron was alpine," I said, bringing myself back to the present.

Annabel was pleased to have awakened this interest in me. "Quite," she said, and she got up to examine the leaves, the petals more closely. When she returned beside me, I put a hand against her back, and then we lay back together and looked up at the sky.

There is very little more story to tell. We married, traveled, aged, moved from place to place. She had money from her previous marriage and I had accumulated enough over the years that we could enjoy a leisurely existence. We did not make love often and did not say cruel things to one another and were content. Her daughter married a literature professor and chose to stay in England. And Annabel and I continued our travels—visited Japanese temples, swam in coves in the Aegean, were robbed on a train in Seville. Once, along a Norwegian Fjord, she identified a previously unknown variety of lily, and named it *Liliaceae annabel*. And so found a bit of immortality. At last we settled on our Pacific island, Kelualua, and she took to studying sea shells — limpets and whelks and coquinas—and lined the balustrade of the veranda with them. And I took up chess and played clarinet and swam in the morning. Performed my life functions in perfect synchronicity with the tides, the moons, the planets.

I am sure there is a lot that I have forgotten. Details. Stories. Laughter. Tears. But what I recall is just the sense of calm. We were two refugees. She had inherited and I had acquired, and we had enough to support our travels and our sea-view and Ugueth. For reasons unknown, and following an ancient tradition that I dared not question, she did the cooking and housework. We were both retired. So why? Did it give her a womanly pleasure? There are some mysteries in life that it is better not to question. And so I did not ask.

Was I never bored? Restless? At times I was. But I was faithful in deed. And near enough to contentment at least to comprehend it.

And then one day we were at breakfast under the agave and her look fixed on me and she started speaking, and what came out was something that sounded like language but lacked any meaning, even any recognizable words. And then her eyes grew confused. She kept trying to talk, knew something was wrong, something wasn't working. She got up, was trying to move somewhere, and stumbled and wound up lying on the floor, on her back. In another time, one might have concluded she was possessed. Ugueth helped gather her into the car. Only by then she had lost consciousness.

- Kelualua -

Prostitute number seven. Clomping on high heels. Out of her taxi cab. Into my life.

"Fuckin' taxi driver."

Her salutation and greeting.

"Hello," I reply.

"Dickface."

"Sorry?"

"Not you. Him. He keeps speedin' up and then jammin' on the brakes. Swervin' around. Almost hits this goat in the road. I'm like, 'This is givin' me a headache, mista. D'ya think ya could slow down or sumpin'?'"

"Sounds frustrating," I say.

"Plus he's like starin' at me in the reeview mirra. I can't look up without seein' these little eyes a' his lookin' back at me." She pauses, does an odd little wriggle, perhaps lifting her bra back over her breasts, or possibly getting her thong back in place, or somehow realigning her parts. "You gotta drink a' sumpin'?"

She slumps back, knees apart, takes her glass without looking up, gulps, collects herself. "Thanks. I'm Carla. I mean. Oops. I'm Violet."

And so Violet.

"Hello, Violet. I'm Hans."

"I don't mean ta complain an' shit. I mean what makes him think he can look at me like that though?"

I become aware of trying to look at her in a way other than how I presume the cabbie looked at her. Violet: Bronze. Overripe. Black hair. Flower pinned in it. Hawaiian style. But sagging. Like the rest of her.

Her behind big and round. Prominent as the rear of a horse. Her accent from somewhere other than our little volcanic island.

"You're very pretty," I say. I often say something like this out of courtesy. Why not allow the girl to feel, at least, that she is appreciated, that she is more than simply a manual laborer?

"Oh yeah?"

I had not planned to say more, but now feel obliged to. I struggle for something more to add. "Quite," I say.

"That's what they says. I got the goods." She swivels sideways, juts her behind in my direction, gives it a beckoning shake, then reaches back and gives it a spank. Whether this represents a sadistic or a masochistic tendency I cannot quite say.

Seven seconds of foreplay. Then hand running down my chest. Accelerating. Beeline for the zipper. And then the act itself. Passionate, heartfelt as someone pumping up a bicycle tire. A few cursory groans emitted. Half-hearted reports of pleasure. Mmmmm. Rrrrrrrr. Mmmmm. Child pretending to be a race-car.

She gets her clothes back in order, does that wriggle again, like a little electric current is coursing through her.

"Stay," I say.

"What for?"

"Talk."

A flop back down on the couch. "I cou'j'use another one of these." Holding her empty glass. Fanning herself to demonstrate heat, and therefore thirst. Or possibly to cool off her scorching ardor.

Glass refilled, she settles back, takes in her surroundings. "Nice place."

"Thank you."

"It looks kinda like Stephen Tyler's place. In Santro Pay or wherever. He's got a really nice place."

"You've been there?"

"I seen this whole article about it. He likes earth tones and shit."

"I didn't know that."

"It's like fuckin' huge. It's got its own corral and lake and heliport and you wouldn't believe. That's what I'd like though. A horse farm. That's what I'm gonna do when I have enough money saved. I'm gonna buy a horse farm and just ride horses and shit all day."

"Sounds nice."

"Yeah. Better than gettin' it up the ass for a livin'." And then, an afterthought, "Do you think your ass gets sore riding a horse all day though?"

"Not as sore as…from the other thing."

"I guess it's like anything else. You get used to it."

"Right."

I have no idea who this person is that she is describing, and am dubious about a horse farm in San Tropez. But I let it go. It occurs to me that I have an interesting piece of intelligence to impart. From one of those idiot magazines beside my watery throne. It is about a model, a so-called supermodel who has been seen with a married baseball player. I am shocked that I know this, and more shocked that I report it is information of some potential interest.

"I didn't hear that. Makes sense though. She kinda looks like that otha' woman type."

"You can see that in someone?"

But she does not respond to this. The drink is downed. And she is up. Readying to leave. "I watched a whole show about her once. She was wearin' like this see-through shit and I'm like, I could do that. I could definitely do that. I got what she's got."

"Yes, you do."

Is it not our white lies, our little social graces, after all, that allow us to continue as a species, to endure one another, to live in this world?

At the door she shakes my hand. "Nice talkin' to ya."

"You too."

"Ask for me."

"I will."

"Ask for Violet. Like the floweh. Violet's a floweh, right?"

"I believe so, yes."

"I knew it."

And so we begin. Dawn by day. Violet by night. Succor to my septuagenarian scepter.

Our meetings follow a pattern.

Houdini-like wriggle out of too-tight dress. Three unpersuasive moans of pleasure. And then the specimen extraction. Is it the very ineptitude that appeals? What is it? Why do I ask for this one? The humanness. The indifference that approaches a kind of honesty. Or maybe I am ashamed after all. Ashamed before my comatose wife. My Annabel. Not three miles away, in our little island hospital. I imagine that she must know. Must sense. And that surely this woman is one she could not feel jealous of.

Violet never asks about me. I am not interesting. In fact, I scarcely exist. Nor does my Violet share anything of her own life. Rather, we settle on, dream of, the only common currency we have: the celestial princesses and demigods of her celebrity magazines.

She worships them in her fashion. At the same time, it is not an admiration based on the great virtue of these larger-than-life figures. Rather, Violet worships them as the ancient Greeks worshiped their pantheon. Full of reverence, and yet at the same time accusing her deities of the most disgusting behaviors. A heaven of misbegotten Gods. Deviants.

She will assure me that some famous actor is secretly having relations with his famous sister.

"How do you know this?" I ask.

"Buzz," Violet says, with a certain, knowing mystery.

It is apparent that Violet is an oracle of sorts.

I learn from her that a certain deceased diva was poisoned by her own family for the inheritance. And that the drowning of a some famous starlet was no accident. Moreover, Violet knows with certainty who is responsible. (She will not mention names, but it is someone who gained fame playing a television detective who drove a talking car.)

"I gotta get goin'."

Our session is over. She wriggles, fixes her breasts into the proper places against her chest, sighs. "You got some dick."

"Thank you."

"I'm not talkin' size. I mean...actually it's...kinda small. I just mean...at your age...."

"I understand."

"I like that it's so fast, too."

"I'm glad that you appreciate that."

"Some old guys it's like, oh my God, are ya gonna die first or are ya gonna cum?"

"Right."

And off clomps my Dulcinea, into the balmy, chirping night.

I am relieved that she is gone. And yet three nights later I call for her again. And there she is, twirling around in front of the bedroom mirror.

"You think I'm beautiful enough to be a movie star?"

"Why not?"

"I auditioned once and this guy says I'm not tall enough. Do you believe that? And I was in like four inch heels! Lousy fucker."

"Not everyone has taste."

She undresses, takes a break from her conversation to perform her service. When she comes back up, as though from a little sip at a water fountain, she continues as though there has been no disruption at all. "He doesn't even mention like, how I moved. My talent. He just says, like, 'Not the right look'."

"I see."

"I like talkin' to you," she says.

In time I learn a bit of Violet's boyfriend. He is named, by some fate with a comic streak, John. John is the name of her one lover who is not a John.

"He's nice to me."

"That's good," I say. "What does he do?"

"He's a rock star."

"Really?"

"Well, he's not really a star yet. He's still…like makin' money… you know…dealin' drugs and shit. But that's just for now."

"I see."

"You know, lots of rock stars go for models. It's like a thing."

Yes, I think to myself. And many drug dealers also go for prostitutes. That is also a thing.

"Do you think I should tell him the truth about what I do?" she asks.

"Probably not."

"Yeah, ya' right. Not everyone would understand."

"Right."

"Because this is just a steppin' stone for me. Only he might not see it that way."

"Exactly."

I am saying goodnight to Violet outside. Waiting with her for the taxi that will whisk her away.

Rustling. Something approaching out of the darkness. Walking up the driveway.

Thrash of a branch. And there she is. Dawn. Right before us. Startled. Apologizing. "Oh! Excuse me. I'm so sorry." She turns away as though one of us were naked.

"It's okay," I say.

Violet looking Dawn up and down. "Who's *she*?" Something suspicious and peevish in her voice. Not, as my vanity might have preferred, some jealousy over me. Rather, simply, Violet's reaction to the fact that such a creature as Dawn dared to exist. This very picture of ease and grace, this child who needed no make-up for highlighting, no heels for lift or wireframe bra for contour or lipstick for sexual analogue. What woman would not have been shaken by this child in ponytail and shorts and t-shirt, this girl for whom being desirable was merely a matter of waking up in the morning?

"This is Dawn. My neighbor."

"Yeah. I sees her. Hello."

"And this is Violet."

"I really didn't mean to intrude," Dawn says. "I just had this invitation to deliver. I'm sorry. It was nice meeting you."

And she is gone.

Violet looks at me irritably. "See ya."

And then a moment later Violet too is gone.

When I call for her, the agency says she no longer wishes to see me. As though just to be somewhere that might recall's Dawn's presence, her scent, was too much for her. Her territory had been taken. There was no going back.

I open the invitation. It is to a party at Cole's.

A week later I receive a call from the hospital. Annabel's heartbeat has ceased. It is over. What does it mean really? A line on a monitor has changed from wavy to straight. The chemical reactions of life have switched to the chemical reactions of biodegrading. I go to see her before they put her in the morgue, and she is the same craw-shaped gnarl of bone as during the previous visit. I run a hand through her hair, squeeze out a single tear for my partner and love of many years, return home, call her daughter.

"It's over," I tell her.

The sun comes the next morning. The waves splash white against the coral. The breeze freshens. The hummingbirds, shiny as Christmas ornaments, zigzag through the poinsettia. Ugueth chops off dead palm fronds with his machete, cracks open coconuts, rakes the high-tide line along beach. I play the clarinet, play something I used to play before the war.

When I tell Ugueth the news he looks down at the sand, makes a swath with his foot. "She a good woman, cap'n." And then, turning away. "It good she miss all de goins' on here."

Late in the afternoon, he serves a cup of iced tea. He is humming *Old Man River.*

"Ugueth," I say.

His humming ceases. "Cap'n, mon?"

"Let me ask you something. Have you never been involved with a woman? Have you never had *goings on?*"

"De woman?"

"Yes. You were young once. Didn't you…ever play the field? Fall in love?"

He seems slightly rattled by this. "De woman is de trouble," he says.

"Always?"

"Always dat I be seeing. De problems of de worl' start wit de pussy."

There is no questioning Ugueth's acquired wisdom. I can only nod and marvel that this savant has come to be my groundskeeper. "So you never wanted to marry?"

"I be married to de work, cap'n. I be married to de, 'do dis do dat.' I be married to doin' what I is told to do. To de way of de world, cap'n. Dat's how I be married."

Suddenly, everything was over. My visits to the hospital. My sexual adventures—that had sustained me through the coma—had begun with the rude swipe of a MasterCard and ended with Violet's chance meeting with Dawn. And soon, my life on Kelualua would be over as well.

- North Africa -

Here is a joke. Do you want to hear it?

Knock-knock.
Who's there?
The Gestapo!

Do you get it? It's not funny at all. That's what makes it funny.
That it's *so* not funny.
Ha ha ha!
Oh come on. It's funny! Maybe I didn't tell it right. Let me try
again.

Knock-knock.
Who's there?
The *Gestapo*!

Ha ha ha ha ha!
You still don't like it? Oh well. Well, *I* thought it was funny.
You know what else is funny? Are you ready? I wound up
volunteering in the *Wehrmacht*. Isn't that funny? Are you laughing
Sylvia, who always smiled and laughed so easily?
Well I guess it is not funny like haha. Or as we say in German,
haha. I mean funny as in peculiar.
Yes, I know. How could I volunteer to fight for…*them*? For the
side that had sent my beloved to a "protective custody" camp? That had
done the same to my teacher Klampf?
Did I not say I have no politics? Did you not believe me?
For a while, I had tried asking my mother about Sylvia, but she

denied everything. "Me? Inform on some girl I don't even know? I wouldn't even know who to inform to!" And then she turned it around on me. "Why do you care so much?"

"I just want to know."

"What does she mean to you?"

"Nothing."

"Find yourself a nice girl, Hans, from a good family."

"I had one. I don't know any others."

"There's lots of nice girls!" my mother declared, and again she went through a long list of possible prospects, some of whom she had not seen since third grade, some of whom were not even familiar names, and who I suspected were really fictional creations, purely theoretical nice, attractive girls from purely theoretical nice, established families.

Was it just my mother's contradictory nature? Or was she trying to change the subject? I was never sure what to believe. And somehow she succeeded in making me feel like I was the one in the wrong, *I* was the one disappointing *her*.

She wanted to be able to go out with me and show me off in a shiny, new uniform. "Schwarzfeldte's son...he's an officer in the *Luftwaffe*," she would say.

Why did I do it, after my father had left me the factory to run, had provided me my excuse? There are so many reasons. Nearly everyone my age had headed off in one direction or another. So what was there for me? Then there was the absurdity of my mother's house with her tiresome Fleulen. The shame of being a young, able-bodied man who had not enlisted. The emptiness of so many weeks and months without word of Sylvia. (Isn't that one ironic though?) The unavoidable desire to make my mother proud.

There was something else as well. The company, Jaegermusik, under my leadership, was in decline. The bugles were no longer in demand, now that the marching had ended and the real fighting had started. We had tried to convert Jaegermusik to manufacturing parts for guns. Brass was necessary for firing parts that require heat insulation instead of the rapid heat conduction of iron. And we were experts in brass. But we had no experience in mass production. And soon the workers themselves were conscripted or volunteered. And without a working assembly line, training of new workers became expensive. And so our parts were easily underpriced. What's more, I had to admit, I was just as clumsy as my father in managing the workers. How could I be telling these men twice my age what to do?

So it was everything. Edelburg felt like a reminder of everything that was sad, stifling, shameful. A reminder of that one, horrible moment. All I wanted was to get away from it. All of it. What better way out of my predicament was there than to sell the factory as cheaply and quickly as possible and march off, head held high, to somewhere a thousand miles away? Only...only where had they taken her? Why didn't anyone know? Why wouldn't anyone say?

Even Hilda did not object to my volunteering. There was a difference between defending the Fatherland, which almost everyone believed was essential, and supporting the regime. And did we not feel just a little pride—even Hilda and I—in our growing empire in spite of ourselves? Our economic miracle? Our bloodless annexation of Austria and Czechoslovakia and the Rhineland? Our nearly effortless conquest of Poland and France? "I guess I better start rooting for us," was what Hilda said. "Now that both my men are in the fight."

I volunteered for the Africa Corps, because it seemed especially far away and romantic. I wrote to my father and told him, and he wrote back, said nothing of my selling Jaegermusik, offered words of encouragement. He was headed to Poland as part of the occupation force, and was looking forward to us both getting home someday and sharing stories of our experiences. He told me that he loved me, and to use my sense and take care of myself. I had a feeling he would have written more about being careful had the letters not been subject to inspection. It was painful to think of him in the army, not just because I feared he would come to a bad end, but also because it was so easy to imagine how far out of his element he would be, how uncertain he would be commanding other men. How could he be the one to give absolute orders? And what would the other officers think of him?

I said goodbye to Hilda, who cried and wiped her eyes and said, "Don't you dare come back with any medals. I mean that."

"I'll try not to," I said.

I kissed my half-brother goodbye, and Hilda held up Georg's hand and pretended to speak for him. "Bye-bye Hans. I'll miss you!"

I was afraid to show my face to Sylvia's mother, but I wrote her a note urging her to write me if she heard any word of Sylvia.

As for my own mother, when I went to tell her the news I was introduced to the new governess she had hired for her baby. How completely we had been replaced, I thought. The munitions manufacturer Fleulen had replaced my father the musical instrument maker, and the baby had replaced me, and this governess had replaced Hilda. Was this new cast superior in her mind? Had the understudies surpassed the original players? Was this baby in fact more skillful, more adept at being a baby than I had been?

And can I deny that I was eager to be done with the introductions so I could tell my mother the news? That I was delighted when she wrapped her arms around me, proud when she hired a photographer to take a picture of me in my Africa Corps uniform—a picture to be placed on the wall beside her parents, her new baby, and her hero, the *Führer*?

Soon she was full of advice about what I should eat in Africa. As though I would have a choice. And as though the greatest threat to my survival would come from having an unbalanced breakfast. She took me around to her friends, spoke favorably of all the services, but still managed to put down the other divisions of the military by comparison to the glorious Africa Corps. "He'll be serving with Rommel!" she declared to the new governess, as though I would be working directly with him, he and I would be going over maps and strategies together.

"Who are we fighting over there again?" the governess asked.

But this infuriated my mother, who had suddenly come to believe that the African theatre was by far the most important, that the future of the Reich depended on it. At the same time I was not sure my mother knew the answer for certain. Was it just the British? Or were the French, and possibly the Canadians, also involved? "We're fighting the enemy!" she exclaimed. "It's our land route to the East. And there's oil! How do we win the war without oil?"

Fortunately for the governess, the baby spat up in the middle of this, and so she was able to trot off for a washcloth with no reply beyond a nervous, "Excuse me." Moments later though, when the baby started crying, my mother seized him from the governess as though this was all the poor woman's fault. *You see! Now you've upset the baby with your foolishness.* But her frustration passed quickly. With the baby now in her arms, my mother was lost in her cooing and kissing and baby-talk.

On the day of my departure, February 3rd, 1940 (for those of you tracking at home), my mother gave me a photograph of herself, and I couldn't help feeling that she was conveying a certain message with it. I was hers again. I was to look at this picture of my mother when I was lonely and homesick, and find solace in it. There was no Sylvia anymore—thank goodness. I was hers and the Fatherland's!

And then, for the first time in life, I left Edelburg behind.

I took a series of trains south to Athens. They were public trains, but full of German soldiers headed out in one direction or another. We checked in at the stations, showed our papers, were pointed to the next train and then the next to link up with our regiments. Did I not feel smart in my new uniform? And proud that all of the countries we traveled through were occupied Germany now? Our empire! In Athens

I was driven to Piraeus, and in Piraeus I was taken by seaplane across the Mediterranean. I remember staring down at the sand-blasted islands of the Aegean, the sparkling blue sea, thinking of the Odyssey that I had read for class, of the wars of Homer, feeling myself, for just a moment, as a latter-day Odysseus. Headed for my own glory.

It is hard to say exactly when I started narrating, in my mind, everything I did, for Sylvia's sake—imagining the way I would describe something to her, the words I would use. But maybe it was then, soaring above the Mediterranean. It was as though I was always composing a letter to her about it in my mind. And the letter just kept growing. Day after day. Week after week. Until it was simply the way I saw things, experienced them, one story and then the next, always imagining her reaction, how she would smile at some particular turn of phrase, how she would recoil at all the horror, how we would share the experience.

Look, Sylvia! I am high above the sea. Descending toward the port of Tripoli. I am looking out at a city of minarets and belly-dancers and dust-filled, coffee-scented streets. I am part of the war! And yes, it is terrible. But does it not perhaps have its own poetry, even the very tragedy itself? Are not tragedies the greatest of all works of art? Do you not think I am handsome at least in this uniform?

My reverie, my excitement, did not last long. We approached the Libyan coastline, the plane skimmed just above the surface of the water, weightless for a few long seconds, and jolted as it met the water. We rocked forward and then back and taxied to a bleak, non-descript base along the shore. I was introduced around, shown my cot and the mess hall and the latrine. This is where you sleep, eat, crap. There. Welcome.

My first impression was of the desert itself—heat and light and constant squinting. And I remember a fleeting loneliness, dislocation, an urge to cry. And knowing I mustn't. And then Colonel Stricker.

Unlike most Germans of the day, my family had had a car, and so I had some experience driving, and was assigned to be a lorry driver. This was hardly the role I had envisioned. And it put me under Stricker's command. I had already heard whispers about him, groans, rolls of the eyes, by the time I met him. "Another *Trottel*, I have no doubt," was his only welcoming comment to me, as I stood there saluting. *Trottel* being a moron. I was assigned repair duty and he seemed infuriated that I had not arrived with a perfect understanding of truck repair. For him it was confirmation of his assessment of me.

Stricker was a big man, chinless as a frog, with a long, sloping forehead covered with blotches like a map of some random archipelago (or perhaps, if you looked at it the right way, of the North African theatre of operation that he considered himself to be master of). He hated the Arabs, the desert, the heat, and above all, us. Once when we had to wait for a group of Bedouins and their camels blocking the road, he ran out of his car and started berating all of us. "If you can't find a way through this nonsense, just plow over them!"

In short, Stricker would have made a superb villain in some American war movie, except that he spoke actual German, rather than English with a German accent. Still, had he been used for American propaganda purposes, he surely would have inspired an earlier Allied invasion.

And yet I am also confident that we enlisted Germans came to hate him more than the enemy ever could have. Whereas the allies could kill him (which we all dearly hoped for), we had no choice but to do as we were told and swallow our rage.

Thinking back on those first days, with the benefit my extreme distance from that period, what also comes to mind is the falseness of the conversations among all of the newcomers. Our pronouncements that ranged from feigned bravado to feigned nonchalance, depending on the moment or the mood. What we were all really feeling, I have no doubt, was some mixture of homesickness and fear and shame that we would have such feelings.

What reminded us that we were really in a war were the air raids that came at night. The sirens and then, seconds later, the whistling, the explosions. The sound of the flak guns going and the bombs exploding, sometimes all of it growing to a feverish pitch as we hurried to the shelter. We felt the ground shake, looked at one another to gauge and calibrate our fear. *No, not that close. Yes, that one was nearer.*

It was airless and sweltering in the shelter, and in the back of our minds we were all surely terrified of being buried alive. Still, until we sent home the first bodies, helped evacuate the first wounded, it seemed impossible that something could truly happen to me—that I, Hans Jaeger, could die, not in some future battle, not after two years of grand and glorious war in my smartly-pressed uniform, but now, tonight, ignominiously, before I had seen a moment of action. Was this what I had imagined when I had volunteered? Cleaning the officers' quarters? Cowering before Stricker? Cowering under the air-raids? Or curled up in my lower bunk, distracting myself with absurd fantasies, pleasuring myself, three feet below the sagging mattress of a fellow dreamer?

Of course you had to believe in the cause, at least a little. Defending the homeland. Because why else would you put yourself through this?

After a few weeks of tinkering with the lorries, learning our way around, the company moved forward to Benghazi, on the eastern side of Libya. There I started my regular duty, bringing supplies to the front.

We loaded up in the ancient, white-washed harbor, dotted with Greek and Roman ruins, drove in convoys to El Alamein, in Egypt, where the fighting was, emptied our loads, and returned. Was it a brilliant stroke of boldness by Stricker that these trips were undertaken during the day, in the merciless Libyan sunshine, our trucks plodding along, as conspicuous and helpless as beached whales? Or was it lunacy?

Each truck came with a driver and a navigator. It was the job of the navigator to peer into the perfectly blue, desert sky for that one atom that did not look right, that might grow into a dot, and then no, a little group of dots, growing, growing, and then suddenly right in front of us, a fleet of fighter-planes, roaring, dive-bombing, headed right at us, raining death.

I have spoken about sheer, heart-pounding terror. The knock on Sylvia's door. Reality itself. *I am coming for you.* This was different. This was a slow rumbling forward. A slow building of tension. This was calm, calm, the ticking of a clock, knowing that at any moment you could be in the midst of it. And feeling it there, just out of sight, hour after hour, day after day. The truck grinding. Roaring. Vibrating. About to explode. Always about to explode. That atom in the sky, or that one, or that one, always about to turn into something that was after you, that wanted to kill you. *I am coming for you.* That single point of azure sky over there. That is the one that will kill you.

What were we even doing, I began to wonder. Fighting for this land that was devoid of life, this land that was neither German nor British, that belonged to the sandflies and the snakes, that could never be conquered by humans. Two great armies fighting over an endless void. The British holding to their vast expanse of sand named Egypt. The Germans and Italians sharing their vast, ever-changing emptiness called Libya.

Of course, the lorries were only lightly armed. So by the time the planes were spotted there was not much to be done but run out into the desert, get away from the trucks, dive face-first into the sand like so many ostriches. That was what our instinct told us to do. Have you ever seen very young children playing hide-and-seek? Too young to realize that covering one's own eyes does not prevent others from seeing you? Covering their eyes and declaring, "I'm hiding?" That was what we brave heroes of the *Afrika Korps* were like. Diving face down into the sand. As though somehow, magically, that would make us invisible.

Where was Göring?   Where was the goddamned *Luftwaffe*?
Nothing. Our sole survival mechanism was to dive out of the truck and
run. Chased like some mindless, defenseless prey. What glory! What
valor! Are you not proud, *Mutti*? And if Africa was so God-damned
important, where was our God-damned air support?

Once the planes were gone, what was left were the moans of the
wounded. We hurried them into ambulances and jeeps, drove the ruined
trucks off the road, loaded the dead into the backs of trucks that had not
been hit. Sometimes, bizarrely, they wound up right next to a load of
rations, two or three bodies, now part of our delivery.

That was it. The convoy was moving again. Creeping forward.
Terror ebbing back to that perpetual tension.

My navigator was a short, beefy boy of nineteen named Dieter. He
had two oversized front teeth that must have looked endearing when he
was younger, and walked with his knees angled away from each other,
like he was waving in one direction and then the next. It all gave him a
rather foolish, and at the same time a happy-go-lucky appearance. He
spoke with what might be called a "low" accent, whistled tunes from the
radio back home.

On our very first outing together, just a few miles outside Benghazi,
he offered this conversation-starter: "I could use some nice, Italian
pussy right about now."

Perhaps this was simply an all-purpose phrase of sorts. It meant
Hello. Goodbye. Shalom. Salaam. Peace be with you.

It will be no surprise that sex, the desire for sex, the lack of sex,
was an ever-present topic of conversation, not just because of our
loneliness, our youth, but also because something was needed that could
hold our attention. Something strong enough to bring us out of that
trance-like scanning of the skies. And, of course, it was a proof of sorts
of our manliness, just as all the false bravado had been in our first days
together.

"It has to be Italian?" I inquired.

"Well, that's about the only kind around here," he said.

I mentioned that I had seen some pretty Arab girls, and this led to a
detailed and entirely predictable discussion of comparative anatomy,
preference, alleged tightness, moistness, olfactory considerations, and
so on.

"You got a girl back home?" he asked.

"No," I said.

"Never?"

"Yeah, for a while," I said.

"She leave you?"

How many times I would be asked this question, and have to evade. "Not exactly. Just didn't work out. You?"

"Yeah I got a girl." He reached into his pocket, showed me a picture.

"Pretty," I said, though she seemed rather plain.

"You ever done it?" he asked. "I mean, all the way?"

"Once," I said. "You?"

"Oh yeah. Right before I headed off."

"Nice."

He flashed his toothy, childish smile. "Yeah."

I sensed that there was more that Dieter wasn't saying, something forlorn, and though he was no younger than me, I felt a sort of older-brother protectiveness with him. I had visited him once in the infirmary after he'd come down with what might politely be described as a severe stomach bug and he'd looked particularly dejected.

"What's wrong?" I'd asked.

What came out was that he had befriended one of the nurses, had mistaken her kindness and sympathy for a romantic interest, had made a fool of himself. "That's the way it goes with me," he'd said, smiling, frowning, sighing.

It was especially unusual that someone would actually confess something like this, not try to mask it in any way—as though he was still a boy, had none of the protective armor the rest of us had acquired.

"What about your girl back home?"

He shrugged and I didn't ask more on that topic. "You know, you're not really at your most appealing right now," I said. "Maybe you should try again when there's not liquid crap streaming out of you every five minutes."

That almost got a laugh. "Yeah, maybe," he said.

A month later, we made it back to Tripoli for a two-day leave (back when we still had time-outs from the war) and miraculously, our collective wish—expressed so eloquently in Dieter's greeting—was granted. The *Wehrmacht* had set up bordellos there staffed with young Italian women to satisfy the needs of its troops. We might die a slow, agonizing death in the desert. Our guts blown out across the sand. But at least we would not be deprived of this.

The setting consisted of a medium-sized bivouac not unlike a very small circus tent. A line of men waited outside it in the baking heat, just as they might have waited for the latrine or for our slop in the mess tent or, in another world, for an amusement park ride. There was even a separate officers' bordello with a separate officer's whore right next to the *landser's* tent, just as there was a separate officer's quarters and mess hall and latrine. Yes, we were all comrades at arms in this great cause. Yes, we were all fighting for *Volk* and *Vaterland* and *Führer*. But how could you expect the officers to share the same pussy with a common soldier? Was it not obvious that they would need their own business-class, officers-only vagina?

I stood on line with Dieter at the *landser*'s whorehouse, awaiting my turn. It was too hot to feel much enthusiasm, even to say much of anything.

"I'm not sure I'm even up for this," I said.

"You should though," he said.

"Why should I?"

"Because…because who knows what tomorrow will bring."

"True."

But that just turned us more thoughtful. We stood quietly, dreaming, visualizing together, stepping forward, watching the men exiting with a little extra kick in their step.

"I hope she has nice tits." Dieter said. Not just to break up the silence, to share this hope, but also, it seemed, to just to say the word, *tits*, to savor it, to make them real, place them before us.

Dieter went in first. And then it was my turn. Inside, the air was still and stifling. There were two girls, separated by a sheet. There was no choosing. You took the stall, the slot, that was available. When my turn came, Dieter was busy with the girl on the right, so I went to the left. I brushed aside a curtain. A girl lay back on a bare mattress, wearing a see-through nightie that came down to her waist. She looked off past me as though I wasn't there. Yet still arousing, suddenly—that little oasis between her legs. Condom sliding over erection. Aerodynamic like a dive-bomber. Nose-cone of one of those Tommy planes. *Jabos*. Plunging downward. Inside her. Inside that hot, sweating, nearly motionless female flesh. How different was it, really, from masturbating to some pornographic photograph or fucking an inflatable doll—plunging into this semi-inert blob of femaleness that did not even speak the same language—even if there were anything to say to one another. Ejaculating, departing, wordless.

I waved goodbye awkwardly, just in the hope of some response, any response, but received none. The girl just kept looking off, as though nothing had happened. I had not even been there. I did not exist.

Looking back on it, I cannot but marvel at the very nature of a man's sexual attraction. What is it for, exactly? A specific set of lines? Shapes? The woman's sex organ itself? Some set of mathematic relations between two points of nipple, arc of ass, elongated ellipse of vulva? But these relations are always changing based on a woman's position. The lighting. The particular woman. And there is so much more to it. Can we not feel the same physiological response to a woman who is clothed? So what is it then? The outline? Can a mere silhouette suffice? Do we not also require a face, the legs, the neck? What then? Some image of *female* we carry from before we were born, from a million years of ancestry?

If so, then of what does this image consist? Can a blind man sense it, so that, if he were to suddenly gain his sight, he would look upon a woman and say yes, of course, this is exactly what I have imagined, dreamed of, desired? And how is it that our internal image of female has evolved just as the object of our desire has evolved? For imagine if we, modern men, still desired the form that female hominids took three million years ago? But no. Somehow, our desire has evolved in perfect unison with the opposite sex's appearance. Kind of strange, no?

Back in Benghazi, back from our leave, we were reunited with our beloved Stricker. He had just returned from a meeting with Rommel, and now carried a baton much like Rommel's—although respectfully, not quite as long. Where he had found this item, nobody knew. Was there a baton-store somewhere for aspiring Field Marshalls? Moreover, he seemed to have assumed Rommel's gait and now spoke as though he and Rommel were the closest of confidantes and friends, as though he knew not only the highest level secrets, but also the in-jokes, the gossip, all the while insinuating that none of it could possibly be shared. He was enjoying the war. Enjoying this power, this ability to torment his fellow Germans. And now, amid all of these other delights, he was enjoying playing with his baton.

Two days later we loaded up a cargo of anti-aircraft shells headed for the front lines. Stricker inspected our loads, made us reload, in the sweltering heat, not because the loads weren't balanced but, so it seemed, because he could. After all the repacking we left late, drove through the midday sun up to the lines—or what was left of the lines. What we were hearing, at least in whispers (because nobody dared say anything negative aloud) was that El Alamein was not going well.

On the way, Dieter talked more about his girlfriend. "She worked in a department store."

"Nice."

"Yeah. She got discounts on all her clothes. She knew how to dress too. That's one thing she learned there."

"Nice."

"Yeah."

I finally asked. "You getting any letters from her?"

"Nah. But what the heck. I just need me another Italian girl."

"You write her?"

"Yeah. Some. But what the heck."

"Hey, when we get back you'll have plenty to choose from," I said.

Or maybe I never finished that sentence. Or only thought it. Because they came at us suddenly. From the wrong direction. From the South. The desert. "Tommies!" Dieter shouted. And then, in what seemed like an instant, they were on us. We were stopped. We were running out into the sand, curled over, explosions everywhere, bombs, machine gun fire, the planes so low you could see the faces of the gunners, rushing by and pulling up, swooping down and pulling up, leaving screams and moaning and chaos in their wake. I was curled up in the sand, wondering if it was over this time, and looking back and seeing them, there in the distance, looping around, graceful as sailing ships, out in the sky, beautiful like that for just an instant, and then coming at us again, coming in to kill us, thinking this time is it, this time I am going to die, getting up to run again, only where, there was nowhere, and so diving, digging into the sand, covering myself, face up, so I could throw sand on myself with my hands, half covered, and then just lying there, motionless, waiting, hearing the strafing again, *tch tch tch tch tch tch tch*, where was fucking Göring and the fucking *Luftwaffe*, how could they send us out here to die like this with no way to defend ourselves, *tch tch tch tch tch tch tch tch*, goodbye Sylvia, if you are looking for me, I am buried here in the sand.

And then, just as suddenly, they were gone. The sky was empty all the way out to the horizon. Had it worked? Had they actually not seen me? Or just missed? Somehow or other, I was still alive. Uninjured. Eight of our twenty-two trucks were ablaze. Mine was still in one piece, but riddled with bullet holes. I went to where I had last seen Dieter, but he was lying face-down. Dead.

I helped tend to the wounded. Helped load up the corpses that were more or less complete. Not exactly there. But moving. Working. We were all rushing, fearing another raid. Some drivers switched trucks, found new partners. And then, as though nothing remarkable had just happened, the trucks were starting up, rumbling on. Giant insects, oblivious to their own dead, burned out comrades. Driving right by them. Not even recognizing them as the same species.

In my own truck my hands were still shaking. It was one thing to hear that so-and-so had died in an air raid. Someone who you barely knew. It was another to lose someone you'd been side-by-side with for so long. I kept starting to say something to him as I was driving, and then I'd look over and it wasn't him. What was I thinking? And then I would see him lying there again, face down. Of course! He is dead! You idiot!

When we arrived in El Alamein it was more chaos. It was night and you could see the fires in the distance long before we arrived. As we approached there were soldiers running everywhere. Fire brigades and ambulances. Most of the anti-aircraft gunners had been taken out, their nests destroyed.

God damn it. Dammit dammit dammit! That was what I kept thinking. And do you know why? Not because of our defeat or our suffering. Not because I had lost my navigator and only friend. No. Because I had all these damned anti-aircraft shells and now there was nobody who would take them. And without that, who would sign my paperwork? And if I came back without my paperwork signed, they would think I'd ditched my cargo in the desert and turned around to avoid the Tommies. For which the penalty—as we were frequently reminded—was death. If the damned gunners had taken out a flew planes they'd be alive now, I thought, and maybe Dieter would be alive too. And I would have someone to sign for my goddamn shells. I shouted at everyone I could find in El Alamein. Argued with one receiving clerk and then the next. Finally got rid of my stuff, got a signature, headed back.

The next night, back in Benghazi, I thought more about Dieter. Because why couldn't that girl of his have just lied to him? Sent him a few letters? Given him something to hope for? Because why break his heart when he was going to wind up dead anyway? She would never have to see him again. And he could have died imagining she still wanted him. And then I wondered about his parents. His mother. I imagined his mother must have been of the over-protective sort. Still feeling like he was her baby. What would this news be like for her?

And then I was filled with more thoughts. What was I doing out here? What was happening? Where had my life taken this crazy turn? I wanted to be home. To be a boy. To be comforted. How shameful! What a pathetic creature I was. It was no longer about whether we were right or wrong or who knew what. I was too absorbed in my own misery to even think like that. The sand fleas that had become nearly unbearable—the fetid water, the heat, the stomach that was sometimes empty and always full with fear. I wanted just to be a child again. To be in my own bed. To be cared for by my mother. And of course I longed for my Jewish sweetheart. My deep, dark secret.

Just to be in her arms again. Every time the mail came I prayed that there would be a letter a from her. She had been let out. She was okay. Or if not that, at least something from her mother, saying she'd found out what camp Sylvia was in, that she was alive. That she was getting by. But there was nothing.

Two nights after he was killed, I received a message that Stricker wanted to see me. I went to the officer's dining room, which was in the former *pensione* that had been requisitioned as the officer's headquarters. The rations of late had been both lean and flavorless, and as I entered the room the aroma of real, cooked food left me feeling weak.

Stricker acknowledged me vaguely and then left me standing there, waiting, watching him eat, watching all of them eat. Did he not understand the torment he was putting me through? Did he not realize how my mind was already swimming with everything that had just happened? Did he revel in it, dabbing his cloth napkin against his lips with particular elan, just for show? For a long while I was transfixed at the sight of this man who held complete power over me—his chinless chewing, the map of birthmarks on his forehead. As I stood there, shaking with hunger and rage, I cared a thousand-fold more for the indignities committed against me by this man than for all of the horrors committed against mankind by the German war machine.

At last he called me over.

"Too bad about your partner," he said.

"Yes, sir."

"Just wanted to say that."

"Yes, sir. Thank you sir."

"No medals for losing your partner. No special privileges."

I just stood there, unsure how to answer.

"Nobody gives a damn," he said.

At least he was right about that. Nobody cared.

I nodded. *"Jawohl."*

"That's all."

And with that I saluted, hailed the *Führer* in whose name we were fighting, was dismissed.

"How's our fearless colonel?" someone asked when I returned to our tent.

I made some gesture, the very inverse of a salute. "I'd love to shove that baton up his ass."

It did not occur to me to think of our losses as a sign of how the overall African mission was going. It was all I knew. The extents of the losses were just accepted. Wasn't that how things went in war? But it was apparent that we had not taken Alexandria or Cairo. Whatever this battle was, it was no *Blitzkrieg.*

Weeks and months passed. The weather turned. Dust storms turned the sky brown and made it impossible to breathe. It felt like the desert itself was rising up and reclaiming whatever humans had built to separate themselves from it. The streets faded under the sand like some lost civilization. We coughed and spat dust. The conveys slowed to a near halt, navigated by the oil barrels along the roadside which, when the road was completely sand-covered, were the only way to know where the road ended and the desert began.

But at least they couldn't fly in it. We were briefly safe.

One night when the dust storms had abated the sirens sounded very late. We all raced out of bed. Whatever dreams we were dreaming were gone. That first shock. Buzzing. Madness. When you are still half-awake. And then running to the shelter. Bright flash. Near the officers' quarters. Dive! The explosion coming a half-second after. Then up again. At last there in the shelter. That one was close! Sirens sounding. Shouting.

In the morning we learned the news. Stricker had been killed! I felt nothing but joy. Everyone was turning to one another. "Did you hear? Stricker got it."

"No!"

"Yes."

Looks of shock. Nobody dared say what we were surely all thinking. We'd been liberated! It was difficult not to flash a smile at one another. And then to laugh at ourselves, our satisfaction in the news. We all fought it. Did I feel guilty for having wished this upon him? Only in the sense of feeling, strangely, that his spirit would haunt me. That he would blame me. Blame all of us. Torment us from the grave. Beyond that I felt nothing. Relief. One less misery.

After the dust came the rainstorms. Desert downpours. Mold spreading through the kitchen. Everything rotting. Roads flooding. Clothing and underwear always damp. Not even the bed sheets dry. The infirmary filled with malaria cases. Once again, it meant the British couldn't fly. We hurried to the front and back again while it was safe, and prayed for it to keep raining.

By the time the weather cleared, and without Stricker's expert guidance, it was finally decided that we should only drive at night, and with our headlights off. And we were spread much further apart. This was both safer and a good deal stranger. Sometimes you could see only the stars, the moon, lights that told you which way the sea was. There was no way to see the road more than a few feet ahead of you. You were constantly veering off into the desert and regaining the road.

Hour after hour we advanced like that. Driving through nothing.

No longer just the dark, the desert, but something less even than that. The black of nothing. And why? To kill these strangers who were out in the same blackness somewhere, out in the same nothing, who wanted to kill us. Where was my life—the people and places and love and music—that I had known? It was as though the world had ended and this was all that was left. A few survivors lurching through the darkness. Trying desperately to kill each other. To be the very last human alive.

I had a new navigator, and now his job was just to keep us on the road. Sometimes, when the road was bombed out, cratered, blocked by wrecks of other trucks, we would head off into the desert to get around it. We drove in soft sand and over dried salt lakes, the surface crunching, half-eroded. It was at one of these dried lake-beds that I saw one of the strangest things I saw during the whole of the war.

There are so many poetic deaths in a war. Ironic, all of them, in their insignificance. A million more like Dieter. Living humans vanishing in a flash. Pilots crashing downward, pirouetting ball of flame like some failed circus stunt, man and machine together exploding, tumbling weightless, reunited with the earth. Heads blown off and coming to rest, bizarrely, looking straight back at the bodies from which they had been severed. Shot up cows and horses—as though even the enemy livestock were evil, must be hated, destroyed.

On the salt lake I saw something strange even by the standards of this strange world—the truck in front of us rolling forward, there, the next ant in the line, then suddenly, bizarrely falling down through the earth. Just like that. Not even close enough to hear. Just there and then not. The salt crust giving way. The desert consuming it. As though the earth itself, the very planet, were alive, could open its jaws and swallow you if it decided it was your turn to go.

Is that what happened to you, Sylvia? Because how could she just vanish? What were they doing with her? And why hadn't I at least looked at her? At least said something? *I love you.* I had never actually said those words. How I dreamed of us now, slipping out of the window together. Silently. Slipping off into the night. Off into some alternative reality.

What I didn't know, as we crunched across the Libyan sand, was that our missions were winding down. The truck that had disappeared beneath the desert turned out to be one of our last casualties among the lorries. The war news, generally, had turned bad for us. Of course, no bad news was ever actually reported. In fact, even hinting that a battle had gone badly, that the war was not going well, was a grave offense. But when the wireless declared that, "The glorious *Wehrmacht* is making a courageous stand in El Alamein," rather than, "Victory In Egypt!" we all knew. What we didn't know was just *how* bad it was. We learned that a few days later when El Alamein was overrun. Tanks and munitions and thousands of men were captured. Benghazi was in ruins from all of the air raids. Africa was all but lost. We fled West, back to Tripoli.

There is your brave, your glorious *Afrika Korps*, *Mutti*. Are you not proud?

- Illyria -

We saw a boat the other day. It hung in the far distance, a barge of some sort. Only really just a tiny dark smudge in the view. A smudge that stayed there near the horizon when you blinked. That moved with infinite slowness from right to left. We fed our fire, leapt and waved palm fronds. But its path was as steady as it was silent and slow. And soon it was gone.

Would you like an update of what else is happening here on our little Island?

We are all blistered and hairy and emaciated. Animals. We are no longer Cole and Conrad and Hans. We are the animal formerly known as Cole. The animal formerly known as Conrad. And so on.

The island of the damned.

For a while, Andreas's bamboo lobster traps yielded fish and crabs. And we learned how to tip over urchins and pick them up and eat out the insides. But it seems most of the urchin beds have been cleared of all but the smallest morsels. And the traps are no longer as full.

"We need to stop harvesting the urchins," Conrad says to Cole.

"Why?" Cole asks.

"We need to regulate the intake. As a group."

"You want a quota system?"

"If we all compete for who can catch more fish, we'll just run out of fish faster."

"Maybe we'll develop better fishing methods if we're competing."

"But then we'll just run out of fish even faster." Conrad rolls his eyes. "You should read, *The Tragedy Of The Commons,* by Garrett Hardlin."

"Good idea," Cole says. "Can you order me a copy? Or maybe I'll just stop by the library."

"The free market doesn't always work," Conrad says.

"Well how fair is it," Cole says, "that I'm supposed to eat the same as everyone else when I'm bigger?   Portions should be according to weight."

"That's socialism," Conrad says.

"How is it socialism?" Cole asks.

"'To each according to his needs.' You think you should *get* more because you *need* more."

"I thought you *liked* socialism," Cole says.

"I thought you hated it," Conrad says.

Monique staggers up, walks off a few steps, starts vomiting.

"Are you okay?" Cole calls out.   But it is not easy to answer while you are throwing up.

"It's that bulb we're eating," Conrad says. "It's poisonous."

"If it's poisonous, why aren't the rest of us puking?" Cole asks.

"Maybe she had more than we did," Conrad says.

"It's not the bulb," Cole says. "She's sick. Can't you see that?" And then, thinking back to Gloria, to the possibility of a contagion, "We need to start quarantining."

We are surprised to hear Cole speak of quarantining his lover. Especially when she is right there. Unable to speak, yes, but clearly able to hear. Things do not seem entirely right between them these days.

Cole's clothing has grown more and more frayed, and now his shirt hangs on by one shoulder, giving him the look of a cartoon artist's rendering of a caveman.   Still there is a kind of vanity, self-consciousness, even to this. Cole has found clay in the soil along one hillside, and has started making things with it. At first it was bowls and plates, which were first rubbed with seawater and then placed in the fire and hardened.   Our culture now has pottery.   Then he turned his attention to his artwork, where he showed a surprising talent. He could make a believable elephant, a lion, cuddly-looking bear, a big-cheeked gnome.   Soon he had gnomes along the outside of his hut, and more gnomes under his crucifix. I have no insight into the cultural meaning of the gnome. Why do these hideous things appeal to people? What does Cole see when he looks at them?   Moreover, will future archaeologists think we were a culture that revered the gnome? Or even that we all looked like gnomes? Or will they realize it was just one guy with a gnome fetish?

Monique is wiping her lips, burying her puke in the sand.

"I'm not sick," she says. "And I'm not poisoned either."

We all turn to her. Cole looks confused. "What is it?"

"I'm pregnant, Cole," she says, her voice lower, searching for a more intimate register, while still letting the rest of us hear. "That's what it is."

For a moment Cole just stands there looking at her, unsure how to react. Why had she not told him sooner, why had she chosen to tell him along with everyone else?

"Well," Conrad says, "Let's quarantine her. By all means. So we don't all get pregnant."

Cole looks at him, then at Monique. He nods inwardly, self-consciously, lets everyone see how inwardly he is nodding, how deeply he is thinking. "I guess we're going to need to make some changes around here," he says. "We're going to need to prepare."

And this is how he attempts to reassert his control, his superior status. We must do it for the baby. We must prepare for the baby. Our future—the future of all of us—depends on this baby. And if Monique has turned on him, if Monique does not wish to think of it as his, then neither will he. It is *ours.* All of ours.

For myself, I do not particularly see Cole's child as in any way perpetuating my existence after I am gone. My genes are far too selfish for that. And I already have my own son after all, out there in the world somewhere.

There is arguing that night from inside Cole's hut. And then, late at night, Monique moves back in with us. Back into Versailles. There is no discussion. She just slips in and we make room on the floor for her and that is that.

Of course, this leaves Cole with his own shelter, all to himself, and this does not sit well with Conrad. The next afternoon I am sitting on the beach with him. The wind is whipping up the ocean and it is suddenly churning and alive.

"So I guess we're quarantining Cole now," I say.

"So we don't all turn into Republicans," he says.

"I have no politics," I say.

"Well, that's fine," Conrad says. "But he's still an ass."

I have no response to this. I look out at the ocean.

"Beautiful view," I say.

"You know what's weird?"

"What?" I ask.

"People pay fortunes for this view."

"Yes."

"They build everything to look rustic. Thatched roofs. Bamboo. They all want to get away from it all."

"I know."

"People dream about being us!"

"Like on that TV show."

"*Survivor*?"

"No, the other one."

"*Lost*?"

"No. The other one."

"*Gilligan's Island*?"

"Yes."

"You know what else is strange?"

"What?" I ask.

"Electromagnetic waves are hitting us from every direction. Even out here. Bouncing off satellites. News broadcasts. Talk shows. Presidential debates. Porn. It's all around us. The world. And we can't even see it. Feel it."

"True," I say. "And you know what else?"

"What?"

"Probably there's some set of waves, some frequency, that's beaming out some old episode of *Gilligan's Island*."

"I'm glad we can't see that," Conrad says.

"Me too. They made all kinds of wheels and machines. It would make us feel stupid."

"They had great huts," he says. "With windows."

"They had Mary Ann."

"And the professor."

"You liked the professor?"

"No. I'm just saying…he was useful. We could use him."

"True," I say.

"I once took the Universal Studios tour," he says. "And they showed you the actual lagoon where it was filmed. Right on the Universal grounds in LA."

"I didn't know that," I say.

"Wouldn't it be cool if we were really on the Universal set somewhere?"

"Like it's all part of some show."

"Yeah," Conrad says. "And we'll get in our skiff and just sail out to a wall that's the end of the set."

"And then we could sell the movie rights to our story."

"And they could make a movie about us sitting here talking about them making a movie about us," I say.

"It would work better if one of us triumphed over an addiction of some kind."

"We could add that in."

"Or if one of us was training for the Winter Olympics."

"And one of us should be gay," I say.

He looks at me.

"An incidental character," I offer.

"I think that should be you."

"Why me?"

"Because you're older.   You're not going to have sex with anyone anyway. So what does it matter who you're not having sex with?"

"So what about you? Who are you having sex with?"

There is no answer.

"You're still dreaming of Dawn?" I say. "I think she's taken."

He sighs, nods, changes the subject.   "I really miss the news," he says.

"What news?"

"I don't think it matters.   Just something about other humans. Wars. Scandals. Celebrity break-ups."

"Serial killers," I say.

"Yeah. I really miss serial killers," Conrad says.

- Italy -

For weeks the wireless had been reporting about our soldiers' courageous battle in Stalingrad. Victory was at hand! *Sieg!* And then there was simply no news. No final confirmation. Stalingrad just disappeared from the bulletins. As though it had never happened. And then something even more unusual. An official admission. Coming through the radio. We had been defeated? How was it possible? Weren't we just about to declare victory? But no. Stalingrad had been lost. The sixth army—an entire army—had been lost. Somber music was played through the static. We grieved our fallen. What it actually meant, we still dared not discuss. It was as though it was acknowledged, but completely isolated, disconnected. Of course our ultimate victory was still inevitable.

The details of how it happened we did not learn until years later, from the handful of German soldiers who had lived to tell about it— how we had surrounded the city, closed in, laid siege to it from land and air, turned it to rubble, and then how the Russians and the Germans battled among the ruins, fought to the death for every last pile of debris, Stalin telling his soldiers there is no refuge behind you, nothing exists behind the Volga, and Hitler telling his army to hold the city *at all costs*, and so the two armies imprisoned there by the orders of two madmen, battling over something that was not even a city anymore, that was nothing, like two suitors so lost in the fight that they don't even realize that the girl they are fighting for has abandoned both of them.

At last the Russians looking about, finding nothing left to defend, and leaving the city's remnants to the Germans, ceding them the putrid corpse of Stalingrad, and the Germans entering it in apparent triumph, only to find themselves surrounded, so now instead of the Germans encircling the Red Army it was the other way around, the Germans trapped within the city, the armies encircling one another like two amoebas, each trying to incorporate the other, or perhaps like that American cartoon with the bird and the coyote, where, ironically, the machinations and devices of the villain must always backfire upon himself, only the German army frozen and starving and unable to see the irony, cut off from their supplies and out of ammunition and at last the entire army swallowed up, devoured, just like that—never heard from again.

Because after that one day of honest news reports, the sixth was never again spoken about. Goebbels held a rally days after the defeat at the *Sportpalast* in Berlin. We all had to listen to it. "Do you want war?" he shouted furiously. And the crowd cheered wildly. "Do you want total war?" he bellowed. Again, they cheered, even more wildly. Yes, of course. *Total* war. *Sieg Heil!* Apparently, what we had had up to this point was not war enough. It was not *total* war.

Now, thanks to our great and wise leaders, we would have the great pleasure of experiencing *total* war.

One thing that continued to function, even amid the chaos of our evacuation from Africa, was the mail. In Tripoli there were letters waiting for me from my mother and Hilda and my father. Hilda sent a box of chocolates, along with a letter that told little stories of Georg's accomplishments. He was four now, and she had told him all about his brave half-brother. "He thinks you get to ride camels, and he plays at camel-riding like some kids pretend to ride horses or fly airplanes." Berlin had been bombed, she reported, but nothing had been hit as far east as Leipzig, and Edelburg was fine. Although she missed having all of the handsome men around. She added that there was no word from any of our other friends. Which I knew, of course, was a reference to Sylvia.

My mother, amusingly, sent me the identical box of chocolates from the same confectioner. Her letter was full of pride in me, worry for my diet and my sleep, confidence in our brave men in uniform and in our ultimate victory, and news about the baby. (I see I have not yet given him a name. Did I so resent the doting attentions my mother directed at him, at my replacement, that I have preferred to keep him anonymous? His name was Stefan. As in, "Stefan is darling as ever...." "I bought the loveliest new train set for Stefan..." And on and on.)

Dare I admit how much—as I lay on my cot, covered in sand-flea bites, as I turned about sleeplessly, as I imagined the air raid siren was at any moment about to start screaming—how much I truly missed my mother?

But it was my correspondence with my father that became the most interesting. It started with the concluding sentence in one of my own letters. "We have just made a truly glorious stand at El Alamein, and I sincerely hope the war is going as triumphantly for you as it is for me."

Since he must have known that El Alamein had ended in defeat, and knew I never spoke like this in any case, he of course grasped the sarcasm. I smiled when he replied in kind. "I'm glad to hear of your great success! And I can report that everything is equally excellent here. I have been transferred to help with our splendid advance against the Bolsheviks, so I am getting to see the beautiful Russian countryside while at the same time enjoying our fine *Wehrmacht* cuisine, which I am pleased to say is keeping my gut completely clear." Which meant, of course, that the campaign was going poorly and he was suffering from diarrhea.

We continued in this vein, back and forth, and so in our way managed to communicate the depth of despair, in spite the military censors, by the degree of false enthusiasm. Everything meant its opposite. Our ever-increasing confidence in victory meant our growing certainty of failure. Health meant sickness. Warm and sunny meant cold and miserable. Love of our majestic *Führer* meant hatred of the lowly scum. My father ended all his letters though with the simple words, "I miss you." And there was an added poignancy to it, because they were the only words that meant what they said.

But I mustn't deprive you, Sylvia, of a description of the end of the Africa campaign. We defended Tripoli until we didn't. Then we drove even further west, all the way to Tunisia on our epic, four-thousand mile retreat, a *Reichsretreat*, as we might call it, as we liked to stick *Reich,* (meaning "imperial") ahead of everything, our imperial army, our imperial schools, the imperial *Reichsturds* we left in our imperial *Reichslatrines* on our way to our imperial *Reichsdefeat.*

By some scheduling malfunction, our unit arrived in Tunisia just in time to greet the Americans, who were busily establishing a beachhead. *What a coincidence! What are you guys doing here? Oh...you're coming here to kill us! Oh well. Gotta run. Catcha later.*

Our unit was soon surrounded by the Americans. Of course, we had done such a fine job of delivering munitions into useless heaps at the front lines, there was not much left with which to defend ourselves. I was part of a last-minute air-lift to "safety" as it was called (meaning of course, more war, misery and death). We boarded a small transport plane, rose up and away from Africa, bid farewell at last to the sand and dust and baking heat. In a moment there was nothing below us but sparkling water. We landed in Sardinia, where I was awarded the iron cross second class for no particular reason other than that, for some odd reason, I was not dead. What better way to pretend Africa had been a victory than to give everyone medals? ("You're all winners!" Isn't that what we tell our children at the end of their American soccer season? Do you know those plastic trophies that proudly declare *Participant*? That is what I wish had been engraved on my medal. It should have read, "Africa Campaign, 1940—Participant".)

I was promoted to corporal and assigned to a new unit that was being organized, destination unknown.

It was May, 1943. I had been a soldier for almost three years. Sometimes it was hard to believe I had lived through the things I had lived through, and then at other times it was hard to believe there had ever been anything else, that the past before the war had been real—the pretty riverbank of Edelburg that I had fished with my father, the Beethoven concert he had taken me to when I was just ten, the ruined castle where I had played hide-and-seek as a child, where, years later, I had passed happy hours after school with Sylvia.

That was another thing that scarcely seemed real anymore. Sylvia herself. Was it all just some magical past that I could never go back to? If she were real, then how could she have just vanished like that? Without a word of her? When I cried, late at night—and it had become a rarity—it was no longer that I felt I was still a boy, stranded in this foreign, terrifying place. Now it was that I was no longer that boy. Would never be. That there was no going back. The war was not just all there was, but in a strange way, all that had ever been.

But of course it is never that simple, is it? Every generalization has its exceptions. Because sometimes, in the midst of never-ending daily survival, Sylvia was suddenly there again, and so real and immediate I could feel her, feel exactly what it felt like to be with her, to hold her in her nightgown, or be alone in my house with her, laughing together at my parents' arguments, listening to my father's gramophone.

We waited for six weeks in Sardinia. It seemed strange, with the war all around us, that they would just leave us there doing nothing because someone up the chain of command could not decide what to do with us. At last, when the allies invaded Sicily in June, our unit was sent to Italy to help defend it. The population had turned against us just as the Americans and British were streaming across from Sicily. Italy officially switched sides just as the Allies landed, joined with the Allies, at which point the Italian army, suddenly our enemies, promptly surrendered to us. Well that is not exactly right. What I mean is that all of the Italian soldiers individually surrendered to us. The Italians did not surrender in any organized way (I know what you are thinking. What did they do in an organized way? But I'm not, as you say, going to "go there." It is too easy. As you also say.)

My job now was to drive an armored troop carrier. In Italy the danger was less from the air. The British didn't want to bomb behind the lines and risk killing their newest allies. It more was from the Italian partisans, who planted explosives along the roads and sniped at us from behind trees and rooftops and out of windows.

More even than before, survival depended on having the right paperwork. And on driving directly to your destination and back. Any deviation could cause you to be seen as a deserter, and executed. This was not just because by then so many secretly longed to desert, and not just because we were now in a land where it was possible—where one could melt in with the Italians and hope to find food, a comfortable bed, a jug of wine—but also because something had changed in the tone of the commanding officers. Even in the *Führer's* speeches themselves. We were disappointing him. Disappointing the Fatherland. Since it was impossible that we, the master-race, could simply be defeated, if we lost a battle, it had to be the work of treachery, desertion. We were cowards not fit to call ourselves Germans. Of course it was understood that the *Führer* himself was infallible. So any failure must be a failure of the ranks. We had all come under suspicion. The numbers of the military police had grown, and their authority had grown with their presence.

And now that it was even more clear that the war was going badly, it was more important than ever to act as though it was going well. Defeatism, like so many other offenses, was punishable by death.

What did most of my comrades think and feel in this year of our shrinking empire; in this year that the carpet bombing of German cities started, and hundreds of thousands of civilians were incinerated, and millions died on the battlefield, and the Jews were vanishing from one city and then the next, all across Europe, and there were rumors so shocking that only the sheer horror of the war itself made them seem plausible? There were the hardcore Jew-hating Nazis. They were generally despised among the *landsers*, the enlisted men, not so much for their politics as for the fact that mostly they were by the book, uptight, foul-tempered, condescending little shits. But what of the rest of us? All I can say is that, in some way, right alongside our doubts, we clung to our faith. Some clung to their glorious Hitler. Others just to the Fatherland. The crimes of Versailles that must be righted. At least the possibility of victory. *We are sorry, Herr Führer. We are unworthy of you!* Just as we had become both heroes and cowards in the eyes of the German public, so we had become both believers and unbelievers.

I still kept up my letters with my father. "Italy is wonderful," I wrote. "It is great to be in another Fascist country. They all love us here so." There was some risk in writing this. Perhaps even the censors would recognize it for the sarcasm that it was. But sometimes you didn't really care. Let them do their worst. How much worse could it be? In the end, we were sure to die one way or another.

"My health is better than ever," my father replied. "The close combat does wonders for one's alertness. We must be thankful we have been given this great opportunity to forge the thousand year Reich that is our destiny."

The war itself had created a bond between myself and my father, now thousands of miles apart, which had never existed in all of my childhood when we had lived under the same roof. It felt like at last we could truly understand one another. And when he ended his letters with, "I miss you," or, "I long for the day we are again together," I invariably felt a pang.

Also, my father's reference to *close combat* distressed me. I had thought he was too old to be sent to the front line. But after Stalingrad the call had gone up for every male from sixteen to sixty. I tried imagining him in actual combat. He did not like getting his hands dirty, literally or figuratively. He did not like even the slight pains and humiliations involved in a visit to the doctor. Poor man, I thought.

And then I thought, that must be just what he is thinking about me. *Poor boy. My poor son.* And then I felt even sorrier for him. And was there also not a premonition in these letters? For how many were really going to come back alive from the East? Surely, he was aware of that himself. The thought of it made me want to write something more to my father. Something more desperate and emotional. *Just run! Just go back home, get away from there, whatever you have to do!* Only was there even any prospect of deserting, in the middle of the Russian Steppes?

I see I have mentioned, in passing, the rumors regarding members of the Jewish faith. It was all whispered. Top secret. Someone had a brother-in-law in the SS, and saw him on leave, and came back with these knowing looks and veiled references. A plan to take care of "the Jewish problem." Someone else had heard, from someone who had been there, about trenches full of thousands of dead bodies with yellow stars around their arms. Civilians. Children even. Nobody dared express an opinion on it. They would just look at each other.

Whenever I heard something about it I felt it in my stomach and went silent. Was this what had happened to Sylvia? Had the "problem" that she was causing been "taken care of," by having her killed and dumped in a trench? For so long I had held to the idea, the hope at least, that she would one day be released. Treated cruelly, horribly, perhaps, but finally, when all the hysteria passed, allowed to return home. Now I was filled with a sickening feeling. So this was why I had not heard from her? Was this the fate I had left her to? And then, had she thought of me in her last moments? And if so, what was it that she thought of? That moment I slipped out the window? The eyes that never looked back at her? Did she dream, in her last moments, of me racing to her rescue, saving her, running off with her? Did she feel I had deserted her? Left her in her moment of need?

Or just possibly...was she still alive somehow? Somewhere? Surely not all of the Jews had been killed. It must only be some subset. Some particular group of offenders. Surely it could not mean all of Europe's Jews were being slaughtered!

But I must continue my travelogue. We lost Rome and headed north up through Italy, slowly but steadily. The main roads were pounded from the air. The side roads were booby-trapped by partisans. We never referred to it as a retreat. It was always a matter of consolidating our position. And then consolidating it again. And then again. Still, it had that same feeling of moving in retrograde that I had come to know in Africa. Firing forward, stepping backward. As though to preserve some optical illusion. Like that dance that pop-singer used to do, the moonwalk. A five-hundred mile moonwalk. *No, we are not really backing up! It only looks that way!*

We all took turns now on sentry duty at night. I had not fired a weapon yet in the war. But now, every sixth night, I had one in my hands. Most of the time this was just boredom and fighting against exhaustion. Peering out into the moonlit fields. But at times you imagined movement and drew to a sudden alertness.

One night I thought I sensed movement in the distance and soon realized it was not just my imagination. Only what was it exactly? It was difficult to make out. Close to the ground. A mass of...what? Now my senses were raised. There was nobody to call to. Any sound would give away my position. But...were they not creeping toward us? A band of partisans? More than a band even. Thirty perhaps. And yet, unusually small-seeming. My finger held to the trigger. Readied. Listened. What was it? Whispering? The wind? What to do? Or rather when to do it. And what were they doing? Crawling closer? Shapeless in the dark. And then...*now!* Scream of the machine gun.

I'd gotten one! Only what a shock when the others rose up, rose into the air, whirring, flew off. No, not Partisans! Not Americans. For a fraction of a second they rose on angels' wings, flew off to heaven, and I was witnessing a miracle. But then they were not angels either. Ducks! I'd killed a duck! How clear it was suddenly. How low and small they had seemed! Only...how difficult it was to tell distance!

In the next moments everyone was up, arming themselves, rushing, questioning me.

"What was it?"

"What?"

It took me a moment as I searched my mind for an excuse. At last I answered. "A duck."

There it was. My first kill of the war. A duck.

The entire camp was furious with me for waking them. But by the next day it had turned more to teasing.

"Hans, you saved all of us."

"Great shot."

"They must have been pretty scary. A whole flock of ducks!"

"It was an enemy duck. It got what it deserved."

And at last, when I went out and found the duck in the field and we cooked it up, when we each got a small taste of it, all was forgiven.

My bunkmate shrugged. "Next time get the rest of the flock."

It turned out to be the last meat any of us would taste for weeks.

Roads and railways had been shelled. Supply lines were interrupted. We were soon told it was up to each of us to find his own food. We headed out into farmers' fields and picked our own fruits and vegetables when nobody was looking. We stole chickens and slaughtered them and cooked them on open fires. We went to farmhouses and knocked at the door and asked for food (strange that we were both overlords and beggars). Or else, when we had to, we drew guns on families and demanded. The locals learned to hide their food, and we learned to ransack in search of it. Of course there were many gradations between begging and threatening, many forms of hint, suggestion, implied coercion. Every method had its dangers. But then starving was also not a desirable outcome.

At one point we survived for three days on some melons we found in an untended field. When the melons ran out I went out scavenging with another driver. I would tell you his name, but what is the point? I barely knew him, and he will be dead within a few pages in any case.

We were driving along quiet roads in our near-empty troop carrier. It was a waste of precious fuel, but fuel was second in importance to food. We were in Tuscany, and the beauty of the countryside, the brilliant sunshine of the morning, registered even in my state of near desperate hunger. It had just showered, and the puddles steamed and splashed, the *terra cotta* roofs shone, the vineyards, still dripping, bounced up and down the hills along the road. We rounded a curve and there, out in the middle of nowhere, was a roadside stand where two young women were selling fruits and vegetables. They were pale, dark-haired, possibly sisters. We slowed, approached. Surprisingly, they showed no fear, waved to us, tried to wave us over.

What was this? A trap? Did they just want to separate us from our vehicle, so their friends could come out from the trees and surround us with their bayonets? Or were they simply trying to sell their produce?

We had no money, but we had cigarettes we could barter, I still had a watch my father had given me, and if necessary, we could also just take what we wanted, apologize, step backward, bow, our arms full of corn husks, and disappear.

There was something about it that felt almost dreamlike. The sun shower that had just passed. The pretty girls. The brightly colored, fresh-looking food. We pulled over a hundred yards down the road.

"I don't like it," I said.

"Neither do I," my comrade said.

But we were both staring back at them, and at that moment we had no powers of resistance. I backed the truck up the road. Back to the stand. All around us it was quiet. The girls waved to us. We waited in our truck, looked around in every direction, then climbed out, waved hello, keeping our hands against our rifles. Our eyes ran hungrily along the display of food. There were grapes, oranges, grapefruits! There were loaves of bread! And there! A sausage. *Meat.*

We tried a few words of Italian. Held out cigarettes. Only they didn't want cigarettes. They rubbed their fingers together to mean money. *Lire.* We held our hands open. No money. Sorry. Here. Take the cigarettes. They smiled, shrugged, nodded no, sorry, no *lire* no can help.

Only just to be smiled at like that. To be something other than hated. And by these pretty young women in their embroidered peasant tops, in this sunny, little roadside glade. I tried to sign that I was hungry. And then I was holding out my watch. *Per favore.* Pointing to the sausage and bread. Holding out the watch. Telling myself, it was fine. It was safe. Why else would they be negotiating like this. One girl reached for the watch and slipped it on her wrist, held her arm out, twirled a little, showing it off for her companion, maybe even showing herself off slightly for us, for these desperate German soldiers. They were enjoying, in their way, our desperation, our lust—for everything that they were and everything they possessed. But in the end the girl removed the watch and handed it back. Nodded no. Sorry. Not interested. And then it didn't feel right again. Why were they in so little hurry to sell anything? Why didn't they want the watch? In the back of my mind it felt wrong.

The rest all happened at once. My comrade started shouting at the girl, *"Wir haben Hunger!"* We're hungry! No games! We need food! Now! Right up in their faces. *"Wir haben Hunger!"* Only they couldn't understand it. And then his rifle was pointing at them, and they were talking fast, hands up, looking from side to side, and I was shouting at my companion, *"Halt! Nein!"* and approaching him, and then I saw that the girls weren't looking directly at us anymore, they were looking behind us, watching something behind us, and then I knew it for sure, knew what I had always known, I didn't have to see the men behind us, guns drawn, because I could feel them, I could see them in the eyes of those two girls, and then I could hear the clicks of their guns engaging and the men's voices and then I could feel the metal against the back of my head and hear the words from behind me, *"Hände in die Luft!"* Hands up!

Instantly we were their captives. My companion was forced down to his knees, like he was about to be executed and he was praying, pleading, and then I was forced down next to him.

They were deciding our fates. The women, it seemed, were defending me, that was what I gathered from the gestures, explaining how I had argued with the one who had drawn the gun. One of them even spoke directly to me, in Italian, as though I would understand. She made a face of tenderness, or understanding, as though it were still a game to them. They were so young. How they had enjoyed luring the enemy, using their youth and desirability and power over these men, the two motives, the sexual and the political, inseparable, so that we could either be killed or made love to and either possibility had its thrill. Only how unfortunate for the game to be over just like that.

And with so much happening at once nobody not even hearing the streaking sound overhead, nobody seeing them coming, the planes, because nobody was expecting to be attacked from the air. Except the pilots—American, by the planes—must have seen the German troop carrier parked along the road, not even cared who the rest were, just focused on the German soldiers, enemy, the planes already diving at us before we realized it, and then suddenly I was shouting and pointing, and maybe I wasn't even thinking about who was next to me, it was instinct by then, grabbing the arm of the man next to me and diving into the trees, the one thing I knew with absolute perfection how to do, dive for cover, just as the strafing started, the machine guns, *tch tch tch tch tch tch tch*, spraying the ground like a hailstorm, one plane, then the other, all the while I was there in the underbrush with one of the partisans, feeling a burst along my leg, a rush of pain, the Italians shouting, frantic, only why wasn't I hearing my comrade, just a moaning, and now I was holding my leg and screaming, seeing him holding his side, or what was left of it, soaked in blood, the Italians all up except one of the girls, the one who had wanted to spare me, or so I had imagined, who had looked at me and had exchanged something human in that look, sitting up, but bloodied, holding her shoulder, the men gathering themselves together, trying to sort out the situation, speaking excitedly, furiously, it seemed like all of them at once, helping the girl, racing from one spot to the next, one of them approaching my injured comrade, holding out a gun to him, looking away, for a second praying, crossing himself, the half-alive thing writhing helplessly below him, and then the shot to the head, echoing for a long moment, silencing not only the one who had been shot, but all of us.

The Italians stared at my comrade who they had just shot.

Quiet. Shock. Maybe it was the first actual violence they had been a part of.

Then they started talking again. Quietly at first. Then more intensely.

My leg was throbbing now. I was sitting up. The men looked at me as they spoke. Was I next? The gun waved this way and that and I followed it with my eyes. Something seemed to be settled though. The gun returned to the belt of the partisan. My spotting the planes, shouting, grabbing of the man next to me—all of it purely out of instinct —had saved me. The Americans, their heroic entrance at just right moment, had saved me.

Now one of the Italians brought me water, shook my hand. We moved away from the roadside, in case the planes returned. I was given bread and a sprig of grapes.

Grazie.

Prego.

How wonderful everything tasted, even as my thigh ached and bled. Even as I tried to absorb everything that had just happened.

We attempted to communicate further. Where in Germany was I from? Where had I fought? They showed me a picture of Hitler and I waved it off, made the hoped-for gesture of disavowal, contempt. They smiled, talked more among themselves, patted my back. Yes, I was no Nazi, they seemed to understand. Just some hapless nobody, caught up in the fucking war. How much more I wished I could say. That, believe it or not, I had once…but I didn't know the words.

I found myself in the back of a wagon, drawn by a pair of mules, the three men and one of the girls were across from me. I was lying back in a bed of hay beside the injured girl. I had no idea where we were going. What I knew was that I was alive. I had a bit of food inside me. The countryside was calm and beautiful. At times I even realized there were birds singing all around us—indifferent as could be. Another universe, superimposed over ours. At other times the pain in my leg came so intensely it felt like it was on fire.

We rode for hours, paused, ate again, the injured girl beside me sometimes passing me slices of sausage or olives or some other delicacy for me to try. I was there I was among strangers, the enemy, scarcely understanding a word, and with a bullet hole in my leg, and yet in a certain way I felt—for the first time in how long—a flicker of happiness. I would try to eat only half of whatever the girl offered me, and then hand her back the rest, as though it was my own gift, as though it had not just come from her. How else was I to convey any friendship back, any gratitude?

We were heading north, I realized. Setting sun to our left. Which meant closer to the German lines. And as we approached nearer, we moved more slowly. I felt then that I knew their plan. They were delivering me back to my army. Or trying to. I was both overcome by their kindness, and half-disappointed that they did not intend to take me home with them. We rested, let the mules graze along the roadside. And then, after a while, the bumping forward started once more. I felt the hand of the injured girl beside me tap my own. A gesture of offering comfort. And then somehow we were holding hands. Squeezing one another's hand. How incredible. We could not communicate more than a few words to one another. And yet that was part of what made it seem so pure, so simple in its meaning. She was nothing to me and I was nothing to her. Or rather, what we were to one another was consolation itself. Peace itself. The wish for peace. An end to killing. At least, those were the feelings that were filling me. Like a dream. Was it all in my own head? Or did she not send me those feelings, thinking the same things when, in the settling darkness, I held her hand up to my parched lips and kissed it, and she squeezed my hand back. I had tears in my eyes. But by then it was too dark for anyone to see.

We were soon close enough to the German line that it was too dangerous for them to continue. They had to leave me. I thought of trying to find a way to tell them I wanted to desert. I am still not sure what exactly held me back. Lack of a common language or some remaining sense of loyalty or duty or authority. Or just fear of the unknown. Who knows. I have sometimes wondered what path my life might have taken had I made a different split-second decision at that moment.

They gave me a last bit of food and water. I embraced each of the men. I kissed the hands of both of the girls—not really knowing what would be considered too familiar or too distant. What were the rules for such an encounter?

They turned the cart around, the mules started forward, and I was alone in the darkness.

As soon as I tried to walk I was in agony. I wound up crawling, three-legged and throbbing with pain, the last mile or more back to the camp. I waved my undershirt as I got close, called out in German so I would not be mistaken for the enemy, collapsed in pain and exhaustion as I reached the edge of the camp.

I would like to say that in those moments I grasped just how mad the war was. Even how I, Hans, was fighting for the wrong side. How could I not have seen it after all? Would the Nazis have shown such compassion for an enemy? And look at what they, my own people, had done to Sylvia. Look at the rumors we were hearing. The havoc we had wreaked. How urgently you must wish me to declare that this was what I felt. But when I had such thoughts they were vague, ephemeral, contradictory. I was just doing. Not thinking. I did not, if I thought about it, support anything whatever about the Nazis. I never had. But somehow that had nothing to do with my existence, my position, my need to fight on.

- Illyria -

It has been a long while since I have spoken of our present condition here.

Monique is due soon, according to the hash marks we have made in the rock face. She is a narrow wisp of human with a sudden bulge, like a snake that has swallowed a cat.

Andreas and Dawn have become a couple, are open about it, have moved into their own shelter.

Andreas, ever busy, has been working on the skiff, building a roof to it so we don't die of exposure while we are out drifting, and building oars and oarlocks so we will be able to steer ourselves, if only slightly. We have been experimenting with materials for a sail, so far without much success.

Our copy of *Vogue* was left out in the rain and turned to mush. It has since dried and now appears to be in the process of petrification.

And the last of Cole's clothes has withered away. He now covers himself with the broad leaves of the eucalyptus tree, sewn together with some fibers from a bamboo stalk. His privacy is largely preserved, but at the expense of looking something like a walking plant in a comedy sketch. Moreover his garment is in need of near continual renewal, old leaves being replaced by newer ones every two or three days. But he had long ridiculed Conrad's abandon to nudism, and so when his own clothes at last gave way—the last of his civilized exterior disintegrating with them—what choice did our former leader have but to find a way to cover himself?

Also, Cole has been caught stealing food. He was hungry, I have no doubt. But it was still a serious offense. Conrad caught him swiping root vegetables from the daily communal pile. His shelter was searched by Andreas and Conrad, and fish bones and crab bones and even eggshells were found in it.

There was pushing. There were threats of violence between Conrad and Cole. At dinner Conrad spoke to the group, while avoiding looking in the direction of Cole. "I think we need to devise a punishment for food-stealing. Something that will make people think twice about doing it."

"It's not stealing," Cole says. "Because it was never owned. The crabs were taken from the ocean."

"But we agreed to divide our chores and share our catch," Conrad says.

"I voted against it," Cole says.

"But you were overruled."

"But I never accepted...."

There is more arguing. Then Conrad addresses us again. "We should take a vote. Who here believes in some form of punishment?"

At first there is silence. Then Monique speaks up softly. "I do." I am surprised to see tears in her eyes. This final break, this betrayal of Cole, is difficult for her.

Cole, leafy and ragged, buries his head in his hands. "Monique!" he exclaims, apparently genuinely hurt.

"My baby is hungry," she says.

"I agree," Andreas says.

I look at Dawn. I wonder what she is thinking, watching this. Seeing her step-father being judged, chastised. At last she speaks. Softly, but with conviction. "I do too."

We all look at her, astonished. There had always been something in her relationship with her step-father that I had been unable to fathom. Or rather, it was the lack, the absence of any visible bond between them, that was most striking. But nobody had ever heard Dawn speak against anyone. I surely had not believed she'd had it in her. And it was more than just what she'd said. It was something in her voice that I had never heard. Something its softness did not quite conceal. Fury. She actually possessed, was capable of this. Only why, I wondered, was Cole singled out for this?

Cole looks back at her silently, and for a moment they are staring into each other's eyes. He starts to speak. "Why you little...." But it is as far as he gets. There is surely some history between them. But it is left unspoken. At last, Cole catches himself, looks away. His defeat is complete.

Conrad wants to discuss sentencing. He is clearly enjoying himself. "I'm against corporal punishment on principle," he says. "And we have no prison. So I would like to propose banishment."

"Aren't we already banished?" I say.

"This would be banishment from the banished."

"Maybe we should just stop talking to him," Monique says.

"I thought you'd already done that," Cole says to Monique.

"Well maybe I'll join," Conrad says.

"Please do," Cole says. "I'll finally get some peace."

It is quickly decided. We sentence Cole to that most aboriginal, most primitive of punishments—the silent treatment. Monique and Conrad are the strictest enforcers, and for a while this creates a sort of bond between two of them. They make conversation in front of Cole expressly for the purpose of excluding him.

In time though, the sentence proves difficult to implement. There are communications that must take place. Discussion of chores. Apportionment of food. And there is the fact that Conrad needs Cole to argue with. That Monique cannot but hope that one day she and Cole will reconcile, that he will be a father to the child she is carrying. Finally, there is the unspoken realization between Conrad and Monique that they really have next to nothing to say to one other. They try various topics. Sporty cars—to which Monique is particularly drawn. Favorite bands. Professional sports teams. But nothing really takes. Andreas, for his part, is not inclined as much to conversation, and so must force himself to contribute to the general discussion to show he is inflicting his silence upon Cole.

Cole, meanwhile, busies himself carving more gnomes, acts like he never even hears us. For the very first time, I see something almost admirable in him. This focus. This unexpected, slightly off, yet oddly impressive artistic streak. True—the subject is idiotic. Who wants their encampment decorated with a bunch of fricking gnomes. But they are well-rendered. There is a technique. They are certainly better gnomes than I could have done.

Monique and Conrad soon reconsider.

"I think he's paid his debt to society," Conrad says, just six nights after the sentence has been imposed.

"What debt?" Cole asks. "And what society? And how did I pay it? By having to listen to Monique go on about cars she'd like to hump?"

There is actually a bit of a smile between Conrad and Cole. A brief, newly formed alliance. Men against the nonsense of a female. Nudity Man and Leaf Man chuckling at the foibles of woman. For a while our civilization finds a sort of contentment.

We are a poor nation, with our sorry-looking thatch shelters, our takeout containers and crude pottery, our dove farm and root vegetables.

But we have developed something like a culture. I have crafted a chess set from different kinds of shells, and Dawn and I have started to play again. We have made a drum from a hollow tree trunk. We produce music by pressing plastic spoons against our cheeks and singing and drumming. In the visual arts we are limited exclusively to gnomes, but is this any less worthy than the Easter Islanders who did nothing but megaliths, or even the Egyptians, with their lines of women, arms pointed to and fro, over and over, scene after scene, through a thousand years of civilization? For the love of God, couldn't anyone invent a new dance step?

Our crucifix is ignored now even by Cole. Once he realized he had no flock, no followers, he lost interest. And here is something I don't entirely understand. How can you worship something that you yourself have created? How can you put two pieces of wood together and then persuade yourself that your creation has magic, that at this perpendicular angle these sticks will bring salvation, whereas when they lay next to each other they were powerless?

On the other hand, our calcified copy of *Vogue* has devolved into a kind of religious icon of its own. Our sacred text. No longer readable. Yet still a symbol of what once was. The other world. Beyond the horizon.

What ends this time of hope, of economic growth and cultural expansion, is Monique's labor.

She is hauling water from Piss Brook late one morning, and suddenly drops to her knees, calls out, "Oh God!"

She is helped back to camp. Dawn spreads her beneath a lean-to on the beach. Dawn is our only other female now that Gloria has gone, and so she has taken it upon herself to assist in the delivery. She has prepared, as much as possible, for this moment. She has water and rags and an oyster-shell blade and that is all. The rest of us wait from a distance. We hear screams. From time to time one of us approaches to ask what we can do. How it is progressing. The sense we get, after some time, is that it is not. Something does not seem right.

Cole goes over to them for some minutes. When he returns he is shaking his head, looking distressed. "There must be something we can do," he says.

"Like what?" I ask.

He doesn't answer. He sits down on the sand and puts his head in his hands. Do I actually feel something for him?

The suffering goes on all through the afternoon and long into the night, pierces the heavens with its pleas. I think back through all of the different screams I have known. Each in a different pitch. Each representing a different proportion of pain and terror. Dieter diving for cover. So many others coming out of air raid shelters. Ditches. Bombed out houses. Of all of them, this one is the most ghostly. That lone, ululating cry. And it is the most prolonged. Hour after hour.

Conrad covers his ears. Andreas goes to help Dawn, returns looking pale and faint. We don't know what we are doing, but we know that this is not how it is supposed to go.

No. Worse than that. It is going very, very wrong. Cole paces, at last heads back to Monique for what I imagine is a protestation of love, a teary farewell, an apology for any wrongs ever done. But then I am a romantic. Who knows what is really said.

What exactly went wrong none of us are even sure. Dawn says something about some kind of breach, the baby not being positioned right, the mother hemorrhaging. At last the screaming wanes to a kind of quiet moaning. That brings back memories too. As the night wears on—and who could say what the hour is, how much night there still is left—the moaning at last dwindles to silence. Dawn emerges blood-spattered and shaken. She says nothing, walks down to the water and wades in and washes herself.

There is nothing to do. No going back to our shelters or trying to sleep. We all just sit there until sunrise. In the growing light, mother and baby lie in the open. Covered in blood and sand. Flies crawling up and down them. Umbilicus dried and gnarled beside them like the staff of a wizard, placenta feeding not the baby for which it had been meant, but a hungry horde of bugs.

If our primitive society ever becomes a diorama in some museum of natural history, I wish it to show the following: our take-out containers, our latrine, our fossilized *Vogue*, and this. This scene of Monique and her baby. This is how we lived and loved and crapped and died.

We bury them beside Gloria. Monique and her unnamed infant. This time there is only a weak attempt at ceremony. There are fewer left to do the memorializing. And no words can really frame our feelings any longer. Dawn is still in shock. Cole pulls at his tangled locks of hair, his leaf-suit, says it is time to get off of this stinking rock. My last image is of Andreas with his arms around Dawn, comforting her, and Dawn calmly accepting his comfort.

A few nights later I find Dawn on fire duty, and sit beside her. Her face has turned gaunt. A front tooth had gone to a grayish color. Her breath is slightly rank. Yet her loveliness is still there, underneath it, or perhaps transcending it, incorporating it. "Game of chess?" I suggest.

"No thank you," she says. "But thank you for offering."

"You okay?" I ask.

She looks off. "They didn't deserve this."

"Monique?"

"Monique and the baby. There should have been a way to save them. I'm sure there was. If only..."

"What?"

"If only I knew what I was doing."

"How could you know? And what do we have here? We have no tools."

There are tears flowing. "We should have been able to save them."

"You should be the last one to blame yourself," I say. "Blame the rest of us. Blame the shipwreck. But don't blame yourself."

I turn a log in the fire. "You're the one who doesn't deserve this," I say.

"That's hardly true."

"You're young. You have your life ahead of you. If I die here, it's no great tragedy, is it?"

She wipes her eyes. "Don't let's talk about that."

"But you...." I let the thought trail off. What is it like to have Dawn's interior monologue, I wonder. To be inside her thoughts. "Aren't you sad at the thought of not getting back?" I ask. "Of ending here? Dying here?"

"Sometimes. Although...honestly...I didn't have much of a life...."

"You never talk about it."

"I know."

"Tell me about it."

She shrugs. "What is there to say?"

"Why did you come on this? Why did you come on the trip in the first place."

"I had nowhere else to go."

"What do you mean?" I ask.

"Why do you think I was sent off to boarding school?"

"Why were you?" And then, since, after all this time she is actually, ever-so-slightly, opening up, I ask what I have been wondering since I first got to know her, "Where is your mother?"

"She died when I was eight."

"Sorry."

"It's okay."

"Do you remember her?"

"Of course. All the time."

We look up at the stars. Listen to the insects. The snapping of the fire.

"You know what I feel like?" she asks.

"What?"

"I feel like she knows I am here. Only there is nothing she can do about it."

"That's sad," I say.

There are fresh tears in her eyes. "Do you believe in an afterlife?" she asks.

"I have no views," I say. "I've given them all up."

"I guess that's a no."

"Probably," I say.

"You're probably right."

I angle the chess board slightly toward her, push forward the little limpet-shell that is the king pawn. And, just as I had imagined, she is looking down at the board. Thinking. Her hand reaches out and pushes the snail that is her king's side knight. Alekhine's Defense. It is not until two moves later that she realizes what has happened. "You tricked me!"

"What did I do?"

"I said I didn't want to play. And here I am. How did that happen?"

"We can stop if you'd rather."

"No. Let's play."

The board is dark, side-lit. The shadows of the shells tremble with the flickering fire. For a while, we manage to lose ourselves in the game. We trade bishop and then queens, parry our knights, are suddenly down to an end-game. "We're going to get out of here," I say. And then, "You are, anyway."

"We all are," she says.

"Tell your mother that. Next time you talk to her."

"I tell her that every night."

I am going to kiss you. Now. Right now.

"This is looking like a draw," she says.

"Yes it is."

"You know what it reminds me of? It reminds me of our first game together. The early queen trade."

"That one ended in a draw too," I say.

"You had a victory."

I think back, try to remember. "If I did, I didn't see it."

"I saw it," she says.

"Really?"

She manages a smile. "Yes."

"Why didn't you say something?"

"I didn't want to embarrass you."

"See? You're too nice."

"If I were that nice as you think, I wouldn't be telling you now."

"You're telling me now because you know it won't bother me. You know I'll find it amusing."

"Possibly." She moves her limpet-rook to cut off my king.

"I'm serious though," I say. "You can't just do things for other people. You should think of yourself sometimes."

She is still looking down at the board. "And what if I don't want to?"

Only what a strange thing to say. "Why wouldn't you want to?"

She doesn't answer.

"You're a mystery," I say. "Do you know that?"

"Why am I a mystery?"

Because you have no reference point, I think. There is nowhere to place you. Only how can I say that. "What about your father?" I ask. "Is he still alive?"

"Yes. But…"

"But?"

"Nothing. I didn't grow up with him."

I am looking over the board for some opportunity, some combination, but see nothing. "So shall we call this one a draw?"

"Yes," she says.

"You're sure you don't see a victory for me?"

"Not this time."

I look at her suspiciously.

"I promise," she says.

I nod, swat a bug off my arm.

She stretches. Yawns. "It's late."

She is right. The moon is sinking. She moves as though about to get up.

"So are you in love with Andreas?"

Why have I asked this? How did those words come out of me? Was it just to keep the conversation going? Because I could think of nothing else? Do I really want to hear the answer?

"Why do you ask?"

Because I love you.

"I don't know. I was just…."

"I don't really want to talk about that."

There is a rebuke in her tone. I have overstepped the bounds. Asked something I should not have.

"I'm sorry," I say. "It's not my business."

But she is already getting up. "Thank you for the game. And the talk."

And she heads off to the shelter Andreas has built for them.

I hear the waves pulled against the sand. Breathing. Hans, you are a foolish old man. What are you dreaming? You must get away from here. You are losing your mind. And now she is cross with you. You must beg forgiveness. You must prove to her that... Or no. You must stop worrying about what she feels.

- Germany -

Something cold on my leg. Ice. Fire and ice. Pain. Shooting through the cold. Was I awake? I was back. Yes. At the base. Injured. Remembering it. The wagon ride. The girl. Whoever she was. The girl whose hand I kissed. The shot in the leg. But was I awake? Had it really happened? Was it a dream? No. It couldn't have been a dream. Because of my leg. That was real. That was still there. Throbbing. Worse.

"Pain killer." I mumbled it out into the dark. "Pain killer."

Then asleep again. Awake again. A shot in the arm. How much time was passing?

"Pain killer." Dark. Or not. Not dark at all. Only I just hadn't been able to see. Now it was light. I was coming to. In an infirmary. My wound was being dressed.

Once I was fully awake I was questioned by the military police. Do you know what I was accused of? Of shooting myself on purpose. Haha! Causing my own injury to get out of the war! Can you believe it? Well, the truth was, I had considered just such a plan more than once. Still, I acted shocked and indignant. Of course, I didn't dare tell them about my real experience either. All I said was that I had been attacked by partisans while foraging for food. I'd escaped into the woods. My comrade had been killed. At last, and somewhat grudgingly, my story was accepted.

The full extent of my great luck only became apparent in the coming days. From the infirmary I was sent to a bigger field hospital. And from there it was decided I needed more time to recover, and as all the hospital beds were needed for more serious injuries, I was given leave to spend a month at home.

Was it really possible? I would have a month in Edelburg? What resentment I felt from my fellow soldiers. Even from the military police themselves. No wonder they were so begrudging of me. Because they envied my blown out leg. I was getting the hell out.

I was placed in a cast from my thigh to my ankle and given crutches and placed on a train full of injured soldiers—many in far worse shape than myself. There was moaning and misery in the train and I remember the contrast between the inside of the train and the peaceful countryside we went through—northern Italy and Switzerland, mostly untouched by the war. It was covered in a late November snow, and just watching it pass by filled me with a kind of yearning, not just for an end to the war, but for some other life from the one I had. Some past that was not my own, not even real.

When we crossed the German frontier it was different. Most of the towns were still pretty and undamaged but some of the cities were little more than rubble. There were blocks where a single building stood, all the others around it toppled by air raids. At one point we reached a spot where the tracks had been bombed. Everyone had to get off and walk forward (or be carried) to the next train, waiting on the other side of the crater. It took hours to move all of the injured. I made my way on crutches.

At last we started again. I looked warily out at the sky, imagined something coming out of it at any moment. Blowing us apart. But there were no incidents. After two days of travel, and another switch in Leipzig I arrived at the station in Tormalund, four miles from Edelburg. I hobbled the rest of the way on crutches, through slush and mud, as the road gradually grew more and more familiar. I was moving at best a mile an hour, my armpits burned with every step where the tops of the crutches dug in. My arms and my one good leg were exhausted and aching beyond anything I had thought I could have tolerated. Every step I told myself, just a few more steps and I will take a rest. At that rock. At that tree. No. At the next one. But the sense of coming home, of this absurdly slow finale to my great journey, urged me onward. When I did stop to lie down, my cast made it almost impossible to get back up again. I felt, at times, like an overturned turtle. Helpless. Unable to right myself. But after great effort, using the crutches to pry myself up against, at last I righted myself. Another mile of thirst, abraded armpits, exhaustion, and I was there.

Edelburg was still just as I had left it. The streets were calm and people were out. There were few men of course. But that was the only recognizable difference. I was headed past a square when a woman with a boy looked up and looked at me and let out a scream. It was *Mutti.*

She made a face of disbelief, horror at my condition, excitement at seeing me, all in one, all while running toward me, wrapping her arms around me. Soon I was at the house with her and my half-brother Stefan, who was now a little boy. My mother chattered away madly, served coffee and a spread of delicacies I could barely believe (apparently immune to the rationing most of Germany lived under). Stefan was frightened of my cast and cried and hid behind her for a long time. The boy's father, Fleulen, was also there. He was plumper than I'd remembered, wore a suit, sat back with a pipe and a child's wind-up toy he was fixing, or maybe just playing with.

For the first hours the sheer comfort of home seemed almost beyond comprehension. The softness of the sofa. The limitless store of food. Coffee! Cakes! And just the sense of safety. Of being somewhere that had not been bombed and that was not about to be bombed. And of course there was the presence of my mother herself— with all her doting concern for my injury, my weight, my generally sorry condition.

"We need to hear all about your medal and how you earned it," she exclaimed. "You can't keep denying you deserved it forever!"

"I'll make something up," I said.

"Stop!"

"I didn't do anything."

"Too modest, you are."

She showed off some little-soldier-boy outfits she'd bought for Stefan that she thought were "too adorable to resist." Then she launched into a story about the price. "I saw the very same outfit I'd purchased two days later in the store window, and it was twenty percent off! Do you know what I did? I went right back and insisted on the same discount!"

I was confused. "But…you'd already bought it. Happily. At the original price."

"Well there's was no way I'm going to pay fifteen marks when they're selling it two days later for twelve!"

Somehow she took it as a personal affront, that they had done this to her, insulted her with this price reduction. They'd devalued her purchase!

As the conversation moved on I found myself staring at an orange that was sitting in a bowl on the table. At first I thought it was fake, a little art with which to taunt the hungry. But it was real. What a miracle! I started wondering where it had been born and plucked, from what distant corner of Europe it had made its way, through a thousand miles of war, to rest in a bowl on our table?

I spent the night in the beloved bed of my childhood and savored my mother's breakfast in the morning. By afternoon she was impatient to hear her son's war stories. It became apparent that just as I had assumed that the reality of the war would have changed her view of it, and of the great man who had led us into it, so she had assumed that my experience fighting the treacherous enemy, defending the fatherland, would have made me understand, at last, our valiant struggle.

"I'm sure you made an important contribution," she said.

"To what? North Africa's lost. Over. We're not there anymore."

Whereas her son had marched off, years earlier, to what seemed the most critical campaign in the whole of the war, now my mother shrugged, surrendered all the Sahara with wave of the hand. "Who really wanted all of that Egypt anyway? They can keep it. Let the British jump off the pyramids."

When I told her the story of how I hurt my leg, the American plane swooping down on us, she wondered why we hadn't wiped out the allied airfields.

"We're low on planes," I said. "We're stretched in every direction."

"And why don't you just round up all the partisans?"

"We don't have enough men," I said, feeling a little impatient now. "Or enough equipment. That's why we keep pulling back."

"Nonsense," she declared. And she listed, as though quoting from some officer's briefing, all of the military assets we had in Italy.

"Mother, I was just *there*," I said. "It's not going the way you think it is. We're losing Italy. And not because we aren't trying!"

I could see Fleulen looking at me, growing more uncomfortable, keeping his quiet out of some deference to the nature of our relationship, but silently discussing me with his pipe.

And there was that orange again. Still in its bowl. And then I realized the other miracle about it. That nobody had grabbed and shoved it into his mouth the instant he saw it. That there was no urgency. It just sat there.

My mother became more animated. "This is just the sort of defeatism that…that the *Führer* is talking about."

"It's not defeatism," I said. "It's just what's happening."

We argued. Fleulen got up and paced. He cleared his throat. Tapped his pipe. Seemed to start countless sentences, as though he was preparing some grand speech but was unsure how to open it.

"Are you doubting that we are going to win?" my mother asked.

Now, in my own home, I suddenly felt like I needed to watch what I said. I didn't know Fleulen. I didn't know who he might talk to, what he might say. For that matter, I scarcely could say I knew my mother. "Of course, in the end, we will win," I said, not sure that I believed it in the slightest.

"Precisely!" Fleulen burst out, his grand, one word soliloquy delivered with gusto. It was just as though he was a bit player in a stage drama, and had been waiting all this time for his one climactic moment.

That night my mother came into my room after the light was already out. She wrapped her arms around me. "I'm so glad you're safe," she whispered.

"Thank you," I said.

There was a pause. "I know...." She started, stopped, started again. "I know it's not going so well," she conceded to the darkness— as though it came from some part of her that was not allowed out in the light.

"You don't know what it's like," I said.

"We can only pray," she said.

Then she gave me a goodnight kiss on my forehead, like when I was a child.

What I came to enjoy most, in my first days, was my young half-brother. My favorite memory is of watching him after the season's first snow. He was playing out front with some other little boys. I wanted to go out and play with them but I was still on crutches, so the best I could do was let them throw snowballs at me. They made exploding sounds like the snowballs were hand grenades, and I died at least ten or fifteen times, only to magically reawaken and receive another volley.

After a bit I left them to their own devices and went back inside. I played cards with Fleulen. When I looked back out I could see them decorating their snowman excitedly. They came in for a comb. Then they ran back out. Then in for some buttons. Then out. What was it they were creating exactly? I strained to see better. And there it was! A was a likeness of our beloved leader! The comb above the mouth was, quite unmistakably, Hitler's mustache. And someone had found an officer's jacket to drape over the shoulders. A mop bottom served as the hair. Almost as comical as this innocent lampoon was my mother's reaction to it when I called her to the window. She gasped, let out a shriek like she had just seen the Red Army approaching.

The children were alternately saluting to their Hitler snowman and then throwing snowballs at him, heaping upon him all of the affection and abuse of any rag doll. My mother ran out and placed herself between their snowballs and her idol, courageously defended *Vaterland* and *Führer* from these six-year-olds.

"Who is that?" she asked them.

"It's…it's *the Führer!*" they exclaimed.

"Do we throw snowballs at the *Führer?*" she asked.

At first they looked unsure. But my mother's scowl was unmistakable. The answer came to them regretfully. They suddenly turned sheepish. "*Nein,*" a couple of them said.

"Right!" my mother said emphatically. "We *love* the *Führer.* Don't we?"

"*Ja,*" they said, looking at one another.

"Good. Now we have to take him apart immediately."

"But if we love him…why are we taking him apart?"

"Because! Because…we love him." And then, at a loss, she offered that logical argument of last resort of all mothers everywhere, since the beginning of time, "Because I said so!"

My visit with Hilda was awkward at first. In a strange way, the war was going so miserably that it was no longer easy being against it. The years of imaginary struggles against the world, of thinking the world was against us, about to destroy us, had brought us to a real struggle. Now the world really was trying to destroy us. And we both knew that actually losing was going to be very bad. And then Hilda didn't want to mention Sylvia and didn't want to ask about whether there was a new girl either, for fear of presuming anything about Sylvia's fate.

I lightened the mood though, by telling her about the snowman and my mothers' reaction to it. "I think I still love your mother," she said, laughing.

"Well, I do," I said. "But I have to. She's my mother."

"Is she happy with that man?"

"I have no idea," I said. "He has money. I think she is happy with his money."

"You might be a little hard on her," Hilda said.

"You know, I think he has put on weight," I said. "All of Germany is going hungry and he is getting rounder. Sitting around smoking his pipe. Playing with Stefan's little wind-up toys."

Hilda smiled. Then she told me about how Georg had been getting in trouble in school for forgetting to salute. "It just doesn't mean anything to him," she said. "How could it, at his age? But the principal takes it as a grave offense."

I asked if it was the same principal from when I was a kid and to our mutual amusement, it was.

"Is he still shaped like an eggplant?"

"Very much so."

" We used to call him *die Aubergine.*"

Hilda laughed, but then she grew serious. "I really hate him. Does he himself say '*Heil Hitler!*' every time he passes someone, or sneezes, or farts? Of course not! But the children are all supposed to. And a month ago I was called to school, and it was no joke."

"What happened?" I asked.

"I got there and Georg was in his office crying. I looked at the principal and he said, "Look at this!" He was practically shouting at me. I looked down and it was a paper of Georg's. The children were all asked to do sentence completions. And one of the sentence starters they were given was, 'What if....'"

"And?" I asked.

"The other children wrote, 'What if we never had to go to school,' or, 'What if I could fly'. And you know what Georg wrote? He wrote, 'What if...we will lose the war!'"

"No!" I couldn't help laughing.

"Yes!" Hilda exclaimed. "And there is this stupid principal staring at me like I'm supposed to be as horrified as he is. And as though I am, undoubtedly, the reason for this abominable sentence. As though this unbelievable, shocking thought has come from me!"

"Your son is a genius," I said. And then, "You know what's funny?"

"What?"

"He just wrote exactly what everybody thinks. Only the more everyone thinks it, the more horrified and shocked you feel you have to act when someone says it."

"I know. Can you believe he had Georg in tears over it? A six-year-old boy? Poor Georg! He had no idea what he'd even done."

"We all hated that man," I said.

"So you called him, 'the eggplant?'"

"Yes."

"Well I hope, when the Russians get here, they shove a cucumber up the eggplant's ass."

We both laughed. Then she said, "You're a grown man now. I can say things like that now."

"I don't think you need to worry about shocking me," I said.

"I suppose not." And then, "You know what else is funny? I'm so worried about Georg getting in trouble again that now I'm teaching him to how to say his *Heil Hitler!* I'm teaching him how to be a good little Nazi! Me. Of all people."

I smiled. At the same time, I was still thinking about what she had said about my being a grown man now. I couldn't help feeling there was more she wanted to say, or ask, on that topic. Or something I wanted to tell her. Instead, we wound up asking one another what we had heard of my father.

I tried to describe the exchanges between myself and my father, the bitter humor, the way we'd evaded the authorities. Hilda smiled, but I also sensed that it had surprised her, that as my correspondence with my father had become more meaningful, her own correspondence with him had grown more distant. "I just hope he's okay," was what Hilda kept coming back to.

After two weeks my cast came off, and though I was still limping and my leave was only halfway through, I was declared fit to return to service. German territory was shrinking rapidly. The glorious, thousand-year Reich was imploding. There was a general call for all men aged fifteen to sixty. And no more niceties about being "able-bodied."

Just before I was to head off again to defend the Fatherland, we received one more letter, not from my father this time, but from the *Wehrmacht*, in reference to him. It came, of course, to my mother's address. I was cleaning my mess-kit in the living room, the parts spread out before me. I heard a kind of a cry and looked up and my mother's hands were over her eyes. She swept past me, dropped the letter in my lap, ran upstairs.

In retrospect I am aware that the radio was playing. A lively swing tune. That the sun was out and the icicles were dripping outside the window. To this day, seeing icicles dripping in the sun, even imagining them, always brings the moment back.

Does anyone ever make it past the beginning of these letters? "We regret to inform you…"

"Field Marshall Guderian, commander of the armies of the East, regrets to inform you…." You get to that point and then you search madly for your loved one's name. There it was.

"Lieutenant Arnold Jaeger…courageously defending…preserving our great…." You look away and come back to it, read a few more words and look away again and come back to it again.

He died outside Kiev. That was what the letter said and that was all we would ever know. There was no body. No funeral service or memorial. Nothing. He was just gone. Not coming back. It had been three years since I had seen him. And yet it is strange how the mind works, what a shock it still is, even after a three-year absence, to feel that your father is no longer out there. How suddenly you remember the feeling of being with him, how much he had loved you, all of the strains that were there for all of those years, how they would never be any different now, you would never reflect with him over those letters you had exchanged, he would never get to know the person you had turned into.

We regret to inform you....

Just that short string of words—and you are flooded with all of those memories.

What I found myself thinking back to was why he had enlisted. Somehow I hadn't thought much about it since he had left. But now I was amazed at how I had nearly forgotten. He hadn't even believed in the war. He'd enlisted to spare me, to leave me behind, managing a factory deemed vital to the war effort. At the time I hadn't really grasped it. But Sylvia had when I'd told her. Why had I been so indifferent to it? Like it was just some words a father might say. Now it gave me a chill. I have made it this far without descending into emotionalism. So let me just leave it at this: Goodbye, *Vati*.

My mother came back downstairs looking pale, face blotchy from tears. Did she still herself feel for him? Or was it just the shock? Of course it must have been both. It was all of the years, her youth, that she had spent with him. Just that feeling that everything was changing. The war was coming closer and closer. Nothing would ever be the same.

"He didn't deserve this," she said.

I said nothing, left her to whatever memories she had.

"Why can't they all just leave us alone!" she exclaimed at last. I didn't respond, not just because I was too distraught, too shocked, not just because it was too crazy to know how to answer, but because I knew she didn't even believe it herself anymore.

I was the one who broke the news to Hilda. I don't remember her saying much. But I remember the tears streaming quietly down her cheeks. The subject of her and my father had always been an awkward one between us, and now with his death, her feelings about it were no less difficult.

"Should I leave you?" I asked. And in truth I had little desire to stay. The last thing I wanted on that day was to worry about what anyone else was feeling—not even Hilda.

She didn't answer directly. "Georg has no father," she said softly.

Neither do I, I thought.

For just a moment, a second even, I forgot that she was not still my nanny. I was suddenly a child again, and I felt a flicker of resentment that she had thoughts for others besides myself. And then I was back in the present. Seeing the tears in her eyes. And yet still wanting to get away. To be alone with my memories.

We gathered ourselves enough to say a warm goodbye, to share the requisite words of hope for better days.

And then, two days later, I was traveling East myself. I was with a new company now, heroic son, picking up the line where the father had fallen. Or some drivel like that.

Hold the line at all costs.

These were our constant orders now.

Dig in.

And then would come our great counter-offensive. And at last, our noble victory.   Shall I tell you how it all turned out? Give away the ending? Or should I leave you in suspense?

- Kelualua -

Cole waiting at the door of his villa. Coolly picking at his gums with a toothpick. Free hand extended.

"How do you do."

Power handshake. Clenching down like a trap. Smart attire. Deftly delivered welcome.

"Coatroom on the left. Full bar in the back."

Then a voice from behind. "Don't leave that open! The cat will...."

Ghostly swish past the feet.

"Oh my! Chou-chou!"

Guests heading out into the night. In gowns and heels. "Here kitty-kitty." Calling into the darkness. "Here, Chou-chou." Speaking to shrubs and rocks.

"Come here, girl."

Flashlights spreading about the crime scene.

"I think it's a boy."

"A boy?"

"Yes."

As though the cat knew one word from the other.

Pointing a flashlight at...a woman. Squinting at the light directed back at me. Two flashlight beams, aimed into each other's faces.

"Hi."

"Hi."

Staring into the blinding light.

"I'm Hans."

"Hi. Monique."

"How do you do?"

Searching together now. A team. Puckering sounds, coos, calls, aimed at a tree-stump. "Come on, kitty."

"How do you know Cole?"

"His neighbor. We just met. You?"

Mrrraaaaooooo.

Clear. Distinct. *There.* Cat! Against the side of the house. "Over here."

Frozen. Illuminated. Ears up and alert.

"Easy, girl."

"Boy."

Grabbing it. Holding it away from me. Hurrying to the front entrance, kitty-cat squirming, hissing, scratching. Almost there! Don't let go. Hideous beast! Snarling, clawing, wild. "Good, kitty."

Biting. "Monster!" Both my arms bloodied. Hurrying inside.

"I've got it."

Dawn standing there, at first smiling hello. Then seeing my predicament. Then distressed. "Take it outside!"

"What?"

"Take it outside. Hurry. It's scratching you."

"But..."

"It's the wrong cat!"

"The wrong...?"

"It's not Chou-chou. It's the wrong cat."

Hurrying the Satanic beast back out. Nothing but teeth and claws. Letting it go. Returning inside, to Dawn.

"We just caught Chou-chou. She's in the kitchen."

A *she* after all.

Dawn frowning sympathetically. "Well, hi. I'm glad you could make it. But...look at you!"

Long scratches down my arms. Raised into ugly welts. Dawn taking me back to the kitchen, bent over me, ministering to my wounds. "That was brave of you, handling that cat."

"Thank you."

Smiling, laughing faintly. "Too bad it was the wrong cat."

"Yes it is."

Was there ever a fairer Florence Nightingale than this girl in her simple, cream-colored wrap? Bent over her work. Dabbing her cotton balls in alcohol. Pulling a stray lock of golden-blonde back behind her ear. Was this fleeting intimacy not worth the wounds?

"There." A final bandage applied.

"Thank you. What do I owe you?"

"Hmm...a promise?"

"Yes?"

"Next time you do something brave and heroic, make sure you have the right cat."

"I promise. I'll consider it a life lesson. Although I thought I was done with those."

Back in the living room. Nautical-themed. Anchor in the corner. Model sailing ships, coffee-table books on yachting, giant marlin mounted on the wall, frozen in mid-*grand-jete*.

"Can you believe we've been neighbors this long? And we finally meet?" Cole, coming up beside me.

Admiring the fish together. "I don't get out that much."

"Well, I'm glad you're keeping Dawn occupied. She doesn't know anyone here. We don't want her getting bored."

"I think she plays me to be nice. I'm sure I bore her terribly."

"She's a beaut, isn't she?"

Odd thing to say. "Yes."

"I caught her last summer."

For a moment I am confused. "Dawn?"

"The fish."

How do you know it's a she, I wonder.

At dinner, regaling my audience with my cat adventure. Briefly the center of attention.

Elderly woman beside me, all sequins and baubles. "Oh my! Look at your arms. What drama!"

"I don't think I've ever known such terror."

"You should get a purple heart."

"My heart is already rather black."

"Oh, you're a cad."

Was I? Had I been a cad? Or was she merely encouraging me to be one?

"So how do you know Cole?"

"I'm here with Dawn."

Now she put her hand over her mouth. "Oh, you're too much! Oh, you're a cad, you are!"

Monique on the other side of me. My fellow cat-hunter, sharer in my glory. "It was a big cat."

"It was," I agreed.

"We had to think quickly."

Nod of assent. Dipping bread in my French onion soup (prepared by the nameless matron in the kitchen who would one day come rest under a cross of twigs on an empty stretch of Illyria beach).

Monique, "So what do you do?"

Now I look at her—looping earrings, plunging neckline, cleavage set out as on a tray.

I read *People* magazine and consort with prostitutes. I play chess with ghosts. "I'm a kidney importer."

Monique starts, is silenced.

"And yourself?" I ask.

Monique chasing a very slippery melon ball across her plate. Toothpick giving hunt. Some miniaturized game of field hockey. Dawn talking to a Spaniard who is declaiming about what a beautiful sport soccer was. "You Americans lack the patience to appreciate it."

Cole introducing me to his cousin, Conrad. To a couple from Sonoma, the Mandels, who own a chain of pet stores and whose son, so we learn, is a math genius. "You're chess players? Our Martin...."

Man to my right advising on investments. Someone asking, "Isn't this terrine absolutely divine?" Others assenting to its divinity. Cole discussing a retirement community he is developing, looking at me as though I might be a prospect. I see buildings numbered 1 through 20. Artificial lake in the middle. Quaint footbridge spanning water-obstacle created so that it might be quaintly spanned by a footbridge. Only nothing on either side of it to come from or go to. Clubhouse. Socials. Movie night. Bingo night.

"Sounds extraordinary."

"I can't quite place your accent."

"Germany."

"Interesting."

Conrad, sipping his wine, "Be careful. My cousin is about to go into sales mode."

And on and on. Yes, the sunsets are beautiful from this side of the island. No, I haven't done much deep sea diving. Yes, Dawn is a remarkable girl. No, I was not a mass murderer. Yes, the terrine is exquisite.

And then afterward. Leafing through the yacht book with Conrad. Each page another glamour photo of some magnificent vessel. Perfectly posed and angled and airbrushed. Yacht porn. Little captions beneath. Name. Year of birth. Length.

"Shouldn't they tell you each boat's turn-ons and turn-offs?"

Conrad nodding. "And its favorite movie."

Moments later Cole joining us. "Want to come out with us some day?"

Describing his planned excursion. Inviting a few others. The Mandels, who regretfully must get back to home to their son. The man advising on investments, who, unfortunately, is going in for surgery on his herniated disk. Monique. Asking her casually. Almost as an afterthought. Monique catching his eyes. "It sounds lovely!"

Only now, staring out at the ocean, at the ever-empty horizon, something suddenly seems clear. Because wasn't that the real purpose of our entire trip? That too-casual invitation to Monique? Isn't that the real reason for it all? Of course it is! Why else this motley assembly? To invite her out on his boat without making seem as though it was just her. To make it a party.

So that is it, after all.   So we are stranded here not as penance for our own sins as I had so long presumed. Our own failures. No. We are here because Cole wanted to fuck Monique! The Mightly Pole of Cole has been our undoing from the very start. Has destroyed us all!

And now here we are. Steered by his carnal compass. Pointed not to magnetic North, but fatefully *South*. South to the steamy rain forest of Monique. Alas, we have followed Cole's penis, and the great conquistador, his lunatic quest for gold, for *oro*, golden honey-pot of pussy, has led us here to Illyria. We are the nameless attendants in his expedition. And now we are half-starved and lost to the world and Monique—his conquest, his triumph—is dead, and I am tired and aching and possibly going mad.

It is late. There is a piece of dried phlegm stuck deep in my nostril. Loose but unreachable. Maddening. I must try to ignore it. Forget it. Sleep. Goodnight.

- Eastern Front -

There were few vehicles left that were drivable. So my previous experience as a lorry driver was no longer relevant. I was handed a rifle, shown how to fire, thrown into a hodge-podge of hungry, bedraggled men somewhere outside Lodz, in Poland. German schools had been emptied of their fifteen year old boys. And now these boys were there among us. Innocents, true believers, fresh from their indoctrination, holding broken old rifles that looked foolishly gigantic in the hands of the smallest boys, and facing artillery guns and tanks and the Russian Air Force.

What was extraordinary was how many of these true believers were mowed down in their first moments of combat. Years of learning and preparation and finally their chance and then mowed down by the thousands. Accomplishing nothing. Slowing the Red Army's advance by an hour or two, preserving the thousand-year Reich for as long as it took to cook a meal.

Hold the line! Führer's direct order.

But there was no line anymore. Just chaos. Retrenchment. More chaos. Soldiers shot from behind for daring to wave a white flag, just hours before the shooter himself waved his own white flag. *Just say the word, O great Führer! We await your order!* Only all you wanted to do by then was just, by some continuing miracle, make it back alive. Slip away and hide in the woods. Crawl your way back home. And then you couldn't help wondering, was that what the others were thinking? Were we all thinking the same thing? Except for the children of course. The believers. Only we were all thrown together. So how could you know anything? How could you know who you could trust? What you dared say? Because now, not only was defeatism a crime punishable by death, but failure to report a defeatist was also a crime punishable by death. And so nobody saying anything. Each watching the other. Wondering what the soldiers all around him were thinking—all of the middle-aged men and miracle survivors like myself. Each calculating the odds of survival if he ran, if he stayed, if he surrendered.

Surrender was the most dreaded of the options. Nobody believed they would ever make it out alive from a Russian prison camp. Nor were we allowed to take our own prisoners. From here on, all enemy must be killed. *Führer's* order. And wouldn't Stalin's order be the same? Just look at how he treated his friends! How would he treat his bitterest enemy? And weren't we the ones who had broken the non-aggression treaty? Weren't we the ones who had gone on about *total* war?

I did make one friend in that time. A lieutenant named Slonimsky. He was from Düsseldorf and had Polish relatives somewhere on the other side of the war. He had a wife and son back in Düsseldorf. That's about all I knew of his past. Nobody talked much about their past anymore. But I liked the way he swore under his breath, liked his mixture of toughness and fatalism. He carried a set of dirty pictures in his pack, and we looked at them together once, as calmly as though we were two boys away at summer camp together. Some nights he took out pictures of his wife and son. Other nights, when it seemed he couldn't handle looking at them, it was these girls.

Of the fighting itself, of actually fighting back, combat, this is my only memory:

Slonimsky and I are tucked behind a stone wall somewhere in Poland—west of Lodz is all I can say. With us was a blonde boy of no more than sixteen, whom neither of us knew. I have no memory of how the boy wound up with us. Just that he had a perfect, Aryan face of the sort that the Nazis might have used for a magazine cover or a poster. I remember the three of us there, and the boy telling us his name was Werner, and Russian eighty-eights whistling by. Shells exploding around us. The boy didn't even have a helmet. And his blonde head kept popping up over the wall to see where the shells were coming from.

"Get down!" we both shouted at him.

"Well, how else are we going to fight them?" the boy demanded.

What the hell does it matter, I wanted to say. But then again, who knew. The young ones were dangerous. The *Hitlerjugend.*

"You're going to get yourself killed," Slonimsky told him, oddly calmly.

"I don't care!" this boy declared, looking both brave and terrified.

"I'm ready to die."

"Well, you'll get *us* killed with you," I said.

But he kept popping up, firing shots at some movement in the distance, too far to have any chance of hitting anything. During a lull, a break, we both tried reasoning with him.

"Hey kid, we're only trying to help. If you can't hit them, there's no point in showing your position."

He said nothing. There was a pause.

"So where are you from?"

"Danzig."

"You miss it?"

We learned that his home had been destroyed. The city had been mostly leveled in a firestorm. He and his mother and sister had survived in an air-raid shelter, had moved in with friends in the country and had been sleeping in a single room together. His older brother was dead. He hadn't heard from his father.

At least the conversation kept Werner down low with us for a while. And maybe it would make him remember something from his past that would make him want to live.

But then there was a big explosion. Closer. And then Werner was up again. Firing.

We're going to lose! Can't you see that? It doesn't matter what you do. So just keep the hell down! Just live to find your goddamn mother!

We were both shouting at him. And then he was down again. At last. "Stop doing that!" we shouted, heads buried in our arms for cover. He didn't answer. I looked at him and saw how he was bent over on the ground. We hadn't heard anything hit him. Hadn't heard him utter so much as a single cry, or moan, or grunt. Whatever sound there was must have been drowned out by all the explosions. But there it was. A bullet had gone through his neck. Blood had splattered his hair and face, and now it was spreading over him as though a spigot had been opened. And as the blood poured out, it was like you could actually see him shrink, like he was deflating before our eyes. He looked even smaller, and therefore even younger. His features were the delicate features of a boy. Germany itself. Shriveling. Deflating.

And then more firing from across the field. They'd seen us.

"Fool!" Slonimsky muttered, with that odd calm and resignation of his. And it was exactly what I had been thinking. I felt nothing about the boy's death. He was nothing to us. There was no time to think. I just hated him for giving up our position.

What to do though? The Russians were advancing. In breaks in the firing, we could hear distant, mechanical sounds now, wheels and engines. Was this, finally, the end? The long awaited, long anticipated end? How could we survive if we left the protection of the wall? But to stay there…we would inevitably be surrounded.

Hold the line at all costs! Ha ha ha. Funny guy.

"Have to run for it," I said.

"Two hours to dark," Slonimsky said.

"We'll be overrun long before that."

"I know."

Once more, we discussed surrender. Only the thought of a Russian prison camp, who knew, maybe years of it, a lifetime of it, held no more appeal than the last time we'd considered it. Of course, we would more likely get executed on the spot. But why not at least try? Escape or death. Just be done with it. We waited until the shooting had died. We moved sideways along the wall to one end and fired two shots back at the enemy, over our shoulders, to give them what we hoped would be a confusing sense of our position. (To the best of my memory, these random, poorly aimed shots were the only ones I fired at the actual enemy in all of my years in the war.) Then we crawled back in the opposite direction to the other end of the wall, hoping they would now be looking for us in the wrong location. At last we slithered away from the wall. Bellies to the ground. Paddling, hands and feet, like a pair of moles. Pausing. Frozen. Then paddling forward again. Only how far could you go like that? Eventually they would see us over the wall. They would have an angle.

"Ready?"

"Yes."

"Good luck."

"You too."

"Now!"

Suddenly we were up, mad prey, bolting, bent over, running, scrambling. *The body says run.* Waiting for it to start. Expecting it. And then there. The firing from behind us. The *shot* from behind us. That one that I had been waiting for all those years. The one shot. Amid all of the thousands I had heard. The one I had been diving from. The end.

Only what? Nothing. Silence. Waiting for it at any instant. *The one.* Running forward. How far now? Two hundred yards from the wall? And another two hundred back to the Russians?

At last the firing starting behind us. Only still alive. And then more artillery. Eighty-eights. That terrifying whistle. Far enough away maybe. A quarter of a mile. Or more. There. Diving into a bomb crater. Heart pounding. Startled. Where was Slonimsky? What the hell had happened to Slonimsky? And what was this, this...something. A body next to me! Almost covered in the mud. Or no. Not a body. Alive. Fucking alive! Moaning. Next to me in the crater. Covered in mud. Part of the mud. But alive!

More mortars. That mocking, inhuman whistling. The ground shaking with another explosion. A pair of eyes was looking at me from out of the mud.

"*Hilf...mir...!*" the thing moaned. Deep, inhuman call. "*Bitte!*"

What to do? Should I try to keep moving? Slip out again? Stay ahead of the Russians?

Or maybe wait until it was dark now. Hope their advance would slow. And wasn't the sky already getting dusky? And what to do about this? Could I leave this creature, this half-human, behind?

"*Wie heißt du?*" I asked.

But it couldn't reply. Maybe it no longer knew. No longer had a name. "*Hilf...mir...!*" it moaned.

I reached for my canteen. Almost empty. I put it to the thing's lips. It drank. Water. Draining down into the earth. A hole in the earth. A mouth. Alive. Drooling. Bubbling spring.

"Where are you hurt?" I asked.

Moans. What was the difference where it was hurt? I couldn't take this thing with me. There was no way.

Minutes passed. Distant creaking of wheels. Clanking. Then a voice calling out. Russian! Far still. But not *that* far. Too late to run now. No way was I climbing out of that hole now. Just enough time to cover myself, head to toe, in mud. Turn myself into another mud creature. Roll in it. Dig deep in it. Play dead.

Voices. Closer. What if they heard this thing moan though? Saw it writhe? The end. And what chance did it have anyway? Could I carry it? Could it survive without me? And Goddamn the fucking thing. It wasn't even human! It had no name! You have made it this far, I thought. At least keep trying. Just make it to the next hour and then the next and then the next. And then it will be over.

I took the bayonet end off of the rifle. Felt with my free hand for its throat. There. Gripped tight on the knife. *Just do it.* What does the doctor say? *You might feel a little pinch now.* And then in. Sliding through flesh. The different feel the flesh has as the knife goes deeper. Tendon. Nerve. Muscle. Artery. Goodbye half-human. Goodbye, somebody's beloved son. Whoever you are.

Wiping the bayonet. Slipping it back on the rifle. Rolling in the mud. Then lying absolutely still. Face down. Better that way. So they can't see you breathe. Or blink. The firing waning with the darkness. Other sounds though. Scraping of machinery. Distant rumbling of a far-away bombing run.

And then suddenly, right next to me, right above me, a voice. Russian. A conversation. More movements. Licking the mud. Just to stay moist. Listening. *Don't move.* Absolute stillness. Pressed against the mud creature. Like that for how long? Two hours? Five hours? Trying to measure time by counting. Only getting lost. Starting over. The mud creature still warm. Comfortingly warm. One with the mud creature. Only needing to pee now. Counting. Voices. Right about me. *Just do it!* Peeing. Motionless. Silently. Into my pants. Hot spreading down the legs. And then cold. Stinging cold. At last the voices, the other sounds fading. Not like they had moved on. More like the Red Army had made camp right above me.

Another two hours of silence. Or three. Middle of the night. Crawling out of the crater. Mud creature, sprung back to life. Taking over its spirit. Climbing out into the night. Not standing up though. Crawling forward. Beast. Looking for sentries. There. Two hundred feet away. Black silhouette. Machine gun pointed out at Germany. Can't make a sound. Feeling with the hands. One knee and then the next. Testing every piece of ground before putting weight on it. Freezing whenever the sentry moved. And then past him. Out beyond the Russians. Only now the most dangerous part. In front of him. Night nice and dark though. Maybe just dark enough. Maybe he wouldn't see. Moving forward. That feeling again. Waiting for it. The *one.* Only nothing. Crawling for how long? A mile? More?

And then suddenly up. Running forward. Trying to slow to a walk. Because why did you need to run? You were far enough away now. Only there was no way to walk. Moving forward, slowing at last but still moving fast, jogging, hurrying, the rest of the night, and then at dawn moving through the shadows and along the tree lines at the edges of the fields, walking finally, walking all of the next day and still moving the next night. And finally far enough ahead of the Russians to walk in the open, look around, figure out where I was. And realizing from the voices, the road signs, and to my amazement…I was back in Germany.

Along a road heading West. People out in the open. And everyone walking the same direction. Civilians fleeing the advancing Russians. Soldiers like myself. Looking for a unit to report to. More and more with every mile. Carrying bundles, knapsacks, pulling carts, loading their possessions into baby carriages. Everyone streaming West. Anywhere that was West. Bandaged and limping. Horse-drawn wagons. Here and there a bicycle. An overloaded car. An ox-cart. And then no longer by the thousands. By the tens of thousands. The landscape itself moving. Streaming westward. Fleeing.

Five years. Three theatres of operation. And through it all, what had I accomplished? I had killed no one but a fellow German. And an enemy duck. In all of it, I had done nothing but retreat. I had retreated across two continents. Four thousand miles of Africa. Seven hundred miles of Italy. Four hundred miles of Poland. And at last, my Sylvia, I had retreated back to Germany. I was coming home to you.

Roads converged. We were on a more main road now. More and more refugees. Some taking their livestock. A mass of humanity. Animals. Everything. Like the land itself was alive, moving. But mostly it was the faces of the people. An endless river of dispossessed humanity. Lethe flowing into the underworld. And the damned all streaming along in it. Children without parents. Old women with walking sticks. Thousands upon thousands of feet. All moving. All knowing the same thing. It was time to go. Time to move. Only where was our inevitable fucking victory?

Where was that miracle weapon we had heard talk of? All those rumors. They were working on a miracle weapon that would save us. Only where the hell was it? And now it was time to flee, to run.

Everyone thinking the same thing. If only to get to the American zone! To surrender to the Americans! What a miracle that would be! Instead of those rapists and thieves. The Americans! That enemy we had been taught for so long to despise. Suddenly our only hope! Our glorious saviors!

That the land had been freshly bombed, "softened," was obvious. Corpses of cows and horses lay in the fields. Pecked at by ravens. Legs pointed up in the air like dead bugs. Burnt out farmhouses were smoldering. We passed through a village of rubble. A warren. Bodies still poking out from the stones. Like one of those children's puzzles. How many dead bodies can you find in this picture? Oh look! There's one up there too, with just the foot sticking out. Funny how it is made to look like the butt of a rifle!

Along the roadside, some of the stragglers had found a puddle formed by a bomb crater, and were drinking from it. What a strange sight—all of them bent over, crowded around it. Like thirsty lions at a watering hole.

We approached a bigger town. An old, wrought-iron bridge. From a distance it looked like it was decorated, festooned, in some way. As we got closer we could see there was a body hanging from every lamp-post. What was this? And then we were all streaming across it.

Looking up in amazement. They were bodies of German soldiers. Around the neck of each was a sign that read, *I am a coward and a deserter.* The work of the military police. In case I needed a reminder of my own precarious situation. Or in case everything was not ghoulish and hideous enough. The bodies turned on their ropes, faces contorted, eyes bulging, mouths open as though screaming. We streamed across the bridge. Our official "Welcome to Germany." Or rather, *Welcome to the Underworld.* Because was this procession anything other than trudging through the gates of Hell?

This was how it would end, I thought, as though composing an epitaph to the war itself. In a crescendo of madness and death. In stink and rot and horror. *Total* war.

And yet, amazingly, it wasn't over. We were still fighting. And I had to find a unit to report to. I saw a gathering of soldiers at the church in town and told them I'd escaped from across the Russian lines, had lost my unit. I was looked at suspiciously, questioned by the military police. But they decided to spare me—perhaps because all the lampposts were already taken.

The soldier assigning duties told me our orders were to hold the town. Hitler had declared it a *stronghold.* He looked worn as he said it. Like he knew it was crap, and he knew I knew, but he had to say it.

Then he reached into his desk and handed me an envelope. "Here."

I opened it. It was a stack of Reichsmarks. "Your pay," he said. "I presume you haven't been paid in a while."

I looked at the stack of bills with astonishment. And where would I spend these? Will the Russians accept them? Am I going to be granted a leave to go and spend it in Berlin? In the next two weeks, before it collapses? What a joke, I thought. This government that had lied about everything from the start, that had sent us off to fight a conspiracy that did not exist, was now rewarding us with this worthless paper and pretending it was giving us something. And all the while, it was setting us up to be slaughtered.

"Thank you," I said, with the same entirely straight face the officer had used.

And then I was off to my new assignment. While the native population of the town was packing up and fleeing, joining the masses heading West, a few soldiers spread out along the square, along the very bridge where our comrades still hung. I was stationed close by the church, and was surprised that in the churchyard were a group of three Russian prisoners. I couldn't imagine how they had been captured, but was told that they had been out on a scouting mission and our soldiers had surprised them. As I came upon them I was drawn into an argument among the captors.

"What are they doing here?" one of my companions demanded. He was a Lieutenant, also with an iron cross—although his was First Class. His neck and ear looked like they had suffered a burn injury. "You know the *Führer's* order," he said. "No prisoners."

None of us responded to him. He said it again. "No prisoners! Those are the orders!"

"So what do we do?" one of the others asked.

"Orders keep changing," another said.

The Lieutenant seemed genuinely shocked by our attitude. "We execute them! That is what we do!"

I looked at the Russians. They were just sitting there, worn and frightened-looking, trying to catch our eyes, to read them. How could you shoot people who are not even trying to kill you? Who are just sitting there?

"I need two volunteers for the firing squad," the Lieutenant said. The veins of his neck bulged. His burns turned blotchy red.

Nobody moved. The Lieutenant grew more indignant, more incredulous. "This is a *direct order*!" he insisted. "Are you disobeying a direct order from the *Führer*?"

Was it the bulge in his neck? The lack of food and sleep? The years of misery I had been put through? The endless lies? Klampf and Sylvia and my father and Dieter, the blonde boy and the countless anonymous corpses I had seen, those ghoulish bodies, hanging from the lamp-posts on the bridge, as though there was not death enough to see already in every direction? I felt myself almost shaking with rage. "So if the *Führer* told you to murder your mother, would you do it?" I exclaimed.

He glowered at me. Approached me. "This is a direct order pertaining to the war. To our victory in the war!"

"You think we'll win the war if we just kill these unarmed prisoners?" I replied, trying to contain my tone, if not my words. "Will that turn the tide in our favor? It's not going to happen."

He approached. Stared into my eyes. Furious. "*What's* not going to happen?"

"I think you know," I said. "It's not happening. It's not going to happen." And now, without intending it, I was shouting. "Everyone knows it!"

He looked at me in horror, "I know no such thing!" and stormed off. He came back a few moments later. His face was still bulging and blotchy red with rage. But now there was also a slight smile on it. "The colonel, inside the rectory, would like to have a few words with you."

It was only then that I realized just how bad it was. What I'd said, in front of everyone. *It's not going to happen.* This was it. The colonel, whoever he was, whatever he himself thought, would be required to turn me over the military police.

I headed toward the rectory. There was no making a break. I knew this lieutenant was watching my back. How close I had come to my home, I thought. Two hundred kilometers maybe. To die so close! And just before the end. I had somehow managed to stay alive all this time. Had kept my head low. Unnoticed by either side. Had survived by sheer, absurd luck. And now this stupid mistake. Only didn't it figure that my end would come as Sylvia's must have, at the hands of our own countrymen? And all because I couldn't keep my mouth shut?

Inside, the air was cool and dull. The room almost completely bare. I stood before a man busily writing at a desk. What could I say? I could plead. Apologize. Promise. Maybe the sheer, desperate need for soldiers would spare me. *"Heil Hitler!"* I said.

I waited for a long moment. At last the colonel looked up. *"Heil...."* But he did not finish his sentence. We looked at each other. Then both nearly jumped with the shock. It was Slonimsky!

"Jaeger!" he exclaimed.

"You're alive!" I said.

"I made it across," he said. "And so did you! I thought we were done."

"Me too," I said.

It is hard to convey (but surely easy to understand) how happy I was to see him at that moment. I briefly described my night in a bomb crater, my escape through the Russian lines, and he described his own, harrowing ordeal.

"You made colonel!" I said.

He waved it off. "It's good for morale," he said. "Promote everyone. Everyone you don't hang."

"Well, congratulations. On not getting hung."

Then he remembered the reason for my visit, turned more serious. "Hans, what the hell did you say?"

"I was just...upset."

He nodded disappointment. "Is it true what you said, about how we can't win the war? About how it won't happen?"

"I don't remember my exact words," I confessed.

"Well...something like it then," he said.

I said nothing.

He shook his head. He put his hands in his hair. His familiar calm and resignation. "What the hell are you doing saying that?"

"I wasn't thinking."

"You couldn't just keep your mouth shut for another two weeks? Another two goddamn weeks, and it would all be over and you could say whatever the hell you want."

"I know."

"Now what am I supposed to do?" he said. "You know I'm required to report you to the *Feldjägerkorps*."

"But you yourself just said…in two weeks…."

"I know what I said. But that was between you and me. There was nobody else to hear it. And we both have already forgotten it. It was never spoken. Was it?" He looked up at me, tilted his head in question.

I nodded. "Yes. It was never spoken."

"Exactly. So…what do we do?"

We were both quiet for a minute.

"You're going to turn me in?" I asked.

"I'm going to tell him you apologized."

"I don't think that will matter," I said.

"Then I'm going to tell him you offered to execute the prisoners."

He looked at me. I looked back at him. Yes, I had killed the man in the bomb crater to save my life. But this was different. They were healthy. They weren't dying. I pictured myself holding out a gun to them, firing. Thought about what that would feel like.

I have said I am not political, that I have no opinions. Perhaps I have overstated. Because there are times you must be either one thing or another. You cannot be in between. You cannot have no opinion. You either shoot the prisoners or you don't. Shooting them made no sense. I had no anger toward them. "You know they're just three Russian boys who someone gave guns to." I said. "Just like us."

"I know," he said. "But there's nothing I can do."

"I can't do it," I said.

"They're going to be shot, you know. Whether you do it or not."

"I still can't do it. I'm not doing it. You can report me."

He looked at me. "You're not giving me a choice," he said.

For a while we both just looked at one another. Measured one another. "Dammit, Jaeger," he said at last. "You can't shoot them, and I can't report you. And I don't want to get strung up on a lamp-post any more than you do. So we have a problem."

"We could stall," I said.

"And hope our brave lieutenant gets blown to bits when the rest of the Russians arrive?"

"Yes," I said.

"It could be another day before they get here. What would I say about why I haven't turned you in? Why couldn't you have just…."

"I know," I said. "I wasn't thinking."

"You need to make a run for it," he said. "Get to another unit. I will say you escaped. And I will write you a note in case you run into any *Feldjägerkorps.*"

"Can you write me a note for the Russian army too?"

He smiled at that. "I can write it. I doubt it will help you."

"I should punch you first," I said. So they don't think you just let me go. It will be safer for you."

"That's okay," he said. "Then they might look harder for you. And besides…."

"Yes?"

"I don't feel like getting punched."

"Oh well," I said. "I tried."

He smiled dryly. "And I thank you for the offer. You'd better hurry."

"I left my pack out with the others."

"I'll let you steal mine. Then nobody will suspect."

We were about the same size, so the clothing—whatever rags either of us had left—didn't really matter. What personal things did I have in my pack? That photograph of my mother. That was it. Perhaps he had a photograph of his mother in his. We could trade mothers.

"Look for me after it's over," he said. "My wife and son are in Düsseldorf. And my parents. All named Slonimsky."

"Okay," I said.

"Good luck," he said. Then he paused, like he was considering whether to say something more. "Another thing."

"Yes?"

"You have those pictures of the naked girls now. They're in my pack."

"Yes?"

"I want them back. When you come visit."

We smiled. "Right."

I took his note, grabbed my rifle and his pack, looked out to see if anyone was watching, and slipped away. The note ordered me to report to the next town, twenty kilometers south, supposedly to prevent a pincer maneuver that could surround Slonimsky and his men. It made no sense of course. As though a soldier, or two, or twenty, could actually make a difference. And twenty kilometers? But it was plausible enough that it could save my life if I were stopped. Communications were breaking down. There was a chance they couldn't even check out the story.

I slipped out without being noticed and headed South, which was perhaps safer for someone in uniform than heading West, the direction of deserters. I tried to look like I was watching the front. When I was a kilometer away, I heard a round of gunfire from behind me. I thought of the prisoners. The lieutenant had gotten his firing squad.

I was on my own again. On tiny side roads, and cutting across fields. With death once again averted, the hunger I had lived with for the past weeks came back to me powerfully. I was feeling pangs, wondered when I had last eaten, realized it had been thirty-six hours since my last, insubstantial piece of bread. I searched through Slonimsky's pack, but there was no food.

For a long while the scenery was calm and peaceful. I heard artillery far in the distance. Behind me, I saw planes in the sky, but too far away to make a sound. I could only feel the slight rumble of the mortars and see the smoke here and there along the horizon. And then, after a while, the peace itself began to feel strange. The landscape so completely empty. I was alone. Completely alone. In the middle of a vast battle. In the middle of an endless war. Where had it gone? And when had I last had that peaceful sensation of being truly away from other humans? I looked down along the ground when I walked through cultivated fields, hoping to find some bit of food someone might have missed. I bent to pick up a lone, dried out husk of corn and sat down and ate it raw, gnawed it desperately and got up and kept walking, through this empty, surreal world.

Where were the masses that I'd seen heading West? The farmhouses were all empty. I was in some strange eye of the hurricane. But it was not all peace either. There were dead, rotting livestock in the fields. I stopped by a farmhouse in a completely deserted hamlet. Outside was a well, and I used it to drink and refill my tin. Then I went in to look for food. The door was open. Inside everything had been smashed and emptied. At first I thought there was nothing left to eat. Then I saw, amid a heap of trash on the floor, a little broken jar of jam. The contents had poured out over the floor. I cleared a space, bent down, and licked it up, spitting out the little shards of broken glass as I encountered them. When I was finished, and had given up on finding more to eat, something—I don't know what—told me to look upstairs. I went up and found two bodies, both shot in the head. One was a young boy, no older than six. The other was a woman, no doubt his mother. The boy was clothed. The mother was bare below her waist. I wondered who had been shot first. What the boy had seen before his death. What the mother had experienced.

A little further, at a crossroads, were three dead soldiers. Germans.

The blood was dried. But the bodies hadn't yet started to decay. I reached in their pockets, hoping to find a piece or two of bread. But there was nothing. Then I realized they had no boots on them. Someone had been there first, had taken the boots, had no doubt reached in the pockets as well.

At the next deserted hamlet I heard the crowing of a rooster. Life. At last. Something else alive, besides me! And then look! There was a fellow German. Not far in front me. A soldier, faithfully manning his machine-gun nest! He was poised, facing away. I ran up to him, feeling a kind of excitement. "*Hallo! Guten Tag!*" But he didn't move. He was dead. Frozen forever in position. Defending the Fatherland. Unto eternity. How could I not have noticed that he wasn't moving? Was I starting to lose my own mind? Starting to hallucinate? I reached in his pocket and this time I found a dried, stale crust and I ate it. Then I looked for the rooster, but it had stopped crowing, and I couldn't find it.

The war continues to go splendidly, father! I'm sure you would agree. I feel victory is very very close at hand now. And if it weren't for this total war our leaders have provided us, I never would known how delicious is nature's bounty—dandelions, weeds, dirt. I hope you are sleeping comfortably out there in the Steppes, and dreaming of our glorious victory!

By now there was no avoiding what I had already sensed, known, for the last several hours. I was behind the Russian line again. There was no other explanation. That pincer movement Slonimsky had worried about—it must have really happened. The Red Army had simply gone around Slonimsky's town and kept going. And had left its mark on the landscape. The war, like the line of a wildfire, had come to this area and had left it, all in a matter of a day, and had destroyed everything in its wake. And now I realized that yes, the artillery sounded like it was to the West. Had sounded that way for a long time. What to do though? There was no point in continuing on to the town I'd been sent to, if it had already fallen. I had to start heading West again. Back to the German line. And I had to be more careful. I rested behind some trees. Slept and awoke. Before moving again I threw away my rifle to lighten my load. I tossed away my medal—my iron cross second class. What the hell had I done for it? And what would this honor, bestowed by a regime that was about to disappear, mean in whatever future we were headed toward?

I started moving West at dusk, stopped in more farmhouses and scavenged bits of food and eventually came to a house with some civilian clothes that fit me tolerably. I changed into them. Then I realized my pack would still give me away as a soldier, and I found a little duffel I could sling over my shoulder, and moved everything from the pack into it. Best look like a civilian if the Russians saw me. I would find a uniform to change back into if I made it back across the line.

I walked for days like that.

Have you heard of those stories about the journey, deeper and deeper, into the strange unknown? Everything keeps getting darker, more macabre. Only imagine that you are living it, except that it is happening during your return home. This is your own land. Little bits, here and there, are familiar, like a nightmare that contains curious details of your own past.

I reached a bigger road and started to see more stragglers again, refugees, headed West. Families and then even larger groups. As though whole villages had left their homes together, were walking together. Once I came across a dead cow that was not yet fully rotten, and cut it and made a barbeque and ate until I was full. My stomach retched with the sudden shock, and the questionable state of the meat. But for the first time in a long time, my stomach was full.

Finally I reached a main road, and again, there were civilians streaming along it, and I did my best to melt in with them. I was shocked when a group of Russian soldiers pulled up alongside us, letting us pass. Soon a Russian tank rumbled by. Reinforcements. Supply trucks. Even horse-drawn wagons. Sometimes the Russians seemed on edge, suspicious, and then I kept a distance from them. Other times I affected a limp to better blend in with the sea of refugees. Only where were they all coming from? This never-ending train. Just as I had seen before. I struck up conversations with some of my fellow travelers and learned a little. (And learned more years later).

They were from all over Eastern Europe. They were German Poles. German Czechs. German Slovaks. German Hungarians. Some barely considered themselves German. Did not even know the German language. Only they had German last names. And all through Europe there was a rage, an uprising against anything German. And so they were expelled from their countries. Fleeing reprisals in the wake of the great German defeat. Driven off their land, and leaving their homes with only what they could carry. Arriving—I would later learn—by the millions, twelve million at least, over three million from Czechoslovakia alone, four million from Poland—into this place that was a foreign country to them, pouring into this ruined land where there was no food and no shelter. Some had even fought against the Germans, fought for their own countries, and were now expelled for

German. Just as Sylvia had been persecuted for her father's ..ishness, even though he had fought for the Germans. Is there any other moral, in history, but that the world is completely mad?

In Czechoslovakia they were massacring German women and children by the tens of thousands. Rounding them into camps. Torturing in ways that showed how ably they had learned from their enemy. Committing their own counter-atrocities against people who had done nothing, to avenge other atrocities against people who had done nothing.

This is why I say I have no politics—even if, perhaps, it is not entirely true. People are animals. Let them do what they will to one another. Fuck all of them.

I caught glimpses of the first days of Russian occupation, passing from town to town. What was remarkable was not just the lack of any law, but also the lack even of any continuity from place to place or hour to hour. It was all just chaos. Sometimes the Russians pillaged and massacred. Sometimes they gave little bits of food to German children. They arrested German males of fighting age, questioned them, shot them or sent them off to slave labor camps, or, sometimes, apparently depending on their mood, just ignored them. They drank and raped at night, and then in the morning, in a wave of sobriety and guilt, they gathered wildflowers and candies to offer to their victims. And then they raped again the next night.

The women hid in attics and under beds. They cut their hair and covered their faces with ash to look old and ugly. They painted on rashes and blemishes to imitate diseases, much as a harmless animal may evolve to look like the poisonous one, in hopes of being mistaken for something toxic. And, at least according to rumors, they committed suicide.

I slept in barns, or sometimes on the bare ground. I fell ill and lost track of time. I would awaken covered in sweat, disoriented. And then I was asleep again. Chilled. Looking for more hay to cover myself with. Was it three days that had passed, or four? How long had I been in this one spot? As though fastened to this same bit of earth until I came to know each separate clump of grass. How long since I had eaten? I came out of my fever to see the mass of humanity heading West was still flowing. And when I was well enough, wobbly still, faint, but able to put one foot in front of another, I rejoined it.

Signs on the road began to name familiar places. Places close to home. Arrows pointing to Leipzig! Had Edelburg fallen already? Would anyone be left there when I got there?

Stories—rumors—ran up and down the road. We heard one of

some Russians who had quartered at the best house in some town, and had never seen a flush toilet before, had no idea what it was, and had used it to wash their potatoes in. These were our conquerors? Our overlords? This was who defeated the Master Race, these drunks, these primitives who shat in the open field and washed potatoes in the toilet? These invaders, some of them with nothing more than horse-drawn carts, had defeated our *panzers* and our *Luftwaffe*?

And then there were stories of the concentration camps that had been opened, clothes and shoes and human hair piled up by the ton, emaciated bodies stacked like cord wood. Was one of those piled bodies you, Sylvia? Were you one of the nameless corpses, buried somewhere in the middle? Or were you, just possibly, one of the survivors who were also whispered of, living skeletons, grown men and women weighing sixty pounds, too weak to walk, yet, somehow, still alive?

And then one day there was a different kind of rumor. Shocking and unbelievable in a different kind of way.

Hitler ist tot!

"What?"

"Hitler is dead. That's what I just heard."

There had been such a rumor once before. But this time it seemed like there were details. It was on the wireless. Everyone was saying it. Confirming it. The piece of garbage had killed himself!

We would not even have the pleasure of hanging him from a tree. Why, O *Führer*, if you were going to kill yourself, could you not have done it fifteen years before? What would the world look like now, had you just taken that one life instead of all the others?

But that was it. It was over. Done. Someone named Donitz had come on the air and declared himself Hitler's chosen successor and said the fight would continue! But hardly anyone gave a crap. It was over. Finished. There had been no miracle weapon. No magical victory out of the jaws of defeat. We had simply lost. There was no great cheer along the road at Hitler's death. Everyone was too exhausted, too focused on just moving forward, getting away, to show much reaction. The moron Donitz would rule what was left of the Reich, a few square blocks of Berlin, for a week, just long enough to get himself arrested by the Allies and assure himself a lengthy prison sentence for war crimes. Imbecile.

Every German male of combat age was to surrender to a Russian unit. That was the next message that went up and down the road. But what did the Russians want? Were they just looking for Nazis? SS? Or were they dumping everyone in prison camps? I decided it would be best to walk the rest of my journey—wherever it would take me—at night. I was not surrendering. I knew by the road signs I saw that it was just two days' walk to Edelburg now, and the thought of it made my heart beat faster, focused me toward that one objective. There was no way I was surrendering now. I needed to make it home. That Hitler was dead gave me some sort of hope.   At least the camps, the exterminations, whatever had really taken place—at least it would be over now. Maybe…just maybe…she had survived it. Maybe she would be there waiting for me.

- Illyria-

There are some questions that are imponderable.   Eternity. Consciousness. Gnomes.

Cole has expanded his whittling endeavors.   He has built a gingerbread-style house and decorated it cleverly with shells and corals and sand, and has created around it a gnome-filled Christmas scene.

"Why gnomes?" I ask him.

He is seated in his leaf-suit, amid a pile of wood shavings. "Why not gnomes?"

"But...why gnomes?" I ask again.

"Well, why *not* gnomes?" he replies.

"But...*why* gnomes?" I   change my inflection as a means of encouraging him to consider the question differently.

He thinks about it. "I don't know. I just start working. And that's what comes out. Gnomes."

You see what I mean? It is one of the imponderables. One has to wonder, is this true of all gnome artists? Do they plan to create gnomes? Or are they just vessels, used by some higher power, some weird god, who takes hold of them for his own purposes, his twisted desire to populate the world with this particular iconography? Maybe they really do mean something after all.

What other tidings have I? There is one of the tide itself. A storm passed by last night, and the ocean is still in a froth. We look out at gray waves, spray flying off of them.

We have learned that often these tempests bring shellfish up onto the beach. Mussels, limpets, crabs, sparkling like jewels along the line of highest tide, strewn amid a thatch of seaweed and stalks and sea fans. We have learned to comb along the tide line at dawn after a storm, competing with the seabirds, gathering a meal. Andreas has become adept at spotting a bird as it dives, using it to find some hidden gem, then chasing the bird away and stealing its quarry. He is fast and agile, and dives into the sand like he has evolved specifically to employ this particular technique of predation.

We are all more dependent on Andreas now. Strong and quiet and uncomplaining. He catches the most food. Checks on all the shelters after a storm and fixes what is needed. He works patiently on the skiff, has tested it carefully and has shown it to be sturdy, at least when the wind is low. He has fashioned two pairs of oars and a small sail made of a sort of twine peeled from a beach shrub, woven into a mat of eucalyptus leaves. The problem is that with supplies, the skiff can seat no more than two of us. And so we have been discussing who should go and who should stay behind, and have concluded that the most sensible plan is sending Andreas alone. He is strongest and most able, and could send help when he is rescued. It would leave enough room in the skiff for fresh water and food, and his rowing would not be slowed by having extra weight in the boat.

How I longed to find some flaw in Andreas's character, something to despise him for, some reason Dawn might turn away from him. But there is nothing.

"There is no reason to hate him," I say to Conrad. "He's a good person."

"Yes, but...don't you just hate people like that?" Conrad says.

With Andreas's ascendance, alliances have shifted. He has built a new shelter for himself and Dawn, superior to ours, and they emerge from it as the young leaders of the island. Cole has quietly ceded his status, scrawny leaf-man, whittler, mutterer. He has befriended Conrad, now that he is one of the downtrodden, has even moved toward Conrad politically. He is willing to concede, for example, that capital gains should be taxed at the same rate as ordinary income. And they agree not all mandatory minimum sentences for drug offenders make sense. At the same time, Conrad has moved toward Cole, so it seems, in terms of actual behavior. He is equally lazy and self-serving. They fail to bury their dove bones, in violation of one of our only environmental regulations. They both eat what they find now, rather than contributing it to the pool of food.

Conrad has started covering himself again. He has taken some material from one of the travel bags that made it onto the island, and fashioned a loin-cloth from it. It was Monique's bag, and so has a rather feminine, floral pattern to it. But it least he has his modesty.

"Why are you covering yourself suddenly?" I ask.

"I made my point, I think," he says.

"What was your point?"

"That....that the need to cover oneself is imposed by society."

"So why did you start covering yourself again?"

"Because I'd proved my point."

"But...if your point was it was imposed by society, then doesn't covering yourself again now, here, where you are on your own and nobody asked you to do it, *disprove* your point?"

Conrad thinks about that. Or at least makes a show of thinking. "No," he says.

I wait for more. But there is nothing. "Why not?" I ask.

"Because it doesn't," he says.

I nod. Another imponderable.

Dawn has forgiven me, so it seems, for my asking if she loved Andreas. We are back to our chess games. Only am I finally losing my grip? Consider this.

We are playing one afternoon. I am feeling weak and slightly confused. I drift off to brief flashes of sleep. Little half-dreams. And suddenly I am the king himself. The idiot black king.   Impotent cuckold. Surrounded by his little guard of eunuchs. Quavering in fear. Pacing. Procrastinating. Doddering old Hamlet. And what am I so afraid of? That moment the queen will break through my defenses. Burst into my chamber.   Pin me. Pierce me with her deadly poison. There is no Dawn. No opponent on the other side of the board. Just a dark force. Trying to unman me. Plotting against me. And then a rook is moved and there is something so familiar in the move, so distantly, impossibly familiar. Where have I seen it? And I actually feel him there. My son. I am playing him. He is trying to destroy me.

I can see his small frame across from me. Little eyes bent over the board. Looking for some solution. I am sorry, I think. I know I was not a good father to you. I tried. Maybe not hard enough. But I did try. You do not need to kill me.

And then, as the scene fades, as I awake to the present, a thought occurs to me. It is my son's birthday. This very day. Is that what is making everything so vivid, so strange?

"Have you ever wondered," I ask Dawn, "why can a pawn never become a king?"

Dawn scrunches up her face in confusion.

"When it crosses the board," I say. "It can become any piece but a king. Why not a king?"

She considers it. "There can't be two kings of the same color. How would that work?"

"Exactly," I say. "This is why my son went off. There cannot be two kings."

She looks at me curiously. Her knight finds an outpost, deep on my side of the board. It is not unexpected. But its effect is grave. More grave than I had at first realized. An electric current flowing right through my side of board. Almost impossible to maneuver around. Is there no way to dislodge it?

I consider limited options. "Nice move."

"Thank you."

"I think you might have this one," I tell Dawn.

"Finally. I might win one," she says. But of course this is just her attempt to maintain a pretense. She wins as many as I do.

Then there is another strange moment. I reach down to the board just as Dawn reaches out, and for just an instant, our hands brush. We touch. And suddenly this game that is purely conceptual, cerebral, fantastical, becomes physical, is suspended, in a state of shame and embarrassment and shock at this most forbidden contact. As though at last my secret desire is revealed. Because just to touch that young hand. The hand that chooses all of those moves. To confess that secret, that forbidden love for one's adversary, that desire to reach forward from that hand that I had touched, to reach up the arm, to her face, her lips.

"Sorry."

"Excuse me."

We both hurry to say it.

And then, as Dawn is demurring further. protesting my apology, Andreas comes over and sits behind her. Places a hand on her shoulder.

Dawn smiles slightly at his presence. This good-natured boy who is now responsible for my survival. My rival. My one true opponent.

"How's it going here?" Andreas asks.

"Not going well from my side of the board," I say. My meaning is lost. Unimagined.

"Well, there's always tomorrow," he says.

"True enough," I say. "Tomorrow and tomorrow and tomorrow. But it won't matter. There is no hope."

"They say you need to exercise your mind just like your body," Andreas says. "To keep it young."

"What are you saying, Andreas? Are you saying I am old? I am an old man?"

Andreas smiles nervously. I smile back, to show I am only teasing.

Sometime later, Conrad and Cole join us.

"How is the skiff?" Conrad asks Andreas.

"As ready as its going to be," Andreas says.

"Really?" Dawn asks. I can see she is worried for Andreas. Is worried about being left without him. "When will you launch?" she asks.

"Maybe in a couple of days," Andreas says. "As soon as the ocean flattens out."

She looks at him. And do you know how mad I have grown? A part of me is eager for him to be gone. Even if it means there will be less food. Even if it means we will perish.

"You think it could handle a storm?" Cole asks.

We all look out at the sea. It looks harsh and grey and unforgiving.

"Not the sail," Andreas says. "The sail would go. The rest of it, yes."

Cole and Conrad look at one another. "We'll all be thinking of you," Conrad says.

- X -

I have a small confession to make. When I said it was my son's birthday, I made that part up. It was not actually his birthday at all. I thought it would be more poignant. More touching. I see now that it is too much. Overwrought. I apologize. I am truly sorry. It won't happen again.

- Germany -

Mutti. Why am I even hurrying toward you? What is this compulsion? Home. Just to make it back home. What else is there? Unless of course...unless...but that is not even possible. There is no point even thinking of it. And yet how could I not think of it? How could I not hope?

It was over. The camps had been liberated. Some had made it out. Would she not have been one of the young, healthy ones? One of the ones with a chance? And being only part Jewish? Could she not have been spared the worst?

I reached Edelburg at dawn after walking most of the night. There was nobody out. The Russians mostly slept late anyway, slept off their nightly victory celebrations. So in the early morning hours I felt relatively safe. And nothing could have stopped me, now that I was so close.

Even as I approached the outskirts, I could see that everything was different. The war had passed through and the streets were clogged with rubble. Houses stood, unharmed, side by side with others that were reduced to heaps of bricks. A few ruins still smoked. And as I got closer in, the damage was worse. Animal corpses, scavenged and stripped and left to rot. The Dorfshenke was another pile of debris. The walk along the river stank of bodies, and I could see two stuck in a thatch of branches, under a bridge. Another floated by slowly. Again, I had that strange feeling like I was dreaming. Like the past five years, the war itself, was streaming by in a dream. The friends and neighbors of my childhood. Dead. Ghosts. Drifting aimlessly by.

There were a few others out on the streets. Not everyone had fled. Heads popped up from heaps of ruin like rodents. All of them filthy, exhausted-looking, awakening with the morning. This was their home now. These piles and pits and ditches. One whole block was burned from what must have been a phosphorous bomb. The old Jaegermusik factory building was just a blackened skeleton. And just past it I saw one of the strangest and most disturbing things I had seen during the war. At first it was just an abstract shape. But then no. It was a woman and child, completely blackened, charred, fused together, soldered to the pavement. Almost like it was a relief, coming up off the street. The woman holding the child. Frozen like that. But no longer even what could be called bodies. Turned to something solid.

Our part of town—the fancier part—was less damaged. And when I reached my mother's house I saw that it was perfectly intact.

There. Home. I was home. Exhausted and hungry. But I had made it. Except I was still in danger. I was young and male and it wasn't safe to be seen on the street. I was supposed to surrender to the Russians. And what would that mean?

I knocked on the door and waited. It was past dawn, people were starting to awaken, and I was nervous showing myself out on the street. I looked around me, then called inside. I knocked again. I looked through a window and was surprised at the disarray inside. Still, it looked lived-in, and there was what looked like a woman's dressing gown on a sofa in the parlor. Which meant that perhaps my mother had not fled. And a child's toy? I went back to the door and knocked and at last heard sounds inside. The door opened. An unshaven man stood in his underwear, looking tired and irritable. He said a few words. At first I tried to make sense of them. Maybe I was just tired. Startled. Who was this man, living in my house? But the words meant nothing. And then I realized why. They were in Russian. For just a moment I froze. Then I ran.

Of course, I thought. A house like ours—one of the nicest in town, and perfectly intact— was bound to be requisitioned by some Russian officer. The man might have made an effort to capture me. But evidently, at this hour, the imperative of arresting all combat-aged German males was outweighed by the imperative of getting back to bed.

I continued down the street, walking, glancing back, half-running. What had happened to my mother? And how would I even find out what had happened? And...what if...where would I stay? In a few minutes I had reached the old town. The streets were busier. The morning activity starting. It was getting more and more unsafe to be out. Were exhaustion and hunger and the excitement and confusion of being back home leading me to take risks, oblivious to my safety? I hadn't slept in nearly two days. And as for food, I had more or less lost track. I considered hiding, waiting again until nightfall. But I was already almost at Hilda's. My stomach was telling me to go forward, and the neighborhood was mostly undamaged, meaning there was a chance she might be there. I reached her building, I knocked impatiently, waited a moment, knocked again. I mentally prepared my escape route, if the door was answered by another Russian, or if a Russian soldier accosted me.

A wary voice came through the door. "Who is it?"

"Hilda?"

Silence.

"Hilda?"

"Hans? Is that you?"

"Yes."

Then a little, excited scream. The door opening. Hilda pulling me inside. Wrapping me in a hug, Georg wrapped behind her leg.

"Hans!"

Then I was upstairs in her apartment, sitting across her little, ice-cream-parlor-sized kitchen table. I gave her a very brief account of my return to Edelburg.

"I can't believe you made it."

"Neither can I."

"You're alive!"

"Apparently."

I asked if she knew anything of what had happened to my mother and she didn't.

You're getting by?" I asked.

"Barely," she said. "We haven't been out of our rooms for two days. We're nearly out of food."

But Hilda shared what they had. Tomatoes and stale bread. A round of cheese. Once the first bit of food hit my tongue, everything in me quickened, and I had to contain the mad rush to shove every speck of food into my mouth as quickly as possible. When I was done I found a couch and collapsed and let the war, the world, everything I had lived and seen in the last how many days, swirl through me, play on my eyelids, dissolve into sleep.

I awoke hours later—there was no way to say how many—to the smell of coffee brewing. The smell made me ache. Hilda had heated the stove with her last pieces of coal. I sat up and took a cup from her hand. How glorious the coffee tasted. That bitterness in the back of the throat.

We talked. Hilda told about the day the artillery rolled through.

"Why didn't you leave before they arrived?" I asked.

"It all happened so fast. I thought we'd have some warning."

"But…haven't you heard the stories?"

"Of course I've heard. But I have no place to go. At least we have a roof over our heads here. We're not sleeping in a hole in the ground like half of Germany is. Although…I think I might be ready to start digging soon. As long as the hole is away from here."

Georg interrupted, was bored, wanted attention. He had a funny, egg-shaped head. It is strange the things one remembers. Like how I remember wondering what he would look like when he grew up. If he would look like my father. Or me. Hilda found a toy to distract him with.

"The American zone?" I asked.

"American zone. British zone. Maybe escape Germany altogether. If there is any way out. Or anywhere that will let us in. I'm afraid to go outside. Afraid they'll come knocking in the middle of the night. I don't want to think of it."

"When was the battle here?" I asked.

"Two days ago. Georg used to celebrate at school when the air-raid siren went off. It didn't mean anything. It was just a break from the school day. Three nights ago was the first time it actually meant something. We spent the night in the shelter. Babies crying all night. The ground shaking with the explosions. Then a fire swept down the stairs. We thought we were all going to die. Somehow we managed to put it out. And then in the morning the tanks rolled through. Shooting everything just for the hell of it. Then the soldiers. I saw them right outside the window."

"So what do you think happened to my mother?" I asked.

"There was no sign of her at the house?"

"There was a Russian officer there."

"I don't know. Like I said, I haven't been outside."

"It's funny. You can't go out during the night. And I can't go out during the day."

"You know we should be celebrating," Hilda said glumly.

"Celebrating?"

"The tyrant is dead," Hilda said.

I nodded. "We lived to see him die. That's something."

She looked off distractedly. "Only his ghost will haunt this place for a long time." Then she seemed to see me again. "So you'll stay here? You'll need a place to stay."

"I can find somewhere," I said, though in fact it had no other plan.

"You don't have to find somewhere. You're welcome here."

There was no point in declining further. "Thank you," I said.

We talked about whether it was safer to flee or remain in Edelburg, where we would go if we left, whether it would be safer to go now, amid the chaos and confusion, or wait until after maybe the Russians' thirst for revenge had subsided. Only that would also give them time to organize, to establish their laws, exert their control. So which made sense? There was no way to know. We decided to wait, at least a few days, and see how it played out.

I needed, in any case, to find out what news there was of Sylvia. And also my mother.

We had been ignoring Georg again. He was playing, as so many children did, with a set of toy soldiers. I joined him for a while. "Bang, bang."

"You're dead! I got you."

"You missed."

"Bang bang bang. Now you're dead."

"Ooooooh. You got me!"

No wonder we fight wars. Look at how children love the idea of them. And do we not all, even as grown-ups, still carry that child's play in us? Bang bang, you're dead. No I'm not. Yes you are. No you missed. No I got you. I'm hungry let's go get a snack.

Hilda starting crying to herself while I was playing with Georg. I had the feeling it was not really anything specific. It was just a chance to cry when she knew Georg was occupied.

"What's wrong?" I asked, after a while.

She wiped her eyes. "It's silly. You know what bothers me?"

"What?"

"The bastard killed himself."

I looked at her, confused. "Hitler? You're upset that Hitler killed himself?"

"The coward," she said. "We never got a chance to hang him from a tree. Like the Italians did. With Mussolini."

"I've had that same exact thought. But…"

She went on. "I mean…I'm sure the Jews would want to get at him first. And no doubt they'd have first rights. Still…I wish it was us. Look at what he did to us. If only the Germans had hung him up themselves…and he didn't even give us that."

I thought about that. "We could have done it. Couldn't we? We just didn't," I said. "Why didn't we? Even in the last months? The last days? What's the matter with us?"

Over the next week or so we almost managed a routine. Hilda went out with Georg during the day. It was safer for a woman to be with a child, and safer when the Russians were sober. Before she left she made herself up to look as old and as homely as possible (in direct inverse to a woman's normal routine, in normal times, of making herself up to look attractive). She knew a farmer family outside town and carried bits of jewelry and other valuables, and traded with the farmer for eggs, beets, whatever morsels the farmer was willing to barter. A pair of pearl earrings was worth a loaf of bread and three eggs. A sapphire ring sold for a whole chicken and a cup of milk.

Georg meanwhile played in the ruins with the other children who had started to venture out. He made a shrapnel collection, picked dandelions for soup, even begged a few scraps from the Russians. He was clever and outgoing, and the Russian soldiers soon recognized him and grew fond of him. Hilda and Georg were back before dark, and then very late at night, at three or four in the morning, I dared to venture out myself. I scavenged the garbage the Russians left behind for uneaten bits. I found myself envying those in the American zone not because of their vaunted democracy or presumed humanity, but because surely the Americans left behind superior garbage. I fished the river at night, and one night actually caught a fish, which was dinner for the three of us, in spite of its having swum among the bodies of our neighbors before I'd plucked it out.

Our schedules solved an additional problem. There were only two beds in Hilda's apartment, so I slept in Hilda's bed while she was out with Georg, and she could get a comfortable sleep while I was out. That I thought about her recent presence in the bed when I climbed in, that it was sometimes warm with her body when I found my way into it, that it imbued the transition from wakefulness to somnolence with a special sensation, there was no denying. But we never shared the bed. If I wanted sleep in the evening, before I headed out, I found a patch of floor, or she snuggled beside Georg.

At last, one night, I headed out and made my way to Sylvia's old neighborhood, to the house she had lived in. I had put it off because I had secretly been hoping for a miracle, hoping that somehow she had returned and was living there again. And I hadn't wanted to have this hope destroyed. By some superstition I felt that the longer I waited, the longer I resisted temptation, the better her chances of survival would be.

I reached the neighborhood just around dawn, as I had planned, and saw that it was badly damaged. Sylvia's house was still there, across from the cemetery, across from the bench from which I had, many years before, waited and watched for signs of her. But the house was missing a side wall and part of its roof. It looked like a doll's house where you could just reach in and rearrange the furniture. I could have just walked in through the missing wall. Instead I knocked at the front, though it felt foolish, since the door meant nothing, it just opened to the same outdoor air. When there was no answer though, I stepped around the side, climbed through the rubble, and went in. I called and heard nothing back. Yet the rooms looked lived-in. I climbed the staircase Sylvia had twice led me up, in total darkness. My heart pounded. Could it be? My miracle?

"Sylvia?" I called. "It's me. Hans."

I opened the door to her room, bracing myself not just to see her, but for how different she might look. It was empty. Of course. Wasn't that what I had expected? Wasn't that the only realistic possibility?

It looked exactly as it had years ago. The rug. The bed. The scent was familiar as well. That was what brought it all back most of all. That scent I had not even been aware of at the time, amid all of those other sensations. Something starchy, clothing maybe, mixed with something sweet and girlish. *Her.* I could actually smell her. "Sylvia?" I said softly. Hoping she was perhaps just hiding, thinking I was an intruder. Hoping to hear some reply, if not from the living person than from her ghost.

I looked at her closet, imagined her hiding inside it, placed her in it, built up a kind of excitement in my mind as I reached for the door and opened it. It too was empty. And yet, there were all of her clothes. Her shoes. I sat down on her bed and ran my hand over it. And then, I felt myself start. I was aware of a movement, and then I was aware of what it was—someone standing in the doorway. A chill came over me. There is no way to describe the feeling. The startle. Before there is any thought at all about who it is. Just some instinctual jolt. Something alive. Very close to you. Unsure of whether it is something to be frightened of. And then the shape forming into something recognizable. Something neither terrifying nor wonderful. Sylvia's mother.

Her mother must have been hiding. Not knowing who had been at the door. And then had heard my voice.

"She's not here," she said.

"Sorry," I said. "I thought…maybe…she'd…returned…."

"No."

"Have you heard anything?" I asked.

"No."

We talked for a few moments. I saw that her face was bruised on one side, assumed it was from when the house was hit, didn't ask. We both wanted some connection between one another. But struggled for something more to say.

"How well did you know her?" she asked at last.

"I was on that bicycle trip with her. That was where I got to know her."

"I see."

"And then afterward...we used to meet after school. Up by the ruin. We played make-believe. She was my princess."

"She always wanted to be a princess," her mother said, almost smiling. "From when she was three. Always playing dress-ups. She loved stories about princesses."

"Lots of little girls do."

"And she was a great one for dolls."

She pointed to the dresser, picked up a doll. "Her father brought this back for her from France. It's supposed to be a little French girl. Oh how she loved it. She called it Sheynda, or something, some made up name. She had all kinds of long conversations with it."

"I can only imagine her that young. I'm sure she was very cute."

Her mother wiped a tear. "Is that where you met her? The bicycle trip?"

"Actually I met her before that. I asked her to be my girlfriend. When I was thirteen."

"Really?"

I smiled. "Yes. I thought she was pretty. Even then."

"What did she say?"

"She said no. Just no. Nothing more. It was very devastating."

Her mother smiled again. "Well, you seem to have survived it. And I guess she changed her mind about you."

"She gave me another chance. On the bicycle trip."

Then her mother was dabbing her eyes again. Putting her hand over mine. Then pulling it back shyly. "You loved her?"

"Yes." And then, "I never said it. I never told her it. But I did."

She took a music box off the dresser and played it. It seemed just a nervous gesture. But for a moment the room filled with tinkling music and I had such a strong sense of it having been the room of a little girl. We both sat quietly as the music slowed to a stop.

She looked away. "I...have a question."

"Yes?"

"It's...difficult. Maybe it's not my business. I just...want to know."

"What?"

"When she was arrested...you'd already...I just want to know. If she died...completely innocent."

"She wasn't," I said, looking away, feeling extremely uncomfortable. "Sorry."

"No," she said, gathering herself. "It's all right. I'm glad she at least had a bit of love. She knew what it was."

Then she broke down completely. Bawled. Collected herself.

"You should get out of here," I said, once she had calmed. "I mean...out of Edelburg. Out of the Russian zone."

"I can't."

"Why can't you?"

"Because what if she is out there? I know it's barely possible. But what if? What if she shows up some day? And I'm not here?"

"But...."

"I'm her mother. I have to be here."

We went downstairs and I told her I needed to go and she wrapped her arms around me and started crying again. I felt every bit of her misery, shared it, and at the same time, was filled with a sense of the awkwardness, this stranger clinging to me as though I were a strand of hope, this emptiness that we both felt, that was at once the same and completely different, so that we would never really know one another, could never really console one another.

That night, after Georg was asleep, I told Hilda about my visit.

"Poor woman," Hilda said.

"I kind of know what she feels like though," I said. "About leaving. I don't really want to go either. Until I'm sure."

"I know you don't want to hear this but...I think it's pretty sure."

"I know," I said. But she was right. I didn't want to hear it.

Hilda put her arm over my shoulder. "I have something." Then she showed me a bottle of schnapps. "I traded away a lot of gold for this. So we better make good use of it."

She smiled conspiratorially. "Come on. It's time to celebrate."

She poured me a glass. "What are we celebrating?" I asked.

"The death of the scoundrel," she said. "With regrets for celebrating so belatedly."

Suddenly it was the most cheerful I had seen Hilda. I saw flashes of her old self. I drank. It was from some farmer's still, and tasted like exceptionally good poison. If she was trying to cheer me though, it most definitely worked.

"To Hitler's death," I said. "And thank you."

"And to Goebbels's death."

"To Goebbels's death."

"To the fact that we are not yet dead."

"To being not dead."

We drank with each toast.

"To soap," Hilda exclaimed. "I got us a new bar."

"To soap," I said.

"Isn't it wonderful being rich?"

"Yes it is."

"To comrade Stalin! Thank you for liberating us from tyranny! And bringing us your paradise."

"To Stalin!"

"And to his paradise," Hilda prompted. "You mustn't forget his paradise."

"Of course. To his communist paradise."

"And Churchill!"

"To Churchill! A hearty congratulations. No hard feelings."

Before long we had drunk to every sacrilege we could think of. We drank to the Czech partisans, to De Gaulle, to dandelion soup and to rat meat. What giddy happiness! This was exactly what I needed.

"I think I've run out of things to celebrate," I said.

"Impossible," Hilda said. "What about God?"

"What about him?"

"To God," Hilda said. "In all His infinite goodness."

"You're crazy."

"Now you realize that?"

"I am just realizing *how* crazy."

"What's wrong with toasting God?"

"It's wrong because you don't mean it. And he realizes that. You think God does not understand sarcasm?"

"I'm not sure he does. He's too thick-headed. Bullying everyone around all the time. Come on. You have to toast."

"Fine. To God," I said.

"You know what I notice now when I go out?" Hilda said.

"What?" I asked.

"There are no dogs anymore."

"Sorry?"

"There are no dogs."

I looked at her suspiciously. "What are you saying?"

"Just that…."

"Do you think people are eating their own pets?" I asked.

"Of course not!" Hilda said.

"What are you thinking?"

"They're eating their neighbors' pets. Just like their neighbors ate their pets!"

"That's horrible," I said, almost laughing. "I refuse to believe it."

"It's wonderful!" Hilda exclaimed.

"You're crazy," I said again.

" Our bountiful God in His infinite mercy has given us our neighbor's pets to eat."

"Hilda!"

"To our neighbors' pets. And to God. Again. Again and again. For all His goodness. And love. And all that good stuff about him. Whatever it is."

And so we drank again.

We were soon drunk. Close to one another. Looking at one another.

I still wasn't quite sure that Hilda was seducing me, had in fact planned to seduce me. I just knew she was looking at me a certain way. Leaning toward me. And there was something to her toasts, some desire to break one taboo and then the next, like she was preparing herself, or me, or both of us, for that next barrier that we needed to break through.

After a while we both became quiet. It had already occurred to me that we had nobody else in the world anymore. There was no need to say it. It was just there. Obvious. Hovering as her face was hovering before mine. We had talked about where we would go, when we would leave, and there was something in it that was never even said—that, in some way, we were together now.

At last she came beside me, arm around me. "To...my soldier boy," she said, finishing off her glass of schnapps.

My words were slurred. "To my...whatever...you...are."

And then we were kissing.

We drank more. Through all of it a part of me was thinking she is still mothering me. She was always mothering. Feeling sorry for me over Sylvia. And feeling sorry for herself besides. And then she was taking me stumbling to her bed, undressing me, guiding me inside her, we were one mass, one fleshy being.

What we became, in the days after that, was in some ways as vague as what we had been before it. Were we lovers? A couple? Yes, we were together, made love, depended on one another. But was it understood that this was just a convenience, that ultimately we were in different phases of life, were unsuited to one another? Or was I only imagining that? Was she in fact attached to me? Expecting an attachment with me? Because in so many ways we were so suited to one another, got along so well from day to day. But as soon as I started to feel comfortable with Hilda, with our being together, I started to wonder. Because if Hilda had planned this, had needed this, did that mean that on some level she was glad that Sylvia had not shown up? And if that was so, was she telling me there was little hope that Sylvia was alive, when perhaps there really was? Was it possible that she was trying to spirit us away quickly, just in case Sylvia might yet appear?

Or did all of these thoughts represent my need to cling to hope when there was none?

Of course, as things with Hilda changed, I also thought of my father. What he might have thought, had he known. Whether he had loved Hilda and whether she had loved him. It was a topic Hilda and I dared not go near. I am not sure whether I knew then of the Jewish-Austrian doctor Freud and his theories. He had fled to London before the war, and his ideas had been banished as well. I must have learned something of them later. But I didn't need to be told of Oedipus and of some theory about marrying one's mother, to sense something uncomfortably wrong in being lovers with my former governess, with my father's former lover.

And yet, was I really secretly longing for *Mutti* in choosing her rival and very opposite? And who else was there left in our town anyway? And was Hilda not also herself? Appealing and desirable in her own right? And what did any of it matter, really? We were together. That was that.

As Hilda and I became more established, I grew more accustomed to the idea of leaving. And in any case, it would have been hard to explain to her, now that we were lovers, that I had to stay in hopes of finding Sylvia. Before I could go though, I still needed to find out what I could about what had happened to my mother. That she was both a Nazi sympathizer and a leading member of the gentry of Edelburg would not have endeared her to the Russians. If she had survived the invasion, she could easily have been interned somewhere already. Only it wasn't like I could walk up a Russian officer and ask. Or even visit that house where I had spent my childhood.

Her lover, Fleulen, had lived by the munitions plant outside town. I knew the plant had been destroyed. But perhaps the man's house was still there. Perhaps my mother was there with him. I set off there one day. When I got to the house though, it was intact but deserted, and appeared like it had been that way for a while. There were mouse droppings everywhere. Fleulen must have been called up at the end, and marched off, and who knew if he was dead or in some miserable camp or maybe sailing off to Paraguay.

I kept remembering that Russian officer who had answered the door at my mother's house. Unshaven, yawning, standing there in his underwear. Something in that image had stayed with me. In the glimpse inside the house itself. The dressing gown across the sofa. Was it just a woman's? Or had it actually belonged to my mother? Yet how at home the man had looked. The king of the castle. The next night I headed back there. It was a moonlit night. I knew there was a balcony window in back without a lock, and I knew how to scale up to it along a drain pipe. It had been a climb I had enjoyed many times as a boy. Even in the darkness, I knew exactly where the footholds would be. I was inside in a moment.

I had a knife out, just in case. But the house was silent. I crept as quietly as I could down the hall. It had a thick, Persian runner along the floor, so it was not difficult moving with scarcely a sound. But something in the air, the smell, was almost dizzying in its familiarity. My home. Where my mother had tucked me into bed every night when I was little. Where my father had taught me chess and music. And now here I was, a trespasser, a criminal, tiptoeing through all of those ancient memories. The door to what had been my parents' bedroom was open. So no need for creaking and jostling. I peeked into it. Two forms lay in the bed. It took me a while, in the darkness, to be sure who they were. I took a step into the room. Studied the shapes, the sounds of the breathing, the faint light against their hair. And then there was no doubt. That man. That Russian I had seen. And *her. Mutti!* So that was it. The house had not been requisitioned after all. My mother had taken a Russian officer for her lover.

Of everything she had done, this was what caused in me the greatest revulsion. I looked at her, sound asleep next to this man, and felt sickened. You can forgive your mother almost anything. In my own case I could forgive her beloved photographs of Hitler and her love of the Reich and her petty contradictions of everyone, her harassment of waiters and governesses, her high-chinned superiority. The one thing you can never forgive in your mother is being a whore. Giving herself away. It turns you, her child, into nothing, shames you a hundred times worse than if she were merely a mass murderer. *My mother is a whore. My mother beds the enemy for favors.*

She had surely done it as a matter of her own protection. She would be spared the celebrations of the common soldiers. She would be spared denunciation for her money and her associations. Was it really so terrible, giving herself to this man? Switching her allegiances so suddenly to the enemy? And yet none of this meant anything. I just felt sickened.

Before I left I could not resist opening the door to my childhood bedroom. I did it slowly, paused with every squeak. And then there it was. That room that had once been filled with my toys. That my father had ventured into to sigh and philosophize to me when he was upset. I started. There was Stefan, my little half-brother, sleeping in the bed I had slept in when I was his age. My mother had moved him into my bedroom! I hadn't really considered what room he would have been in.

I just hadn't expected him there. In my bed. What did I feel at that though? Like I had been displaced? Or like I was looking right at my childhood self.

I slipped downstairs and lit a candle and found a piece of paper to write on.

Dear Mutti,

I'm alive. Staying with Hilda. Wanted you to know.

Hans

I left it by the front door and let myself out.

I must admit that I secretly hoped that my note, in spite of its air of indifference, would elicit an immediate response, which it did. I returned to Hilda's, and late the next morning, there was mother at the door. She looked disheveled, tired, threw her arms around me, wept.

"My baby. You made it!" she exclaimed.

Hilda and Georg hurriedly headed out, left my mother and me alone together. She asked how I was, if I was hungry, exclaimed over and over about how horrible everything was.

For a while I was quiet. I felt myself burning inside. "You seem to have found a way to get by," I said at last.

"Hans…I…look at the times we're in."

"And whose fault is that?"

"Is it my fault?"

"You supported this."

And suddenly, within minutes of our reunion, we were arguing.

"You want to get into that *now*? When I have just discovered that my son is alive?"

"Yes."

"I didn't support *this*," she said. "Not the way it happened."

"So what did you support? Just murdering some…undesirables? Just…."

"No. I'm sorry. Look…you can't talk like this. To anyone. You know what could happen to me."

"What happened to Sylvia. That's what could happen to you."

She buried her face in her hands. "Look at me, Hans. I'm your mother. Can't you forgive me?"

"Tell me. Will you at least admit that it was wrong? What happened to her? That she had done nothing?"

"Yes. It was wrong. Of course it was wrong." She cried. "Please!

I'm not perfect. I made mistakes. And believe me, I'm suffering for it now."

"You seem to have found some consolation," I said.

There was a long pause. "What would my son prefer? Would he prefer that I were raped by every Russian private in Edelburg, one by one? And then executed for my sympathies? Or that I find a way to avoid that outcome?"

I had no answer for that.

"I need you," she said weakly. "I need you to understand. I am trying to stay alive. That's all I'm doing. And...you should know...he can help you, too. I was thinking about that too. You can stay with us and...at least you'd be safe."

"I don't want his help."

"Are you hungry?"

"I am. Shall we go out to the Dorfshenke for a sandwich?"

"It's gone," she said. "That whole block is gone."

"I know," I said.

"So...." my mother hesitated. "So what...*did*...happen to her? To Sylvia I mean."

"No word of her. Since the night of her arrest. She was killed. I'm sure. What else could have happened to her?"

My mother went quiet. Sobbed again. "I'm sorry. That's awful. That's very awful."

"She hadn't done anything! What did she do?"

My mother held her hands to her face. "Nothing. She didn't do anything."

Only, did she mean she was sorry personally, because she felt responsible, or just sorry in general for what had happened? Whatever it was, it was good at least to hear her say it.

Only then I had other thoughts. She is just playing on your sympathies, I thought to myself. Just using that weapon that women have. Tears. But it is surely a lethal weapon. I felt myself beginning to soften. Was she not still my mother? Did she not have her own suffering and loss and disappointment, her own confusion and misery?

"I'm sorry," she said again, this time little more than a whisper, a plea, through her tears.

I had no words for a long while. "Forget it," I said at last.

After a while her tears subsided. She swallowed. "So...so I am wondering...." she seeming afraid to ask it. "So what are your plans?"

"Hilda and I are heading West. With Georg. That's all I know."

"You can stay with us, Hans. He can protect you."

"I don't want that," I said. "There's nothing left here. I need to get out of here."

"I've barely had a chance to see you. Is this...right away?"

"It's soon," I said. "A few days."

For a while she tried to persuade me to stay. She had just seen me. She was hoping that we could get to know one another again. Hoping we could start over. Hoping I would learn that my mother wasn't such a horrible person.

I sighed. My anger had left me. "I would stay if I could. The borders are going to be closing. It'll get harder."

She chose to let it go. "I hope you'll be careful."

"So you're staying?" I asked.

"For now. I have the house. I've never slept in a barn before. Or on a floor. Or in a field. I've never had nothing. I don't think I'd be very good at it."

"I suppose not," I said, almost smiling at the thought.

"Maybe once you are settled you can write me and I can...."

She was afraid to finish the thought, didn't want to know whether I would want her to be near me, whether the suggestion would be rebuffed.

"I'll write."

"And Hans, he...Petrovsky...that's his name...he can write something for you that will allow you to get across the checkpoint. To the American zone."

She was eager for me to take advantage of this connection to the conqueror, to share in this compromise and so accept it. And I knew I would be an idiot not to. "I guess...that would make sense," I said.

She took my hand, squeezed it. "So what happened to Fleulen?" I asked.

"Nobody knows. I got a letter from him a month ago. He was fighting in Bohemia. Then nothing. Just gone. Like your father." She nodded her head. "It's all unbelievable."

"I hear the Bohemians are even better at butchering Germans than the Russians are," I said.

"I hope he didn't suffer," my mother said. "I can't say I ever really loved him. But still...too much suffering...."

There were many questions to ask on that score. I almost launched into a whole new round of accusations. But I let them go.

"And Stefan?" I asked. "How's he doing?"

"It's been difficult for him. All the changes. But he's good. He's a smart boy." And then, "So how's Hilda?"

"She's surviving."

"I'm glad you two at least...have each other." I felt like she must have sensed that our relationship had changed.   Or perhaps she was trying to figure it out, hoping I would offer some hint.

"We still get along well," I said.

She smiled. "You always did.   From when you were two."

We talked a while longer. About who was alive among her friends. Who had not returned. About what the Russians might or might not do. Rumor was they had promised to leave after some period of occupation. But could this be believed? And if it all became Communist, what would become of my mother's beautiful home? Where would they have her live? But she preferred these risks to fleeing. Hoped for the best. Assumed if the worst came, at least she would have bribe money and could make her way out when the time came.

And then, at last, it was time for my mother to leave. Apparently there was someone waiting, a Russian soldier, to provide her escort back to her house. She took a few foods out of her pocketbook. "I hope you're getting something to eat."

"A little."

"My poor baby."

"I'm okay."

"Thank Hilda for me. For taking care of you. Again."

I smiled. "I will."

"I hope she doesn't hate me."

I shrugged by way of answer, gave her a goodbye hug, and she was gone.

Two days later she returned with the documents for me and Hilda and Georg. I knew it was hard for her. She didn't really want me to leave her behind. I understood that her helping us flee was to her an act of contrition. The one thing she had left to hope for, that at least her son would make it back alive, had come to pass. And yet, after a couple of short visits, I would be gone again.

"He's not that bad," she said, as I looked over the meaningless, Cyrillic sentences, the official-looking seal, the officer's signature, *Petrovsky.* "He's not a Communist. Actually, he comes from an old family, they had lots of land before the Bolsheviks."

In some ways, though chastened, softened, she was just the same. Vanity about her race, about the master race, had been replaced with vanity about this officer's wealth and birth. It was still *Mutti.* Her love affair with National Socialism had ended badly. Had hurt her. But in its wake a new world view was already rising. One that served the same pride and allowed her to move on. When I thought about it in this way, I felt like I was once again able to see her as the difficult, slightly absurd, but ultimately forgivable mother of my childhood, as a comic character and not a malicious one.

"I thought the Russians were all sub-humans," I said, unable to resist a last dig.

"Not *all*," she said. "Anyway…I've admitted I was wrong, Hans. It was all wrong. Are you ever going to forgive me?"

We made plans for how we might get back in touch after Hilda and I had settled somewhere. We would try the mail service or we would go through my mother's sister in Leipzig. Then she reached into her handbag and took out a handful of gold jewelry. "Take this with you," she said. "It's one thing that will always have value. Wherever you go."

I looked at her. This was it. Goodbye to my mother. "Thank you," I said.

"You're welcome, Hans. Be careful."

"I will."

I thought about telling her something more, that I forgave her, would miss her. I was close to it. Surely, if I'd known that I would never see her again, I would have said it. But how could I have known that? Only the plans we made to get back in touch never worked as they were supposed to have worked. We never heard from her. Perhaps she was arrested after all. Perhaps her Russian lover lost interest in her. Or was unable to save her. Or who knows. I wrote letters. I never heard back.

There was one more errand I needed to make before we could go. It was a last visit to Sylvia's mother, to tell her we were leaving.

The Red Cross was tracking missing people, helping them to reunite, and I told her that was how she—or Sylvia—could reach us. I would register with the Red Cross and she just had to write to them and give them my name and the town I was from and they would find me. Because we still weren't sure where we would end up.

There was no more sharing memories of Sylvia on this visit. We both kept our composure and kept it brief.

"Good luck," she said.

"You too," I said.

"I'll write if I hear anything."

"Thank you

- Illyria -

It is my night for fire duty. The night before Andreas's planned departure on the skiff. Conrad is keeping me company.

"Do you ever feel ready to die?" he asks.

I think about this. "No," I say.

"Can I ask you something though?"

"Sure."

A pop. A burst of embers float up into the night.

"Why should rescue even matter so much to you? I mean, how many more years could you have?"

I am mildly offended. But answer seriously. "It's human nature, no? The heart wants to keep going. As long as it beats, it wants to keep beating. Each beat contains the wish to make it to the next."

"I'm ready," Conrad says.

"Really?"

"Yes. I have lived. It is time. And…and you're past eighty already."

"Not all of me is."

"What are you talking about?" he asks.

"My left kidney is only fifty-eight," I say.

He looks at me.

"It's true. I bought it from a Brazilian woman. She was twenty-eight when she donated it. And it was thirty years ago. So my left kidney is fifty-eight. In fact, I am something of a medical miracle. The kidney was expected to last perhaps ten years. And it has lasted thirty. It turned out to be a bargain."

"You bought it?" he asks, surprised. "From some impoverished woman? You left her with only one kidney?"

" Yes."

"And that…doesn't bother you? You think that's okay?"

"Absolutely," I say.

He slaps at an insect, scratches under his arm.

"It was a simple transaction," I say. "She was a mother of five and her children were hungry. She had two healthy kidneys and I had none. And I had money and she had none. So I gave her money and she gave me her left kidney."

"And you don't think that's exploiting her poverty?"

"No," I say. "I think it worked out well for her. She was very pleased."

"That's it?" he asks. "Just like that?"

"It's called Organ Tourism," I say. "Travel to exotic location. Return with native body-part. A lot more authentic than some hand-carved bamboo flute. No?"

For a moment he just seems amazed. "How did you…even know how to do this?" he finally asks.

"I paid a broker. He found a woman in Sao Paolo, Brazil, a hotel maid, who was a match. Only do you know something? The purchasing of organs, it turns out, is illegal in most countries. But what is legal is receiving them from family members. And so this Brazilian maid and I were officially married, in Portuguese, in a little chapel in Sao Paolo. I lifted her veil and kissed her. We had to make it look real."

It all comes back. My son might have offered to donate his kidney for me. But chose not to. I would have refused, of course. It would have been my final gesture of love that would have brought us back together, united us on my deathbed. I would have savored the self-indulgence of such a death. The sacrifice. The proof of a father's love. But he made no such offer.

That my son never offered, that instead I was receiving years of life from a stranger, made my kiss with her seem oddly poignant. Suddenly I was remembering the way she looked up into my eyes at the ceremony, and how, in that instant it had felt completely real, and I had the strange sensation that she was feeling the same thing. That just the veil, the ritual, had produced the illusion of love, that if I had told her then that I wanted it to be real, that I wanted her for my bride, her eyes just might have beaded with little tears. And yet we had no language in common. No way to know what one another really felt. Who our mock-beloved was. And two hours later I was back in the Sao Paolo hospital for another round of dialysis.

Two weeks later was the operation. We met in a dingy clinic on a side-street cluttered with bars, a tarot-reading room, a shoe-repair place. We saw one another in the waiting room. Shook hands. Smiled. She brought her sister with her, and her sister shook my hand eagerly and said thank you in Portuguese and then English and then we sat for a while and read and they chatted. The doctor came over with a translator, and at last, through the translator, I wished her good luck, and she said the same to me.

Then we were in the operating room. The walls were a dull, under-sea green. The doctor smoked a little stub of a cigarette as he probed me and spoke to the nurse and Madeira in Portuguese. The masks came over both of us. We went into a dream.

And then awoke, and divorced.

I describe it all for Conrad. "Her name was Madeira. Like the wine. Isn't that a pretty name?"

"But it was a fraud," he says. "The whole marriage was a fraud."

I lean back. Look up at the stars. "It was a successful marriage. I owe her everything. How many men can truly say that about their ex-wives?"

"You can joke," he says. "But it's wrong. You exploited her."

"Did I?"

"Yes."

"So we should tell poor people they have no right to do what they need to do to feed their families? That we know what is best for them? That they are letting themselves be exploited, and need to stop degrading themselves? That it makes us uncomfortable, seeing how willing they are to degrade themselves? 'Your starvation, your desperation makes us uncomfortable. You must stop showing it.'"

The breeze is soft, the waves lap gently, make a sound like a stage-whisper.

"So this is what the third world has come to mean?" Conrad asks. "Junkyards of spare body parts for us to rummage through? Picking and choosing until we find an organ that is to our liking?"

"She made what she could have made in five years at the hotel," I say. "So tell me who is exploiting her. Me or the hotel company? Which should be illegal?"

"It doesn't seem strange to you, to have all of these people walking around with missing body parts that they have sold? Just to feed their families?"

I think back to things I saw in the war. To Annabel, who I met in Annecy, while recuperating from my kidney transplant. To Dawn rising up from the sea that very first time. "The world is strange. The fact that we are here is strange." And then, "She was grateful. She thanked me again on the day we signed our divorce papers, showed me her scar, signaled a little thumbs up, how well she was healing. I thanked her in return, even gave her a little extra money. Was there ever a happier, more mutual divorce?"

"I need to get sleep," Conrad says, starting to rise.

"Let me ask you something," I say. "Wouldn't you sell a kidney right now, to get off of this island?"

He pauses. Considers. "Yes. I would."

"And should you be allowed to make such a deal, if it were possible? Or should you be forbidden from it?"

He is standing, has turned serious. "If anything happens to either of us...." he says. He pauses, starts again. "If anything should happen... I've enjoyed our conversations."

Then I am alone. Tending the fire. The insects chirp. My mind traverses my eighty-six years of memories—yes, eighty-six now, I have celebrated a birthday here on the island—picking at random bits.

Clear skies. Gentle breeze. Calm ocean. Perfect weather for Andreas, I think to myself. Tomorrow will be the day.

- Germany -

What plan did we have? The truth is, we hardly had one. We just wanted out. Out of this ruined land. The people were already starving. And still, more and more refugees were pouring in. Streaming in from the East. Now by the trainload. Car after car. Train after train. The Germans. The despised. The damned. Beaten and starved and dumped into Hell.

Our idea was to get to the American zone. And from there to get away. Illyria. Oz. El Dorado. If any of them were accepting Germans.

What actually happened, the last comic act of the grand *opera buffa*, was remarkable not for its artistry or comedy or even its random cruelty, but for the sheer shock of it. Because by then the violence had finally begun to subside. There was still a drunken gathering here and there that was to be avoided, that could turn at a moment's notice. The Russians were still armed, after all, and far from home, and emboldened, intoxicated with their power. Law and chaos swept back and forth across the countryside with the shifting wind.

There were rumors that the trains had started to run again. But there were no schedules. And then we heard other rumors—that trains were rumbling through without stopping. That they had closed the station. That there were shootings there. Was it true? Nobody knew. It was what someone said that someone else said. We decided to try our luck on foot. Hilda knew we might be sleeping outside, worried about lice, and so she shaved Georg's head before we left. With it shaved, it had an even funnier, egg-shape. We packed what we could, loaded up Georg's old baby carriage with a couple of bags of clothes.   And walked away.

It was the 6th of July, 1945. The day Hilda and I left Edelburg behind us.

We walked North toward Berlin for three days without trouble, slept where we could, ate the bits of food we had packed. Georg alternated between a kind of daydreamy quiet, and some rambling story that was so silly it actually had us laughing. Something about some make-believe bear named Siegfried that the school children could ride to the bakery. We were leaving our home forever with nothing, and this was what this funny-looking little boy was blabbering about! If only we grown-ups could enter that make-believe world whenever we felt like it!

"What do you think about Africa?" Hilda said one night, as we lay together under the stars.

"Like where?" I asked.

"I don't know. Maybe Chile," she said.

"That's South America."

"I know. I switched continents without telling you. Sorry. But what do you think about Chile?"

"I don't know much about it. It's far."

"I think it's on the ocean."

"I think it might be cold, though."

"Well, we should go somewhere with good weather."

"True," I said.

"And meat."

"That too," I said.

"And good schools. For Georg."

"I always wanted to see Iowa," I said.

"Is that South America?"

"No. That's North. It's right in the middle of North America."

"Let's go there. I like mountains. Do they have mountains there?"

"I don't know. I just know there are Germans there. Lots of German farmers."

"They're not throwing them out?"

"I don't think so."

The stars faded behind a thin halo of cloud. We fell asleep, and were awakened in the middle of the night by a rain. We got up miserably in the dark, got back on the road and started walking. Later in the morning the sun came out again, we took a break and spread everything out to dry, and actually enjoyed an hour of peace and calm. It felt good—as it always did for me —to be moving. Dreaming.

In the afternoon we came to the last town in the Russian zone, just outside Berlin. It was half-ruined like Edelburg, crowded with refugees, and had the feel of a frontier. Campfires and drink and singing. And then, amid all of this, we passed a body that had not been cleared from the streets. Gunfire. Like we were moving backward. Descending back into chaos. We headed anxiously away from the center of town, to a quiet street away from the commotion. But as we walked we came on just the sort of scene we had hoped to avoid.

Did we not both feel a tightness come over us? A little wave of anxiety? I'm sure we did. But it was no different from a hundred other times. A hundred other little things to be wary of. Because how could we have known? And we had the papers from my mother's Russian officer. Wouldn't that help us? Only we just turned a corner and there they were, right in front of us. Russian soldiers beating on a German. Like they had accused him of something. Stealing? He was emptying his pockets. Or trying to.

This was no victory celebration. One of the soldiers angry. Drunk. Staggering. The German dropping to the street. *Back up.* Hilda and I watching, backing, holding Georg. And now the soldier pausing, taking a swig from a bottle, pouring out the last drops over his victim. Taking out his gun.

Why didn't we run? Before we were noticed? The three of us just frozen. Would it be worse to run? To be seen running? Calculating furiously. What to do. Only what you wind up doing isn't really based on the calculation. You are just frozen. Or you are just running.

Slurred words. Russian? German? Then the shot. Deafening.

Maybe it was that it was so unbelievable. So unreal. That was what kept us there. What kept us always doing something wrong. Always choosing the wrong door. Always wondering if only…. If only this. If only that. If only I had taken Sylvia with me. If only Hitler's mother hadn't screwed that night. If only Hilda and Georg and I had slipped away.

The three of us just staring. Georg pulled out of your dreams of riding bears to bakeries. You should not have to see this. And then the Russian swinging around to see who was there. As one naturally does, perhaps. After committing a murder.

Seeing us. Right there. Staggering forward. Approaching. Hilda fumbling to get at the papers. No, no. It's not a gun. Papers. Russian. See? Look! The soldiers all there now. All before us. Everything happening at once. And then…he had been so quiet. That was the thing. So quiet we had almost forgotten about him. But he must have just been staring at that soldier. At that freshly fired weapon. Georg. Back from his little daydreams. Back in the world. Seeing that man shot by those soldiers. Right before his eyes. And then pure instinct, pure fear taking over. Hand shooting up in salute. In deference. To one in uniform. To one with such power. Speaking loudly. Firmly. "*Heil*

Hitler!"

The Russian staggering. Cold-eyed. Waving his gun.

"No no! No...he doesn't mean that!"

Both of us shouting at once. In German. The Russian shouting back in Russian. What did it mean? What was he saying? Did the Russian feel he was being mocked by this little boy? Or just that here was an actual, unrepentant Nazi! One of the enemy. This little child. Did he think, perhaps, that we must all have been Nazis, to have such a child? Did he think anything at all?

This man, who had just killed another civilian right before our eyes? Staring down at the boy. Only that just heightening Georg's fear, and Georg holding his salute firm. Trembling. Brave little boy. *"Heil Hitler!"*

At last! At last Hilda had taught Georg how to do it. How to say it so he wouldn't get in trouble. And now he was doing it. Perfectly. Just as he was supposed to. Only why wasn't it working? Why was this man still looking so angry? Hilda kept pleading helplessly. Sobbing. The gun aimed at her. Fumbling for the papers. But shaking. Not able to get them. The others calling out in Russian behind the drunk one. Only what were they saying?

My own arm reaching over, pushing Georg's arm down and Georg finally panicking, lost, exploding in tears. Hilda holding out the documents, pleading, only nobody taking them, the Russians, all of us, talking all at once, nobody hearing anything or understanding anything, and the gun moving from Hilda to Georg, from mother to son, and the boy screaming and crying, *Hilf mir, Mutti,* and then the one Russian grabbing the other's arm, trying to stop him, so when you heard that sound, that deafening, irrevocable sound that you did not want to hear, it was impossible to say if the shot was even intended or if it had gone off accidentally. You just knew that at that moment everything exploded, everything shattered, Hilda and Georg and everything that had happened since the night they took Sylvia, those two moments seared on each end, closing off the years between them, blocking out everything, always there, always real, always wrong.

Hilda falling over the Georg's body. Screaming and sobbing. The Russians shouting among themselves. Taking the gun from the drunk. Pushing him. One of them coming up to us, looking somber. Distraught. *"Bitte. Bitte."* Possibly his only German words. Motioning to the boy. Switching to Russian. Pleading. Realizing at last that we could not understand. Would never understand. And so the three Russians heading off. Leaving us. The two others still shouting at the drunk. Pushing him. Leaving Hilda and me to our little boy corpse.

What can one say about a mother's grieving for the loss of her child? It requires words that are not a part of the language. Nor do I dare try to explain what I myself felt—that he was my father's and my half-brother and that the death of any child is seems so unsettling, so against one's sense of what should be, that all you can do is just reject it, refuse to believe. Only it just keeps coming back, and each time it is just as real as the last.

I covered the little body and carried it to a field, and we stayed by it all night. In the morning, without asking, I brought it to a churchyard and borrowed a shovel and found a corner to bury it in. At least Hilda would know where to find it, I thought. If she ever came back. She watched me silently. When we were done, I dragged her to the checkpoint for "processing." We showed our papers, and walked across some unmarked, imaginary line, and were in the American zone.

"I can't do this," Hilda said.

"What?"

She wouldn't say directly. But I understood. She wanted to go back across to be with Georg at that church. But she also knew it didn't make sense. And there was no Georg anymore. There was nothing to go back to. Nothing to hold and love and protect. Nothing. And he was in the Russian zone. It would be madness to go back there. There was only forward.

- Illyria -

I awaken from strange, unsettling dreams, to a feeling that something doesn't feel right. I rise slowly to my knees, then, one at a time, my feet. I stumble outside.

It is the quiet. Not just the perfectly flat ocean. But...the emptiness. Where is everyone? It is early morning. Dawn is still in her hut. But what of Cole? Shouldn't he still be on fire duty? The fire is low, but still lit. Strange. I get the fire going better, and look around more. But there is nobody there. There is nobody at the log with the gnome scene, or by the dove coop, or at the brook or along the reef or up or down the beach. What's more—and this I see only on passing it for the third time—our store of fruits has been removed. And then there are no dove eggs. And then I go back to the beach again. Andreas is there, looking off in disbelief. And that is when I see it. Or rather don't see it.

The skiff.

The skiff is gone. And Andreas is still here. It comes over me gradually, like a feeling of vertigo. Conrad's last words from the night before. "If anything should happen...I've enjoyed our conversations." And then it all comes together.

Conrad and Cole have left together. Have taken the skiff, have taken whatever food and supplies they could and left.

I look out at the sea, scan in every direction and wonder if I can make them out in the farthest distance. A little mark just below the horizon.

Later I am sitting on the beach with Dawn and Andreas. Just the three of us now. "I hope they die," Andreas says.

"If they die, it's the end for us," I say. "We'll be here forever."

"I still hope they die."

I have to admit it is a pleasing thought, the two of them drifting in the middle of the ocean, arguing about malpractice insurance premiums, slowly baking, running out of food, vanishing into nothing.

"Why did they do it?" Andreas asks. "It was just stupid. I would have had a much better chance."

I think back to how the two had asked Andreas about how sturdy the skiff was. I think back to my conversation with Conrad the night before. "Maybe they thought they'd die here without you. Or maybe they didn't want to give you so much food, so many supplies, like we'd planned. I think Conrad just wanted it to be over. One way or the other."

"Fools," Andreas says.

"Can you imagine the two of them on that tiny boat together," I say.

"They're probably already fighting," Andreas says.

Dawn is shaking her head in disbelief. "I hate him," she says. They are the harshest words I have ever heard her say.

For a long while we look out in disbelief, imagine there is something to be done about it, express our outrage and contempt. But there is nothing to do about it. And we need food. In time we have no choice but to start scavenging, to go on. How strange, though—this sense of their absence. This sense that there are only three of us now. Three of us at our lunch of snails and roots. Three of us at dinner, splitting a small fish among us. Only three to take turns tending the fire. Only three to provide a human presence for one another.

After dinner, Dawn heads to the brook to wash out our utensils. I am alone with Andreas.

"Maybe it's a good thing," Andreas says. "Maybe they'll be rescued. And then they'll send someone to look for us."

"Unless...." I don't finish the thought.

"Unless what?" Andreas asks.

"Unless they are too ashamed of what they have done to send someone after us. Because they don't want anyone to know."

"You mean...they'd just leave us here?"

"Who knows."

"I don't think they would do that," Andreas says.

"I can believe Conrad did this," I say. "But Cole...to his own step-daughter."

"That's just it though," Andreas says.

"What?" I ask.

"*Step*-daughter," he says. "No blood relation. Conrad is his cousin."

"But they always hated each other."

Andreas nods, sighs. "We misunderstood them from the beginning."

"I suppose you are right."

So this is it. We are down to three. And I am the narrow end of the triangle. The lonely end. From here on I will sleep alone. I will be the odd one out. Tribal elder. Dependent on the benevolence of my youngers. Am I ready to die, as Conrad said he was? Not yet. The heart wants to keep beating. That is all. I should have died sixty years ago. In the war. But here I am. Each beat beating. Urging on the next.

The next night Andreas goes to bed early and I have Dawn's company. She is as close to despondent as I have seen her. Monique's death had been terrible. But somehow this is deeper, more unfathomable. "I always wanted to believe in him. Do you know that?" she says.

It is a beautiful, cool evening, just enough breeze to keep the bugs away. The sky is midnight blue.

"Cole?" I ask.

"Yes."

"My mother acted like he was my father. I was so little when she married him. But I always knew underneath. I had some confusing memory. Some other father. Only...."

"Only what?"

"Only I wasn't supposed to say anything. I was supposed to act like he was my father. I was supposed to look up to him."

Suddenly, with Cole no longer there, no longer exerting his presence, she wants to talk about it. About him. This story I have so long wondered about. I nod. She goes on. "When she got sick, she would ask me if I had been good with him, if I had done this or that the way he liked it. And I always had. I was always trying."

"I don't doubt that," I say.

"I'm sorry," Dawn says. "I'm sure this is boring. I don't even know why I am saying it."

"I'm interested," I say. "Tell me."

She apologizes again, protests, at last goes on. "I knew it was what she wanted and I knew she was sick. And I wanted to believe her. I wanted to believe he was this amazing man. But you know what she was really worried about?"

"What?"

"I didn't realize it until...I don't think I realized it until I went to live with him again after boarding school. She was worried about who would take care of me after she died. What would happen to me. And she had no faith in him whatever. And her only hope was that I would be so good to him that he would want me, would want to raise this little girl. Would accept this burden. So she was always telling me how to be around him. What to say and do. How to please him. And when I was little I kept trying. Even that summer I met you."

I think of everything Dawn is saying. And then I think of Cole making off with the skiff, floating somewhere out beyond the horizon. "You know I never actually hated him," I say. "Until now."

Dawn does not even seem to hear me though. She is lost in her story. "I just kept wanting to believe in him. Like I would be disappointing my mother if I gave up on him. So after school I went to stay with him for the summer. I had a friend from school I could have stayed with. But I was still hoping. Maybe right until the day he was caught stealing food. And Monique was pregnant with his child."

"You surprised me," I say. "Speaking out against him."

"That was it. That was the moment I understood. I finally saw him."

"What about your real father?" I ask. "Did you ever try to find him?"

The moon has risen, hovers big and low over the ocean. It is the sand-crab hour. The undead. I watch them rising from their graves. Scuttling across the sand. Pale, insubstantial as ghosts.

"I did," Dawn says. "One summer when I was at school. I tried to track him down."

"And?"

"I found his parents in Chicago. They showed me pictures of him and my mother with me as a little baby. It was strange, because I could see my features in the pictures of him."

"So where was he?" I ask.

"He had some kind of breakdown. I don't know. He wound up in a hospital. And then he became an addict. That's what they said. And moved to Europe. They'd lost touch with him. They were nice. They told me I could stay with them. My grandfather was a mathematics professor. And I guess so was my father, before he fell apart."

"I'm not surprised," I say.

"They had Dutch accents," Dawn says. "I'm half-Dutch, it turns out."

"It's quite a story," I say.

"So am I still a mystery?"

"You are," I say.

"Why?"

"Because I still cannot figure out how all of that produced you."

"Well, let me know when you have it figured out," she says.

It is strangely quiet, unsettling, empty with just three of us. Closer and closer to solitude.

"I will. We'll have a lot of time."

"And someday maybe you can tell me *your* story."

I think about that. Was I not even more private, more secretive than Dawn? Who had I ever shared my story with? I might joke how I killed a duck in the war. Or how we traded my mother's jewelry for a warm meal. But...that one moment. That one that has followed me. That has followed me even here. That left me thinking, over and over, *what is the point of shame.* I had never told that story. Not once. Not ever.

A man in his eighties on a deserted island. Who claims to no longer believe in shame. *What does it matter what people think*, I say to myself. *Let them judge.* And yet...what a fraud you are, Hans!

"I will tell you," I say. "One of these nights."

It is almost fully dark now. The sand-crabs are just the vaguest impressions. Fleeting little wisps.

Have I ever felt closer to this girl? More desirous of her? Just to settle a warm, protective arm over her shoulder. Kiss her hair. My rival asleep in their shelter. Does she not feel even a faint shadow of this connection? Alas, there is no actual contact between us. We observe the rule of touch-move—as in our chess games. We say our good nights.

- Germany -

At last, we were in the American zone. With the good, kind Americans. The Americans! Such young, wholesome faces and clean uniforms! They fed us and helped us to find good shelter. Clothing was donated to us through American charities. We learned, at last, about democracy, freedom of speech, the sanctity of the ballot box and alas, the importance of treating everyone, no matter their race, religion or creed, as equals!

Oh my poor, deluded reader! Did you really believe that stuff I just wrote? I really had you going there, didn't I? O, poor sad, naive reader! So ready to feel proud of that great, noble, American goodness! And that bit about, "the importance of treating everyone as equals?" Your army was *segregated.* Hello? Did you forget? I mean what the fuck—as you Americans say. We were given starvation rations! Do you know what the ration was in the American zone? Nine hundred calories a day! And that was for the "good" Germans. The ones the Americans didn't like...seven hundred and fifty calories per day. Have you tried living on seven hundred and fifty calories per day? And why? Because you were short of food? Not at all. It was to punish us. To punish people like Hilda and myself and our little children. Millions of ordinary German soldiers were shipped off for a year or two to work in labor camps in France and Britain and yes, the United States. Did you know that? Did you ever think that this was...umm...what is that phrase I am looking for? Slave labor?

I'm sure I am not saying this right. What I mean is...if we are all so fucking equal...why was it okay to create massive firestorms that wiped out our cities, that left countless children orphans, never to see their parents again? Do you have any idea how many Hitler-haters you killed, how many anti-Fascists, lovers of Democracy, how many Jews that had gone into hiding, how many five-year-old children, too young to have any politics whatever, too young to be anything other than completely innocent, all of them incinerated in firestorms by the tens of thousands, and all for no military purpose whatever? Were the babies also guilty because they were German?

Sorry. Sorry sorry sorry. You were way better than the Russians. And look. Way way better than us. There. I said it. Is that better? Plus in the end it all kind of worked out. We both agreed to hate the Soviets. We drank to it, became friends, allies. And then of course there was the Berlin airlift. We mustn't forget the Berlin airlift. Because suddenly, once the Soviets started starving us, instead of you starving us, it became extremely important to rush food to us. So we wouldn't starve.

So let's let bygones be bygones, as they say. No?

Because after all, as I have said, I have no politics, personally. There is nothing that I believe. Let them all kill one another. What does it matter? Okay maybe that's not true either. Maybe that's actually a pile of crap. Or let's just call it a narrative convenience. A trope. At least it has gotten me this far. What I really mean, of course, is just that political beliefs imply hope and hope is futile. Because why should God, even if we accept His existence, care whether we are good or not? Why would He give a crap? If He wanted us to be good, wouldn't He have made us good? He could have given us free will, but still tilted us slightly more toward good and away from bad. Right? It makes no freaking sense. And it makes no sense for me to care either, whether people are good or bad. Why should I care? They can all kill each other. I will be gone soon anyway after all, and I am stuck on this sandy spit in the Sea of Limbo. So who gives a crap if mankind is good or bad or destroys itself in twenty years or is destroyed by an asteroid in twenty thousand? What does it signify? This tiny speck of a planet among trillions in some vast universe. What does it matter?

- X -

My curriculum vitae:

Hans Jaeger.

Retired Refrigerator Salesman. World War II German *Landser,* winner of the Iron Cross, second class.

Previous Work Experience: Musical instrument manufacture and repair. Human Organ Dealer. Dove farmer.

Additional Areas Of Expertise: Diving for cover.

Core competencies: Chewing soft foods, peeing, crapping.

Hobbies: Masturbation.

- Germany -

The rest of my story.

Before Dawn. My pre-Dawn hours.

By the way, have I used that play on Dawn's name enough yet? Personally, I don't think so. Actually, just to let you know, I plan to continue to use it, possibly many more times, in fact as often as possible. I'm eighty-six. Can I not do as I please?

Speaking of my years, I am thinking I better speed this up. One never knows. I may wake up dead tomorrow. And wouldn't that be ironic, if I die of natural causes, after all of the unnatural deaths I somehow escaped? I think I'll have to use that. Although, not sure how I will write about my death. Maybe I'll just imply it. We shall see when we get there. Or here's an even better idea. I could have mankind wiped out from an asteroid impact at the end. But...you would know that didn't really happen. Because how could you be reading about it? Okay, bad idea. I'll just die of natural causes. What would you prefer? Kidney failure after all? Which kidney then? My own? Or the one that had belonged to the Madeira, my kidney-less Brazilian protector, my princess of peace? Or maybe not kidney failure at all? Heart disease? The big C?

As I said... the rest of my story.

At last we were in the American zone. But aside from that one fact, everything seemed wrong. There was no more Georg. And without Georg, Hilda had no direction. And without her direction, I had little of my own. So we just wandered, for no particular reason, and with no destination. Berlin proper was just a half-day walk away, but we'd run out of food, and we'd heard the city was in ruins, so we started looking for work where we were. We went to a farm looking for food, and wound up working there for a meal, and then another, then they took us in. There was no money exchanged because there was no currency worth paying in. The Reichsmark, along with everything Reich, was dead. The Deutschemark had not yet been issued. We were paid in potatoes and barley and milk. We slept in a barn behind the house. In the winter, when there was no work in the fields, we helped repair the farmhouse. There was no heat in our barn, and no coal to be found even if there were a stove to burn it in. A little wooden separator kept us away from the animals—cows and pigs—but could not keep away the smell, the flies, the tramping of hooves and sudden nighttime lowing that woke us sometimes with the urgency of a train whistle.

What can I say about that time? We were always hungry. That is what I remember. Never having enough food. All of that year. And then in the miserable winter of 1946 to 1947 we were always cold. Frozen. And somehow we had gotten stuck. What had happened to our dreams of fleeing this wasteland? They had faded with the death of Georg. And what was left of them vanished amid the airless chill of that shed. The day to day drudgery. We got lice from sleeping with the hay and the cows and had to wash our hair out with kerosene to get rid of them.

Most of all, through all of it, was that one overwhelming need that must be satisfied—that need to eat. It seemed to fill every bit of consciousness. It turned us into mindless animals. We slept beside them, and we had become them. We ceased to imagine the future any more than a starving wolf imagines the future. There was just the day. The frozen night. The next day. The plate of potatoes. The bowl of soup. The crust of bread. Night again. Perhaps a few gasps of sexual union, under a pile of old blankets. Then sleep. Fighting the drafts of cold that came in through the cracks in the door. Through the cracks in the walls. Through the walls themselves, the blankets themselves. Awakening to icy morning. To not enough to eat.

The change in Hilda was there in everything she did. It was hard to even see in her the warm and vivacious soul, the same gregarious person who had once been both my mother's confidante and my own. Maybe there was just less to talk about. Maybe we were too tired and cold and hungry to talk.

And then there was that one fact. Georg had been shot in the face. She had seen it happen. We never spoke of it. But how many times every day, I wondered, did she relive that image? Even if she found a reason to smile and laugh, I sometimes saw how instantly her happy mood vanished, as though she remembered that no, she was not supposed to be happy. She was a mother who had left her child behind. How dare she be happy. Because wasn't that still tugging her, even if unconsciously? Keeping her back? That Georg was there in that churchyard. That she mustn't want to be too far from him.

The couple we rented from blamed all of Germany's hardships on the Jews. We assumed they'd been Nazis, although we never asked— and nobody would admit to it now anyway. It startled me to hear them —even after we all learned of the camps, learned that the truth was even more horrible than the rumors. Or perhaps it was because of the camps. Because now here they were, this old couple, defeated and miserable, full of their own problems. And now the world was judging them too. And wasn't it all because of...you see? Hitler had been right! They were vermin. At least my mother had admitted her mistake. This couple refused to. Clung to their delusions.

True, the posters denouncing Jews, the anti-Semitic laws, the enforced hatred were all gone. But you still overheard it. Under people's breath. *They got what they deserved.* Because was it not even more important, even more essential, now, to hate the Jews? To think that surely they deserved what they got? Surely they *must* have done something. Because if not...then...then we murdered millions of innocent people over nothing? Over something we just imagined, dreamed up out of thin air? A delusion? That couldn't be! We are a civilized people! They must have...done *something.* And now they are playing the innocent victim! Trying to deny it! You see? You see how duplicitous they are?

"I am so tired of hearing about *their* suffering," our landlord had said. "Haven't we suffered? Haven't we all suffered?" That was the other side of it. The incomparable suffering of the Jews. Wasn't that itself a brand new reason to hate? To resent? Must we always be reminded only of *their* suffering? Must it be so infinitely superior to our own? Are we not, in the end, allowed even our last refuge—self-pity?

"What's wrong with these people?" Hilda said.

But what answer was there? I just shook my head.

We were all required to fill out questionnaires provided by the Americans as part of their de-Nazification program. The questions were designed to determine who had Nazi sympathies and who could be trusted. Any misrepresentations, we were assured, could result in imprisonment. Had I volunteered for military service? Did I have any close relations who were Nazis or Nazi sympathizers? Had I attended Nazi rallies? What was my highest rank in the military? What was the nature of my service? And so on.

I lied about whether I'd had close relations who were sympathizers, assuming that the lie could not be easily disproved, since I had come from the Russian zone. But for a while it filled me with anxiety. What if they discovered that I'd lied?

One night we heard a commotion and went out to find a band of people, two or three families together, had showed up at the farm looking for food. They had nothing to trade. They were trying to force their way into the house. My landlord saw me and called to me to help chase them off, and soon I had joined him and we had succeeded in driving them away. Only afterward I felt ill over it. I saw their children in memory. How hungry, how desperate must these people have been to go out wandering in the night like that? And I had chased them. And on behalf of whom? This man we could hardly bear the sight of.

"We have to do something," I told Hilda.

"I know," she said.

"This isn't living."

"I know," she said again.

The frozen fields of winter had at last turned to mud. It had become clear that I would not be shipped off to a prison camp. So I sold most of my mother's jewelry and packed up our few clothes and headed the last short distance to Berlin. The city was half destroyed and overwhelmed with refugees. We spent three days searching for a room to let and sleeping at the train station. At last we found a single room in a building that had a ladder at its entrance in place of its bombed out front staircase.

Hilda attempted to start a business scavenging old clothes and cleaning and fixing them and trading them. I found little vestiges of the Berlin music scene around the old symphony hall, which was still standing. Remarkably, the Berlin orchestra was being reconstituted with the support of the Americans. I put up my own signs offering to repair musical instruments. I gathered brass scraps from junk heaps, purchased a few of the most basic tools, found an abrasive sponge for polishing, and attempted to start a business, not knowing at all what to expect. But nobody came.

I wound up looking for work as a day-laborer, working for the Americans, helping demolish destroyed buildings, running this way and that, piling the materials into stacks—bricks, piping, wooden beams. The city was still mostly in ruins. Nobody had nearly enough heat or enough food. We received our nine hundred calories a day in rations. We had hardly any clothes. No mattress. No furniture. We slept on the floor, on top of our few clothes, and used a pile of rags that Hilda had collected for our pillows. Outside, the whole city looked like we felt.

Cold and hungry and exhausted.

And then one evening, when I had practically forgotten about the business I had wanted to start, someone actually brought me an instrument to be fixed. A frail old man with an oboe. What a remarkable feeling that was. Looking up into the eyes of that very first customer. Someone was thinking about something besides food! Life —not just existence, but actual life, civilization, was trying to awaken! I showed the oboe to Hilda, played a few notes once I had it playable. "You see this?"

"Yes."

"This means we're not dead." She looked at me strangely. I went on. "Someone wants to play this again. To make music. We're alive."

She cried.

Gradually, more customers started arriving and I bought more tools, tinkered in the evening and stacked bricks during the day. Word of me got around. I found someone who could fix violins and cellos, which had started arriving, and someone else who could go out to apartments to fix pianos.

There was still no currency worth saving so we were mostly paid in barter. But we had a few clothes, and had started to eat better. Not well, but more bearably. I had the first grapefruit I had tasted in years. We had a bit of coffee and bread and a very occasional piece of sausage. And in time I was busy enough to leave my day-labor jobs behind.

In the fall there were signs around the old symphony hall for a Beethoven concert.

"We should go see it," I told Hilda.

"What does it cost?"

"I don't know. But...you will hear some of the instruments I repaired. I will have played a little hand in it."

"We should buy a mattress. Plates. A pot."

"It's Beethoven. My father used to play his music on the record player. I've always wondered what it really sounded like."

What I didn't tell Hilda about was my other memory—listening to Beethoven with Sylvia that day we slipped into my house together, how captivated she had been, how I had promised to take her to a symphony someday. Was this not part of the urgency I felt? Was I not attempting to fulfill, in some limited way, that dream we had had?

"We can't afford it. We need what we have to live."

"This is part of living," I said. And then, "Please. Just this once. This was the orchestra on the records we listened to. The Berlin Philharmonic. And now we're actually here!"

With that, she didn't resist any further, and somehow we managed to come up with the money for it.

When the night of the concert arrived, we dressed as best we could, which was shamefully shabby, and bought tickets at the box office and went inside.

The concert hall was lit, but there was still no heat in it, and it was cold enough inside that you could see your breath. Everyone, the players and the public, wore coats. The audience was a mixture of American officers, German civilians, even some American soldiers with German girlfriends—these mixed couples no longer hiding their affections as they had at the beginning of the occupation.

For a while the Americans had had a policy of no consorting with the enemy. Posters went up with the English words *No Frat,* which, I learned, was short for, *No fraternizing.* We Germans were being punished, after all. It was not a party. But this American rule had proved impractical. There are times, situations in which young men and young women will be drawn toward one another by nature itself—and no mere language barrier or army regulation will keep them apart. And as the rage toward the Germans—pitiful as we were now—had started to subside, so the rule against fraternizing had been relaxed, and then gradually abandoned. Here, in the concert hall, was the result.

I couldn't help noticing how proud some of these German girls seemed beside their American men—healthy, victorious young men who had all their limbs intact. Who knew how to fight. Unlike us lowly Germans. And, moreover, who had so many treasures to offer their *Fräulein*—chocolates, peanut butter, ham. Do I dare admit how much I envied these men? Not just for their status as conquerors, for their swagger and confidence—but also for the pretty young women on their arms? Yes, Hilda and I had our bond still. Yes, I was extremely lucky compared to so many German men. I was alive after all. My injury had healed. I had even been spared a labor camp. But who really dwells on being thankful for what one has? The human mind is an organ of discontent.

And when I thought about it…where had my youth gone? Why had I never had a chance to love a pretty young woman? Two nights with Sylvia, so many years ago, in another world. This had been the extent of my youthful romantic experience. How had I, who had fought for six years to defend the Fatherland, suddenly become inferior, in the eyes of these girls, to the once-despised enemy? And was it really possible not to blame Hilda in some way for my plight as well? Hilda who seldom smiled anymore? Who…who had chosen me when she was so many years older than me? Yes. There. I had admitted it to myself.

As the maestro came out and the lights dimmed, all of these thoughts faded—disappeared into the darkness, along with the images of the pretty girls themselves. I took Hilda's hand and turned thoughts toward wondering what a live symphony might sound like. Applause. Silence. And then the music started. Beethoven's Sixth Symphony. Instantly, this was nothing at all like what I had heard over the gramophone. Now it sounded so full and alive, so real, just the opening strains took my breath away.

In all my years of tinkering with instruments, of playing the clarinet, I had never heard a symphony but in a distorted little sliver of sound that whistled over the radio, or crackled from the needle of the record player. I thought to myself, *so this is what real music sounds like*! This is what all of those instruments are for! The melodies were all familiar, distantly, but it was still as though I was hearing it all, what it really sounded like, for the first time.

This is it, Sylvia! Can you hear this? Can you believe it? This is what I dreamed of taking you to. And now here we are!

Unlike most of the Beethoven I had heard, there was nothing triumphant or heroic in this piece. No doubt the conductor had wanted to avoid anything that could seem military. Only, was it possible something could sound so purely beautiful? That a human could create something so beautiful? And so happy? What was it like to feel as happy, as carefree, as that opening movement sounded? To feel the calm of the second? How could these sounds even coexist in the same world in which I had been living? How could the same species that had given us the camps, have created this?

It swirled inside me, and I felt my heart filled with a kind of hope and at the same time an unbearable sadness. Because how long had it been that life had been nothing but bleakness? When was the last time I had seen or heard or known something beautiful? Something that existed purely for the sake of its beauty? And because—of course—*she should have been there*! Next to me. Sharing it. Like I had promised. Just to have shared that one hour with her, to have been granted some magical, hour-long reprieve, just so she could have heard it!

The thunderstorm movement was both frightening (I had grown jittery at sudden noises, but at least I avoided diving under my seat!) and thrilling. And at last it seemed extraordinary that something frightening and dramatic could also be beautiful, pleasurable. Or was that part of why it was pleasure? Because you knew it was only a piece of music, because it had been tamed, elevated into something melodic and magical.

The storm soon subsided, the sun came out, and soon we were in the joyous finale. The last movement, the celebration after the storm, was surely, in this dark and cold building in this dark and cold city, about the rebirth of life itself after so much death. Listening to it, I felt I understood why the conductor had chosen this piece of music—specifically for this glorious last movement. Calm after the storm. Peace after war. And there was something else in it too—in all great music perhaps, but especially in this music, at this moment—that message of one's common humanity, not just one's bond with the one who could create this, but with the rest of humanity that could understand it, who knew its language without having to be taught it, who were born with that understanding, those feelings of sadness and happiness and the capacity to love.

If those customers of mine taught us that we were still alive, then this, this night, seemed to say that it mattered. It mattered that we were alive. We still had beating hearts. We still wanted and ached. And then another thought came over me in a way the was overwhelming. Why? Why did we have to do this? Why did we have to kill so many millions of people to prove some demented idea about our race? Wasn't this enough? Wasn't it enough just to have produced one Beethoven?

And then, as the music hurried toward its end, at last, I thought of my own father. How he would have felt, had he been here with me. How he too never had a chance. I squeezed Hilda's hand, tried to communicate some message to her.

At last the lights came on. The audience rose, exhaling steam, and applauded. The spell— ever-so-slowly—lost its grip, ebbed away like the wearing off of a soothing narcotic.

"You liked it?" I asked Hilda.

"It made me think of your father."

"Me, too."

On the surface the concert had drawn Hilda and me closer. We had gone home full of conversation, felt a mutual passion, excitement at the evening, had made love. But perhaps Hilda saw into some of my less than faithful thoughts.

The next morning she seemed morose. "I'm keeping you back," she said at last.

"From what?"

"From…from starting your own life."

"No," I said.

"I've felt it lately. I felt it during the concert."

"Not at all," I said. "I felt the music pulling us together."

"Yes. I felt that too. But I also felt the opposite."

"What do you mean?" I asked, though I knew exactly what she meant.

"I mean...like you were swept up in something, and I was left behind. I don't want that. I don't want to keep you back."

"You're not keeping me back."

"I don't want to lose you," she said. "But...you must sometimes wish you were free. Or wish...I were younger. Or...that you were with someone younger."

"No," I said. "That's not how I feel. We have each other." I felt a lump in my throat as I spoke though.

"But...you are young enough to start over. I'm not. I just want you to know...if you want to go, you should go."

Yes, at times I had thought of it. Only at that moment, what I truly wanted was to make her feel better. "I'm here with you," I said. "That's what I want."

"Do you love me? Tell me the truth."

"Of course," I said.

Is it ever really that simple though? In my more private thoughts, I wasn't quite so sure. What I really thought was how much I cared about her, admired her, how at times I had grown tired of her, how at other times I loved her, didn't want to hurt her, how completely alone I would be without her and how even more alone she would be if I were to leave her. And...how my youth had been stolen. And how pretty those girls had been the night before. And how much I despised them and longed for them. And how I envied their American boyfriends. The conquerors. And a hundred more thoughts like that. All spinning around.

We spoke no more of it that day. But later in the afternoon I checked again with the Red Cross, as I had done several times over the last year. Imagining some word from Sylvia.

A black market had sprouted up at the train station—row upon row of racks and shelves and hawkers bartering clothes and supplies. I would go there to look for basics we needed to get by, or sometimes, when there was no repair work to be done, just to walk around and take in all the busy activity. To get out. One afternoon I was just leaving the station when a figure came toward me.

"Hans? Is that you?"

She looked familiar. But it took me a while to place the voice, the face—so much older than when I had last seen it. "Alika?"

"You recognize me. I'm impressed."

The Herman Hesse reader. From the bicycle trip. I had seen her in school after the trip, but had not stayed friends with her. She was gaunt and weak-looking now, her hair scraggly and her clothing nothing but rags—real rags in place of the simple, unkempt look that had once been a matter of style for her. "Yes, sure I recognize you," I said. "I'm surprised you recognize *me*."

"You're alive!" she said.

"Yes, I know," I said. "People keep reminding me of that."

We sat down for a while and talked. I told her a bit of my war experience. "You look thin," I said.

She told me she had been living with her mother when they both were arrested for anti-Fascist activities.

"What were you doing?" I asked. "Why did they arrest you?"

She had the same voice. But if it had had a trace of affectation years earlier, now that was gone. Replaced by something immediate and direct. She sat close to me. "We were given away."

"By who?"

"Remember Klampf? The teacher who was arrested?"

"Our trip leader?"

"Yes."

I couldn't quite believe it. "He exposed you?"

"He was tortured."

"How do you know this?"

"I don't. But he's the only one I confided in. And I know he was tortured."

"That's horrible."

"He's dead now."

"But…you were young. What was there to confide?"

"It was after the trip. I looked up to him. I went to him not long before he was arrested."

I remembered that time I saw them—Alika and Klampf—alone together by that waterfall outside Salzburg. That absurd accusation I had made. How particularly childish and imbecilic it seemed now. "I think I misjudged you," I said. "Not that it matters now."

She brushed it off.

"Are you hungry?" I asked.

"I'm staying at my aunt's. They have enough to feed me. We have the better coupons. Because I was in a camp. I'm getting a little weight back."

Soon we were reminiscing about school and Edelburg and our bicycle trip. Whereas she used to wander off to meditate, kept her distance, now she had the somewhat opposite habit of sitting just slightly too close. But we talked for a long while. An hour later I still didn't want the conversation to end, so I made a plan to have her to dinner at our place.

Two nights later we had little party, myself and Hilda and Alika and my assistants in my business, the six of us crowded into our little room. We sat on heaps of blankets, on cinder blocks covered with quilts. Everyone brought a bit of food and Hilda had managed to trade a dress she had made for a chicken and a bottle of wine at a corner market.

We talked about changes in the city, where there were still piles of rubble and what had been cleared, about the Americans, about who had survived and who hadn't, not just among our relations but among the former elite, this famous writer, this well-known actor, that opposition politician.

Our musical guests picked up a couple of woodwinds and started improvising a bit of jazz. And I started a side conversation with Alika.

"You mentioned you were arrested with your mother."

"Yes," she said.

"What happened to her?"

"She didn't make it out. She died."

"What happened?"

Alika looked away and then back. "Do you really want to know?"

"Yes."

"I'm...not sure you do."

"It's okay," I said. "I've seen a lot. Not much can shock me."

"She gave me all her food. In the camp. She kept saying she wasn't hungry. Pretending. And she let herself starve. So I could eat."

"That's horrible."

"Yes it is."

"Awful."

"More than you know."

I sensed Hilda and the other guests glancing at us, but went on. "What do you mean?"

She seemed frustrated suddenly. "You don't understand."

"What?"

"I haven't told you the horrible part. I mean..."

"What?" I asked.

"Nothing. Let's drop it."

"What?" I asked again.

"I mean...there's nothing more. It's just...you don't understand. And I'm not sure I want you to."

I left it at that, at least for that night. There was something else I had been thinking, had wanted to ask her about.

"Do you remember Sylvia from the trip?"

"Sure," she said. Now she managed a faint smile. "You liked her, didn't you?"

I nodded. "I did. Was it that obvious?"

"Only to all the people on the trip, and the squirrels, and the trees. Oh, and the rocks."

I smiled.

"She was a nice girl though," Alika said.

"Do you know she disappeared on *Kristallnacht*?"

"I think I remember hearing a rumor about that. I never knew if it was true. What happened to her?"

"I have no idea. I never saw her again. I was just wondering. Do you think Klampf could have denounced her too?"

She shook her head. "It's possible."

"I just...would love to understand what happened. Why they chose her."

"It's...it's possible," Alika said at last. "People can be made to say anything. I don't blame him."

So perhaps that was it. So perhaps my mother had been telling the truth all along. It made me long to reach out to her. To reach a peace with her. (I fear I am dangerously close to employing that repellent cliché about just wanting resolution. What fucking difference would it really have made? I have no idea. Something about closure. Only my letters went unanswered. And so a debate with my mother would go on in my mind for many years. A cross-examination. A verdict at once triumphant and merciful. A longing just to know.)

The musicians played another tune, and now Hilda joined us.

"Alika was a big Hermann Hesse reader," I said, looking for a way to include Hilda.

"That's right! I forgot that," Alika said.

"It seemed very mature when we were high school," I said. "I was very impressed."

"Do you still like to read?" Hilda asked.

"I haven't," Alika said. "I would like to again. Someday. I'm not sure I could focus on it now."

"I was so unfair to you back then," I said, think of the absurd things I had said to her.

"Sounds like there's a good story," Hilda said.

"Only if you both want to embarrass me," I said.

"It's okay," Alika said. "You were fine. We were kids."

"Well, I was not always a very mature kid."

She looked at me dryly. "I've been treated worse."

"I suppose," I said.

The musicians finished their piece, and there was applause and laughter as they bowed with a little flourish. We called out another tune, and they stumbled into the next number. I turned back to Alika. "So what are you going to do?" I asked.

"I want to get to America. I've heard of a place called Iowa."

"Hilda wants to go to Iowa."

"I do," Hilda said. "But I'm not sure why. I don't know anything about it."

"I don't either. But my aunt lives there."

She talked about a place was called Amana that had been founded by Germans as a kind of experimental community. Everyone worked together, raised their families together, believed in community. Not the *Volk* and *Volkssturm* and *Hitlerjugend* in which we had all been indoctrinated. But, so Alika described it—real community. Helping one another. Elevating oneself through...well, I will not attempt to reproduce Alika's way of putting things. But it was good to see that she had not changed entirely.

We said our goodnights that night, Hilda and I standing at the apartment door like actual party hosts offering actual well-wishes. We went to bed feeling animated by the party, the conversation, the meal. We talked about the place Alika had described in Iowa, and we had her over again soon after, and this time we talked about it more seriously. "But how will you get through immigration?" Hilda asked.

"I wrote to a family through a connection of my aunt's, and they're willing to sponsor me."

"So you're going?"

"I haven't decided."

Alika was looking a little better already, not as frail. Something about her way of speaking and thinking, her independence of mind, impressed Hilda. Afterward, Hilda and I talked about it.

"What do you think?" I asked.

"Utopia sounds good to me," she said.

"It has to be better than hell," I said.

"Maybe the same family could sponsor us too."

"Are you sure you want to do this?" I asked.

"Germany is done," Hilda declared.

I thought about this. "Forever?" I asked.

"Forever," Hilda said emphatically.

And so we decided on a continent, a destination. We were off to the mountains of Iowa. Because Germany had no future. So were the great moments in one's life decided.

Getting sponsored was not easy, but Alika's aunt evidently had the wherewithal to write to her senator, and some weeks later we heard back that it had been arranged.

Before we could leave, I needed to make a promised side-trip to Düsseldorf, to see Slonimsky and return him his pictures. I brought Hilda along on this little detour. There weren't many Slonimskys in Düsseldorf, so he was easy to track down.

Hilda and I arrived by train. On the way she asked more about my war experiences, and I told her what I could bring myself to talk about —some of the early parts in North Africa. She asked about my friend, wanted to make a good impression, but I stumbled for anything to say. I barely knew him. That was the truth.

Slonimsky lived with his wife and son in a modern-era, brick row house that had survived the war. We embraced at the front door, sat down politely in a small living room with him and his wife, tried to rally up stories of our last days of the war.

"Let's drink to our victory!" he said. He took out a bottle of bootleg whiskey and we toasted.

"Our *inevitable* victory," I added.

His wife was pregnant with their second child, and seemed worn and physically uncomfortable. Hilda made small-talk with her about children, watched their little boy running around, pretending to be a Banshee. The American Western, along with so many other bits of Americana, was making its way into Germany, right behind the American GIs.

"How's everything going?" I asked Slonimsky.

He was a smart man, had wanted to study chemistry, but he was working as a car mechanic.

"It's going," Slonimsky said. "We're eating."

"That's a start," I said.

"He didn't recognize me," Slonimsky said, nodding to his son.

"Didn't recognize you?"

"When I got home. He had no idea who I was. I looked pretty scary, I'm sure. He ran away crying when I tried to reach for him."

"And now?"

"I bring him treats. His mother keeps trying to get him to do things with me. Keeps saying, 'This is your father, Helge.'"

"And?"

"And he's still a little afraid. Maybe in time."

"A lot of changes for a little boy."

"Yes."

"You never told me you had a lady," he said, nodding toward Hilda.

"An old family friend," I said. "We're together now. Heading to the U.S."

"Good for you."

Hilda knelt down and played with their little boy.

"I brought your card deck back!" I said. "I told you I would."

He smiled.

"They're a little worn and yellowed."

"Ah. They got a lot of use then?"

I laughed. *"Kein Kommentar."* No comment.

I flipped through the deck. "I don't think she would approve," he said, nodding toward his wife. "Still, they make a good memento of the war. Better than some pointless medal. Don't you think?"

I looked over at Hilda playing with Slonimsky's little boy and had a distant flashback of her on her knees playing with me when I was very young. And when she herself was so young!

Slonimsky's wife offered us tea, but when we declined she started folding laundry. We couldn't help feeling in the way. Slonimsky and I struggled a bit more for conversation topics. We had never had to make conversation before. Everything had always been about the immediate. We stayed an hour, and then Hilda and I were looking at one another and saying our goodbyes.

"Well, good luck," Slonimsky said. "Come visit when you get rich."

"And if I don't get rich?"

"I thought everyone gets rich over in America," he said. "And if you don't get rich...well then our friendship is over."

We laughed. At last, once we were all standing, we remembered our remarkable meeting in the rectory, after I had been accused of being a defeatist. Of his letting me escape. This, finally, made for a good story, and Hilda and his wife both laughed, established a warmness, making the goodbyes easier.

"You know," I said, "I really should renew my offer to punch you before I leave."

"Alas, once again I would have to decline," he said. "But thank you just the same."

- Pacific Ocean -

At first the voyage has its pleasures. The weather is calm. The boat sways gently. Ice tinkles in our drinks. Dolphins gallop gamely alongside us. Far in the distance, we see whales breeching. The water flying up, here and again, like a series of far-away fountains, like a game of connect the dots.

We anchor outside luxury resorts with names like *Xandara* and *Zaliq* (which, so says a sign in the lobby, is the Samoan word for *paradise*.) And then we make our way further out into the ocean. That great leap of faith—pointing out toward nothing, toward the horizon, pure and blue and sweetly feminine. Yes, the boat itself is "she" to the lovesick yachtsman. But is not the ocean itself the ultimate *she*? The vast, all-consuming mother, mother sea, the womb from whence we all came?

Monique sunbathes nude on the deck. Conrad sets up fishing rods trawling behind us. Gloria and Andreas, the underclass, work away below. In the evening there is karaoke night. Flashlight tag. Billiards (because what would a yacht be without a billiard table?) And there is poker. Cards turning over like a flashing of private flesh. Piles of chips before the players. Cole and Conrad playing late into the night. Cole's stack rising and falling, according to his condition. Conrad opposite. Rising and falling in inverse. Locked in male battle.

And then, off in the distance, there they are. Chain of deserted atolls. We swim in turquoise coves. Cole skinny-dips, splashes merrily, pecker flopping, flaunting, alpha status phallus. Monique and Cole exchanging furtive glances. Monique Oblique. And when we are all cooled and contented, Andreas is allowed his dip in the water. Gloria wading, waddling in her one-piece. How immediate and strange it is

among such a small group—this notion of privilege. Of class. Because
somehow, in the everyday world of millions and billions of souls, we
take it for granted. But how strange, how perverse, when there are but
seven of us in a watery wilderness, that there are those who serve and
those who are served.

Cole though is in his element—captain, benefactor, conquistador—
opening a bottle of champagne, resting an impressively casual hand on
Monique's shoulder, explaining to her the finer details of all of his on-
board gadgetry. Dawn, meanwhile, spending long hours apart from us.
Helping in the kitchen. Reading.

One afternoon I find myself out on the deck with Dawn. Water
splashing below us. Wind in our hair.

"Are you okay?"

"Yes."

"So where did you live before you came to the island?" I ask.
"Who did you live with? If not Cole?"

"I'd rather not talk about it. I'm sorry."

How little I know of her, after all of our chess games. I try to
imagine what she thinks of Cole and Monique. I watch her watching
them.

The next day I am scuba diving with Dawn along an empty island.
Drifting through a coral sculpture-garden, through vast schools of little
fish, shimmering bright as newly minted coins. Each of us pointing this
way and that. Motioning to one another. Exploring. A row of squid
passes in front of us, single file, in perfect unison like a ballet. Eyes
appearing beneath us in the sand. A ray. Basking. Camouflaged.
Invisible but for the eyes. And no sound at all except our own
breathing. In and out. *Shhhhhhh. Shhhhhh.* Bubbles rising by the
thousands. Sea fans flapping in the current. Angel fish suspended in
place, zebra-striped, perfectly elegant wedges, as though designed not
by the rigors of evolution but by the demands of excessive vanity.
Dawn herself motoring past, chimera of oxygen tanks and breathing
tubes and streaming blonde hair.

And then swimming back to shore with her. Water four feet deep.
Rippled sand bottom. That silvery play of light along the surface. The
crystal water roiling with sand, fine as smoke, when a little wave passed
overhead.

And then how startling! What was that? Something big. Fixed.
Dawn coming up beside me in her wet suit. And both of us pausing.
Looking. There. Standing in the sand. Human legs. Human feet.
Bottom halves of two humans, cut off like the legs of a pair of sunken
statues. Yet the legs themselves alive. Familiar. Even recognizable.

Cole and Monique. Toes touching. Entangled. How very startling. This other world. Spied upon. Proof of something dark and secret, some ancient, subterranean connection. And how strange, that Dawn and I would share this discovery in our present situation, unable to say anything to one another about it even if we had wanted to. And so just looking, observing, moving on. As though we had seen nothing remarkable at all. Just life. That hidden life that is there, always, beneath the surface.

Andreas picking us up in the skiff. Taking us out a half-mile from our cove, back out to the yacht. And that evening, as the atoll itself recedes away to the horizon, the weather turning. The waves building. That feeling of becoming aware of something, something ominous, that is already before you. Aware not of its arriving, but of something already there, upon us, a darkness, not of evening but of overcast. The bits of distant islands in the distance disappearing one by one behind a darkening gray. Far-away veil of rain. And now the wind building. Ruffing the water. The ropes and canvas flapping. Out on the deck, the *Vogue* magazine flipping through its pages on its own, as though read by a ghost. Or no. As though all of our existence, all of our past life, our world of luxury and vanity, were flashing before us in the very last moments in which we would be in that world.

Cole looking at Monique. A sign. Heading inside. And then a moment later Monique following. The delay calculated. Did they not sense the coming storm? Did they assume it would be just a passing squall? Did the danger excite them in some way? Inspire them? Andreas lifting anchor. Starting the engines. Turning the boat into the wind.

Roll of thunder. Prow rising high and falling. Deck of cards flying up into the wind and scattering. And then a few fat droplets smacking us.

"Shouldn't we get inside?"

"Yes. In a minute," Dawn says. "I like seeing the ocean all churned up."

And so standing there with her. Watching the raindrops pelt her. How alone she seemed. Or did she want it that way, want to feel that way? Standing there in the rain. Yes, I still had no idea who she was. And yet the sense of her standing there is so strong, has scarcely changed since the first time I met her. Except for this. She is motherless. Belonging to nobody. To the sea alone.

The image doesn't last. Can't, really. The rain picking up suddenly. Sweeping over us in a sheet. Thunder rumbling closer, louder, lightning illuminating a sudden tableau, tempest over the ocean, back-lit like some romantic painting.

Dawn starting to move, pausing, trying to balance. And then what was that? Brilliant flash. Explosion. All of us thrown. For just an instant, a glance—or was it a dream?—inside that dark room where Cole and Monique had gone. Their shapes, wrapped together. Lit up. Copulating. Wasn't that what it was? Lightning flash. Nightmarish. And that...glimpse...or...was it even real? Imagined? That Halloween light. Orange like they should have been something else. Skeletons. Demons. And then dark again. Screams. *Fire!* Andreas shouting. Smoke coming up from somewhere. Black and acrid. Everything happening at once now. Smoke and wind and downpour and screams. And something else. Something stopping. The vibration. The hum.

"We're stalled!"

Eerie. Like something had died. A minute just to figure out what had happened. Struck by lightning. Engines dying. Heartbeat stopped. Just the storm now. Drifting. Billowing smoke.

Sparks. Flames. Andreas yelling. "Everybody out." Banging doors. Life jackets. Survival pack. There. Broadside to the waves. Rolling. Helplessly rolling. Cole on deck now. Shouting into the radio. *Mayday.* Conrad and Andreas fighting the fire. Monique coming out arms full of clothes. And in the next flash of lightning we could see something else—a line of white-water. Waves crashing. What was it? The reef. And then a shoreline. Far away still. But approaching. What do we do? Moving toward us. The air full of spray. No way to know what was rain coming down and what was ocean flying up. All of it just water. Water and wind and smoke and shouting and now the reef coming toward us.

And then, somehow, we have all made it into the lifeboat. The skiff. And we have pushed off from the yacht. And we are paddling.

But here is the miracle—what saves us from all getting torn apart in the coral. Because it is right there in front of us. And somehow, at the last moment, the skiff seems to lift, glides over the reef, borne by a great steed of a wave. We scream, hold on, are settled down almost gently, into the calmer waters inside the reef. We look back and see the yacht aflame, raking against the reef, boiling down into the sea.

And then we are shivering in the sand. Looking out at the line of white in the distance, where the waves are crashing. The yacht almost gone. Where were we?

- United States -

At last, many months after Alika's aunt first contacted her senator, and four months after we first started writing to the consulate, our visas cleared. Hilda and Alika and I packed up our belongings and followed the corridor out of Berlin to the British zone. From there we boarded a train to Hamburg. And from Hamburg we said goodbye to Germany and took a ship across the Atlantic.

For a long, grueling week, we cut endlessly through the waves. There are surely many accounts of such crossings—the cramped quarters, the squalor and seasickness and anxiety and hope. There is no need for another such account. As to the seasickness, in our own instance, Hilda got it the worst. She turned white as a ghost, was unable to hold down any food at all. Alika made friends with an elderly couple headed for Wisconsin and discovered they had some distant relations in common. And she wrote in a journal she kept. I spent long hours looking out over the sea, which of course I had never seen except in glimpses at the Mediterranean from an seaplane. Nothing in the paintings, still photographs, black-and-white newsreels, can prepare one for the endless tossing, the view that is always forever, always out to the horizon, always alive, moving, pulling your eyes every which way. Is there any other view that one can look at for so long, without growing tired of it? How good it felt, how exciting, not just to be moving, retreating, advancing, but to feel the sea moving all around you.

It was sunny and calm the morning we approached New York, and the blue sky made a perfect backdrop for its triumphal appearance. Not merely intact, undamaged—unlike any city we had seen in years—but reaching proudly upward into the sky. There is one little detail I still remember. As we drew closer a little wisp of low cloud actually crossed

the top of the Empire State Building—its spire piercing the cloud like a
Cupid arrow.

The seat of our conquerors. The new empire.

We checked in to the cheapest hotel we could find in Manhattan.
We were exhausted and hungry, but still went out for a walk, dazzled by
all of the lights, by the storefronts full of new fashions, by the hundreds
of restaurants and bars and diners, the taxis and corner groceries and
heaping fruit carts and street vendors and jewelry stores. Of course, we
had expected to be dazzled, had expected a world of plenty, undamaged,
full of life. Yet its appearance was still miraculous, as the arrival of
spring is miraculous, even though it is just what you have been
anticipating.

The three of us shared a single queen-sized bed in our hotel room.
And in the morning we made our way to the Grand Central Station
where we boarded a train headed for Chicago and then Des Moines.

This is what I remember most of the train. I was sitting beside
Alika while Hilda slept. It was warm on the train, a hot summer
evening, and of course before the days of air-conditioning. Alika took
off her sweater, was in a sleeveless dress. And there it was—tattooed
on her arm. Her number. Her emblem. Sign that she had been through
the slaughter-house.

"I never asked what camp you were in," I said.

"It was in a few. The last was called Auschwitz. Auschwitz-
Birkenau."

The name itself was not yet so much a part of one's consciousness
then. It had not yet become a synonym for hell, for the most desolate
place on earth—the vortex of death that inhabits one's darkest
nightmares. But I had certainly heard of it, knew something of it.

"Are you glad to be in a new country?" I asked.

"I'm hopeful," Alika said. "I wouldn't say glad."

"Things will work out for you," I said. Though of course there was
no way I could really be sure of it. It was something to say.

She nodded.

"Does this remind you of anything?"

"What?"

"Being on a train together?"

"You mean when we were kids? On our way to Austria?"

"Yes."

"I envied you and Sylvia. Do you know that?"

"Really? I assumed you thought I was very childish."

"You thought of how I acted as some kind of sophistication. But it
wasn't. I was just lost. And you two knew what you wanted. You

wanted each other. You seemed happy together. I envied it."

The train rattled us into fatigue. Lights flashed outside. Another train memory came back to me. Returning from Italy with my injured leg. How much it had meant then to be returning home. Alika went on. "I was involved with a boy when I was arrested. He'd wanted to be an artist. He painted."

"What happened to him?"

"He wound up fighting in France. He had no idea what had happened to me, wrote letters that I only received after I got out of the camp and made my way home. I got them all at once when we were liberated."

"What did you do with them?" I asked.

"I arranged them chronologically and read them one by one. At first they were just talking about what he was doing. Then he wondered why I never wrote. He was hurt. Then he wondered if something had happened to me. He grew more impassioned. Started confessing his love. In the end he wrote that if I was still there, he wanted marry me. You know what's strange?"

"What?"

"I think the reason he decided he wanted to marry me was because I never wrote back. I became this fantasy he started to construct. He needed me more and more. Because I wasn't loving him back. When in reality I had no idea he was trying to reach me."

"What happened to him?" I asked.

"I heard he got injured and married a nurse where he was recuperating. He was married by the time I read his letters to me. Isn't that odd? I'm reading about how he wants to marry me, and the letters are so old he has already moved on, married someone else. Like we're in two different time dimensions."

The train slowed. We heard the tolling of a road crossing, passed headlights staring out of the darkness like cat's eyes, went on.

"What did you feel?" I asked. "When you read that he'd wanted to marry you?"

"It was just strange reading all them all at once. Like I was reading something that might have been. From some alternative life. A love story I was a part of without ever having actually experienced it. Without having even known it."

"Are you sorry he married?"

"I've thought about him some. But I don't think he was right for me."

"Why not?"

"Honestly?" She smiled to herself. "He laughed at his own jokes."

"That's it?"

"Well, it was a sign of something more, I think. Some insecurity. I don't think he was very mature."

"See?" I said, smiling. "I knew you thought that about people. Judged people for their lack of maturity."

But Alika wasn't ready to joke. She was never really one to laugh at herself, even before. "I just was looking for something. Something I thought there was an answer to. And I looked up to people who I thought had the answer. And tried to imitate them."

That firm, bronze skin that I had remembered was almost back. Alika's strong, attractive features. Her hair had bleached in the sun. I couldn't help feeling an attraction, feeling like I wanted to kiss her. It was so many things at once. The night. The newness of the surroundings. America, racing by outside the window. And also, maybe, some desire to save, to right everything that had happened to her, reach back to that youth that had been stolen from both of us. But we just sat close to one another. My eyes returned to the number on her arm, and I felt an urge to touch it, to run my finger along it.

I have since read of how, among the prisoners, a hierarchy of sorts had established itself. The politicals, like Alika, had felt themselves superior to the others. It was not impossible to imagine Alika giving that impression—whether intentional or not.

"You never explained something," I said. "You never explained what it was I didn't understand. About your mother."

"What about her?"

"About her giving you her bread. When you were in the camp."

"Giving me her bread," Alika said, immediately tense again. "When she was starving."

"Yes," I said. "I mean…of course it was horrible. What you both went through. But…."

"Yes?" she said.

"What? What more is there?"

She closed her eyes and opened them. "You still don't see."

"What don't I see?" I asked. "Tell me."

What was it that made me press her then? The exhaustion? Some vague frustration toward her that was still there, mixed with everything else?

What was horrible…." She started a couple of times. "What was horrible…was that…don't you see? What was horrible was that I took it. I *took* the food that she was offering."

"But…you were starving! And she…she told you she wasn't hungry. How could taking what she offered you be horrible?"

She looked out the train window. Out into the night. Her voice went soft. "But I knew she was lying. She was lying about not being hungry. And I knew it. She said she wasn't hungry but...I wasn't a child. I *knew* it was a lie. She was *dying*. And I took her food anyway. I let myself believe it. That's what was horrible."

It took a moment to formulate an answer. "You were starving. You can't blame yourself."

"Hans...."

"What?"

"I chose a piece of bread...over my mother's life." She wiped away tears. "There was my mother. And there was the bread. And I chose the bread. And every night I wish I could talk to her. Give her back that piece of bread. And she's not there. She's not there to give it back to. Now do you understand?"

I could think of no response, sat silently.

"Now you know. Since you insisted on my telling you."

- Illyria -

My beloved. My rival. My declining self.

For a while we held out hope for Cole and Conrad. They would find their way to safety. They would send a search out for us. I found myself scanning the horizons. Dawn made a daily trek around the back of the island, hoping for some sign of a plane, a boat in the other direction.

"See anything?"

"I did. Look!" And trying to be cheerful, she would hold out a pair of conches that would be our dinner, or a plastic doll (disfigured Barbie) that had washed up on the beach.

Our second anniversary on the island. Sad and lonely celebration, without any of the others. I could not be said to have truly admired, enjoyed, been one with any of them. Yet we are a social species. Just to see them. To hear their cloying, annoying stories. So empty without that. Does the cow have to admire its fellow cows to want to be near them? To want to know they are there? How I miss their presence. Even the despicable Cole. Even Conrad, my false friend and betrayer. Especially Conrad! How I missed sharing fire-watch with him. How I missed his philosophizing, his sniveling, the absurd wrap he wore like the mantle of a barbarian king.

We have stopped thinking as much about Conrad and Cole. Or when we do think of them, it is Andreas and me imagining two sun-dried corpses, still afloat in the skiff. Drifting on endlessly, petrified in mid-debate.

"Who do you think died first?" I would ask.

"Conrad."

"Why Conrad?"

"Because Cole would have killed him when the food started to run out."

"Interesting."

We have stopped maintaining Cole's shelter and it has caved in. Foliage has begun to grow around it. The gnome garden is choked with weeds. Almost hidden. Our civilization has seen its golden age and is in decline. And your chronicler is declining with it. The knees and back and ankles are aching. The pee drips out as from some broken, medieval fountain. Do you know how they say you cannot smell yourself? Well, I can smell myself. My old-person smell comes back to me in the wind. I can smell my own decline. My impending death.

What's more, I have started to wonder if my mind is growing cloudy. I find myself dreaming in German. And is Dawn just letting me win now? Am I still a challenge for her? Or does she play me out of compassion? I see obvious mistakes a move too late. I confuse who I am playing against. And here is something else: I cry. I never used to cry. Now it just hits me. Just remembering anything. The taste of *spaetzle*. My father putting a record on the gramophone. Annabel attached to her tubes in the ICU, hands gnarled like the feet of a dead bird. My grandmother teaching me to swim at Lake Constance when I was only four.

It all blurs together. Dream and reality. Senescent descent into the surreal. It is all one. Sylvia. Hilda. Annabel. Dawn. Was it with Annabel that we picked wild berries along a mountain rill? Or was that with Sylvia—bicycles leaning against a nearby pine tree? Or, perhaps, did I just place the pine tree there because the bicycles needed something to rest against? Was there really an Annabel? Did we really dive in the turquoise Aegean, and ramble high above Annecy? Or was my Annabel of the Alps just a dream? A reshuffling of fragments? She disappears behind a cloud that sweeps across a mountainside, throwing a shadowy chill across the snowfields, and then the mist clears and it is Sylvia. She heads down to the sea from our villa, casts off into the waves, and Dawn rises up out of them.

Or this: I say goodnight to Hilda in our frozen barn, and awaken in a recovery room, moaning, to a dazed Madeira, my Brazilian bride. And what of Madeira herself? Our marriage forever unconsummated, but for the kidney, the second life she has given me. Who sent her? Who was she? And are we not one now? Is her fate, in some way tied to mine now? Does she feel a faint pain when I cry out in agony? It is all   a   blur.   A   continuum.   One. MotherNannyLoverCompanionDelivererDream.

Conrad was right. I should be dead by now. I should let go, end it, cede this world to these young lovers. I am fully dependent now on my rival. He gathers food enough to share, fetches feed for the doves, keeps the shelters strong—theirs and mine. Do you know what is strange? I not only admire him. I have come to love him as well. His calm and kindness and endless capacity for work. And yes, perhaps even his youthful beauty.

Dawn has her chores—root-gathering and washing, cooking, tending the fire. What am I then? I am nothing. I am the lookout for passing ships. But this last is a job that Dawn invented, a sinecure intended to spare me the shame of what I have become—a burden.

There is something else to my decline as well. Something I did not mention before, when listing my ailments. It is this: I have known my last erection. The brain, addled and blurry as it is, needs the blood, evidently. Or so my body has decided. There shall be no more attention given this organ that, in truth, has served so little utility. That spilled its seed ten-thousand-fold and produced a single thankless heir. This organ that, in the end, has given me so little pleasure. Is it shame that I did not mention this sooner? My wounded pride? The tower hath crumbled. It is my time. Our third Christmas here on Illyria.

Have you not wondered, have you not asked yourself: How did we celebrate our Christmases here? Because, after all, is the answer not sure to be poignant and bittersweet? I will tell you. Our first Christmas, when we were all still together, we gathered crabs and slaughtered two doves for a special meal. Gloria led us in singing carols. We each shared a story (again, Gloria's idea) of our favorite Christmas. My story was of Edelburg, of a bright red tricycle I was given when I was five. Then we gave each other presents, all necessarily of the homespun variety. Cowrie necklaces for the women. New fishing spears for the men. Sundial for our gathering spot. On some level it truly is the thought that counts, and on this level it was uplifting. Because at least we tried. But on another level, it is not the thought at all. It is everything else besides the thought. And on this level it was pathetic and sad and lonely.

By our second Christmas Gloria and Monique were both dead. There were no presents. We worked to put together a decent meal. Managed a little singing. There was still unspoken tension between Dawn and Cole, after Monique's death, and there was no miraculous Christmas truce. This time we were each to tell a story of our worst Christmas (excluding the present one, of course). This was a lot less painful, ultimately, as the contrast to our present circumstance was not so cruel. I chose the one I spent in North Africa, my first of the war, Dieter and I filled with homesickness, despair, every kind of misery, getting drunk together, puking in the latrine.

Now, on our third Christmas, it is just Dawn and Andreas and me. We have stopped declaring the days aloud. But we still mark them on our calendar rock. We all surely know what day it was. Only at first none of us mentions it. At last, the three of us sitting together after dinner, Andreas breaks the silence. "Guess what?"

"What?" I ask.

"It's a week until New Year's Day." Andreas cannot quite bring himself to name it.

Dawn blinks away tears and bravely smiles. "Merry Christmas."

"Merry Christmas to both of you," I say.

We reach across and all hold each other's hands.

"Shouldn't we do something?" Andreas asks.

"Like what?" I say.

"Like sing."

"I can't sing anymore. You go ahead."

At first he is too shy to sing though. So he hums. He hums *Silent Night* and Dawn joins him. And then they add words. I join in. There is no way around what a sappy song it is. How contrived it feels. But soon we are singing other songs. Not just Christmas ones. We are each to sing our favorites. Dawn cannot decide. First she tries *I Will Survive*.

"That's really your favorite song?" Andreas asks.

"I just couldn't think of anything."

Andreas makes a buzzing sound, buzzes her out. "That doesn't count. You're just singing the first song you thought of."

She tries again with *Here Comes The Sun*.

Somehow I recognize both of these songs, have absorbed them from the air.

Then it's Andreas's turn. He gets up and prances around singing something I don't remember, except for some part that goes, "Scaramouche, Scaramouche." Perhaps it needs the instruments behind it, because his rendition is scarcely discernible as music. But his voice dips and leaps, he starts throwing himself into it like a madman, playing air-guitar and mimicking its sound, and Dawn and I find ourselves laughing for the first time in a long while. We demand an encore, and soon he is belting out *Satisfaction*. Another song I have become miraculously familiar with.

> *...Baby better come back later next week*
> *Cause you see I'm on a losin' streak*
> *I can't get no...*

I can't get no…

When it is my turn I realize there is nothing in English I know well enough to sing. I choose *Wenn die Sonne hinter den Dächern versinkt.* *When the Sun Sets Over the Rooftops.* The melody I had whistled outside Sylvia's window. And then I am briefly back to tears. Suddenly I am remembering that night in Berlin at the symphony. What it meant. What it means now. To play music. To sing. To be alive.

At last, Andreas and Dawn each give me a little hug and say goodnight and retire to their hut.

I stay up alone, tending the fire. Imagining the world around me, far far away. Celebrating, opening presents. Sitting down to Christmas dinners. And not only that. What of the rest of the world? The endless oceans. Endlessly tossing. The hot, dry North African night as I had known it. The screeching bullet trains of rush hour in Tokyo. Skiers in Gstaad. Rigoletto in mid-performance at La Scala in Milan. Shoppers on Fifth Avenue in Manhattan. An Amazonian Jaguar slipping down from a tree. Or this: A couple picking wildflowers, high above a Norwegian Fjord. *Liliaceae annabel.* All of it going on at once. All around us.

I head into my shelter, bend slowly down to the ground until my hands make contact, and from there climb my way into a sleeping position.

I used to dream of one more adventure before I died. One more romance. One more trek into the unknown. And then, when that seemed impossible, one more conversation with my son. One more glass of wine. One more anything. One more joke about a sheep. Now I have a new last wish. My last fantasy. Have you ever listened to two old people trying to out-complain one another with their health problems? I wish to be subjected to such a conversation, not because I am interested in what the other has to say (for who in such a conversation ever is?) but so I can interrupt with my own, superior litany. I wish to awe and astound with my list ailments. What is this list, you ask? Let's see, O Reader, if you can match me. Dry mouth. Boils. Diarrhea. Starvation. Bug bites. Weird rashes. Flaking skin. Restless leg. Listless penis. Irritable bowel. Vague shoulder. Constipation. Cataracts. Corns. Delusions. Arthritis. Osteoporosis. Wimpy peeing. Allergies. Insomnia. Crappy mood. German Mumbles. Moody crap. Fungal sores. Cold sores. Chapped lips. Back itch. Shortness of breath. Toothache. Sand In The Ass-Crack II (chronic variety). Sunburn. Hunger pangs.

There. I win! I should get a trophy. Bronze of old geezer bent on all-fours, retching. Hans Jaeger. First Prize. Symptoms competition.

Speaking of retching, did I mention this? Dawn is pregnant. It happened before Christmas, evidently. Only I learn of it after, just as she is starting to show. Just as her morning sickness sets in. Just as the rains come.

We are used to the gusty island shower. The sudden explosion of tropical waters, pouring from the heavens, soaking everything, then minutes later the sun back out, the birds singing, steam rising up through the dripping foliage. And we are used to the ocean storms. The days when the wind is steady and strong and the rain pelts the island and big hunks of driftwood, fish skeletons, brain corals wash up.

This is different. This is monsoon. Day after day. Gigantic, fat drops that splatter against the rocks. Fine mists that come down like a thousand veils cast down by the heavens. Sheets angling in with the wind. Every kind of rain there is. A hundred sallow rivulets pour down from Mount Piss—more aptly named than ever. New stream beds form, new passageways through the sand and out to the ocean. Our shelters grow dank and moldy and there is no hope whatever of anything being dry. The drips are too many. The water creeps in through the walls, rises up from the ground. You must accept, in the end, living soaking wet, eating soaking wet, sleeping soaking wet. We have had to relight the fire many times now, are in danger of running out of lighter fluid. And what then?

And is there anything at all closer to utter emptiness than lying in the dark and wet of my shelter, knowing that at least Dawn and Andreas have the warmth of one another, of their young bodies, holding one another? Or tending to the fire, hearing the dripping all around, the rain pattering the thatch, feeling that I am the only creature left alive, staring, as the day comes up, at the dull gray sunrise, the endless gray ocean, forbidding and empty as ever? Or getting up to pee in the night, stepping out into the rain, dribbling a little, two little squirts as from an eye-dropper, old-man pee, knees creaking, back aching, last drops dripping out unmercifully slowly? Not even caring if I pee on myself. At least it is warm. And wouldn't it just get washed away anyway? At last stepping back into my shelter, wet and tired and unable to sleep, waiting for the dawn, wondering if my kidney—Madeira's kidney—is giving out at last.

And finally we must let the fire die out. There is no dry wood. And our lighter fluid must be preserved. Now there is nothing at night but dark and wet. The doves stop laying. We are not sure why. We guess it is some bacteria that thrives amid the dank and rot. It becomes more urgent when we start finding them dead. It means Andreas spends most of the day out in the gloom, searching for something for us to eat. And he must look especially hard now that Dawn needs more. And whatever is found must be consumed raw. He is lifted though, it seems, at the prospect of becoming a father. At being so entirely responsible for supporting this new life.

"I cannot continue to eat," I tell them one night.

"What are you talking about?" Dawn asks.

"I'm taking food from your child. It's wrong. Why am I still here?"

But Dawn won't hear of it. "There's plenty for all of us."

"This place would be lonely without you," Andreas says.

"I think it's pretty lonely with me," I say.

"It would be lonelier," Andreas says.

The water is too murky to see through, so Andreas has temporarily abandoned his spear-fishing. He goes into the interior and gathers ass fruits—although the bigger, riper ones are all gone. Then he scavenges the beach for something that has been washed up in the surf. When there isn't enough, he tries trapping fish with netting made from thatch. He knocks little sea urchins loose with sticks. Anything to keep us from starving.

I try again when Andreas is off looking for food—as he is so much of the time. "You should poison me," I say to Dawn.

"Stop," Dawn says.

The rain is falling silently, in a mist, draining everything of color, adding to the dreariness.

"I mean it. I'm too old. Don't tell me you are going to do it, though. Just do it. There is nothing left. And you need the food."

"Stop. Stop even talking about it."

"But we have to talk about it."

"No we don't," Dawn says. "And we won't."

"You'd have food," I say. "You'd be alive. You'd have each other."

"There's nothing to say. I won't do it. Andreas won't do it."

I know this is so. Andreas, who I so long tried to despise, now assumes, unquestioningly, that I am part of his responsibility. And do I even mean it? Or am I only proposing it because I know they will refuse?

"Someday…." I begin.

"Yes?"

"Someday you should think of yourself. Put yourself first."

"That's not the way to start," Dawn says. "With…I can't even say it."

"Okay," I say. "Maybe not with that. But you should."

"Did it ever occur to you," she says, "that I don't *want* to think of myself? That it can only remind of...things I don't want to think about?"

"Such as...?"

"Such as...all of the things I don't have. Will never have."

I run a finger over my cracked lips. Why the endless rain would make my lips crack, I can't say. But it does. Dawn rises to get me water. She is showing already, her abdomen distended. Her weeks of sickness have passed.

"Thank you," I say.

We have both turned thoughtful, sit together quietly. The rain gradually picks ups, whispers through the leaves, a dull static, like a radio that is not tuned to a station.

"Do you know I invented a cure for my mother?" she says.

I look at her. "What do you mean?"

"When she was sick. I must have been six years old. I had this idea that I would come up with a cure for her. So I went to the refrigerator and mixed whatever I could find. Orange juice and ginger ale and Cool Whip. Something like that. I don't know. I'm sure it was incredibly revolting. I mixed it all together and poured a glass and brought it to her. And I said something like, 'Look, Mommy. I made some medicine for you.'"

What does one say to something like that? "That's very sweet, in its way," I say. "But...sad."

"My poor mother. She had to sip it and thank me and pretend it was making her feel better."

Have you ever seen a glimpse of someone as a child, and suddenly felt you truly saw the person, saw the adult, because you saw the child inside? That was what it was like at that moment—the sudden feeling that at last I knew her, could make sense of her. She is still that child. Forever frozen in the act of trying to save her mother. If only she could be the right daughter. If only she could invent some cure, some magic, to bring her mother back.

I hesitate to even say it that way. Nothing is ever really that simple, right? Couldn't someone else, with exactly her experience, have come out completely differently? Replay her own life, and change just a single molecule along the way, and maybe she would wind up unrecognizable, a different person entirely, cold-hearted or petty or compulsive. So perhaps it doesn't really explain anything. But I can only say how it feels—that sudden sense that, at last, I know Dawn, know who she is. Is she any less remarkable? Not really. But at least it is slightly easier to discern her, to comprehend her.

I sip the water she has brought, run it along my lips with my finger. The rain has picked up. The volume of the static, the million droplets falling through the leaves, has risen very gradually. It is dripping through the overhang we are perched under. And then, suddenly, it all blurs, drifts off into a dream. I am hit by one of those sudden, old-man naps. When I awaken, Dawn and Andreas are by the fire together, holding hands.

The mood seems different now, on the other side of this nap. What is it? What has awakened me? The light. That's what it is! Everything is shining. Dripping. Dawn and Andreas are sitting in sunshine. Looking cheered.

At first we don't know whether to trust it. We have celebrated the sun prematurely before, only to descend back under more days of rain. But this this time it is real. The weather has finally broken. And my own health seems to come back a little with the sunshine.

For a few weeks we recover our spirits. We relight the fire and celebrate its rebirth, as though in some pagan ritual. And even make little improvements to our camp. Only it is a false sense of reprieve. One day Andreas comes back with his leg bloodied and in pain. He has lost his footing in a wave and landed against a razor-sharp tongue of fire coral. The next day the leg swells and the day after that he comes down with a fever. The wounds turn mauve and brown.

Now Dawn, slowed with her pregnancy, takes Andreas's place searching for food, and then tends him when she returns. I feebly take up gathering fire wood, pick roots from our garden, and look for anything that will pass for fruit. But there is no avoiding our worst fears. Andreas is sick. And seemingly—dare we even contemplate it? —getting sicker. He is too weak to work, to do much of anything but lie back and moan, sit up briefly and eat what Dawn and I bring him and lie back down.

I am helping to provide now. But just barely enough. We are finished, I think. Unless Andreas recovers.

So this is how it will end. Too weak to gather enough food. Slowly starving. The foliage wrapping all around us. Sprouting everywhere with all the water. Twining around our shelters. Devouring our hearth. Choking our gnomes, our shelters, our corpses.

Dawn and I are preparing what will pass for breakfast one morning, and Andreas appears. Leg swollen at the base like the trunk of a palm.

Dawn looks up in shock. "What are you doing?"

"Going back to work."

"Andreas! You can't."

"I'm better."

"You don't look better."

Andreas trying. Half walking. Half crawling. Eyes red and foot brown and the rest of him white. Emaciated. "I have to."

I am overwhelmed with his purity. His determination. "You need to rest," I say. And I am up. Helping. Trying to get him to lie down.

Did I mention how skin is jaundicing? My piss is the color of tea? I am clinging, twisting, like the last, dying leaf of autumn. About to break off from its lifeline and sail downward, deathward. I must speed this story to its end.

- Iowa -

There is an old axiom that we think by association. By comparison. Is this not why we are ultimately so limited in our creativity? Can we ever really imagine something completely new? Is it not always like something else, but with this or that changed? Is this not why our science fiction creations always have eyes and ears and mouths? Why our storytellers write the same character over and over, now in a knight's armor, now in a serape and a sombrero?

I have sometimes wondered: if there had never been a tiger, would we have had the imagination to create so regal, so remarkable and magnificent a creature? By comparison to the tiger, aren't all of the make-believe creatures we have imagined in some way inferior? Overdrawn and unsubtle? Poorly designed for survival? Nonsensical? Can any compare in beauty and grace and terror to an actual tiger? Do you see what I mean?

And if there had never been a Hitler, would we have had the imagination to invent him? This embodiment of evil, this comic-book villain—and yet so much fuller than the comic-book villains we have conjured out of imagination. Complete with his own absurd gait and his own idiotic black plug of a mustache, his own bizarre worldview and philosophy and motive, his dabblings in art, his mysterious mistress? And yet, for all of it, much like a villain from a spy novel, appearing to be guided by the motive of simple evil? And could we have had the imagination to invent the rest—the columns of marching jack-boots, the comical salutes and special greetings hailing our villain, the Jew-hating propaganda, the fiery rallies, the Russians, the war, the gas chambers, Ann Frank and Dresden and the kamikazes and that great, cinematic spectacle, the transcendent denouement of the atomic bomb?

And if there never had been an Iowa, could we have imagined such a place?

We saw it first from the train. The sun rose and we awakened to the light and there it was out the window. What I remember was that nothing looked real and everything was new. Not new in the sense of being modern or beautiful, but new like it had been laid out for a child to move the pieces about—all the houses and silos, all the stores and delivery trucks and gas stations, even the cows out in the fields, as though they were on a board, and could be controlled by magnets underneath. Perfectly plain. Everything so clearly its own distinct thing. Declaring what it was by its shape. Crow. House. Farmer. Tractor.

"So much corn," Hilda said.

It was true. Endless fields of it—so flat and so endless the wind ruffed it into waves like a sea. "I didn't know land could be so flat," I said. "Like the ocean."

"And the farmhouses are like ships floating in it," Hilda said. "Way far away."

Along with the corn, there were all sorts of crops we didn't recognize. "I wonder what those are," I said.

"Maybe peanuts," Hilda said. "For all of that peanut-butter they sent us."

"It looks like the sort of country that would have good schools," Hilda said. I wondered why Hilda would still say that, without Georg, and when Alika got up to stretch her legs I asked her. "Why did you mention that about the schools?"

"Didn't I tell you?"

"What?"

"You're going to be a father."

It was the first time I had seen that mischievous smile from Hilda in a long time.

"Funny," I said. "I think I would have remembered that."

"You see?" she said. "All that awful work in bed with me has finally paid off."

A new country. A new life. And now this. I put my arm around her, squeezed her, made all of the right exclamations. But what was I really feeling? Of course I felt a certain excitement at the thought of having a child. But did I want one with Hilda? And now?

The train pulled to our stop, and we were met at the station by Alika's aunt.

My impressions of couple who sponsored us, and whose home we settled into:

First Alika's Aunt Marta. Skinny, stern, upright woman. Sturdy chin of the faithful. Her atheist husband, Uncle Hermann—wide-bellied, recliner in posture and life. What I remember of Hermann was how he used to quote from the Bible, not out of piety but out of bemusement at its contradictions. He was a Mark Twain reader, and I remember looking at him in confusion as he translated his favorite lines from Huckleberry Finn into German for our benefit—his belly rocking with laughter.

They'd raised three children who had all married and moved out—to Des Moines and Omaha and Chicago—and so the house felt like it was empty and waiting for us. Hilda and I were given one of the little empty bedrooms, Alika the second, and the third would be for the baby—a symmetry Aunt Marta must have found to be a sign from the Lord and Uncle Hermann, who needed his space, no doubt found miserably claustrophobic.

Hilda was soon showing, and no longer doing manual labor. She volunteered at a daycare, received no pay, but was served breakfast and lunch, as much as she wanted to eat (what a remarkable notion) while she learned the language and made friends.

Alika helped her uncle with the farm, helped her aunt with the house, took classes in English and attended prayer meetings. At first it seemed maybe she was just trying to fit in, but soon she was showing surprising concentration, a kind of devotion. She baked for her meetings like she had been a part of this place all her life. And how strange to watch her transformation. She started to spend time with a bearded man named Gustav who worked as a carpenter at a furniture shop—a place that would have seemed perfectly ordinary in Germany but here had the charm of something quaint and antique. He seemed to fit in the store, had the look of shopkeeper. But I couldn't help wondering. What did Alika find attractive about him? I asked Hilda about it. Was he really someone for Alika to love?

"She needs someone," Hilda said. "Don't forget what she's been through."

For myself, I found work at the assembly plant at Amana Refrigeration, the single biggest employer in this part of Iowa. I remembered our first refrigerator in Edelburg, before the war, a big wooden base with a long tub atop it, modeled to look like a sideboard in a dining room. And now in my new job I was assembling these things that looked like shiny, space-age marshmallows, that shipped to kitchens all across America. Was this absurd, white refrigerator style not perfectly emblematic of my entire adopted country? This country without a history, where the cheese was orange and kitchen tables were trimmed with chrome and toilets shined like polished sculptures?

In winter the wind was always blowing. One night Hilda asked me, "Why did we have to leave for somewhere just as cold? We went five thousand miles straight West. Couldn't we have just gone a few hundred miles South, as long as we were already traveling?"

"I thought you wanted Iowa," I said.

"What did I know? I thought there were mountains."

Still, there was plenty of food, even in the cold months, and the rooms were kept warm, and I don't even remember learning English so much as one day feeling like it was all a mystery and then the next day understanding it.

I tried to answer the questions of our baffled neighbors, who had emigrated decades earlier. Why had I volunteered? Why had I served so long? Why hadn't we fled? Didn't we realize Hitler was a madman? Questions I had neither the command of the language nor of my own thoughts to respond to. On some level, I was an embarrassment to them. A German who had been a part of it. Yet in other ways they were welcoming. Good and resolute and resolutely good. Was that what was most trying of all? Even more than the plains and the wind and the foreignness? All of that decency? They would teach me, by way of example, the right path. And then they would search my eyes for that gratitude that might affirm not just their faith in me but in themselves. O thank ye people of Iowa, thank ye for teaching this wayward soul about God and Faith and Freedom, about America. Heil Hitler.

We named our son Serge, which for some reason we thought was a common American name, but turned out to be French. We moved, now three of us, into our own little house whose single decorative gesture atop a white clapboard box was a weather vane in the shape of a cow. It was hard to understand the need to add more cows to the landscape as a decorative motif. There was a white fence along the back that separated our yard from the cornfields. A pair of big willow trees and a clothes line filled the foreground—the clothes always canted sideways in the breeze. In memory, the background of sky is always perfectly blue in this scene, but of course this could not have been so.

People brought us presents. *This is for the entryway. This for the nursery.* Two different pillows, from two different neighbors, both with the embroidered words, *Home Sweet Home.* See what opportunity there is in this great county? Just work hard and look what you have already. And how could I say, *Only do you know the house I grew up in, do you have any idea, do you have any idea how I have come down in the world, how alone I am, how I don't belong here at all, I am not good like all of you, I am not welling with gratitude for Iowa. And*

Serge, my son, my only child, look at you, poet or philosopher or whatever you will be, is this really where you will grow up? What you will know?

What was it exactly that went wrong? That started it unraveling?

It is true that Serge was not really drawn to his father even from the start. Wanting always *Mutti*. Because what child would not have preferred Hilda? But why did it get worse from there? Where so many sons one day discover their fathers, was it just that Serge never did? Was it that Hilda did not even really try to include me, that we had grown apart by infinitesimal increments, scarcely noticing or commenting on it any longer, and so Hilda and her little boy formed their own unit, complete in their love?

Because there she was, devoting herself now to the third Jaeger generation, this time in another language and in another world—a world of little three-room schools with their swing sets, sitting right there at the very edge of windswept infinity. And once again, she was leaving the previous generation behind. Because what was I now? I was a full-grown man, and Hilda loved boys, she loved injured soldiers she could nurse back to health. For a while she could love even an insecure, indecisive man like my father for his very foolishness. But look at what I had become. What was there to dote on, to support, to reform? And had she not grown into this new landscape in a way that I had not, could not, could never, and taken her son with her, and left me outside, blaming not only her, but —cruelly—him as well? So was it not Iowa's fault for stealing Serge? And Serge's fault for stealing Hilda? And Hilda's fault above all?

Still, we held on there. As barren and wholesome as the land itself. The heartland. Heart of America. Hearty and heartfelt and free and good and true. Sunny and golden and empty to the horizon. Dotted here and there with little towns identified from a distance not by their lovely, stone church-steeples like in the Europe I had known, but by their shapeless, aluminum water-towers. Towns of laundry waving on clothes lines and septic tanks parked above the ground and skeletons of ancient cars withering out in the yard, just left there, because there was more land than anyone knew what to do with, and so why not just leave your old stuff out front, out back, wherever, and because wherever it was you were supposed to haul it to was too far to bother with in any case. Beautiful, glorious, shameless, naked, graceless towns, reeking of manure, tiny outposts of humanity.

Alika's aunt Marta, we came to realize, was something of the social life of the town, and one of its more prominent citizens. She seldom spoke about her beliefs. In fact, it was not exactly clear what she truly believed. The literal word of the Bible? Just some sort of benevolent deity? She refused to say. But something—something to pray forgiveness to—was there in her core. She was a big believer in charity, donated to everything from literacy programs in the South to relief programs for Jewish orphans, to CARE packages for hungry families back in Germany.

She was a Sunday School teacher who could still fix you with her gaze—that schoolteacher's penetrating look of disapproval that she must have cast ten thousand times at one or another misbehaving student, and that always froze you in the act, filled you with shame. It never really filled you with fear, because everyone knew that underneath, Marta was a forgiving soul. But it surely filled you with shame. Because you knew that you had disappointed her, and that she represented, by her own example, the ultimate moral authority, and that you must do better.

She was thin and erect and frail as a corn stalk, wore plain clothes buttoned to the neck and never lowered herself to engage in gossip. If there was something bad she knew of someone, something she was inclined to say, she just froze, lips closed, eyes looking off.

We soon realized how people from all over town gravitated to her. Women sought her advice, or just wanted her company. Children, former students, came by to say hello, to show off how grown up they had become.

Marta greatly admired cleanliness. One of her highest compliments, reserved only for a very few, was, "Her house is *spotless!*" She was fond of word games and puzzles in her adopted English, spoke with a pedagogue's precision, baked the same three or four pie recipes week after week, until they lent the house its own distinctive smell, just as the porcelain cats and silver tea set and oval mirrors in the entryway lent the inside of the house its characteristic appearance.

What Hilda appreciated most about Marta was her remarkable way with Serge. She wasn't what one would typically think of as fun or lighthearted. She just had a way of seeing the world through a child's eyes and making it seem fascinating. "Isn't that the most beautiful drawing of a sunflower! May I put it up on my wall?" she would exclaim, with such awe that the child could not help but see it that way, and fill with pride. I remember Serge following behind her and helping her with her tomato plants, Marta asking him his considered opinion, "Where do you suppose we should plant the next one?" and taking his answer extremely seriously.

If Marta was the center of the town's narrow social life, Hermann was her eccentric, remote other half. He preferred sitting alone and reading his newspaper, doing his word puzzles, slouching back with his paunch aimed not just outward but upward. He had made a living replacing wooden counter-tops with modern, chrome-trimmed Formica, and now gloried in his beloved retirement, not wealthy but reveling in whatever means and scope he had achieved. He found a kind of ironic pleasure in Marta's religiousness, her prayers and Sunday rituals and visits from this or that church group. He rolled his eyes, whispering to me that it was all a bunch of hooey, had himself a good laugh.

One thing I enjoyed about Hermann was his contempt for most of the town. When he didn't like the company that was over, which was nearly always, he showed it by disappearing into the back corner of the house to read from his Twain or Sinclair Lewis. If I had any ally or companion in all of Amana, it was Hermann. We were the male outcasts. The pair of miscreants who could never live up to Marta or Hilda or Amana or to women in general, who didn't belong, who didn't want to belong.

If there was any sign that my heart had started to wander, it was this: I not only continued to check in at the Red Cross office to see if there was any news of Sylvia, I started to do so more and more frequently. Each visit I was impelled by some new small reason I had given myself to hope. Maybe she had been in a hospital, recovering. Maybe she had not wanted to contact me, and then had changed her mind. I always left feeling a blow like a lover's rejection. No word. Nothing. What a fool I was. Because just suppose there really was a letter someday? And just suppose we really met again? Would we even still love one another? Would we still have the same things in common? Was I not holding on to some hope that, even if it were realized, would wind up leading nowhere?

The end, in retrospect, began with an opportunity at my job. It was noticed that I showed facility both with the mechanical assembly and the business end of the production. I moved quickly into a role as foreman and from there into sales, and this last position was what finally started me on my future course, as it set me traveling for weeks and even months at a time. I visited appliance stores in Missouri and Kentucky and Illinois, drove into every town and every small city in the region, every shopping center with a plastic sign at the parking lot entrance and a mom-and-pop appliance place, every brick-lined main street with its diners and coffee shops and laundromats and clothing stores, its railroad yard or riverfront, its street urchins and its starch-suited insurance salesmen.

And what a strange mixture of yearning and regret and desire filled all of those miles. To be a driver again. Like in North Africa. In Italy. Alone again. To be reunited with all of those years. To be out in the world, moving, seeing all of those strangers' faces, only knowing this time that my own son was out there in that same world, that his mother was out there, that there was a home that was always pushing me away and tugging me back.

Sometimes the war was still replaying itself in my mind. The letters from my father. And the last one that was not from him but about him, from the *Wehrmacht*. The frozen winter in that barn outside Berlin. Or, increasingly, this: I would find myself imagining hearing from Sylvia at last. Playing out scenes of our reunion. Long, elaborate, highway daydreams. And even if I wasn't remembering the war, the aftermath, there was still something left over from it. The great retreat. The feeling of movement. As though I needed it now. Just to be on the run.

Is there such a thing as a good heartache? That was what it felt like. The sense that you are a stranger everywhere. A stranger to yourself. As homeless as the moon, racing alongside your car window, as a howl in the prairie night.

In the summer I scanned all the people as I drove past. Silent vignettes. Children playing in lawn sprinklers. Little games of catch on front lawns. And how I remembered driving on long winter nights— nothing out there but a light or two in the far distance, the lights calling to one another, yes I exist, yes I am here as well. And what an inexplicable mixture of feelings I felt during those drives. Overwhelming loss over something I could not precisely identify. A life I half wanted and knew I could never truly fit into. A yearning to be back with Hilda and Serge. A yearning to keep driving forever. As though expecting somewhere—in Brazil or Alaska or Bora Bora—I would find something; something completely intangible and nameless— my *real* life. Whatever that was.

And then this: Once, after another fruitless Red Cross visit, I run into Alika at her aunt's, and somehow we wind up in a back bedroom together, folding linens.

There is the cedar smell. The old, four-poster bed. The embroidery across the top of the bureau, covered with little knick-knacks. A room that had not been used in years. And I remember my mood, desperate and aching and bitter and wanting something. Alika proud and worn now like she belonged in Iowa, like she had always lived there. And I remember thinking wasn't it all a lie? Wasn't it really just a facade, and did she not yearn for something else, something more, as I did? Because there it was as we folded. Those numbers on her arm. That other world. And—dare I admit it?—did it not hold a kind of perverse fascination? Did it not urge me toward her in some way? Arouse so many contradictory desires—to hold on to the past, to not relinquish it so entirely, however horrible it was, and at the same time—to rescue her from it? And did she not secretly wish for the same things? Wish for this bond between us, whatever it was, to finally be acknowledged?

The muffled voices from the kitchen. Sounds of running water. Dishes being washed. Our hands—Alika's and mine—taking the four corners of a quilt and drawing them together. Folding the quilt in half and then in half again. And suddenly my hands over hers. Enfolding hers. Squeezing. Looking into her eyes.

"Alika...."

Alika startled, pulling back. But not pulling her hands away. Not right away. Looking back at me. "Hans?"

"Do you...." How to say it? Everything inside me swimming. "Do you not ever wish...."

"What?"

Clinging to her hands—like I am holding on to the rungs of a ladder.

But do you know what is strange? I was so sure of it at that moment. Everything else was chaos. But suddenly this seemed what was right. What she wanted. What she *needed.*

"Alika, do you remember...when we rode the train out here together?"

Hesitating, looking me over. "What about it?"

"Remember....watching the scenery go by? If you can even call it scenery. All of that endless space?"

"Where is this going, Hans?"

"Did you not feel something then? Something between us?"

Pulling her hands away then. Staring at me coldly. "You can't talk like this."

"But...didn't you?"

"It doesn't matter what I did or didn't feel. Does it!"

"Alika...."

"Hans, don't say anything more. Please. It's not possible. You know that!"

Closing my eyes. Feeling the darkness. Everything turning around. Upside-down. What had I been thinking? "I'm losing my mind, Alika."

"I can see that."

"No. Not like that, I mean...."

"You mean what?"

"I mean here. I'm losing my mind...living here."

Her expression softening, if only slightly. "That doesn't make it okay."

And then reaching out. A hand in her hair. Already given up on whatever it was I had imagined. But still wanting *something*. Just to touch her. To feel...*something*. And what was it that I had even imagined? Wasn't it just another illusion, another mirage like Iowa itself? If she actually had wanted me in return...what then?

Her voice gentler this time, "Please stop, Hans." She didn't even lift my hand away. Just waited for me to withdraw it. And that was what drew me back at last. The shame of her letting me leave it there, senseless, un-received.

"I'm sorry."

"What are you thinking?"

"I don't know. I'm not thinking anything."

"What about Hilda?"

"I know. I know I know I know."

It hit me fully only afterward: that I had done it again. I had misunderstood Alika yet again. Said one more idiotic thing to her. Just as when we were young. What was it? What was it in her that brought this out in me? Did I still feel she was trying, in some subtle way, to keep herself apart? Did I still need, after all this time, after everything she had been through, to bring her down in some way? To conquer her? For didn't those numbers somehow make her superior all over again? What could possibly compare to them? Were they not the ultimate proof of what I had always felt?

Now she looked up at me, hesitating at first. "If you must know...."

"Yes?"

"Gustav and I are engaged."

Startled at that. "Alika...."

What to say though? Apologize again? Ask her if she really loved this man? How she could be doing this? Only what if it was true that she didn't love him? What if she didn't love him, and knew it perfectly well, had still decided to do this for her own reasons? What was the point of asking in that case, of forcing such a confession?

"Yes?"

"Nothing. Only...."

"Yes?"

Why, Alika? What do you really feel? Deep down? Who are you?

Only there was something in her eyes, some defiance. As though she had already imagined whatever reservations I might express, and was already prepared to dismiss them. There was nothing to say. Or too much. A hundred thoughts passing through me at once. None of them quite worth expressing.

I found my voice at last. "May we forget this?"

"I would like to. Yes."

And then a voice outside the room. Marta. "Is everything... alright?"

What could she have heard? She must have heard something. Sensed something. How to face her. That gaze of hers. And Hilda.

Alika opening the door, replying back. "We're fine. Just finishing."

And then it was over. Just like that. Nothing. Erased. And yet not at all. Because what I was thinking, suddenly, was—*run!*

This was it. This was the moment. Run, dive, hide. That is what you know how to do. Run from all of them—Martha and Alika and Hilda. Most of all, or rather most horrible of all, run from ...your own son. From those eyes that look up at you, dark and impenetrable. Run from the emptiness itself—that vast, all-consuming emptiness. It is time. The feet are telling you.

And was that not also part of why I had done this? Had I not wanted some turmoil, something irrevocable that would force a change? Some finale, even if it was my shameful retreat?

Hilda knew nothing of what I had done. And yet she felt it all falling to pieces. She spoke, just days later, of our having drifted apart, possibly too far apart to find our way back. Or probably it was not exactly as I am describing. Probably I had been acting in such a way so as to provoke this conversation. Offering hints. Because I was afraid to raise the topic myself.

"It's not working here for you," was what I remember Hilda saying. "It is working here for me and Serge and Alika. But this is never going to be your home."

"I know."

"So what do you want to do?"

Pause. Just say it. Say the words. "Go."

"Where will you go?"

"I don't know."

"Is that what you want?"

"Yes."

"Then just go."

"We could all leave together."

"To where?"

"Anywhere. I have no idea. Someplace new."

"Do you even want us to come?"

But I have no answer to this. No idea. "Why does he hate me?" I ask.

"He doesn't hate you. He's a different sort of boy. You have to be patient."

"Have I not been patient?"

"I'm not saying that." And then, again, "Where will you go?"

"I have no idea."

- Illyria -

Would you like to hear of Andreas's death? How the gangrene climbed up his leg? The delirious stumbling down the beach, imagining a rescue ship, waving it down, at last collapsing? And is that the most horrible part? It isn't. Here is the most horrible part. We didn't even bury the body. We were too sick, both of us, to dig that much without a shovel—Dawn near the end of her pregnancy, myself feeling like I was simply near the end. And so the two of us dragging the body into the waves instead. Only finding it two days later washed back up on shore. The sea-birds swarming around it, plucking at it, screeching over their feast.

How recently it was that I had asked to be poisoned. And now I must live. I must live so Dawn is not alone. She needs me now. The baby will need me. What would become of them if I die? Dawn alone on the island. Delivering a baby. Completely alone. How infinitely cruel. The thought of them starving alone. Mother and baby. Dying alone. Dawn who in a way had always been alone. Dawn who cared for all but herself. Who had tried to save all of us.

Rescue seems more imperative than ever. Not for me of course. So near to the other shore as I am. For her. For her baby.

We are sharing a shelter now. Dawn fell asleep in my shelter one night and has moved back in since. Does this mean she loves me now a little? Just a little? Not in any way but the most innocent, platonic, but…is it possible…at last? And if that is so, has this, just possibly, played out according to some delusional plan? Some dream? Did Andreas really die of his infection? Or did my own wish to see him dead cause his death? Did I murder him with the power of my thoughts, with some devastating chess move?

That is all in the realm of the dream though. Madness. And how shameful are such thoughts now. Now that my darkest wish has come to pass. For in reality, did I not weep, in the end, for Andreas's passing? Did we not squeeze hands, and did I not promise to take care of his child for him, and to take care of Dawn herself? And did I not truly mean it? He placed his trust in me, considered me to be his friend. And how sad that he did not get to see this new life that he had provided for tirelessly, even as his wound festered. He was noble to the end. Hard-working and uncomplaining, handsome and gentle, trying still to provide, to find food, worrying for Dawn's comfort, even in his agony. Of course she had loved him. In the end, we both did.

At first we did not know what it was that had washed up on the beach. It was just a cluster of gulls. Pecking at their carrion. Then we saw. The horror. Dawn ran at the birds, protruding belly and all. She scared them off, then screamed, hands to her ears, at the sight of Andreas's bloated, pecked-at corpse, ran back, burst into tears, wept bitterly while the birds went back to their meal. Soon Andreas was nothing but a ragged skeleton on the beach. The bugs taking over after the birds. And then even the bugs gone. The bones bleaching. The sand blowing across, covering part of his spine. Dawn suffering quietly at her loss.

"I'm sorry," I say. What else is there to say?

And what will become of us now? Dawn is expecting any day. Is barely able to care for herself. I am the pitiful provider. Only I must outlive her. That is my one imperative. At least give that to her. Be there. I cannot leave mother and baby alone. To perish alone.

And then, one night, a great wind blows through, rips down branches, and tears at the shelters.

We listen all night to the hissing and thrashing, feel the shelter pulling away, pulling apart. The next morning it is half-collapsed. And now we sleep under what is left of it. Too weak to put it back up.

The doves are nearly gone. Everything is nearly gone. The gnomes are tipped over, hidden in the brush. Maybe they will be found one day. And carbon-dated. And their meaning will be speculated upon. And our discoverers will wonder who we were and how we lived.

We have ceased playing chess. What is the point? I have surrendered. The king is unmanned.

I have considered poisoning us both together. But with what poison? How would I do it? This is not even the real issue though. The issue is, there is no way I could bring myself to do it, even if I had the means.

Delirium has come to our little settlement, the last ruins of Delirium. As we had always known, inevitably, it must.

- Iowa -

He's going through a phase. That was what Hilda used say when he was young. When we were still together.

"He's always in a phase," I would say. "There's no other phase."

And then I have moved out to Des Moines. Only the conversation —argument, whatever you want to call it—just continues by telephone. Our voices straining, grating. What had started out more or less amicably has grown tense, full of accusation.

"Well maybe he's having a hard time with his Dad gone."

"You're saying that because you want to blame everything on me."

"I'm just saying what I see."

"You see it the way you expect to see it."

"It was your choice, Hans."

"Maybe you are not letting him grow up, Hilda. You want him always to be your baby. You don't want anyone else to be close to him."

"That's not so."

Each argument following a different sequence. The claims and counter-claims following a different order. But all of it much the same.

And then I am visiting for his birthday. Hilda and Aunt Marta and Alika all gathered around Serge, opening his presents. Alika a mother now too, her toddler off in a bedroom, napping, Alika and Aunt Marta barely managing to be polite with me. Filling the room with their high chins, with the unspoken wrong I have done. I have left not just my family but them. Rejected them. Rejected the town.

Serge is sitting on the floor, opening presents with two other children. Hilda has managed to round up these children to make it a party. She serves fruitcake and coffee to the parents, makes conversation, looks for ways to flatter them, to ingratiate herself. And why? So that these parents will encourage their children to stay friends with Serge. Or at least to not pick on him. To be considerate of him. Because of course they— the other children—have sensed that he is different, are inclined to shy away from him. So it is her task to befriend the parents. To turn them into her allies.

Hard to watch. That is what I remember thinking. Hard to see Hilda performing like that. Hard to think about my son needing that. And does it even matter? Does Serge even play with the other children when they are there? At his own party, he opens the new book on astronomy Hilda has given him, turns the pages, seems to forget where he is. He enjoys scrunching up the wrapping paper. Sniffing it. Then he turns to my present.

"Go ahead," I say. "I looked all over town for it."

He looks up at me, goes to work on the package. Handsome boy, I think. At least he has that. Big, gentle eyes, looking over the present— a set of drafting tools and graph paper. Triangle, straight-edge, compass. I had thought the precision, the mathematics, would appeal. "You can design all kinds of things with it," I say. "Cars. Houses."

"*Neat,*" he says. Perfect, eight-year-old American English. But soon he is back with his astronomy book. It is hard to compete with the arresting pictures of far-off galaxies.

"Serge, aren't you going to say thank you?" Hilda encourages.

"Thank me," he says.

"Serge! Say thank you to your father."

"Thank me to my father." Meant as a joke. But Hilda is unsatisfied.

"It's okay," I say. How meaningless, when those words are produced at someone else's insistence. "Why force him?"

She offers me a look of regret. Friendlier at least than Marta and Alika. *You are better than them, Hilda. You were all full of life, once. Don't you remember?* But who is full of life in a land as empty as this?

We sing, *Happy Birthday.* Cut the cake. Am I the only one who feels there is something heart-breakingly sad in it all? In trying so hard?

When it is over I try to kiss him goodbye, but he squirms, runs into his room and closes the door behind him. I make a face at Hilda. Frustration and plea.

"I keep telling you," she says. "He doesn't like it if you haven't shaved. You should before you come over."

"I should shave for my eight-year-old son?"

She doesn't answer. I head into Serge's room, explain that I am going. I wish him a happy birthday, tell him how great it was to see him.

Serge looks away. Eager for me to be gone.

Afterward I am back on the phone with Hilda.

"He's reacting to your being gone," she says.

"How do you *know* that?"

She pauses a moment. "Because I feel like doing the same thing when you visit."

"You're overprotective. That's the problem. It's suffocating him. All he knows is you. Because you don't want him to know anything else. That whole town is suffocating him."

"He's not you," Hilda says. "Just because you felt suffocated...."

"This isn't about me. Why are you changing the subject?"

Then there is the conference his teacher has asked for. It is in the evening, and I agree to drive in to town and pick up Hilda so we can go to the school together. Present a united front. Two people working maturely in the best interests of their child. When she climbs into the car she is all done up, blue chiffon dress and stockings and heels. Perfect mother of that perfect, mid-century decade, in that perfect town in the bullseye of America. She is smiling bravely.

"I recognize that perfume," I say.

"You should. It's the only one I ever wore."

We are soon on what has become our only topic. "How's he doing?"

"He's doing fine," Hilda says. "You just can't expect...."

"Then what is this about? If he's doing fine?"

"I just mean...just love him for who he is, Hans."

Only have I not loved him? What is she implying? And how many times have I heard the same thing? Do I need to hear it again? Suddenly we are arguing. And then we are arguing about arguing. About who started it. Who said what first. Who used what tone.

"Enough," Hilda says finally. "We're two minutes away. We need to stop. For a little while. Do you think you can manage?"

"Fine." And then, "You need to manage too."

"I wasn't the one who said..."

And so the ceasefire is broken. Or rather fails to take hold.

"And I don't want you undermining me when we go in there," Hilda says. "There are things I need to say."

"What does that mean? That I'm not allowed to express my own opinion about my own son? That I'm not allowed to disagree?"

"Did I say that?"

"Well, what the hell else does it mean?"

"Hans, I've spent a lot more time with him than you have. It's just a fact."

"He's still my son."

And then we are inside the school. Silenced. Poised. Putting on our show.

Simple poems up on the walls. Children's drawings. The alphabet. Seeing it, being inside this world, I am struck by how far away I am from my son's life. Hilda is right. What do I even know anymore?

There are three teachers in the school. We meet the teacher for the younger years—Mrs. Mueller. She is friendly, chipper, dyed-blonde woman in her fifties. She talks about all of the different groups she has taught. How each develops its own personality. How much she likes teaching our son's age range. "We just love having Serge in our school. He's such a nice boy."

"That's great," Hilda says.

"He's very studious. Polite with the teachers."

Mrs. Mueller stomps in place, moves her arms heartily as she speaks, like she was coaching a sports team.

"I think he really likes your class."

"Good. Good. We try to stick to the basics." The sports coach again.

A moment more of pleasantries. Mrs. Mueller takes out a pile of Serge's work. "Work-wise, Serge is not doing badly."

What did that mean? That she expected him to do badly? That it was an accomplishment for him to not do badly?

"Here," the teacher goes on. "He did this story for us. I thought it was cute. But you can see...he's not really spelling yet. Not so unusual. But something to watch." I listen for words like, "exceptional" or "superior." Is he not a remarkable boy? Is his chess playing not remarkable for his age? Extraordinary? Surely that means something. Does this teacher just not see it?

"And mathematically?" I ask.

"His math is good," the teacher says. "Although...he needs to work on writing his answers more clearly."

Well, handwriting isn't math, I think. Is it? Hilda glances at me, briefest smile, reading my thoughts, wanting to keep me in check.

"And finishing his problems," the teacher says. "He gets distracted. Focuses in on one problem and then seems to forget where he is."

Hilda nods. "And socially?"

"Well, that's what I notice." At last, the reason for this meeting. "He doesn't really play with the other children. Does his own projects. He likes...he likes sniffing things. Sometimes, one of the other kids will go throw something out and he'll go over to the trash and see what it is. Does he do that at home?

"Not exactly," Hilda says. "But...."

"He likes drawing," the teacher says. "But almost always he chooses the black crayon. Sometimes that might mean he's unhappy. Does he seem unhappy?"

Suddenly my mind is swimming. I think of these laughing children all around him. Playing with each other. And Serge off by himself. Why can't he just play with other children? Why can't he just be happier?

From the corner of my eye there is Hilda—looking proper and composed. How does she manage it? "Is he just shy with the other kids?" she asks. "Is there anything else?"

"Have you thought of other schools?" the teacher asks.

"What other schools?"

"You'd have to move, of course. It's a very small school here. A bigger place there might be more kids like him. Kids he might make friends with. And a program that might fit him."

Hilda turning to me. Nodding. Showing the teacher that we are a team.

Does he have friends outside school, the teacher wonders. Cousins? Maybe a change would be good for him.

No, I think. He has no cousins. He has no friends.

We all nod, agree with one another, assure one another. Growing up isn't easy.

Soon enough we are back to small talk, signifying that our meeting is over. "He's a handsome one," the teacher says. "He's going to be a heart breaker."

"Thanks."

And then Hilda and I are back in the car. Silence. What is there to say? To do? Hilda there in her make-up and lipstick and swishing dress. Only looking sad now. How she tries, though. Suddenly I am thinking of everything we have been through together, have an urge to pull over and put my arms around her. *Hilda let's just try it again. This is wrong. It's wrong for Serge. Let's be a family again.* Only I have learned not to trust this feeling, have learned how quickly it can dissipate, drift mysteriously into, *what am I doing here? I don't belong.*

"I can't bear it," I say.

"That's the problem, isn't it."

"Did you hear what the teacher said?"

"About what?"

"About a different school. Moving him out of here."

"He doesn't need that."

"How are you so sure?"

"This is his home. Our home."

"You're not letting him grow up," I say.

"He's all I have now, Hans. He's all I have to think about. There is nothing I wouldn't do for him if I thought it would help."

"But you won't listen," I say. "You think you're always right."

For a long while we just sit in the car, silent.

"Did you notice what the teacher said about him?" I ask. "That's he's going to be a real heart breaker?"

"What about it?"

"Do you remember you once said that about me? That same phrase? When I was thirteen?"

"Yes. But when I said that...I didn't know it was going to be my heart you would break."

I try one more time, dare to say what I have been thinking. "You just want him like that forever. Just him and you. Do you know why? You want Georg back, Hilda. But he's not coming back."

"Stop the car!" she shouts suddenly.

I keep driving.

"Stop the car! Let me out! I can walk from here!"

I pull over. The door slams behind her. I am alone.

And then I am driving through the night. Wanting what? To run back to them? Or to get more and more miles between us?

I am not meant for this. Not any longer. I am meant for running. Dodging. Diving for cover.

- Illyria -

"It's your turn," Dawn says one night.

We are lying together in what is left of our shelter. We are looking up into the darkness, weakened, wondering, waiting.

"My turn?"

"Tell me," Dawn says.

"What?"

"Your story. Whatever it is you haven't told me. I told you about my mother. It's your turn."

"I see."

"You promised. Remember?"

"I suppose I did."

I feel something coming over me—strange, like a warm wind, a gust of distant memory. I try to focus. Follow the breadcrumbs back. All the way back. To that very moment. How to begin though?

Have you ever heard of Kristallnacht?

Or

Once upon a time there was a boy growing up in a little town on Germany....

Or

Once I met a girl named Sylvia who had pretty eyes like yours. She had dark hair and she was always smiling. Only....

I don't know the words I used. But at last they formed. Formed into sentences. And the sentences into a story. A story I had kept to myself for all of those years, for two generations.

When I finish, Dawn reaches out, reaches across the dark, squeezes my hand. Are we not one now in the darkness—neither young nor old, beautiful nor hideous?

It is done. I have told her. Only how weak her hand feels. As though just squeezing mine requires effort. And who will be strong enough to gather a meal tomorrow? And tomorrow after that?

We no longer track the day of the week. We have lost even the month. There is no time anymore. Just the two of us in our dark shelter, on our deserted island. We are joining with eternity.

- United States -

Do you believe in miracles? Shall I give you this then? Are you so credulous that you would accept it, at least for the sake of closure, denouement, satisfying of expectations? What of its improbability?

Here it is.

It is 1951. Serge is still a little boy and I have just recently moved away to Des Moines, am working as a traveling refrigerator salesman. On the road for days and weeks. And always feeling that same tug, pulling me home, and that same resistance pushing me further and further away. Feeling the miles accumulating behind me. Wanting a thousand different things— experiences, lovers. Thinking of all the parts of the world I wanted to see. Just to be free. To go anywhere.

And then one day I make a stop on one of my visits. Pulling up to the curb. The Red Cross office.

Asking the man behind a counter. "Hans Jaeger? Any messages?"

Some recognition in his voice. "Actually...let me see...." Searching behind the counter. "I seem to remember...."

Feeling my heart start to pound. Is it awful to say I prayed it was not just my mother? Of course I was eager for word of what had happened to my mother. But...if it was my mother then it was not what I wanted it to be.

The man coming back up with an envelope. "Here, I need you to sign this."

Hand trembling. Scribbling my name.

This isn't possible. You are mad to even imagine it. Don't even think about it. It is a mistake. It cannot be!

And then, amazingly, there was the envelope in my hand. What terror then, that I might flip it over and see the return address and see that it was from someone else. Slonimsky. Anyone. Only...Slonimsky would not have used the Red Cross. He knew where I was headed. Who else?

Just look at it.

At last I allowed myself just a glance. And there. That moment. Sylvia Moscowitz. First name Sylvia. Not her last name. But....surely it was her? Married? My Sylvia?

It wasn't real. It couldn't be. And yet...what was this name doing on a piece of paper in my hand? How had it gotten there?

I opened the envelope in the car.

Dear Hans,

I will keep this short, since I don't know if it will reach you. I hope you are well. Yes, I am alive. Don't ask me how because I'm not even sure myself. I hope you are well. Sorry, I already said that. I do hope you will reply if this makes its way to you. Tell me how you are and what you are doing.

Your old pal,

Sylvia

p.s. My toes are freezing! (smiles)

I drove out of town until there was nothing but endless cornfields on either side of the road. I stopped the car and took the letter out and reread it and tried to absorb it.

The new last name suggested she was married. But what of the reference to her toes being cold? Something we had laughed about, her toes always being cold, when we were together. Something that nobody else could have known, that proved without doubt that it was her. And then, was such a reference to our past intimacy more than just a fond recollection? Was she not hinting she wanted me to warm her toes again, as I had done long ago?

I still didn't know if she wanted to see me or just establish contact, find out what had become of me. And why it had taken her so long to write. Had my own letters reached her? There was no reference to them. Still, here was this piece of paper, in my hand, and there could be no other explanation for this extraordinary circumstance but that she was in fact alive, had in fact written these words I was reading.

1950. Sylvia would be twenty-seven, like myself. Did she have

children?   Why had she not written for so long?   I recognized her new
last name as most likely a Jewish one.   Did this mean she was in another
world now, unavailable to me?

From my car, pulled over onto the narrow verge between the road
and cornfield, I considered a response.   I hurried back to Des Moines,
crafting my reply in my mind as I drove.   And suddenly, without
realizing I had been making turns, directing myself, paying the slightest
attention to the world around me, I was back in my apartment in Des
Moines, writing.

Dear Sylvia,

*Is it really possible?   Is it really you?   I keep thinking someone
is playing a cruel prank.   And then I think no.   That is just as
impossible*

*How wonderful that you survived.   No thanks to me, I'm afraid.
How many times I have thought back to our all-too-brief time
together.   How many times have I wondered what became of
you.   If you found your mother, who was waiting for you back in
Edelburg—and I assume you did—then you must know I
survived as well.   Did you get any of my messages?   I hope you
know I did wait for you.   Look for you.*

*What are you doing?   Are you married?   Do you have children?
I worry that what you remember of me is our last moments
together.   I guess saying how sorry I am doesn't really...there is
too much to say really.   I don't even know where to begin.   I
have long wondered if you hated me for everything that
happened.   You must have heard I was in the Wehrmacht.   Can
you forgive me?   Perhaps you would allow me to warm your
pretty toes again.   And beg forgiveness?*

Always,
Your Only Hans

I have little to say of my days waiting for my next reply.   I kept my
travels brief, wanting to check the mail as frequently as possible.   I
sorted through telephone listings of appliance stores, made phone calls,
updated records.   I listened to the radio and took long walks and made
friends with a middle-aged waitress at a diner.   I called Hilda and asked
after everyone.

Mostly though, I just waited for a reply. Only what if I never heard from her again? What if it was only that one little miracle. How long would I keep everything on hold, waiting? What if it had been a lark, if she'd decided she didn't want to be in touch, if her husband had found out, if she took ill. Any of a million reasons why that one short letter might be all I would ever hear. Just as I'd previously come up with reasons why I might yet hear from her, after all these years, now I tormented myself with reasons why I might not.

It took nearly a month, and then, one day, there was a letter in my mailbox at the entrance to my building. And it was in the same hand. With the same return address.

Dear Hans,

It's strange, I dreamed of a reply to my last letter to you, but I never really knew what it would feel like to get one. To hold something written by you. To be transported back to that world. How unreal it would feel. Now I know. And it is quite overwhelming. Yes, of course I thought about you.   And yes, sometimes I felt angry and hurt. Sometimes, through everything I went through, I dreamed you would rescue me. But I knew it was just wanting to believe in magic. Something to distract me, to give hope. Still, it was one of the things I used to help me make it through. So maybe in a way you really did help me survive. But at other times I fell into despair. What if, in that one split second, I had leapt out of the window with you? Maybe we would be together now. Or maybe we would both be dead. Who knows. In any case, there is no point in blaming yourself over that night. You reacted in a way that was perfectly human and I know you would have tried to help if you could have.

As for the Wehrmacht…I'm not sure what to say on that score. Maybe you didn't understand what was really happening. But then after what happened to me…how could you not? But on the other hand I think I know who you are inside and I have no time or energy to think about it or worry about it. Not…if you are serious about warming my toes (more smiles). And if you are not, then please tell me now.

You asked how I survived. I will tell you very briefly. My status as being of mixed race spared me the death camps through most of the war. I was sent to a labor camp outside Dachau and worked as a servant for one of the German commandants on the base. I should say slave rather than servant but it is not a very nice word. It was harrowing and horrible and a hundred times better than so many other stories we both have heard. I was beaten and toward the end the rations declined and I started to truly starve. Shall I say at least I was not raped? For some reason, I do want you to know that. I stayed faithful to my German boyfriend!

Later on in the war, the camp was to be liquidated, and we were all to be sent to somewhere far worse, somewhere nobody left alive. And now this commandant chose to spare me. At least I think he did. He dragged me (I was weak and could only walk with some effort) to his car and took me to his home, outside the camp, where he told me I was to begin work. His wife and children were shocked at the sight of me. I was given a converted closet to live in, and a bare floor to sleep on.

But this is the strange thing. They soon started leaving me there alone. I stole food enough to gain a little strength, and then one day, I fled. I wasn't even sure if he had wanted me to escape, or didn't care, had simply forgotten about me, or was actively hunting me.

The food helped. I had gorged myself before fleeing, and then took as much as I could carry, and headed East. I found myself somewhere in occupied Poland and hid in the woods. When I thought I was again going to die of hunger, I knew I had to do something so I took a risk. When nobody was looking I slipped into a church in a little village and threw myself at the mercy of the priest. There was nobody else in the church. I knew at that moment my life rested entirely with this complete stranger. Would he take pity on a poor Jewish girl? Or would he turn me in? I planned, if I were turned in, to resist, not because I had any hope of escape, but because I was ready to die. I was tired of running. Tired of starving. And at least if I resisted I could get shot on the spot instead of winding up on another transport.

I spoke no Polish, but managed to communicate with the priest. He kept looking away nervously to make sure there was nobody else with us. But I could see, although he did not understand my words, that he understood my situation, and that I was winning him over.

At last he showed me to a little hiding place in the back of the church behind the organ. When I made motions of putting food into my mouth, of begging, he left and came back with a bowl of borscht. He managed to explain, mostly through hand motions, that I was to spend the night, and he would be back the next day. I slept curled up in a tiny enclosure *behind the church organ. When he arrived in the morning it was with two men. At first I was confused. Was this it? Was I being arrested? But they were friendly. And I soon realized they were with the Polish resistance. They moved me to an apartment with a woman-friend of theirs. From there, it was another ten months of heatless hiding places and empty stomachs and close calls. But I was also given work, which was a great solace. At times I felt like I was actually fighting the Nazis. I was actually doing something…besides just trying to stay alive. They taught me how to mix chemicals for explosives, and I worked at it from a laboratory in an unheated basement. Isn't it strange Hans, that we were fighting on opposite sides of the war in that time? I never went outside for months on end, had little food, but I actually had friends. Some Jews who were hiding and helping the resistance, and some Poles. And at times there was satisfaction, hope, a twinge of happiness.*

We were in Krakow when the Russians finally overran the German positions. Do you know I gloried in watching every German death? Every enlisted ordinary soldier like yourself? Every terrified seventeen year old boy with a rifle? Pleasure in revenge. This was what they did to me. This was what they reduced me to. It was only after it was over that I thought of you. Thought back and thought maybe one of them was another sweet boy underneath. How I escaped the Russians, as the borders were closing, is another story, for another day. Another letter, I should say.

To your questions. I was married, but no longer am. Those resistance fighters I mentioned before…well…I'm sure you know how war is. One fell in love with me, and I thought I loved him back, and we married in hiding.

Of course, with the borders closed by the Russians, we had to plan our escape, and so it took a long time to find my way back to Edelburg. I did eventually make it back. With my husband. I didn't know what I would do if you were there. Of course, I hadn't told him anything about you. But it turned out that by the time I reached there you were gone.

I did find my mother though. Thank goodness. About you she was very discreet. She didn't mention you. Because I was married. But then one night when my husband was out I asked if she'd heard what had happened to you, and she told me how you showed up one day, after the war, and asked after me. It meant a lot to me, Hans. And yes, I knew from this that you survived. What a relief that was. Just to know.

We spent over a year in Edelburg, helped my mother rebuild, but there was no happy ending, I'm afraid. She was already feeling sick when we arrived. We had a wonderful, tear-filled reunion, and I'm glad she knew that I had survived, but her illness progressed and she passed away within the year. At least I was there to take care of her.

And as for my husband...what shall I say? Once the war was over, it seemed we had less in common than when we had something we were both fighting for, this cause we believed in. We had no children yet. And so we decided to go our separate ways. Last I heard, he was in New York, and saving money to open a restaurant. Isn't it strange how people adapt to their surroundings? One day planting bombs. The next day opening a restaurant.

I guess that answers your question about whether I have children.

You will wonder why I didn't write. Obviously, at first it was because of my situation. My marriage, I mean. It wouldn't have been right getting emotionally entangled with you again. It is one thing to return to the town I grew up and hope, in my secret heart, that you might be there. And it is quite another to actually try to find you when I am with someone else.

Then, after he and I had parted ways, I needed time. At last though, I realized that the relief I had felt in knowing you had survived—did you not deserve the same?

There is more to say here. But tell me more of your situation first. You ask if I can forgive you. But if you are the same person...well, I just want to know if you are.   .

So tell me what has become of you. I have to believe you are married and a proud father by now. But I suppose I would like to know for sure. Before I start remembering you too fondly.

Sylvia

I read it over and over. First in my apartment. Then in the diner. Then sitting at a bench in a little public park.

My heart leapt at certain phrases and sentences. "...It would only interfere with my desire to know you as I once did." And, "Not...if you are serious about warming my toes." And that last sentence. "Before I start remembering you too fondly." There could be no doubt. She was available. And wanted to know if I was. Was hoping. Surely, she was interested in meeting.

The words brought back a flood of memories. Times that had seemed so distant were suddenly up close again, right there behind me, right over my shoulder. Amana was what became distant. A blur. Lost. I had one purpose now. I hurried to compose a reply.

Sylvia,

I race through your words and then have to go back and reread them just to re-experience them. To absorb them. I probably should have waited longer before replying in order to gather my thoughts. Right now they are everywhere. I am so sorry for everything you have been through. Yes, I stopped by your house more than once after the war, hoping you might come back, or hoping that at least there would be some word of you. I didn't forget you. You know that now. I could not have if I had wanted to. Of course I have many more questions. But... do I dare imagine asking you these questions face to face? And reminiscing about that life we had that was so completely obliterated that this new life seems like a kind of lesser reincarnation? Do I dare imagine visiting you, actually seeing you, alive, for real? I have dreamed of it for so long, told myself always it was an absurd notion, just some impossible idea that my mind wouldn't let go of.

I must tell you one thing. I am married. And separated. Do you remember Hilda, my former nanny, who later became my friend and confidante? Well, I guess lover was the next step after that, and then wife. Although, technically, we never married. But we have a son. He is with her. I have left. I would like to say there is a long story here. But it is long only in my own mind. The facts are simple enough, and too sad and distressing to go into here.

Do you remember Alika from our summer trip to Austria? She was with us in Iowa, and is soon to be married. She was imprisoned for being an anti-Fascist but survived, and I ran into her on the street in Berlin. Speaking of reincarnation, I think she really does believe in it, and I suppose in a way has lived it. Klampf, that nice teacher who was our leader, died in the same camp Alika was sent to. My father died somewhere in Russia. My mother survived, but I have not heard from her since leaving Germany.

I am a salesman and am traveling often. I need to see you. I have never believed in religion much or thanked God for anything, but maybe there is a reason we both made it. You wonder if I am the same person you once knew. I cannot answer that, but you can see for yourself.

Always,
Your Hans

The remaining letters were more about the mechanics of how we would reunite than anything else—mixed in with little memories of moments together, statements of the imperative of our seeing one another again. She was living in Baltimore. It was a four day car drive East, out of the prairie, through hills and past run-down little farms. Through coal country. Across rivers and gorges and mountains. Working class cities with their Woolworths and Sears, their ball fields and cemeteries.

Once I approached a town from the distance and saw smoke rising and suddenly I was headed toward a bombed out ruin. And for a few moments I was there. Back in time. As I got closer I saw it was a smoke stack from a factory. There was no war. Nobody killing anyone. Just miles of this one endless country. I had spent so many miles dwelling in the past, thinking of Sylvia. Moving toward it. No wonder I suddenly found myself inside it. Trapped.

I was somewhere in Pennsylvania. I pulled the car over. Opened the door for air. Forced myself back to the present. Drove on. One more tank of gas, seven hours more on the road, and I was there.

Sylvia lived in a city neighborhood of connected brick single-families, all wedged close together on a steep hill. Each home had a little front lawn no more than a few square feet in front of it. Tricycles and garden hoses cluttered the sidewalk. Big, fat Chevrolets lined the street.

I had tried to imagine, for the last month, what Sylvia must look like now. With her figure filled out and her smile—innocent as a child's even when we were teens—lost to the years. What would it feel like? What would we say?

Shall I mention that it was a brisk, fall day? That a group of girls were out playing jump-rope on the sidewalk? That I made a conscious effort to notice my surroundings, to feel like I was just visiting a friend, enjoying a pleasant afternoon? That even as I turned up her front walk, as the ironically imperious tones of the doorbell sounded, I looked about for something else to notice, to think about, other than what was about to happen?   There. A man tinkering under the hood of his car. Toolbox at his feet. And there. A woman in heels, walking a pair of terriers.

What if Sylvia was changed in some terrible way?   Her looks. What if.   Was it a terrible, superficial thing to worry about that? To wonder?

And then all of the wondering and the build-up was over. The door was open and there she was.

How remarkable is the human mind. Rushing madly to compose the image before it. To locate what it is, what has changed, how it is still the same. All of it accompanied by a rush of emotion. The senses flooding. Consciousness seizing. Telling you this image, this pattern of light that you see before you, is of some great significance.   Its properties, unique only in the most subtle, undefinable way, belong to something important.

On the surface though, we were just looking at one another.

"Sylvia?"

"Hans?"

"Is this real?"

"I'm not sure."

There were many more first words that went back and forth between us. In English and then, more familiarly, in German, and then back to English.   What was said exactly, the awkward stumbling between past to present, between amazement and more quotidian concerns of whether I would like tea or coffee, cannot be reproduced, and in any case are best left imagined.

What mattered more was the impression, or rather, the gradual resolution of the impression—the mind placing the face, the voice, focusing it, aligning it with that past world, that girl, and at the same time merging it with the present—the cooking smells from the kitchen and the Wedgewood on the settee and the warm, dark furniture that looked like it could have come from our childhoods. The reaching across the infinite distance between us and taking her hand—a belated form of greeting or rather a second greeting, required now that we had brought one another into focus, now that we were each surer of the other, sure who we were with.

As we settled in her living room, across a coffee table, I looked into her eyes. Held them. "You look the same."

"Liar."

"You do."

"I can't. You're crazy."

It wasn't just flattery though. What I meant was, it felt like I was with her. Of course she was different, but she was enough the same that it felt entirely like....like she was her.

Her shape was that of an attractive woman in her late twenties. All of the indefinable effects of the years were there. Her eyes had lost a certain lightness. But they were soft and warm and it was a pleasure to look into them.

"Aren't you going to say that I look the same too?" I asked.

"Why should I say that?"

"Because it's polite. Because you're supposed to."

"But you don't. You look...old!" She smiled a little at that.

"I do not!"

"Oh yes. Extremely old." She laughed. "Ancient, in fact."

"Well, then I take back what I said about how you look."

"You can't take it back. Unless you want to admit you were lying in the first place."

"I wasn't," I said, more seriously. "You look...great." I wanted to say beautiful. But I held back.

"And you look...hmm....like someone whose intentions I shouldn't trust."

"I have very evil intentions. To warm your toes."

"Suddenly they're extremely comfortable," she said. "They're just the right temperature."

"That's too bad."

"Yes it is."

"Sylvia."

"Yes?"

"I don't know. I just wanted to say your name."

"Hans?"

"Yes?"

"I think your name is a better name for a boy than for a grown man. At least in this country."

"Should I change it?"

"Yes. To something American. To Joe. Or Steve."

"It's really you. I mean...it has to be. Because we are already joking together. Just like..."

"You really missed me? You're not just saying that?" she asked.

"You know I did."

"I kind of know. I just wanted to hear you say it."

"I missed you. There. Is that good?"

"Now I feel foolish. Making you say it like that."

"It's okay."

"You were sweet, Hans. I can tell you still are." And then, "It wasn't your place to save me. If it was even possible."

"I can't really imagine what you've been through."

"Let's not talk about it. I'm alive. I don't want to think about it now." She looked off, blinked it all away, or tried to. "So what about you? Where did you fight?"

"Fight? I didn't really fight. I drove trucks in North Africa. I retreated through Italy. Then I retreated through Poland. I shot an enemy duck. Are you proud of me?"

"Very. Very well done. My hero!"

We smiled. Then I turned serious again. "You must hate me though in some way. You must hate all Germans. How could you not?"

At that she looked almost uncomprehending. "Hans have you forgotten? My mother was German. Not Jewish. German. And she was my mother. How could I hate all Germans?"

I covered her hand with mine.

"Your skin feels a little rougher," she said.

"You remember how my skin felt?"

"Yes."

"I remember yours."

"I remember how all of you felt," she said.

"How did all of me feel?"

"Like...like...I'm going to cry."

"That bad?"

But she was still serious. "You know, I used to think about it, about sex, about you and me, when I was most sure I was going to die. Just a way of trying to block out the moment."

"Did it work?"

"No. But maybe it helped."

"The story in your letter was amazing," I said.

"I never have told anyone all of it before like that. But once I started writing, I just wanted to get it out." And then, "Everyone's story from that time was amazing. Yours certainly was."

I hadn't yet told her my war experiences. So I wondered what she meant. "How was mine amazing?" I asked.

Here she laughed again. "Oh, come on, Hans. You married your nanny!"

"I think I mentioned...technically, we never married."

"Oh fine. And that matters?"

"And it's hardly a story...unique to that period."

Sylvia was smiling, teasing, but it was not an easy subject for me to laugh about, given how I had just left Hilda, how horrible I felt about it, how I really had no excuse.

Sylvia seemed to sense it. "What should we talk about?" she asked.
"Anything."

"Let's get outside," she said.

"Where?"

"I have an idea. I just...I'm feeling too full of energy to be sitting still in here."

I put my jacket back on. We headed up the hill outside her door. She was in a skirt and sweater, looking quite at home—so it seemed to me—in Baltimore. We turned a corner and headed up another long slope and at last came to a public park at the top of a hill. The walkways of the park were full of fallen leaves that our feet swished through. And more leaves, bright yellow and orange and brown, were still in the trees, in the air, pirouetting down, swirling back up in gusts.

We came to a more-or-less secluded bench that looked out toward the city, and sat together. "What does this remind you of?" she said.

"I don't know."

"You don't know?"

The view was at once beautiful and bleak, tinged with late afternoon, the coming sunset, the coming winter. I put my arm around her. "I'm not really thinking of the view. I'm thinking of you. Of being here with you."

"That's what I mean," she said.

"I'm not following."

"This is our castle," she said. "Up on the hill. Remember?"

"Yes."

"Remember this?"

And then she turned to me and we were kissing. Just like that.

"Yes, I remember that too," I said.

"The view is not quite as perfect, I'm afraid."

"It doesn't matter."

"It still feels good though."

"Yes it does."

We watched the sunset crossing behind the black branches of the trees, watched the rooftops melt together in the dusk.

"Is this really real, Sylvia?"

"I'm thinking it is."

"I hope so."

"How did you wind up here?" I asked. "Why Baltimore?"

"I have family here. On my father's side. They started taking me to the synagogue. I guess I'm actually Jewish now."

"Do you like that?"

"I better. I've suffered enough for it." And then, "They've been nice. They paid for my apartment and got me settled. It's a nice community."

"I doubt they would like me very much."

She smiled. "They keep trying to set me up with these men from the congregation."

"And?"

"And my mind is open. But none has been right. You know how they say Jewish men make good husbands?"

"I think I've heard that," I said.

"Well I think it might be true. Only the good husbands already *are* good husbands. To someone else."

"So there's nobody?"

"There is somebody, Hans. There is you."

We were holding each other tightly. "Oh by the way," she said, "you're welcome to convert."

"I could become a Jew?"

"Sure. If you want them to accept you." She was smiling. But maybe partly serious.

"I don't really believe in religion," I said.

"In that case it should be easy."

"It would seem like I was trying to hide something. I am who I am."

We stayed a while more, until it was dark, and the cold had settled through us. Then we headed back down to her place. We arrived inside to the warmth of the stirring radiators in her apartment.

"You haven't told me what you do now."

"I'm a bookkeeper. At a local bank."

"Do you like it?"

She took off her sweater. Put her head against my chest. "I don't want to talk about it."

"What do you want to talk about?"

"Nothing."

So we were quiet for a while. Barely moved. Then she took me by the hand. "Come with me."

And I was going up the stairs with her. Into the dark of her bedroom. Onto her bed. And then we were embracing. She got up and pulled down the shades and came back and we were in near-total darkness.

I had a sense of why she wanted that—not just that we were older, imperfect in our physical forms, and not just as a gesture to how we had once tiptoed in darkness up the stairs of her mother's house, but so that there might be no present. Or rather no time. No time between our last night together and this one. Nothing at all had happened. This was just the next night.

Of course it could never be perfectly so. Consciousness itself had changed. The awareness of her arrest. The endless ordeals that filled the years between our last meeting and this one. Even the different feel of our forms—not just of each other's bodies, but of our own bodies. But for all of it, still, there was a way in which the darkness merged all of it together, the feel of her, the whispers and kisses. There was a way in which it was just us. Nothing bad had happened. It had all been a dream. *See? We are here still. In bed still. In love still.* And now here we were. How shockingly close to perfection.

I wanted it to linger just like that, wanted us to just whisper and hold each other and tempt ourselves with desire. But at last I was shushed, was pulled over her, inside her. For just a moment a thought passed through me. That she knew I had been living as someone else's husband. And that she didn't let it stop her. Or more than that. She wanted us to do this as quickly as possible, to be done with it, so there would be no doubt about it. And it occurred to me how this was something different. A different Sylvia. A Sylvia who had done enough suffering. Who wanted what she wanted. And then desire overwhelmed everything else. Surreal moment, making love to a ghost, to someone who cannot be real, somewhere that could not have been earth.

Afterward we lay in the dark together for a long while. "Let's go away somewhere together," I said. "Somewhere far away."

"I feel like I've heard that before."

"But...I mean it. I can finally do it. I can finally do what I promised."

"You're done with Iowa?"

"Yes."

"Your son?"

"I will visit them. I cannot live there again."

"It's not right. I don't want you to leave them for me."

"I've already left."

"Really?"

"Yes. Really. Truly."

"I just don't feel like I can keep you from your son."

"I'll go back and visit. I can't live there anymore."

"Where should we run away to?"

"I don't know," I said. "I was thinking of Africa."

"Seriously? Africa?"

"Or the South Pacific."

"What about South America?"

"Yes. There too."

"Let's get something to eat first. Then we can plan."

"Good idea."

We dressed and went down to the kitchen, turned on the lights and let our eyes adjust. Sylvia took cold-cuts out of a brand new refrigerator (Frigidaire, our competitor) and made sandwiches.

We ate them and listened to the radio, a big console in her dining room. I remember The Weavers' *Goodnight, Irene,* and Nat King Cole's *Mona Lisa.* The same songs I had heard so many times on the car radio driving East.

"What about Iceland," she suggested.

"If that's where you want."

"My feet would get cold."

"I could warm them."

"Did you notice how well I set that up?"

"Yes. It was ingenious."

And then we went back to bed.

The next day was our last together in Baltimore.

She took me down to the Chesapeake and we looked out at the sea, busy bay of trawlers and tugboats and gulls floating effortlessly like they were dangling on a mobile. She told me the rest of the story of her escape with her husband from Poland, which involved paying off a series of officials and stowing away in a boat headed to Copenhagen.

"Thank goodness for bribery," she concluded.

"For corruption of all varieties."

I told her more of my mother, of how I had suspected her, of my letters with my father. I told her of running out into the Libyan desert and diving for cover, of being shot in Italy and saved by a little group of Partisans. We walked past some docks lined with bigger ships, and dreamed of finding a berth on a liner and heading off to points unknown.

"I hope," I said, "we can get a room with a ceiling a little higher than the one I had coming over."

"That's okay," she said. "I'll keep you horizontal." She smiled devilishly at this.

We walked up from the harbor, back to the car, and I asked what she wanted to do next.

"I don't know. How about a movie?"

"Sure," I said, and followed her directions to a local cinema. We didn't pay much attention to what was actually playing, as there were no other choices. We just took our seats in the dark. Music started. A white cone of light slashed past us, illuminating a million specks of dust.

Sylvia leaned over and whispered to me. "This is kind of a backwards date."

"How is that?"

"First we go to bed, then you take me out to a movie?"

"True," I said. "And when the movie is over, I'll get up the courage to ask you out."

We held hands. The music started. *Our Feature Presentation.* Then military music. An airfield. Americans in uniform. Somehow, we had completely missed that it was movie about World War II. Now a heroic bit of American History.

Firm, gritty voices said things like, "I'm ready, Colonel!" and "Cover me!" and "Aye, aye, Sir!"

Such handsome, brave, hale soldiers, even when covered, as they often were, with artfully placed dabs of grime and sweat.

We watched the Germans get outsmarted and blown up, over and over. We watched the plucky Americans, undermanned, find creative ways of destroying us. We watched German machine gunners fire hundreds of rounds, possibly thousands, and yet still manage to miss their targets.

"Wow, we are even worse in the movie version," I whispered.

"I'm glad you're losing again," Sylvia whispered back. "I was afraid you might win this time."

"Look at us! We couldn't beat a troop of American Girl Scouts!"

We laughed and were shushed more than once.

"Why are the Germans speaking English with German accents?" I asked. "They sound ridiculous."

"Hans?"

"Yes."

"That's what you sound like."

"Is it?"

We broke into more laughter, kissed, squeezed each other's hands.

At the end of this particular movie, the flyer, played by Tyrone Power, takes a hit in mid-air. He is wounded, his plane is damaged, but he manages to bring it down safely, valiantly, to the airbase from which he has started. He taxis up the runway to meet the woman he is to marry. She is waiting for him as he gets out of the plane. The music swells. The credits roll. Sylvia and I kiss in triumph at our defeat, at our miracle, at our laughing at the war, the world, at our finding one another.

We return to her apartment where she packs her things and we set out, destination unknown.

We stay at a motel somewhere in Virginia. Shady Lane Motor Court. Or something like that. Doorways opening on to the parking lot. Little yellowed outside lamp above the door, a confetti-heap of moths piled below it. What might be called tacky now or cheap, but was then a wonder of uniformity and simplicity—the clean rectangle of the room, the sheets of the bed tucked in so tight they had to be pried apart like opening a vacuum-seal, the mass-produced landscape paintings on the walls.

Wrapping my arms around her from behind.

Sylvia pretending to resist. "The German is not supposed to get the girl."

"I'm American now."

"Ah. In that case I want you inside me."

Our romance had never really been what one might think of as lustful, until that night. It was something in our flight. Our exhaustion. The anonymity of that cheap motel room. Even the water stains on the walls that the paintings did not quite conceal.

What I remember was both the squeaking of the bed and the feeling of not caring about it, savoring it, the luxury of love, of Sylvia, more than a man had a right to.

From there we drove off to eternity.

The car heads into the far distance. Silence. Nothing. Everything. Fade. Credits roll.

- Illyria -

This is how we have come to estimate the passage of time: by Dawn's belly.

One month until she is due. That is our estimation. Five months since Andreas died of gangrene. Five long months of just the two of us. And yet we are still alive. Or suspended, somehow. Between alive and dead. Between sanity and delusion. Yet providence, or dumb luck, or whatever you wish to call it, has provided for us somehow. The storm that slashed open our shelter has left a windfall of ass fruit. They must have been growing back, with fewer of us to eat them now. The root vegetables have come back a bit as well. I have even managed to snag a few bigger crabs, with patience and stealth and the rudimentary tools of some pre-human species. I try to keep Dawn off her feet now. Gather what I can for her. Fetch the water from Piss Brook.

For months I had been thinking how I needed to live now, how I cannot let her be the last one left. Her and the baby. But now I think, what if she dies in childbirth? What if I am the last one? What then? How will I bid my farewell to it all? To this life? One last chess game against the universe. Against time itself. One last game that has no end, that goes on forever.

- United States -

He is sitting cross-legged on a bare mattress in a bare room in Oakland, California. It is 1970. His blonde hair comes down below his shoulders. There is a single chair next to the bed, stuffing spewing out as though from open wounds in the fabric. Beside the mattress is a bookshelf made of cinder-blocks and bare, wooden planks.

"How can you be giving me advice?" he asks. "After what you did?"

"What are you referring to?" I ask.

"What you did," he says.

He pulls his hair back behind his ears. Looks at the wall. He still has those penetrating eyes, would be striking if he would only smile. But instead he looks away. Carries himself oddly. Does something strange, asymmetrical with his jaw when he speaks.

"What did I do?"

"You know."

"I don't know. Tell me."

I am expecting him to bring up my leaving him. But it is not that.

"You fought for the Nazis."

Startled. Trying to keep an even tone of voice. "That's not so."

He has dropped out of college, just as he was nearing graduation. He had been a physics major. At least I had been right about his mathematical abilities. Now he is working at a record store.

"It *is* so," he says.

"Where did you hear this?' I ask.

"From her."

"From your mother?"

"Yes."

"I don't think she meant it like that."

"How do you know how she meant it?"

The room is in a shared, four bedroom apartment. I have met at least eight people in the living room and kitchen. I have no idea who lives in the apartment, who merely sleeps in it from time to time, who is just visiting. I am not convinced there is a precise answer to this.

"Your mother and I were both against it. I'm sure she told you that too."

"But then you joined them."

"I was a lowly private. A *Landser.* That's what we were called. That's all."

I glance over the books along the shelves. Physics. Math. A sci-fi section. *Dune. Stranger In A Strange Land.* Something in a mustard-yellow binding, called *One Dimensional Man.*

Serge shakes his head as though he his shaking me away, shaking away the idea of me. "How can you say you didn't?" he asks. "That's just a lie."

"It's not a lie."

"Did you not fight in the war?"

"Yes but…"

"On the wrong side?"

"It wasn't like that."

"Do you deny it was the wrong side?"

"No. I don't deny it was the wrong side. But…it wasn't like that."

Music coming in from somewhere. Echoing through the bare rooms.

> *It's the same story the crow told me; It's the only one he knows.*
> *Like the morning sun you come and like the wind you go.*

"What was it like?"

"I was against all of it! I never supported…."

"Isn't that what they all say? Somehow nobody ever supported it. They were all against it. But it still happened. It still had lots of support. Didn't it?"

"Just because some people supported it, and then lied about it after, doesn't mean we all…."

"A fact is a fact. You did what you did."

There are posters on the walls, peeling down. Icons. Peace symbols. Stencil of some important leader with bushy hair. Che or Jimi or Angela Davis. How we have gotten from the ten-year-old Serge to this, I cannot say. But this is where we are.

"I...Serge...listen to me. I was involved with a girl who was Jewish."

"Mother told me."

Mother. Never just *Mom.*

"How could I have supported...."

"So that makes it better? That you fought for the Nazis even after...after this girl? That makes it worse! It should have been obvious to you!"

Covering my face with my hands. "I...I was just a soldier. I experienced horrible, awful things. I hated it. I hated all of it."

"You could have deserted. Did you even consider it?"

"I was your age, Serge. They stuck a gun in my hands. I lived through things you cannot imagine. I saw friends getting...."

"Mother said you volunteered."

"Yes. In a way, yes. But..."

I live in a silver mine and I call it beggars tomb
I got me a violin and I beg you call the tune....

"What did you do to stop it?" he asks.

"What could I have done?"

Where do these accusations come from, I wonder. Is this really about what I did before he was born? Or about something more personal, some hurt and shame he cannot confront directly. On the other hand, maybe I am just looking behind his words, in order to avoid looking right at them. Aren't his accusations the same ones I leveled against my mother? How did she support it? Wasn't it obvious how evil it was? And now, here I am. Thinking back. Wondering.

I have said that sometimes you must be one thing or another. Only what was I? Which thing?

"What should I have done?" I ask, almost looking for a suggestion.

"You could have deserted."

"Not so easily."

"You could have helped that girl to...."

"You don't know that!" I say, suddenly more emphatic. What does he know though? What has Hilda told him? I don't even want to find out. I cannot talk about it. We are at an impasse.

I take him to dinner at a Chinese place. He pushes, the food around his plate, at first like he is sulking, and then more intently, like he is daydreaming, lost in some game. Afterward I tell him I need to go. He lifts a hand up, blank wave goodbye. I reach to hug him, feel him squirm out from it.

And then years later again. The very last time I will see him. At Hilda's funeral.

It is fall and the wind is whipping across the cemetery—a plain, little rectangle on the edge of town. Stray leaves are flying out from a lone maple tree and scattering about us, whirling around our feet.

Serge, having moved up and down both coasts, and having drifted through philosophies and religions and occupations, has moved back to Iowa. He has gone back to school in agronomy and consults for a company promoting hybrid seeds and controlled-release fertilizers. He has a fiancé, Julia, there beside him, small, round-cheeked Midwestern girl, holding his hand. I have seen Serge a few times since Oakland. Have even gotten him to play me a chess game once. But it is never right.

Now Marta is on the other side of him, looking frail, thinner than ever, leaning against a cane. But still alive. She has outlived Hilda. And Alika and Gustav are there, now with two grown-up girls. All of them huddled together amidst a small gathering around the grave.

At the head of the grave there are two hands holding up a Bible. And above it a voice speaks of what a kind soul Hilda was, what a strong member of the community, what a devoted mother—the Hilda these people know.

The gravestones are in neat little lines like rows of teeth. Beyond them is nothing but open prairie, out to the horizon. So this is it, I think. This is where her journey ends. Hilda who helped raise me and lived through the war with me, who starved with me and made love to me and traveled across the world with me. This is where she will rest.

A gust of wind scatters leaves around our feet. How is this possible? Why here?

I think of her first child. Georg. The shot that killed him. The little churchyard he is buried in on another continent. How strange that they should be so far apart. *It's not that I stopped caring.* That is what I keep thinking to myself.

Serge is as expressionless as the land. Alika puts a hand on his back, but he steps away from it. Still avoiding being touched. He has become one of them. I can see it now. But he is also still entirely himself. And I can't help feeling that, in becoming one of them, he has hardened against me.

The voice is speaking of Hilda's good works in the town. Baking for the church sale. Her friends in the sewing circle. *God.* All of it watched over by God. Taking care of us. Designing this simple world that is like a children's storybook. Corn and cows, silos and farmers.

Blessing it and watching over it. You only have to close your eyes and think of Him. Isn't that right?

But where was He for you, Sylvia? That is my question. And for Georg? And all the others?

Then the man is done speaking. We are all leaving little mementos in the grave. I have brought my own for this. It is a photograph that somehow made it with me across the Atlantic. The photograph is of Hilda and my mother and me at a bench by the river in Edelburg. Of course it is black-and-white, but it is perfectly clear. I am perhaps seven years old, standing behind Hilda and pulling locks of her hair straight up to make her look crazy, and she is laughing and trying to swat at me. The young and lively and lighthearted Hilda I knew. The Hilda who these people never knew.

And then everyone is shaking Serge's hand. Expressing their sorrow at his loss. He receives them rigidly, formally, like a boy in a school play. And then we are back at Serge's house. Just me and Serge and Julia. We talk about his job with the seed company. Her family, who are from Nebraska. He still doesn't look straight at me when we talk. But we manage to make conversation. About how the town has changed. It has its first fast-food restaurant. Its first stoplight. At the same time, its population has started to shrink. The old are dying and the young are moving away and here and there houses are sitting empty. There are abandoned storefronts along Main Street.

After some time, Julia puts on an apron and heads off to the kitchen, and Serge and I are alone together in his living room.

Spindly wooden furniture. Little, braided throw-rug, pulled up to a fireplace.

"Nice girl," I say.

"Thank you."

"How are you doing?"

"We're well, in fact."

Strange thing to say, under the circumstances. But he is trying to make a point. I wonder, who is *we*? Is he including just Julia? Also Alika? Marta? Some unnamed group from which I am excluded.

"That's good."

He is leaning forward, holding the tie he wore at the funeral. "I have a question."

"Yes?"

He takes out an old photograph, puts it on a table in front of me. "Who is that?"

I am startled. Answer slowly. "That's your mother. With...Georg. Her...her first son."

"What happened to him?"

"He was killed. Where did you get that?"

"I found it cleaning out her dresser. Why didn't you...why didn't anyone tell me about him?"

"She couldn't bring herself to talk about it."

"Can you imagine my finding it though? This picture? This other boy? Who I never knew existed?"

"It was a horrible thing. She just...she tried to block it out."

"That's what Alika says. Only...it feels like it explains a lot."

"What does it explain?"

"What she went through. She'd already had this happen. And then...what you did."

"What do you mean about what she went through?"

"She kept it in. People didn't see it. She suffered though."

I am taken back to the funeral. The voice from above the Bible. "I'm sorry to hear that."

"Then how could you?" he asks. At last he looks directly at me, into my eyes.

"I tried."

"Did you?"

"Yes."

There is a long pause. He is looking down again, wrapping his tie in his fingers. "It's just like...."

"What?" I ask. But I already feel something building in me. Something I am trying to suppress.

"Like in the war."

And now my voice is constricted. Everything feels like it is changed. "I don't even understand what you are talking about. How is it like...."

"Alika says you could have resisted."

"Do you really want to talk about this now?"

"Well, could you have?"

"Look what happened to Alika," I say. "She was sent to a camp. She nearly died."

"All you do is run. Run away. It's what you did in the war. It's what you did with Mother. And...and me."

I feel a strangeness, a sickness settling over me. What to say? There is no answer. "Serge...I am sorry. I wanted your mother to...she never...."

Then we are both silent for a while. I want him to reply. To say anything. But he has gone dark. Just like a light has gone out. His head is turned away. Julia comes out, serves us tea, kisses the top of

Serge's head, retreats back to the kitchen.

Should I tell him what I really think? That Hilda did not really want him to grow up? Because of what had happened to her? What is the point? How will it help?

"You have no idea what we lived through," I say. "I was a kid. I saw things nobody should ever see."

"And then you left Mother," he says, as though continuing his own thought, as though he hasn't heard anything I have said.

Here we are again, I think. Around and around.

"What does...what does the one have to do with the other?"

"It has to do with...."

I wait. He looks away. Speaks calmly, evenly, like he is reading an essay in a class. "It has to do with the fact that you're a coward."

Does he mean this? Or does he just know the exact words to use. The exact words that will cut most deeply?

Suddenly, I am nearly shaking. Raising my voice. "Damn you!"

If he is frightened—by his own words or by mine—he doesn't show it.

I can feel my voice cracking. "You have no idea what I have been through!" Am I not entitled to some anger toward my son? Must I never allow it? Was he not the one who pulled us apart? Did she not turn against me when she devoted herself so completely to him? It all floods through me. I hear myself shouting. And then he is talking over me.

"You left us. You ran. Just like...."

"You wouldn't even look at me! Nobody would! You still don't."

"Did it never occur to you...?"

There is a rare flash of emotion—contained, but showing through. "What?" I ask.

"That...."

But he cannot say it. That he was just a child? That I needed to love him more? That all ever he needed was...? Whatever it is, he cannot say it.

"I can't do this," I say.

"Fine." Serge is looking off. His face is turned away, dull and expressionless. "Then just go."

Burying my face in my hands. "I can't do that either."

"Yes you can. It's what you do best. Just go!"

"Please...."

"Bye."

Like that for a long time. Waiting for him to say something more. "I'll call you."

No reply.

"Serge...no. Not like this."

No answer.

"Just say goodbye. Please."

"Goodbye. Please."

Getting up at last. Putting on my coat. Goodbye. Goodbye my son.

You see? I warned you not to like me. Yes, I have suffered. But I have also been the cause of suffering.

- Illyria -

It's a boy!

Isn't that what one is supposed to say?

Only there is nobody here to announce it to. Still, it is itself a small miracle, is it not? Dawn has given birth and I have assisted, received this child into the world. And somehow—and I am not entirely sure how—we are all alive. Moreover, did my assistance in the delivery of this baby not confer upon me some special role in its life? As though I not only delivered it, but I received it as well, it came to me, was delivered to me, the next in line to care for it. It became mine. My charge.

I am trying, Andreas. Your bones have been washed away by the tides, scattered back into the sea. But you are not forgotten. Your child lives. Dawn lives.

Strangely, my own health has been lifted as well. In receiving this new life, I somehow have been given new life. It cannot last forever, of course. But maybe it will hold out long enough. Maybe we will yet be rescued. In fact, a little dot of a ship passed along the horizon this very morning. No, it did not see us. It did not come close enough. But it was our first sighting in many weeks. Is that not itself cause for hope?

And in my restored state, I have managed a few repairs. The shelter is back as it was. Amazingly, even the doves have made a bit of a comeback. They have recovered from the rains, and are laying again.

Dawn's health has also returned after her ordeal. She is able to smile at the baby, hold him, nurse him. And just in the last week, he has started to smile back. To coo.

We are alive!

I come back from foraging with an armful of fruit, and we feed the baby together. Is he not truly mine? My responsibility? My son? And has it not lifted our hearts? Is my own gaze not fixed upon both of them, mother and child, with a kind of contentment, watching the baby's tiny fingers wrap around his mother's pinkie, watching her nurse him, heading into the interior to gather more for them, peeling and cutting with our oyster shell knife, and passing little bits to Dawn to feed to the baby? Are we not a family of sorts now?

Would you like to know the baby's name?

Before the delivery, I had asked Dawn if she was thinking about any names, but she had not wanted to discuss it. I wondered why at the time and then I realized. What if it did not survive? Better that it just die anonymously in that case. Join its father. But then he was with us, alive and suckling, and so I brought it up again when Dawn was well enough to talk of it.

"I can't decide," Dawn said. "What do you think?"

"We should call him Illyria," I said. "Future king of Illyria."

She smiled wistfully. "Not sure you can make a good nickname out of that."

We considered other names. Absurd ones. Darius the Great. Names that spoke of the island surroundings that he has been born into —Coral or Dove, as an indigenous people might have chosen to call him. Names that the Puritans might have considered, that spoke of him as a gift—Miracle or Providence. And, at last, names that might have appeared in our copy of *Vogue*—Justin, Sean, Brad. Sergio Carbajal.

"What about Friday?" I suggest. "From Robinson Crusoe."

"It's already taken."

"Okay so how about Thursday?"

But this only brought to mind that we had no idea on what day of the week the baby was born. Nor what day of the month. Nor even... what month. We had lost all track of time during the rains, the time of near-death.

The discussion lasted days. I could not help wondering at times: does he really need a name? Who will need to call him by his name? There are only three of us. Each its own type. Old man. Young woman. Baby. Aren't names only required when it is necessary to distinguish individuals among their types? But here, we are each unique. Old man. Young woman. Baby. King. Queen. Pawn.

It is strange what we will name. Summer homes and yachts. But not refrigerators. Not even fancy ones. Not appliances or garments or plumbing fixtures. My villa had a handsome sign in front declaring it to be *Summer Breeze*. But there was no sign by my toilet, proclaiming it *Windsong*, or *Mystic Waters*. Pets are given names. Except for pet fish. Why boats but not cars? Why summer houses but not winter houses?

Important things, beloved things, get names. So why not parents? Our parents *have* names, but we don't use them. We address them, no matter the language, no matter the culture, by their roles, their relation to us. Mother. Mutti. Maman. Mum. As though this is the essence. Not the individual. Just the role. Mother. Mother of all. And so it is with this baby. He is just Baby. That is all.

"Maybe we don't need to name him," I suggest.

It is a passing notion though. There is no doubt that the baby must be named. There is too much of our past lives, our civilized lives, that is ingrained in us, to consider otherwise. And in the end it is my suggestion that is chosen. We have named him Andre, in memory of Andreas, his father.

And does it not say something that it was a mutual decision? That Dawn didn't want to choose a name I did not approve of?

We have found that this desire to track time, this need to measure, to know how many days have elapsed, is a powerful one. And so, now that the fevers have passed, we have started a new calendar. We set Andre's birth date as the first date of our new calendar—January First of Year One. And we are again scratching in the days on a rock. Today is May 18, 0001.

Here is something else. I am becoming that odd, contemporary character—the stay-at-home father. Or in this case the stay-at-hut father. Now that Dawn is healthy again, we have agreed that she is far more able than I am to gather food. And so I have many hours of tending to Andre. Holding him. Talking to him and listening to his babbling replies. *Look, Andre. One of the doves as laid an egg! Are you going to help me cook it? How should we prepare it, do you think? Scrambled? Eggs Benedict?*

There is no time or energy for chess anymore. And Dawn and I seldom speak of the past as we did. We have shared what there is to share. She knows the worst. I sometimes think back to stories she has told. Especially that one. The imaginary cure she made for her mother. I cannot help but think, if only everything worked by magic like that, the way a child imagines it. I remember back to Dawn tending after Monique when Monique herself was pregnant, Dawn trying to assist in Monique's delivery. Mostly Dawn's reaction afterward. And how clearly I see her now. This child forever trying to save her mother. Reliving it, over and over.

Dawn allows me to rest a hand on her now. To touch her shoulder as we settle to sleep. Gesture of compassion. My compassion toward her that compels me to touch. Her compassion toward me that she permits it. I have reached my peace with her, with this mythical girl who rose up out of the ocean one day and sat down with me to a game of chess.   We are joined now, in the darkness.   All three of us. Shapeless and ageless and one.

We do talk sometimes, Dawn and I, when Andre is sleeping. But it is about the present. Or even, most remarkably, the future.

"Next deserted island I'm on, I want there to be mangos," I say.

"And hot water," Dawn says.

"And people."

"Then it wouldn't be deserted."

"Just a few nice families. Kids for Andre to play with."

"That would be nice."

I am not entirely free from darker thoughts. Is anyone? Shall I tell you my darkest? My most private? It is this: That there is nobody here to know. To judge. And so what is to stop me from forcing myself on her? From finally conquering Dawn? Completing the act? But alas, I cannot. Cannot do it physically and cannot do it mentally. How fitting, that such an opportunity would come to me when my ancient obelisk has finally given way, has crumbled. When I am incapable of managing the act I still so vividly imagine. But of course it is not just physical impossibility that saves me. It is humanity. Conscience.   And yes, even this: shame. And is it not enough to lay beside her? To feel that she prefers my proximity to my absence? And as she drifts off to sleep, is it not enough just to lean over and kiss the back of her hair and think of the baby sleeping beside her?

Do you see? I was wrong after all. There is a purpose to all this shame.

May 18, 0001: Ocean startlingly calm. Boat in the far-away distance all morning. Andre turns at the sound of his name. I touch Dawn's hair.

- Germany -

My mother dressed in black. High heels clicking. Wiping her eyes.
Dabbing them.   My father, dressed in his best, hair slicked down,
bringing her tea. How young they are. My mother's face sad and
smooth and pretty. The same age I was, more or less, when I left
Germany. And yet I felt like my life hadn't started then. And the two of
them in that elegant old house, so admired in Edelburg. No wonder my
father had seemed uncomfortable in himself.

On the floor of the drawing room.   My mother sweeping in.
Dabbing her eyes. Crying. *What is it Mutti? What's wrong?*

My father, adjusting his tie. "Don't bother your mother now."

"What's wrong, Mutti?"

My mother turning to me. Kneeling down. Wrapping her arms
around. "It's *Oma*." Grandma.

"Why is it *Oma*?"

Arms tight around me. Enclosing me. "She had to go away, Hans."

"Why did she had to go away?"

"Because she did."

"Where did she had to go away?"

"To Heaven."

Heaven must be very terrible. Why else would *Mutti* be crying?

What a strange, unsettling feeling, seeing my mother like that.
Fighting back tears. *You're a big boy.* That was what she said. *What a
big boy!* I would make her a present. That was it. That was what I
would do. I would make her a present and I would make *Oma* a present
for when she got back from Heaven.

Taking out my papers and my wax crayon-sticks from my room.
Finding a corner in the drawing room. Sketching flowers and birds.
Like I liked to draw. A little turtle-shaped boy with a big semicircle

Dan Blum

smile. Me. Hans. And a little river. Like the little river in the middle of town that *Vati* says flows into the Danube. What is the Danube though? Vati says it is a great big river that flows into the ocean. What is the ocean? It is something that is just water everywhere. Everywhere you look. I draw a whale in the river. Next to Hans I draw *Mutti*. Big round blob with a great big smile. Why was she crying though? Because *Oma* had to go to Heaven. *Oma* taught me to swim in Lake Constance. *Look at him swimming already! A regular fish!* I draw a fish next to the whale.

My father above me. "Come, Hans. We have to get ready."

"What do we have to get ready?"

"We have to get ready for *Oma*'s funeral."

"Where is *Oma*?"

"She's in Heaven."

"Isn't she coming to her funeral?"

Hurrying to finish the drawing. Flowers. *Mutti* likes flowers. Drawing them in.

My mother coming over. "What are you drawing?" Gathering herself. Perfume. Lipstick. My father zipping up the back of her dress. "You can finish later."

Huddling over it so she couldn't see. Because it's a surprise. Hurrying with the next one. For *Oma*. What does Oma like? Cookies. She is always making cookies. And horses. She is always reading stories about horses. Drawing furiously. Farm. Horse. Plate. Cookies. Big smile. Hurry hurry.

More feet arriving. Kisses on cheeks.

"I'm so sorry."

"Thank you."

"Hans…come on! Put it away!"

Oma is *Mutti's Mutti*. *Mutti* is sad because *Oma* is away in Heaven.

Drawing Heaven. Only what is it? Big circles. All different colors.

"Are you going to go to Heaven, *Mutti*?"

My mother wiping tears. "Hans! No! I mean…I'm not going anywhere. I'm right here. Put it away, now."

Done! Jumping up suddenly. Big smile on my face. "Look, *Mutti*. I made it for you!"

My mother looking at it. A new burst of tears.

"What's wrong?"

Doesn't she like it? Did I do something bad?

My own tears bursting through at last. My mother kneeling down. Wrapping me in all of her perfume and softness. "My little Hans."

Mutti looking at the picture again. "Thank you. It's beautiful."

Reaching down. Holding up the next one. "And look! This is for Oma!"

"For…?"

"When she comes back from Heaven!"

Showing it to *Mutti*.

More tears. My mother breaking down. Now what? What did I do wrong? What? What did I do wrong, *Mutti*? *Why aren't you saying anything? Say something!*

If only one could go back in time! Just for a day. An hour. To see them so young. To see Edelburg and the house and feel the air and smell it and hear the sounds. Back before any of it. Before all of the atrocities. That last moment before I knew what death was. Before it existed. If only one could just stay that way. Like it was all just a dream and they would all reappear. My parents. Sylvia. The countless millions. How many times, through the solitude and the rains the fevers, I have had this thought. To undo all of it. Find some little warp in time and replay it all differently. Shouldn't there be some higher judge to appeal to? Some alternative sentence to beg for? Sometimes, in my wandering, withering mind, it is even more than just a dream. It is almost real. God will answer my appeal. They will all be back. It can still be undone.

And then the procession to the grave. The sunlight hitting our faces, turning our tears to salty streaks. People along the curbs and leaning out the windows. The church bells from up the way and behind us and all around us. The box.

What is inside the box, Mutti?

Nothing.

Nothing?

No.

The cemetery in the middle of town. Stones surrounding the grave. And suddenly knowing somehow. Realizing it in that moment.

Is Oma in the box?

She's in Heaven.

What did I do wrong?

Nothing. She's in Heaven.

Do you see now what an idiot I have become? My dreams are a child's. My emotions are a child's. My lachrymal glands are incontinent.

I have lived too long. It is time to die.

- Illyria –

Scattered clouds. Steady breeze.

Health is wavering again. Feet are swollen. Sign of kidney failure. At last. But there can be no thought of slowing. Must be there for Dawn. For Andre. My son. Cannot leave them here alone. Not ever.

There is a boat out near the horizon again. Very tiny. They have become a little more frequent. But still, we can but watch. Hope. My sight is not perfect. But Dawn has come over and pointed to it, and now I can make it out as well.

Of course, I never really did hear from Sylvia. She perished, no doubt, in some horrible camp. Emaciated. A stick figure among a million anonymous stick figures. My darling. But nothing to those who killed her. A rotted-out body to be bulldozed. A number to be counted. Of course there was no hope from the start. Not for one arrested at the very beginning. On *Kristallnacht*. How many years would she have had to survive?

I can see it all, the real ending, just as vividly as the make-believe ending—the one I have constructed and lived, over and over, until it was almost real. How they slowly starved her to death. How they bulldozed her naked, starved, anonymous corpse. Heaped it in a pile with the others.

Did you really believe? I warned you. I told you it was just a dream. Didn't I? Did I even deserve it? Did I deserve a happy ending? I fled. Escaped out the window. Left her to her fate. That is all. If only perhaps I had....

If only, if only. I have spent my life wondering if only. But that is all there is. The feet say run. You run.

Now Dawn is standing, holding the baby, looking out at the ocean. Is it definitely a boat? Is it coming toward us? Or are we imagining it?

I cannot see well enough, Dawn. What do you think? Is it approaching? I think so. Come, Andre. Hurry. Let's add some firewood. This is for you, my son. Come, build up the fire. I am exhausted. But there is no slowing now. There. Do you see that, Andre? It's called a boat. Can you say *boat*? That is what will take you to your new home.

- Illyria -

June 22, 0001.

This will be my last entry.
The day is fair. Lovely and almost cool. The waves are rippling
gently across the corals.   Dawn is waving. Calling out at something.
Something out in the waves. The fire is crackling.   Smoke rising. And
yet I am tired. I am fading.

Farewell.

Auf Wiedersehen.

- Acknowledgements -

No novel is written in a vacuum and this one is certainly no exception. It went through many iterations and received much support and assistance along the way.

In no particular order, I would like thank Karen Evans for her friendship, support, and always honest and thoughtful feedback; Janet Linder, likewise for her enthusiasm and critical judgement; Cimarron Buser for his support and acumen in all my writing endeavors (and a couple of business ones as well); Joel Shames for his always excellent counsel—legal and otherwise; Ann Basch for her friendship, her important ideas regarding this book, and her scene-by-scene advice; Carey Caccavo Wheaton, who was in my creative writing class in 12th grade and has been selflessly supportive, inspiring and helpful ever since; Debbi Klopman, who could not have been more generous with her time and support, and whose suggestions were always on point; Roz Warren, John Spears and Benji Rubin for their long-standing support with my writing; Erica Evans, who gave much needed assistance with the German phrases; my parents, Harold and Elsa Blum, who were believers in the book from the outset; as well as my brother and sister, Larry and Linda Blum, for their support in all ways—brotherly, sisterly and literary.

And finally my wife Kate, who has had to endure the many drafts of this, and my many associated moods, and who has provided her own helpful criticisms—both of the work and of the author!

I received excellent professional advice from Stephanie Delman and Heidi Lange at Greenburger Associates. The book is a better book for their involvement. I should also mention Simon Lipskar, of Writers House, for his belief in my writing and support of a number of my previous works.

Lastly, I must express my great gratitude to my publisher, Laura

Vosika of Gabriel's Horn Press. She has provided assistance in countless ways, from her friendship to her always helpful editorial advice, but most importantly through her sheer will and determination to get this out to the public.

In addition to the many people who assisted along the way, I should mention a number of books that were helpful with the sections that involve historical elements related to World War II. It may not be customary to provide a bibliography for a work of fiction, and I do not intend a complete bibliography here. But in this case, where the fiction is infused closely with history, mention of a few of the sources might be of interest. While a vast amount has been written about this time period, I was most interested in works that illuminated how the Nazi era was experienced, contemporaneously, from the German perspective. First-hand accounts and memoirs provided a remarkable perspective that one does not get in history books, and taken together provide a mosaic of the range of viewpoints and experiences of the time. While some of these, written after the war, may be challenged as revisionist, or white-washed, in general it did not seem difficult to distinguish embellishment or post-hoc recollection from actual personal history. In general, writers seemed more interested in simply sharing their experiences than in sugar-coating them.

The War Of Our Childhood: Memories of World War II, by Wolfgang Samuel provided an excellent survey of the war as experienced through the eyes of German children. *No Longer Silent: World-wide Memories of Children During World War II*, by C. Leroy Anderon provided a similar if broader perspective. *Soldat, Reflections of a German Soldier, 1936-1949*, by Siegfried Knappe provided insight into the mindset and experience of a higher-ranking officer. *A Mind in Prison: The Memoir of the Son and Soldier of the Third Reich*, by Bruno Manz was a compelling first-hand story, told by the son of an ardent Nazi and anti-Semite who only gradually came to doubt his father's worldview. *Defying History: A Memoir*, by Sebastian Haffner was particularly fascinating—a diary written in the 1930s by a German intellectual and anti-Nazi, where he relates his views about the catastrophic path his country was heading down. (Haffner eventually fled to Britain with his Jewish fiance, and was promptly imprisoned for eight months as a possible dangerous enemy. The story of his flight, and of his diary's discovery and eventual publication, itself makes for a fascinating bit of history).

Finally, I owe a particular debt to The Memoir of Werner Mork – A Private's Life in the Wehrmacht During World War II, from which I found a framework for the overall arc of Hans's war experience and for a few of the specific incidents and encounters along the way.